TWO
WIDOWS

LAURA WOLFE

TWO WIDOWS

Bookouture

Published by Bookouture in 2020

An imprint of Storyfire Ltd.
Carmelite House
50 Victoria Embankment
London EC4Y 0DZ

www.bookouture.com

ISBN: 978-1-80019-005-4
eBook ISBN: 978-1-80019-004-7

For my family.

CHAPTER ONE

Gloria (NOW)

I'd grown desperate for company since the discovery of the dead woman in town. A pit weighed in my stomach every time I thought of the gruesome news flash from a few days earlier, the lifeless young woman lying at the edge of the public beach only a few miles from where I stood. I'd been glued to the local news ever since. It wasn't a drowning as one might have expected, but strangulation. The poor girl, who they guessed to be all of twenty-five, remained unidentified. No suspects had been named, although I supposed the authorities held that kind of information close to the vest.

My fingers opened and a clump of weeds fell to the dirt. I peeled off my rubber gardening gloves and dropped those too, my weary eyes following the truck. My new tenant drove a candy-apple red pickup truck across my field, a miniature log cabin trailing behind her. I squinted past the branches of the oak tree that wavered above Charlie's ashes. It was probably foolish to rent her the land. My ad in the *Petoskey News* had been for the apartment above my garage, not for an overgrown field.

My throat dry, I stepped away from the weed-filled flower bed and made my way toward the field, placing each foot deliberately so as not to twist an ankle.

I smoothed down my jacket and refocused on the truck crawling toward me. A fresh-faced woman leaned forward, clutching the steering wheel with both hands. She concentrated on her task but slowed as she neared to offer a wave through the driver's window. The truck was the heavy-duty type I'd normally expect to be driven by a burly man or a construction worker. It eased to a stop, the engine cutting.

I trod closer, the ground becoming more rutted and my balance less reliable. My pulse quickened as I approached, the sticker on the truck's rear window coming into focus. *Not all those who wander are lost.* I'd seen the same sticker the other day affixed to the back of a beat-up Volkswagen outside the IGA. The words shot a pang of longing through my chest, reminding me of something my son, Ethan, would say.

The woman got out and stretched her elbows back. Her eyes darted across the landscape as she waited for me. "Hi. I'm Elizabeth Ramsay." She extended a slender hand. "You can call me Beth." The wind whipped a band of dark hair across her face, her skin as smooth as tulip petals. A tangle of wooden beads hung around her neck. She wore tight-fitting jeans and a navy windbreaker that said Patagonia in the corner. She couldn't have been more than thirty.

"Nice to meet you. I'm Gloria," I said.

She grasped my weathered hand, bulging veins and all, in a firm shake, then motioned toward her trailer. "Is this a good spot?"

"You found the right field." I offered a smile, although my insides jittered. I'd spoken to her on the phone two days earlier, but it had been a while since I'd had a face-to-face conversation with a real person. "How was your trip?"

Beth shrugged and motioned toward her vehicle. "Good, I guess. I mean, considering the load. I drove up from downstate."

"You were smart to wait until after Memorial Day." I inched closer to her vehicle. A number of insects stuck to the windshield and a scrape marred the back bumper. "That's quite a truck you have."

Her smile faded. "It's a gas guzzler." Beth crossed her arms and glanced away. "There's no other option for hauling my house, though."

"I suppose you're right." I swallowed against the dust gathering in my throat. I hadn't meant to bring up a sore subject.

In truth, I chose the field to the north of my farmhouse for Beth's truck because I feared a strange trailer would interfere with my view of the oak tree from the front porch. The few months of the year when the weather was warm, I enjoyed sitting in the rocker at dusk, sipping my Scotch, and marveling at the fireflies as they floated above the tall grass like tiny lanterns. The bats would appear around the same time, and that was a whole different show. Oh, how Charlie and I used to marvel at the bats! They'd flit this way and that, guided only by their personal sonar systems. It was a wonder they never crashed into each other.

Ten acres of land was plenty of room to spread out, and Beth seemed nice enough, but there was no need for her trailer to taint the landscape.

"This looks like a good spot." She meandered along the perimeter of the field, pausing every so often to adjust to her new surroundings. "You have a beautiful piece of land."

Her head tipped back, the sunlight casting shadows across her face. She was thin and twisty like a sapling, but there was nothing frail about her. She seemed to put down roots with every step she took. Her skin glowed with youth, but her dark eyes were hard and determined. I'd expected her to be somewhat of a drifter, but—just as her bumper sticker proclaimed—she didn't seem the least bit lost. If anyone could handle that leviathan truck, it was her. I stopped myself from staring and trained my eyes on the trees.

"You're here at the right time of year, that's for sure. The winters can be long." I'd unknowingly wrapped my arms around myself at the thought of last winter. Northern Michigan had seen three weeks straight of record lows, the frigid air seeping through my unsealed windows and keeping me homebound and alone. I'd been down to my last can of beans when the thermometer finally broke zero.

"I'm sure," Beth nodded. She tipped her head toward the garage. "Have you rented out your apartment yet?"

"No. Not yet." A rock turned over in my gut. I wouldn't tell her, but I hadn't received a single call about the apartment. And, of course, I wouldn't mention how I'd found the metal handle of the apartment's front door banging against the siding of the garage, the darkened doorway gaping open when I'd been so sure I'd turned the deadbolt. The discovery felt as if someone had scooped out my insides with a melon baller and sent a cold wind blowing through me. I'd almost dialed 911 thinking I'd found a clue, that the unlocked door was evidence of an intruder. I wondered if the person who'd forced open the apartment door was the same person who'd killed the young woman in town. But then I laughed at myself. I was a hermit who'd grown afraid of her own shadow. The discovery of the lifeless woman on the beach had made me jumpy, freezing up at every creak of a floorboard and rattle of a windowpane. We'd never had a problem with break-ins, or any crime for that matter. It was probably nothing more than a loose screw. That latch had always been a little wobbly. My repair list had been lengthening since Charlie passed away two years earlier.

"I would have rented your apartment if I didn't have the house already." Beth nodded toward the trailer. "Should I back it into place? You can direct me."

"Yes. Of course." Stretching out the kink in my back, I reminded myself to think positive thoughts about the apartment. *Thoughts become reality.* That's what I'd read in my latest self-help book, *The Thirty-Day Life Coach.*

Beth climbed into her truck and started the engine while I directed.

"A little to the left," I yelled.

She glanced at me through the lowered window and turned the wheel before reversing a few more feet. The metal hitch groaned with the weight of the load.

"That's good. Right there." I held up my hand, signaling for her to stop.

Beth cut the engine again and hopped out. "Thanks for your help, Gloria." She stood next to me as we admired the positioning of the trailer. "I'm still getting used to hauling it."

"It's a very nice trailer."

"Not a trailer." Beth faced me, eyes straining against the late-May sun. "A tiny house." Her voice was sharp, and I sensed that I'd offended her.

"Yes. Sorry." I leaned back on my heels. She'd mentioned some nonsense about a tiny house when we'd spoken over the phone, but I had no clue what she was talking about. Beth had explained she was a writer who used to work for a newspaper but now wrote freelance pieces on resorts around the world. This summer she'd been commissioned by a major magazine to profile destinations in northern Michigan—Petoskey, Harbor Springs, Charlevoix, and Traverse City. Maybe even Mackinac Island. She needed to park her house somewhere in the vicinity while she researched. I happened to be in the perfect location, close enough to the towns but several miles inland from Grand Traverse Bay where the land was cheaper and the tourists fewer.

I'd rented out the garage apartment a couple of times over the past two years but had never let anyone park a trailer on my land, not even temporarily. My pocketbook was light though, and it would be a relief to have another person nearby. *The Thirty-Day Life Coach* recommended I take at least one action a week that was 'outside of my comfort zone.' Being two weeks behind already, I'd agreed to let Beth park in the field.

"I'm afraid you'll have to explain the difference between a trailer and a tiny house to me," I said, feeling my age.

Beth blinked her round eyes at me as if I'd dropped out of the sky. "A tiny house is a lot nicer than a trailer, for one." Her head swiveled toward the tiny house, and I could see she was right. The structure resembled a miniature ski resort on wheels, complete with a front porch. Half of the roof was constructed of metal, the same shade as the dark green evergreens in the distance, and half was covered in solar panels. A white door rose up at the edge of the porch, and three windows lined the long side of the rectangular box. Above the first row of windows was another smaller row of hexagon-shaped windows.

"Also, tiny houses are super-efficient. Everything inside is built with multiple functions: storage inside of chairs, walls that fold out into tables, a lofted space for sleeping. Things like that."

I picked at my fingernail and smiled, still not having a clue why a vibrant young lady like Beth would choose to live by herself in a trailer, even a glorified one.

She continued as if answering my question. "And living tiny lets me focus less on things and more on experiences. I only have what I need, nothing more. Leave a small footprint, and all that. It's kind of a movement right now."

"Well, that's admirable." I thought of my son, Ethan, again—a thirty-six-year-old free spirit who lived in San Francisco. We'd hit a rough stretch over the last several years, but I imagined he and Beth would get along well.

"It's nice to live off the grid, too." Beth tucked a few strands of her windblown hair behind her ear.

"Off the grid?"

"You know, no bills." She pointed at the roof. "I get my electricity from the solar panels, my water from your well, and I have a portable Wi-Fi booster for my internet connection." She rested her hands on her hips. Her eyes reflected something familiar as if I'd glimpsed myself in a puddle after a spring rain.

I stared at her, lost for words. It was a brilliant arrangement, although something about it seemed borderline illegal. I'd never heard of anything so freeing and terrifying all at the same time. This fearless young woman was taking on the world all by herself, just the shirt on her back, not tied to anything or anyone. She hadn't told me that, exactly, but I noticed she wore no rings on her left hand. I could see now that the garage apartment wouldn't have been a good fit for her at all.

Pressing my lips together, I turned away from Beth, hoping she hadn't noticed how different we were. How I'd hitched my own trailer to the past, content to watch film clips from my younger days play out in my head—five-year-old Ethan popping his head out of the chlorinated water of the Grand Rapids YMCA swimming pool, his eyes finding me and Charlie from behind his too-tight goggles as he passed his first swim test; or sixth grade Ethan arriving home from school, smiling wide as he told me how he'd won the 'Student of the Week' award. It was the small moments I treasured most. Those were happier times from a life already lived. Unlike Beth's adventurous spirit, I'd anchored myself to this land for the remainder of my days, this ten-acre parcel of rolling fields and meadows encircled by a safe barrier of forest. The decision had been made the moment I'd buried Charlie's ashes beneath the oak tree.

Beth wandered to the back of her tiny house and unscrewed the hitch behind her truck.

Her independence fascinated me. She was a rare find for a beleaguered old lady like me; it was as if my rusty garden shovel had accidentally hit a gilded treasure chest. I'd barely scraped away the top layer of soil. She peered at me from behind the tiny house, her bottomless eyes scanning the surroundings and landing on me. My breath snagged like a stuck zipper. I had so many questions, but I clamped down on my tongue, stopping myself from asking any of them.

I tended to talk too much. At least, that's what the ladies in my Bible study group had told me. Mary Ellen Calloway complained that I talked too much about Charlie and my feelings, and not enough about the written word. Now I made sure to not speak more than necessary, to not share too much, or seem too eager. I didn't dare go to Bible study anymore. Not after everything that happened. Instead, I read verses to Charlie under the oak tree whenever the mood hit me. On the loneliest days, the unopened book rested on my lap, my eyes fixed on the trunk of the sturdy tree while I harbored visions of reconciling with Ethan, utterly mystified how a book that could provide a lifetime of comfort could also cause so much pain.

I stepped closer to Beth, feeling a lightness in my step that hadn't been there this morning. Maybe because I'd never had a daughter of my own and Beth was about the right age, I was drawn to her. Or perhaps it was because I'd been without companionship for so long. Regardless, I hoped we could become friends; not just casual acquaintances who go shopping together and chat about the weather, but something more substantial, the sort of friends who keep each other safe and share their deepest secrets.

CHAPTER TWO
Elizabeth (BEFORE)

The storage room in the basement normally gave me the creeps, but today I didn't care. I shouldered open the door and pulled the string dangling from the light bulb before inching inside. A cobweb brushed the side of my face and I waved it away, trying not to breathe in the dank odor of the room. It was even messier than I remembered. Towers of musty boxes surrounded me. I wondered how Jason and I had accumulated so much stuff in barely two years of marriage. They were his things, mostly, along with some unused wedding presents and containers from his mom's house that he refused to throw away. If it had been up to me, I would have gotten rid of ninety percent of it. But now I was happy we'd saved everything.

The light bulb flickered, exposing an intricate spiderweb stretching between the rafters. My muscles tensed. I scanned the bare sections of the concrete floor, expecting a mouse to scurry into a crevice, but nothing was there.

My hand drifted to my abdomen, where I let it rest for a second, regaining my courage. These few moments of unpleasantness would be worth it to see the look on Jason's face when he opened the present. A square of turquoise caught my eye from a high shelf in the corner, and I exhaled. It wasn't labeled, but it had to be the storage bin from my mother-in-law's house. I'd helped Jason carry the unusually bright bin out of her attic last year after she'd passed away.

An oversized box blocked my path, so I bent down and pushed, sliding it a few inches to the left. Turning sideways, I squeezed through the space and stood on tiptoes to reach it. I grasped the handles on the sides and pulled it toward the edge of the shelf, causing a cloud of dust to rain on me. My eyes closed, temporarily blinded by the debris. The container was heavier than I remembered, and while I tried to lift it down gently, my arms gave way. The weight of it knocked me off balance as it slammed to the floor. Had Jason been home, he would have come running, but instead, I found myself splayed backward across a large box labeled *Good China*.

"Shit!" I said under my breath. We hadn't even used our good china yet, and now I'd probably broken some of it.

I looked over my shoulder, inexplicably worried that someone had witnessed my clumsiness. It was only 4 p.m., though, and Jason wouldn't be home from work for at least another hour or two. I regained my footing and brushed the dust from my pants. The china—broken or not—could wait for another day. Besides, it might be years before we got around to eating off it.

A long-legged spider skittered across the side of a box just inches from my hand. I jumped back, overwhelmed by a sudden urge to escape the enclosed room. But first I needed to be sure I'd taken the right bin from the shelf. I tried not to think about how many other spiders might be creeping toward me, or the number of mice that might be hiding in the corners, under the old hoses and extension cords, or behind the mountains of cardboard containing Jason's ratty toys and clothes. I slowed my breathing and focused only on the turquoise bin in front of me. My hand grasped the lid and peeled it open, revealing the treasures inside.

I smiled at the familiar contents—a tattered bunny lay on top with two brown button eyes staring up at me. *Peter Rabbit?* I think that's what Jason had told me, although he said he'd called the bunny Floppy. Spots of fur were worn off Floppy's tummy, one ear was ripped, and the stuffed toy had long ago lost its clothes. Beneath the bunny were a few of Jason's baby blankets.

My fingers sifted through the crocheted blankets until they hit something hard beneath. I pushed the blankets to the side, finding stacks of picture books. They were Jason's favorites from when he was a toddler. His mom had saved these things, showing them to me with a proud gleam in her eye one day after we'd gotten engaged. The memory of my mother-in-law, Mary, seemed so fresh that I sometimes forgot she was no longer with us.

"Liz, come over here. Look what I happened upon in the attic," Mary had said, her watery eyes the same deep blue as Jason's. She'd acted as if her discovery was just a coincidence when I knew she'd dug out the keepsakes for the sole purpose of showing them to me. I understood that she'd wanted me to see another part of Jason, a part that she knew better than anyone and I barely knew at all. Despite our differences, I'd loved her for that. We'd giggled at the raggedy bunny and laughed even harder when Jason grabbed the toy from the box and called him Floppy. He'd been a good sport about the whole thing, chuckling along with us, but I could tell by the way he hugged the bunny to his chest that it still meant something to him.

"And this was his very favorite book," Mary had said, holding up a *Goodnight Moon* board book with worn edges.

"Oh, yeah. I loved that one." Jason snatched the book and read through the pages, a hint of a smile on his lips.

The bulb flickered again and I froze, terrified of being caught in the dark. I piled everything back into the container and dragged it straight out of the horrible room, turning off the light and pulling the door closed behind me. One step at a time, I heaved the bin up the stairs to the main floor, grinning at my good fortune.

I'd found out I was pregnant less than two days ago while on assignment in Aspen. Although Jason was thirty-two and I was approaching thirty, we hadn't planned for a baby—not yet, anyway—but we hadn't been too careful either. I'd written off my morning nausea to too much coffee on an empty stomach, but when the queasiness didn't go away I'd taken a pregnancy test. Minutes later, two lines had appeared on the stick and it seemed as though an inexplicable magic trick had taken place. Two lines meant positive. I reread the instructions on the back of the box and then retook the test with more sticks. Two lines appeared each time and the realization that we were going to have a baby, that we'd created another human being, slowly set in. My heart had pounded, but whether it was from excitement or fear, I wasn't sure. Jason would make a terrific dad, no doubt about that. On top of being a great provider, he was patient and loving and goofy. *But, me? A mom?* It was a role I'd never tried on myself and it was difficult to wrap my head around. Yet, I felt as if I was floating above my body, as if I was witnessing something slightly beyond my comprehension.

I'd called Jason right away, bursting to share the news that would change our lives, but my initial calls had gone to voicemail. My fingers fumbled over themselves, anxious to text him, but then stopped, remembering hearing about all of the fun ways my friends had surprised their husbands with the news of a baby: a onesie with the words *I love my daddy* written across the front; a plate filled with jars of baby food presented for dinner; a box of diapers wrapped in fancy paper. That's when I thought of Floppy and the box from my mother-in-law sitting in our storage room, and came up with the plan to dig out Jason's most treasured items from his childhood. I'd wrap them up and give them to him as a present when he got home from work. It would be the most meaningful way to tell him and to start the next chapter of our lives. His mom had saved those keepsakes for a time just like this and it would be a present he'd never forget.

I dragged the plastic container to the center of the living room, lifting it slightly so as not to scratch our newly refinished hardwood floors. Our 2,500-square-foot house in Royal Oak had been a fixer-upper when we'd bought it a year and a half ago and it was still a work in progress. The main floor was complete though, and now we'd have a good reason to finish the improvements to the two extra bedrooms upstairs. I bit my lip, suppressing the smile that was permanently plastered to my face. We could start the upstairs renovations right away. Jason's investment business had been booming, the deposits hitting our bank account growing larger and larger by the month. We'd paid off the construction loan and Jason's student loan, and there was still some money left over.

While the financial windfall was nice, I worried Jason used his long hours at the office as a coping mechanism—a way to deal with his pain since his mom's sudden heart attack last year. It was obvious that he hadn't completely dealt with the loss, his moods shifting with the wind and a frequent vacancy glazing over his eyes. Whenever I tried to talk to him about her, he brushed me off and said he was fine. I didn't believe him, but I didn't know how hard to push.

My phone buzzed on the table and I hoped it wasn't my editor, Gwen. I was a journalist for one of Detroit's major publications, *The Observer*, where I contributed to a column on vacation destinations and local events. It kept me busy and allowed me to travel for free, but my salary barely paid the bills. Now with a baby on the way, maybe I'd have to make some adjustments. I'd talk to Gwen about it when the time was right. The number on my phone wasn't familiar. I sent it to voicemail and refocused my attention on the storage container.

I laid the blankets aside and dumped the board books out on the living room rug, singling out *Goodnight Moon* for Jason's gift box. The book went into the cardboard box first, followed by his tattered bunny. No note. No other hints. I wanted him to be confused for a minute before he figured it out. I taped the box closed and folded some blue-and-white-striped wrapping paper around it.

My hand wandered across the shag rug searching for the Scotch tape, but something else poked my thumb. Sifting through the long strands of carpet, my fingers uncovered a tiny silver object. I pinched it, inspecting the blue topaz center and hooked backing. It was an earring, but it wasn't mine. It must have fallen out of the storage bin when I'd dumped the contents across the floor.

My chest heaved, realizing it must have been Mary's earring. I envisioned it snagging on one of the old blankets or falling into the container when she'd leaned over to pack it for the last time, not knowing she'd soon suffer a heart attack and never see her keepsakes—or her family—again. A wave of heat rose up in me, stinging my eyes. *Poor Mary!* She'd never get to meet her grandchild. I surveyed the piles of books and blankets and stuffed toys surrounding me and steadied myself, my breath trapped in my throat. The best part of my mother-in-law's life had been packed away into that turquoise bin. I held the earring between my fingers and gently placed it in my pocket. Jason would want to save this.

CHAPTER THREE

Gloria (NOW)

The watering can tipped further forward than I intended, dousing the purple-and-white petals. The flowers hung limply over the soil. "Oh!" I sucked in my breath staring at the flattened pansies. Hopefully they'd survive. I probably shouldn't have splurged on the flowers, but it had been too hard to resist the bright pops of color after such a long, gray winter. It was almost June—safe enough weather to plant some hardy greenery to spruce up Charlie's final resting place.

Clutching my back, I lowered myself onto the bench underneath the shade of the oak tree. I stretched my neck toward the tiny house that had appeared in my field a few hours earlier. It was difficult to make out much through the foliage and I wondered how Beth was settling in.

"We have a new tenant." I spoke in a low voice in case Charlie was there with me. "Not for the garage apartment yet. This woman has a tiny house. It's like a trailer, only nicer," I said, explaining what I'd recently learned. "And it's only temporary," I added, in case he was irritated by the activity in our previously quiet field.

I suspected I wouldn't have had the courage to live and travel alone when I was Beth's age. I was already married to Charlie by then, and he'd always been by my side guiding our life choices and planning for the future. He was a few years older than me and happy to lead the way. But I thought we'd have more time.

Now here I was sitting by myself under an oak tree talking to my dead husband.

The craziest thing Charlie and I had ever done was relocating from Grand Rapids to retire on this piece of land out in the middle of nowhere, and even that had been planned years in advance. *A lot of good that had done!* I pictured the unpaid bills stacked on my kitchen counter and the drafty windows that needed replacing. Charlie had been a mathematics teacher who'd eventually become the principal of the high school where he taught. He'd been magnificent at his job, admired by students, parents, and teachers alike, and had enjoyed his position as principal for nearly twenty years before retiring. The security of his pension had informed our decision to move, but finances had been tight since he'd died two summers earlier. Now that he was gone, I only received a quarter of the monthly payout we'd been collecting when he was alive.

I pushed my lower jaw left, then right. The stress of not renting out the garage apartment was causing my neck to ache again. It would be so freeing to not have to pay a mortgage or utility bills. Maybe Beth was on to something.

A door banged closed in the distance, and I discerned some movement beyond the trees. Moments later, Beth cut through a shadowy gap between two evergreens and waved when she noticed me. My knees creaked as I raised myself off the bench and returned her greeting.

"How are you settling in?" I asked as she neared.

"Great. Thank you." She wore a pink nylon backpack that had strings for straps. "I realized I haven't paid you anything yet."

"Oh, I wasn't going to let you forget." I waved my finger at her.

Beth removed her satchel and dug through it. "Here's the first two months' rent, like we talked about. I probably won't be here that long, though."

I nodded, happy to have at least two months of her company and some extra money.

Whispering numbers under her breath, she pulled out a stack of cash and counted through the money before laying the pile in my hand. "Here you go. That should be six hundred dollars, but let me know if I miscounted."

"That's fine, dear." I tucked the money in my pocket without checking the amount. I wanted her to know that I trusted her.

Beth nodded toward the waterlogged pansies. "Your flowers are pretty."

"Thank you." I glanced away, flattered. "You'll get plenty of sun out in that field. You could plant some flowers, too."

Beth shifted her weight. "I've never been much of a gardener. I'd probably kill them."

I nudged the ground with my toe. "I can help you. I've been working with this sandy soil for years. If you have time, I'll wander back with you right now and show you a good area."

Beth straightened her shoulders. "Okay."

We meandered up my dirt driveway past the detached garage, the empty apartment looming above us. Tall shadows passed over us as we foraged through one of the many gaps in the trees. Beth had removed the hitch from the tiny house and parked her truck several feet away. Her heavy-duty hose ran along the ground. She'd already connected the water, too.

I pointed out the sunniest areas around her tiny house and advised her to avoid the rocky soil at the far end. "Feel free to borrow my shovel. It's usually resting on the fence next to my vegetable garden."

"Thanks, Gloria." She turned toward me, her hand shielding her eyes from the late-afternoon sun. "Planting flowers is a good idea. It might even be therapeutic."

Her gaze, once again, stuck on the horizon as if she were searching for something. I wondered what kind of therapy someone like her could possibly need.

"Yes. It is. Therapeutic." I bit the inside of my cheek and stared at my hands. Gardening had been my one escape, my one source of joy, since Charlie had died and I'd lost touch with Ethan, but I wouldn't tell Beth about that now. I didn't want to say too much too soon.

Beth refocused on me and cleared her throat. "So, since you've never seen a tiny house, would you like a tour? It won't take long. Two hundred and seventy square feet." She offered a sheepish grin, her teeth straight and white.

I chuckled. "You've got me curious. I'd love to see it."

I followed her up the three steps to the front porch, which was big enough for the two of us, but not much else. The porch was covered by an overhang. She opened the door and waved me ahead of her. Once inside, it was as if I'd been transported into a dollhouse where I was one of the slightly off-scale dolls. To my surprise, the space was bright and airy. Gleaming hardwood floors stretched out beneath my feet and white planked walls reached up two stories above me, drawing my eyes toward a ceiling fan perched above my head. Light poured in through the second-story windows.

"This is the living room." Beth waved toward the walls next to us. A denim-colored couch rested along one side of the room and a square table built of wood filled a nook beside it. "Watch this." She lifted up the wooden table, only to reveal another wooden box under it. Then she lifted that one and another wooden box appeared.

"It's like the Russian dolls," I said, still unsure of the purpose of all those boxes.

"Extra seating." Beth pulled one of the boxes behind her and sat on it, a satisfied look on her face.

"Isn't that something?" I placed my hands on my hips, awed by the ingenuity of it all.

Beth stood up and marched a couple feet past me. "The kitchen is over here."

Underneath a lofted space was a two-burner stove. A microwave hung above it and a compact sink on the other side. On the opposite wall stood a refrigerator, only slightly smaller than the one in my own house. A wire basket hung from the ceiling, holding onions and potatoes. Her kitchen, though mini, was beautiful, the kind designed by a professional. The appliances were newer than mine, all stainless steel and probably energy-efficient, and her countertops were the color of stone.

"I have a few cupboards under here." She bent down and opened two doors between the stove and the sink. "And when I need extra counter space, I can do this." She pushed a button and a large plank came loose from the ceiling. I stepped to the side, my mouth gaping, as two cables lowered the board. Beth grabbed it, unclipped the cables, flipped out four metal legs attached to the topside of the board and, in seconds, turned it into a long table.

"Oh, my heavens!" Maneuvering around this tiny space was more complicated than I'd imagined. My worn Formica counters suddenly seemed just fine.

"The bathroom's back here." She pointed to a door at the end of the kitchen. "It's small, but it works. And the composting toilet doesn't require any plumbing."

"Composting toilet? Doesn't that…" I hesitated, not knowing how to ask the question without offending her.

"Smell bad? That's what I thought at first, too. But, no. It's not like a porta-potty. It flushes by vacuum and breaks everything down in the tank. Ninety percent of the waste evaporates and the rest can be emptied out and used as fertilizer."

"I see. As long as you don't empty it next to my house." I laughed nervously.

"I'll find a good spot in the woods." Beth waved me back toward the living room. "I sleep up here." She pointed to the lofted space above the kitchen. A staircase with no railing led to the second level.

I noticed holes on the side of each step, and reached out to touch one, but stopped, not wanting to overstep my boundaries.

Beth nodded. "That's a handle. Each step is another storage space." She pulled the handle and a giant wooden drawer on rollers slid out filled with folded clothes.

"Good gracious! You have plenty of hiding places, don't you?"

Beth climbed the stairs to the loft. "Watch your step," she said over her shoulder.

I followed, my body unbalanced and exposed without a railing to hold onto. It wouldn't take much of a slip for me to tumble to the floor. My muscles relaxed once I stepped off the top step and into her bedroom. Like the rest of the tiny house, the room was immaculate and free of all clutter. The walls were painted a misty gray color that felt both soothing and sad. Framed black-and-white prints of flowers decorated the walls. There were no photos of people. Above the bed, a built-in shelf held a row of books. Some of them I recognized: Thoreau's *The Maine Woods*, Kerouac's *On the Road*, and a hardcover copy of Stephen King's latest novel. Others I didn't. There were a couple of books related to tiny houses, like *Tiny House Basics, Minimalist Living, Organized Living, Organized Life*, and one that simply said *Karma* in large red letters down the spine. A handful of travel magazines and a laptop rested on top of the shelf. No self-help books like the ones that sat in a messy pile on my nightstand.

Beth gestured toward her bed. "It's not much, but it's all I need."

"It's lovely. Really. Thank you for the tour." I inched my way back down the open stairway and exhaled when both feet touched the ground floor. "You'll have to come over to the farmhouse for tea sometime, although you'll find it terribly cluttered compared to this."

"I'd like that. I'm sure it's great."

I'd barely met the person in front of me, but I was becoming more and more entranced by her. Or maybe it was simply the possibility of living vicariously through a fearless young woman that intrigued me.

"It will be lovely having you here, especially after what happened to that poor girl in town. Just terrible," I said as the headline from yesterday's *Petoskey Times* reeled through my mind. *Unidentified Woman Found Murdered on Public Beach.* The horrid news clung to my thoughts like a bad stain.

Beth lowered her eyelids. "Yeah. I heard about that."

I shook my head, making my way outside to the miniature porch, Beth following a step behind. "I'm sure we're safe way out here." I motioned toward the wheels below us. "You can always make a quick getaway if you need to."

Beth crossed her arms, my joke failing to lighten the mood.

I glanced in the direction of my farmhouse. "It's been so quiet since my son left. And my husband passed away almost two years ago."

"Oh. I'm sorry." Her eyes flickered out toward the trees, and her mouth turned down at the corners. She flattened herself against the siding as if she were teetering on the edge of a cliff.

The ladies from First Lutheran had been right. I had a tendency to talk too much. That's probably why Mary Ellen Calloway suggested I take a break from Bible study, and why she left my name off the committee list for the church's yearly fundraiser. Now I'd done it again. I'd overshared too soon. Instead of making friends with Beth, I'd made her feel uncomfortable. I certainly hadn't meant to dampen the mood.

"It's okay." I patted her on the shoulder, hoping she wouldn't think of me as a wet blanket. I began to step away, but before I could Beth's hand grasped my arm, her bare nails pinching my skin.

"Wait." Her voice was stretched thin. Something weighed in the back of Beth's eyes like pebbles sinking to the bottom of a murky pond. She stepped closer before she spoke again, her face just inches from mine, and her warm breath fogging my face. "I lost my husband, too."

CHAPTER FOUR

Elizabeth (BEFORE)

The present rested in my lap, my hands clutching the box so forcefully the sides began to cave. Anticipation tightened inside me like an un-sprung trap. I leaned back into the couch and reminded myself to breathe, grateful for the fresh breeze that rushed into the living room through the open window. Outside, the buds on our maple tree were beginning to sprout—a sure sign of spring. Jason was supposed to have been home an hour ago, but he'd called and said he was running late because of a last-minute phone call with a potential investor.

I tapped my manicured nails on the foil wrapping paper and thought of all of the things I should have been doing for the last hour: proofreading the recent article I'd written on Aspen's newest ski resort, sorting through the last three days of mail, cooking dinner. Instead, I sat on the couch squeezing the life out of the wrapped box I could hardly wait to give to Jason, imagining the look on his face.

At last, the familiar rumble of a motor sounded through the window. I peeked out and spotted Jason's SUV in the driveway, the door of our detached garage opening in the distance. He'd had his own surprise for me a month ago when he'd arrived home driving his shiny new toy. A Mercedes.

"Do you like it?" he'd said when he saw my jaw drop as he pulled into the driveway. The driver's window had been open despite the cold day; the March sun reflected off his black sunglasses.

"Is this… yours?"

"Yeah." He removed his glasses and flashed his irresistible smile at me, dimples forming behind the stubble on his face. "My fund is going to take off, Liz. We're living the good life now."

"What happened to the Hyundai?" *The one we just finished paying off three months ago*, I wanted to add, but I bit my tongue.

"I traded it in." He gave no further explanation, just pointed to the passenger seat. "Hop in. Let's take it for a ride."

I'd been pissed he hadn't consulted with me on the purchase, but it had been the first time I'd seen him genuinely happy since his mother died, so I didn't make an issue of it. Really, though, I thought we should have been keeping our expenses down, saving all that extra money for a rainy day. Or a day like today, when we'd start our own family.

The back door clicked open. I started to get up but stopped when I heard him talking.

"I know. That's why my fund is different. It's a mix of stocks and real estate." A shuffle of footsteps echoed from the kitchen, as Jason fumbled with something on the counter. "Right. Well, I learned from the best. I worked for Goldman Sachs straight out of business school."

I cringed, my blood prickling at his lie. Jason was embellishing his résumé again. He hadn't worked for Goldman Sachs. Ever. He hadn't gone to business school either. From the stories he told me, he'd barely made it through undergrad at Eastern Michigan. I'd challenged him on misleading his investors once before when I overheard him claiming he'd graduated from the Ross School of Business. He'd brushed me off, believing the lie was no big deal. "No one's ever going to check it out, Liz," he'd said, rolling his eyes at me. "These people only want to invest with people like themselves. They want the best."

I didn't agree with the lying. He'd promised me he wouldn't stretch the truth anymore.

Squeezing the box even tighter, I sank my weight deeper into the couch. It was a mystery to me why he couldn't be honest with them. Jason was great at his job. He'd been a commodities trader in Chicago after college and had started his own business as a financial adviser when we'd gotten married a couple of years ago. He had a knack for trading, his investments often returning fifteen or twenty percent. He'd developed his own proprietary formula for analyzing the markets, and unlike most other investors, his funds combined stocks and real estate. He had the personality and looks to make people trust him, and the returns to prove them right.

No worthwhile investor would pass over Jason's fund just because his competitors outshone him with fancy degrees and work experience at New York institutions. I wished he had more confidence in his abilities.

"Yeah. Yeah." Jason cleared his throat. "They made me earn my keep, that's for sure. Anyway, I've already raised over four million, so that fund is closed now. I might be able to get you in on the next one though." Laughter, although I knew Jason well enough to recognize it as a fake laugh. "Alright. Go talk to Ken and ask him about his return. Mm-hmm. Fifteen to twenty percent. I think you'll be impressed." Jason stepped into the living room and noticed me sitting on the couch, the present in my lap. He raised an eyebrow.

I drank in the sight of him. His tall stature and boyish grin commanded whatever room he stepped into. Tonight, he looked especially handsome in his charcoal suit and a blue pinstriped shirt that accentuated his eyes. He ran his hand through his thick brown hair, leaving it messy and spiked in front.

"Sure. Sure, Bill. You too. Bye." He placed his phone in his pocket and sighed. "Hi, babe. Sorry I'm so late."

I stood up and he met me by the couch, encircling me with his arms and kissing me on the forehead.

"Goldman Sachs?" I asked, tilting my head.

He shrugged, a sheepish expression overtaking his face. "I know. It's just that… that's what they want to hear. Besides, I'm going to make these people so much money. They won't care that I never worked at Goldman, even if they do find out someday."

I looked away, hoping he was right. "You said you weren't going to lie anymore."

"I know. I'm sorry. It just slipped out. I promise to stick to the facts from now on." Jason gave my arm a playful squeeze and winked. He pointed at the box which I still clutched in my hands. "What's with the present?"

I held my breath, the excitement returning. I wouldn't let Jason's white lie ruin the night I had planned. "It's for you. You might want to sit down first." I lowered myself onto the couch and patted the cushion next to me, the smile stuck to my face.

Jason hesitated but recovered quickly, "I love presents." He grinned and rubbed his hands together, ready to dig in.

He slid his finger under a piece of tape and ripped the shiny, striped paper off the box in a frenzy of pulling and tearing that reminded me of a child on Christmas morning. I clenched my hands together and leaned toward him as he lifted the lid from the box. The stuffed rabbit lay in front of him. He stared at it before picking it up, confused. Then he lifted the *Goodnight Moon* board book up with his other hand.

He cocked his head to the side and looked at me. "These are mine."

"Yes."

He studied the items in front of him, a vertical crease forming on his forehead. "I don't get it."

"Well, I wrapped them up because… because we might get to reuse them soon." I smiled at him, willing him to understand.

"What do you mean?"

He wasn't making this easy. I drew in a breath and held his arm. "We're going to have a baby." Saying the words made it real, and my voice cracked. "I'm pregnant." Emotion swelled from within me, and my eyes watered. I gazed into Jason's eyes, a shield of blue that gave nothing away.

"What?" He set the book down. Sweat glistened on his forehead. "Really?"

"Yes." It was taking him longer to celebrate than I'd hoped, but I remembered how I'd felt in the hotel room in Aspen when the two lines appeared—shocked at first, too.

He flopped backward on the couch, covering his face with his hands.

I froze, trying to contain the anger that bubbled inside me. *Was he upset? Was he crying?* This wasn't the reaction I'd envisioned. "I know we didn't plan it to happen so soon," I said, "but I was hoping you'd be…"

Jason sprung up off the couch and screamed, almost knocking me to the floor. He pumped his fist in the air. "Woohoo! Yes! I'm going to be a dad!" He grabbed me and pulled me close. "I love you," he whispered. Then he kissed me. A long, slow kiss, the kind we used to share when we first started dating. "We're going to be parents. You're going to be the best mom. I can't believe it."

"I'm so happy you're happy." I couldn't stop staring at my husband, at his movie star smile, and wondering how I'd gotten so lucky. "It's surreal, isn't it?"

"When did you know? How are you feeling?" He brushed the pieces of wrapping paper off the couch. "You should sit down."

I laughed. "I feel fine. Just nauseous in the morning, usually. That's why I took the test two days ago when I was in Aspen."

"Two days! You've known for two days and you didn't tell me?"

"I wanted to tell you in person. In a meaningful way." I nodded toward the stuffed bunny and the book.

"That was really cool." Jason laced his fingers through mine, still smiling and shaking his head. "Have you seen a doctor?"

"Not yet. I'll make an appointment."

"When are you due? What's nine months from now?" He began counting on his fingers. "May, June, July—"

"January," I interrupted. "I already counted. Although I'm probably already a couple of months along, so it would be more like November."

"November. November. That's great. This is so amazing." He clapped his hands together and paced back and forth. "We should celebrate. What do you want to eat? What do pregnant women eat?" Jason was talking so fast, like someone who'd downed five too many cups of coffee.

I laughed again. "I don't care, but I'm pretty sure I'm not supposed to eat sushi. And no alcohol."

"Okay. No raw fish or booze. How about Chinese? I can pick up something."

"Chinese sounds great." My stomach rumbled and I realized how hungry I was. "Double veggie egg rolls for me."

"I guess you're eating for two now." Jason winked at me as he pulled out his phone.

He ordered our usual favorites from Lucky Kitchen. I lounged across the couch now, almost in a dreamlike state. I couldn't believe that this was my life, that Jason and I were in this together and so many good things were happening.

"We're going to have to finish remodeling the house, ASAP," Jason said, as soon as he ended the call with the restaurant. "No expenses spared! I want the best for my little one."

"I can't wait to set up the nursery." I edged closer to him. "I was thinking of painting the walls a light gray. That way, it could work for either a boy or a girl."

He raised an eyebrow at me. "Is gray a normal color for a baby's room?"

"I was searching on Pinterest yesterday. It looks really cool and elegant. Trust me."

He threw his hands in the air. "Whatever you want, babe. You're the one doing the heavy lifting." He massaged my shoulders. "Or maybe I'll buy us a new house. Maybe that castle in Bloomfield Hills. Remember the one with the moat?"

Before Jason had started working such brutal hours, we used to take long drives after dinner, using Realtor.com as our guide. It was fun to locate the most expensive houses on the market and cruise past them, voyeurs into the lives of others. The castle house had provided us with a particularly entertaining date night, as we envisioned what our lives would be like if we lived there. How we'd have to start dressing in medieval clothes and eating gigantic turkey drumsticks for dinner. We'd discussed which of our co-workers and relatives we'd raise and lower the drawbridge for. I'd doubled over in pain, my stomach aching from so much laughter.

"I don't want a new house. I like this one," I said, smiling at the memory of the castle house. "But we need to declutter. That storage room is a complete disaster. I almost killed myself getting your mom's box down."

"I wish you would have asked me to help."

"That would have ruined the surprise."

Jason ignored me. "Have you called your parents yet?" he asked.

"No. Of course not." I sat up, my hand resting on my abdomen. "I wanted to tell you first. Besides, we should wait a little longer before we start telling other people about it. You know, just to make sure."

Even if I'd been close with my parents, I wouldn't have told them first. They lived a few hours away, in Kalamazoo, where I'd grown up and where I'd left as soon as I'd turned eighteen. My younger sister, Caroline, had stayed, foregoing college in favor of heroin. Now she was an addict, in and out of rehab, my parents completely consumed with her "recovery," but mostly dealing with her relapses and what was quickly becoming a long criminal record. She'd stolen my favorite necklace with the emerald pendant last time she'd stayed with us. It had been my only good piece of jewelry, other than my wedding band and engagement ring, which I was certain she'd cut off my finger if given the chance. That was two years ago, when Caroline was supposedly clean. Still, my parents defended her, refusing to hold her responsible. *The drugs were to blame.*

I was hard on her. I knew that. Maybe too hard. But I'd given her so many chances, been burned too many times. My time with my parents usually turned toxic in one way or another. I'd call them tomorrow and share the news, but I hoped to keep our baby at arm's length.

"I'm glad I was the first to know." Jason dipped his chin at me, but the vacant look in his eyes I'd been seeing so much of in the last few months since his mom died had returned. I knew he was thinking about her, and how she'd missed the opportunity to meet her grandchild. Her death had stolen so much. I reached into my pocket, the metal clasp of the earring I'd found on the carpet pricking my fingertip. I grasped it and held it in my palm, offering it to him.

"I found this today. When I emptied the storage bin from your mom's house."

He stopped pacing and stared at it. "Is it yours?"

I shook my head. "No. Do you recognize it?"

"No."

I batted him on the arm. "Look at it. It belonged to your mom. You should keep it." My palm hovered inches from his face. He took the earring between his fingers, inspecting it.

"You're right. This was my mom's earring." His hand quivered as he placed the earring in his pocket, his mouth drawn downward. I stood up to comfort him, to let him know it was going to be okay, that I was sure Mary was watching us from heaven, but he turned away from me.

"I'll go get the food." His voice was flat as if our conversation about the earring hadn't just taken place. In a few steps, he was out the door.

CHAPTER FIVE
Gloria (NOW)

Beth's hands fidgeted in her lap. She hunched forward in a wicker chair on my front porch, shaken by the mention of her husband's death. After her initial revelation, she'd had difficulty sharing any details, so I'd ushered her over to the farmhouse and dug out a bottle of wine from the back of my refrigerator. The bottle now sat between us, the label turned toward me to hide the orange clearance sticker. Beth's glass was nearly drained, but the words were trapped in her throat.

I remembered how devastated I'd been after Charlie passed away. The only thing that eased my pain was telling stories about him. Anything to keep his memory alive. Ethan and I had each other to lean on for the week of the funeral, but then he'd gone back to his life in California, refusing to answer my calls.

Then I'd turned to the ladies at First Lutheran, the ones in my Bible study group, but even they'd grown weary of the subject after several months. Mary Ellen Calloway announced midway through one of my memories of Charlie that we should cut back on personal anecdotes and stick to the Bible. Jane Perkins had mumbled "agreed" as she stared down her pointy nose at me. To her left, Barbara Grant nodded along with the other women at the table, a self-righteous sheen in her eyes. It was clear they hadn't wanted me there.

A few uncomfortable Bible study meetings later, Mary Ellen announced they'd created the committees for the church's annual fundraiser, The Fall Carnival, and posted it in the hallway. After the meeting ended and the members had gone their separate ways, I'd stayed back, my eyes traveling down the lists, scanning for my name. My chest heaved when I realized it wasn't there. I'd been omitted. They'd excluded me, even though I'd made a point to turn in my form a week early, even though I'd served on the decorating committee the previous three years. It could have been an oversight, I supposed. That's surely what Mary Ellen would claim if I'd confronted her. But there'd been something about the edge in her voice and the twist of her lips when she'd announced the lists. She hadn't been able to meet my gaze. She'd done it on purpose. That's when I'd stopped going to the meetings, although I should have quit long before that. Those women were the reason I'd lost touch with Ethan in the first place.

I studied Beth's busy fingers. She was here all alone, and she needed someone to talk to. "How did he die, dear?" I leaned toward her, encouraging her to open up. I hadn't meant to pry, but she'd agreed that talking about her late husband might make her feel better. The wine was meant to help her words flow easier.

"He—I mean—Jason, my husband," she paused, biting her lip, "there was a freak accident." Beth squeezed her fingers around her opposite arm, her hand quivering. "We were on a boat, a yacht, actually, on Lake Huron and something happened. A wave hit the boat. He fell into the lake and drowned." She shook her head and glanced away, her eyes brimming with water.

"I'm so sorry." I gave her hand a squeeze. What a tragedy to lose the love of her life so suddenly, and while he was in his prime. Her entire future had been torn away, just like that. "How long ago did it happen?"

"About ten months ago." She turned to face me. "It seems like a bad dream sometimes."

"My heavens! It's still so fresh for you."

Beth suddenly appeared more like a broken little girl than an independent woman, and I wondered if I'd pegged her all wrong. She lifted her glass and swallowed the last of her wine.

"I know how you feel," I said, refilling her glass. "It's already been two years since I lost Charlie. Colon cancer got him. He was in stage four by the time he was diagnosed." A rush of emotion filled my throat and I gulped it back. "I wish I could say it gets easier."

A gentle wind bristled through the leaves of the trees on the other side of the front meadow. Purple and yellow wildflowers rippled among the tall grass, and the afternoon sun shone across the pearly bark of the birch trees. Charlie had brought me to a beautiful spot.

"Was your husband a writer, too?" I asked, making a conscious effort not to hog the conversation.

Beth coughed out a laugh. "No. He was in finance. He had his own business." She closed her eyes and paused before she opened them again. "The yacht we were on that day belonged to one of his investors."

"Did you ever find out what happened? I mean, how he fell overboard?"

"No one saw him go in. Jason had been drinking." Beth set down her wine glass and lowered her voice. "We both had."

My gaze traveled to the bottle, and I feared the wine might have been a bad idea.

"The police said he'd been smoking and must have wandered to the back of the boat when he lost his balance. He hit his head on the boat before his body went into the water." She inhaled deeply, then peered at me. "At least, that's what the autopsy showed."

"I'm sure there was nothing anyone could have done."

"I should have been there for him. Instead, I was in the cabin above making small talk with a bunch of people I barely knew. I didn't even notice he was missing until we were almost back to the marina." Beth covered her eyes with her hands and breathed in and out deliberately several times, the way people do at the doctor's office.

"There, there. It doesn't have to be anyone's fault. Sometimes horrible things happen to good people." I'd read a whole book about that, so I knew it was true.

She looked up at me, her eyes wide and pained. "After the funeral, as if it hadn't been bad enough losing my husband, people started posting horrible things online. People who didn't even know me. I had to shut down all my social media accounts. Even my friends stopped asking me to hang out, like I'd done something wrong."

"That's terrible!" I stood up and hugged her. "You poor thing." Beth's body was radiating heat, her muscles twitching. She felt fragile, as if I were to squeeze her any tighter, she might fall apart.

Beth pulled away from me. She smoothed her hair back and straightened herself, wiping the moisture from her face. "Thank you for listening, Gloria. I'm sorry to lay all this on you, especially on the first day we've met. You just seem like such a nice person. And when you said your husband had died... I thought you'd understand."

"Of course I do."

"I bought the tiny house to get a fresh start, so I can travel around to places where no one knows me." She glanced in the direction of her trailer. "I spent five months in Colorado and Utah, but work brought me back to Michigan."

All at once, Beth's nomadic lifestyle made perfect sense. Of course she'd want a change of scenery after what she'd been through.

"Well, this isn't Colorado, but you never know, you might like it here." I winked at Beth. "It really is a nice place to spend the summer." As I said the words, the awful, murderous headline about the unidentified woman surfaced in my mind again.

Beth bit her bottom lip as her watery eyes flickered toward the horizon.

"Now, I don't want you to worry about that woman on the beach. They're saying her death was an isolated incident. That's what I heard on the news. Someone must have had a personal vendetta." I patted her arm. "We're perfectly safe way out here in the boonies. You should try to settle in a little bit. Make some friends while you're here." *So you don't end up old and alone like me*, I thought, my jaw tightening. I forced a smile and cleared my throat. "There are plenty of nice people your age, especially closer to town with all the city folks here for the summer."

Beth frowned. "I'm not sure I'll be here long enough."

A whisper of despair blew through me at the thought of Beth leaving. The empty apartment hovered in my peripheral vision, and I turned toward it. "The woman who used to rent the apartment over the garage was about your age. She was nice enough. Amanda. Amanda Jennings, or Jenkins, I think. She only rented from me for a few months. She works over at The Tidewater in Petoskey."

Beth slid forward in her chair. "The Tidewater?"

"Yes. I believe she was the concierge."

"That's one of the resorts I'm profiling for my new article."

For the first time since we'd taken our seats on the porch, I detected a glimmer in Beth's eyes. She was passionate about her career.

"Ask for Amanda. Tell her that you know me. I bet she'll take you on a tour and give you the inside scoop."

"Thanks, Gloria. I'll look for her tomorrow."

"My son always liked the food at The Tidewater." I thought of Ethan and the two years he moved back in with us after he'd graduated from college and couldn't find a job. He'd majored in Buddhist studies, so it wasn't a wonder. Ethan had always marched to the beat of his own drum. We'd taken him to The Tidewater on his birthday and he'd raved about the fried perch. That was before he'd told us his secret and moved to San Francisco. Before the women at First Lutheran started asking questions about him and giving me sideways glances. Before I'd pushed him away one last time. I wish he was here on the porch with us now. Maybe then he'd understand how much I'd changed.

"Does your son live nearby?"

I studied my hands. "No. He moved to San Francisco seven years ago."

"Cool city. I've been there a few times. Only for work, though." Beth looked at me expectantly. "What does he do?"

"Something for an online book sales company. He's explained it to me a number of times, but I don't really understand it."

Beth smiled. "Ah. One of those jobs that nobody understands. I love those. Do you get to see him much?"

"No. Not really." I could feel the smile disappearing from my face, and Beth's face mirrored my own. "He came back for Charlie's funeral, but we haven't spoken much since then."

Beth frowned. "Why? I mean, if you don't mind me asking."

I stared out at the rippling leaves dancing in the sky. "He made some lifestyle choices that I disagreed with."

"Drugs?"

"What?" I straightened up in my chair, as I realized what she meant. "No. It's nothing like that."

"Oh, sorry." Beth shook her head.

We both sipped from our glasses, the wind brushing against my skin and the birds chirping in the distance.

"Is your son gay?" she asked.

I swung my head toward her, amazed at her forthrightness. With my palms, I flattened down the wrinkles in my pants. "Well, I guess you can put two and two together, can't you?"

Beth set down her glass. "Being gay isn't really a decision, though. It's like being born with blue eyes, instead of brown."

"I've come to realize that." My face swelled with heat. "A little too late, I'm afraid." This wasn't a subject I was used to discussing, especially with a perfect stranger. Yet Beth didn't seem uncomfortable in the least. I swallowed the last of my wine.

"I have a few gay friends," Beth said. "Most of them said they knew from a very early age. I'm talking four years old."

I nodded, finding her bluntness strange and refreshing like she'd cracked open a jar that had been sealed shut for years. Ethan had said as much to me the night he came out—that he'd always known—but I hadn't wanted to hear it. What I wouldn't give for Beth to have been there to counsel me back then before I'd listened to the not-so-subtle hints from Mary Ellen Calloway. She'd made a point to mention the Bible's warnings against homosexuality at every meeting, her clique of friends nodding along. She'd never said Ethan's name directly, but, in hindsight, I could see what she'd done. I'd been outnumbered, made to feel ashamed. They'd all been so sure of their beliefs, and I'd remained silent, not having the courage to question them.

*

One day before Charlie passed away, someone had left a pamphlet sitting on the table in the church hallway directly beneath my coat. The pamphlet wasn't from First Lutheran. Pastor Mark wouldn't have approved of that type of thing. The ad was from a ministry over in Kalkaska that claimed to cure people of homosexuality through prayer. My hand had been shaking as I raised the pamphlet close to my eyes, reading the promises of "complete transformation" and "eternal salvation," along with glowing testimonials from relatives of people who'd been successfully converted. The words made my stomach convulse as if I'd swallowed a bad piece of chicken.

I'd rushed away in my Buick, my face twitching in anger at the thorny situation. I'd been torn, not knowing who was right and who was wrong, but not strong enough to take a stand either way. I arrived home and tucked the pamphlet underneath a stack of real estate fliers, deciding not to mention anything about it to Charlie. He'd been very sick by then, and I hadn't wanted to burden him with anything else.

Ethan had expected us to accept him instantly, to be proud of the fact that he was gay. Charlie was more adaptable, but I hadn't been able to jump on board as fast or as completely as Ethan wanted.

Then Charlie died. Ethan had immediately flown back for the funeral. He rose above our differences and acted as the perfect son, comforting me, sharing his favorite memories and listening to mine, and tying up loose ends with the funeral home. The morning before he was scheduled to return to San Francisco, I felt closer to him than I had in years. I'd wandered down to the kitchen tightening my robe around me. He'd been eating cereal, his spoon dinging against the bowl every few seconds, followed by loud crunching.

"Good morning." I plodded toward the coffee maker comforted by the familiar noises of everyday motherhood I'd taken for granted for so many years.

Ethan shuffled through a pile of newspapers as he ate. "Morning."

I poured my coffee and turned toward him just as the papers became still. He stopped chewing, the room silent. The brightness in Ethan's eyes faded like the sun disappearing behind a cloud. A look of disbelief stretched over his face. The silverware dropped from his hand and clattered against the porcelain cereal bowl, letting out the hollow ring of a broken church bell.

My eyes followed his gaze to the newspaper in his hand, wondering what could have knocked the wind out of him so fiercely he couldn't hold onto his spoon. Only it wasn't a newspaper he'd been reading; it was a stack of old real estate fliers.

My breath stuck to my lungs. My body felt like it was plunging through the kitchen floor into frigid water. He'd discovered the pamphlet. I couldn't move or think of any words to say. The pain in his eyes paralyzed me.

"Is this a joke?" His voice was strained and his features sunken. He waved the brochure in the air. "Is this what you really think? That you can convert me?"

"No, honey." I shook my head. "Someone at church… I don't know why I kept that."

"This is who I am, Mom. It's not something you can pray away. Don't you get that?"

I couldn't speak.

He slammed the literature down on the table and stormed upstairs, refusing to meet my eyes. He'd gathered his things and called a taxi to take him to the airport while I crouched in the corner like a potted plant, silent and motionless.

Now almost two years had passed since I'd seen him.

*

My hands trembled at the memory of the wound I'd inflicted on my son. I splashed the last of the wine into my glass, and then looked at Beth. "A couple of the women in my Bible study group led me down a bad road with Ethan. I guess I was to blame, too." Even with the alcohol loosening my tongue, I couldn't bring myself to tell Beth about the pamphlet. "My views have changed since then. I still have my faith, of course, but I don't go to Bible study anymore." I pulled in a long breath and looked at Beth. "I'm afraid it's too late to repair the damage I've done. Ethan won't even pick up the phone when I call." It had been Christmas the last time I'd attempted to contact him. I'd hung up in a panic when I'd reached his voicemail, not knowing the right words to say.

Beth lifted her glass and swirled the liquid around. "It's not too late." She leaned to the side and rolled her eyes. "Besides, everyone knows the Bible is meant as a guide, not taken literally. If the people at your church are your friends, then they should understand and support you."

I swallowed, realizing what different worlds Beth and I must come from. I envisioned Mary Ellen Calloway's pinched face, her matching jewelry sets, and her chipper voice that always carried an air of superiority. "They're not true friends. They use my son as gossip. They whisper about me behind my back. Do you know how terrible that feels?"

Beth stared off toward the horizon for a moment, her lip quivering. "Yes. I do."

I held my breath. I'd said the wrong thing again. "I'm sorry. I didn't mean to—"

She held up her hand. "It's okay. I know I just met you, but, for what it's worth, I think you should reach out to your son. I realize I don't know the whole story, but if I had a son, I wouldn't lose touch with him for any reason."

My muscles stiffened at Beth's pronouncement. *What did she know about raising a son?* I clutched the arm of my chair, reminding myself that Beth was only trying to help. But her words had ignited a fleeting pain somewhere deep inside my flabby belly, a prick of a needle tearing open a wide, gaping hole. The branches of the oak tree creaked in the distance, the noise filling me with the sickening realization that it might not be many more years before I'd be buried under the tree right alongside Charlie. Then it would be too late to make amends with Ethan. I swallowed, my throat scratchy and dry. Suddenly, the only thing that seemed unnatural about Ethan was that he had a mother who hadn't chosen love, a mother who hadn't been able to reach out and admit she'd been wrong. Wrapping my arms around myself, I shuddered.

"I suppose you have a point." I lowered my arms and steadied my hand long enough to raise my glass to her. "Some things are too important to put on hold."

Beth smiled at me, her dark eyes pulled down by the weight of her own loss. We sat in silence, staring at the swaying tree branches in the distance and sipping what was left of our wine. Our conversation left me feeling simultaneously invigorated and drained. Still, I was thankful for her company. Beth had opened up to me. She'd listened to me and offered advice. That's what friends did. It felt like we'd known each other much longer than one day.

When Beth had taken her last sip, she straightened up and turned toward me. "You know, if you're not busy tomorrow, you should have lunch with me at The Tidewater. We can take two cars, so I can do my research after we eat."

I raised my shoulders and tugged the edge of my shirt, not wanting Beth to see how flattered I was by her invitation. "Well, I'll have to reschedule my plans to weed the garden, but I can push that until the afternoon."

Beth giggled.

I smiled back at her. "Lunch at The Tidewater would be lovely."

A chill bristled over my skin at the thought of eating lunch so close to the spot where the woman's body had been discovered, but I shook away the uncomfortable sensation. This was the second thing outside of my comfort zone this week—going out to eat with a new friend. I was making up for all the weeks I remained safely inside the farmhouse, taking no risks whatsoever. And since I was on a roll, I wondered if I should push myself to do one more thing. Maybe Beth was right. Maybe it was time to give Ethan another call. This time when I reached his voicemail, I'd leave a message.

CHAPTER SIX
Elizabeth (BEFORE)

Last night's Chinese food weighed like a rock in my stomach. I handed Jason a steaming cup of coffee. The aroma, which I normally found luscious and intoxicating, now made me gag. My morning sickness was in full swing.

By the time Jason had returned with the carry-out bag from the restaurant, his spirits had lifted. He managed to shift his thoughts away from his mom's recent death to visions of what our future baby would look like—whether he or she would have Jason's blue eyes or my brown ones. Jason admitted he wanted a boy and I confided I was hoping for a girl, but we both agreed a healthy baby was the most important thing. Then we debated baby names for a solid hour. Jason said if our baby was a boy, we'd name him Jason Jr., and if it was a girl, we'd name her Elizabeth Jr. After laughing until my gut ached, I objected on both counts. Jason Junior would inevitably lead to people calling him JJ. I had a thing against names that were initials. And my name, Elizabeth, had too many variations: Liz, Lizzie, Liza, Beth. I argued for a simple name, like Helen or Jane. Something people couldn't manipulate.

When 11 p.m. had rolled around, my head sank into my down pillow, eyelids heavy. I wanted to tell Jason that if the baby was a girl, her middle name could be Mary, after his mom, but I knew any mention of her would send him plummeting into a depression. At some point, he'd have to deal with her death. His sudden retreats into silence, increasingly long hours at the office, and late nights in front of the TV drinking beer were beginning to take a toll on both of us. He needed to work out his issues before he became a dad. Maybe a few trips to a therapist could help if I could convince him.

Now the morning sun shimmered in his eyes as he looked up from his phone and took the hot mug from me. "Thanks. None for you?"

"No." I inhaled a few deep breaths, hoping to control the queasiness. "It doesn't smell good." I pinched my lips together, placed my hands on the counter and walked myself over to a kitchen stool. My stomach swirled and I thought I might retch.

"You should eat something." He shuffled around me and grabbed a banana from the wire basket on the counter.

"I don't want that." The words slipped from my mouth more sharply than I'd intended.

Jason held up his hands. "Okay, I'll take it." He brushed something off his jacket. "How do I look? I have a big meeting today."

"You look handsome, as always." It was true. He was consistently handsome, even when he wore an old T-shirt and shorts. In the black suit, pressed gray shirt, and blue tie he wore today, he looked like a million bucks. Meanwhile, I resembled a rat's ass.

He stepped toward me, and I straightened his tie which hung slightly to the right. His warm lips met my forehead.

"Who are you meeting?" I asked.

"Some guys Robert introduced me to a couple of weeks ago. They're the real deal. If they buy into my fund, we'll be living the good life."

"I thought we already lived the good life." My voice croaked like an old woman on her deathbed.

"That's true," He smiled at my unfortunate state and took a sip from his coffee mug. "Then we'll be living the *really* good life. Word about my fund has spread to some heavy hitters."

He was playing it cool, but I could tell by the way the muscle in his jaw twitched that he was pumped. Maybe even a little nervous. Jason didn't need to worry, though. I'd seen his business prowess in action many times before. He possessed chameleon-like social skills, effortlessly blending in with people from any background and adapting to whatever audience sat in front of him.

"Where's the meeting?" I struggled to sit up straighter.

"Pine Hills Country Club. They invited me to lunch."

I squeezed his arm. "Good luck. You're gonna kill it."

"Thanks, babe." He set his mug in the sink and slung the strap of his laptop carryall over his shoulder.

I gave him a pathetic wave. "Eat some lobster for me."

Jason chuckled. "Feel better." He waved and closed the door behind him.

Groaning, I lifted myself off the stool and filled my water bottle. It would be a slow day, as far as work went, and I envisioned myself getting back into bed until the worst of my nausea wore off. Balancing myself on the edge of the counter, I stumbled toward the stairway. Three steps into the living room, my stomach lurched. I darted to the first-floor bathroom and heaved into the toilet, a cold sweat erupting over my body. *Breathe in, breathe out*, I told myself. *This will pass.* This was what pregnant women went through all the time, and it would be worth it. I placed my hand on my queasy stomach, already feeling indescribable and all-encompassing love for the baby inside me. We'd get through this, the baby and I. Every muscle in my body tensed involuntarily, and I threw up again.

Minutes later the retching and heaving had passed, and I lay strewn across the living room couch, water bottle in hand. I turned to one of my favorite shows, a reality show about people moving from regular houses into tiny houses. A couple building their dream tiny house played out on the screen. The energetic host toured them through their unfinished home, pointing out where the refrigerator and bathroom would fit. The future residents stared at the walls and the ceiling wide-eyed, almost as if they were in shock.

"It's smaller than I envisioned," the woman said. "I need to be able to host parties."

"I'm not sure where I'm going to put my tools," the man said, shaking his head.

The smiling host stepped between them, draping his arms around their shoulders. "Two hundred and fifty square feet isn't a lot of space, is it?"

My phone buzzed from the coffee table in front of me, as a text appeared on the screen. It was Gwen, the editor of *The Observer*. I popped up, a bubble of guilt forming in my gut because I'd been watching TV instead of working on the revisions to my article. I read her message: *I have a new assignment for you. Burlington, VT. Need to profile Smithson Manor B&B. Leave tomorrow a.m.*

I flopped back into the cushions and stared at the ceiling. There was nothing I felt like doing less than boarding a plane to Vermont, especially with my morning sickness to contend with. Gwen couldn't know I was pregnant, though. Not yet, anyway. She was all business, all the time, and didn't have any children of her own. I'd need to fit in as much traveling as possible before the baby arrived. I typed in my answer: *Okay. I'm on it.*

A second later, Gwen responded: *Great. Jackie will send you flight info by this afternoon.*

Jackie was Gwen's assistant. I was thankful, at least, that I didn't have to organize any travel plans. My jaw clenched at the thought of telling Gwen I was pregnant. I rubbed my belly, which hadn't yet protruded beneath the elastic waistband of my sweatpants. Maybe a career change would be okay, though. I'd have new projects to fill my time, like playdates, mommy-and-me swim classes, and Gymboree. I'd find a way to do some freelance writing on the side. Perhaps I could start a travel blog. Then I could work for myself. Besides, if Jason was right about his fund, maybe I wouldn't need to worry about money at all.

Holding my phone close to my face, I shifted gears and googled Burlington Vermont Bed and Breakfasts. Gwen generally provided me with the names of hotels and resorts to profile beforehand, but sometimes she left it up to me to locate some additional hidden treasures once I arrived at the location. I wanted to be prepared. The search results spanned five pages and included everything from quaint farmhouses to Victorian mansions. I saved the most intriguing ones to my favorites. Then I pulled up the Smithson Manor website and read about their comfortable rooms and farm-to-table breakfasts. Hopefully, I'd be feeling up to sampling the food.

By the time I glanced back at the TV, the show had reached my favorite segment—the big reveal. The couple's tiny house had been completed, and they were touring it for the first time. The outside was trendy, with a rustic and urban feel made up of stained-wood paneling and corrugated metal. The happy owners made their way inside, where the house appeared much bigger now. Some of the walls were painted a soothing blue color, while others were lined with panels. Storage cubbies separated the living area from the kitchen, and a ladder led straight up into a lofted sleeping area where natural light flowed in through a skylight. More hidden storage pulled out from under the bed and held the few clothes that had survived the journey from the big house.

At last, the host waved goodbye to the gushing couple who hooked their arms together and bounced up and down. The camera panned out. The tiny house sat perched near a meadow with mountains rising in the background. I couldn't help smiling for them.

As the credits rolled, I propped myself up. My nausea had passed. I'd get myself showered and revise the article I'd written on the Aspen resort. Then, I'd drive to Lowes to pick out sample paint colors for the nursery. I clicked off the TV.

For me, living tiny would be one of those alternate realities that every adult left behind to enjoy the life they'd actually chosen. I'd selected a different door to walk through, one with a loving husband, a new baby, and a beautiful house on the other side of it. My palm sank into my midsection and I smiled. Sacrificing the idea of a tiny house was easy, considering all my other dreams were coming true.

CHAPTER SEVEN

Gloria (NOW)

The waitress plucked my drained iced tea from the table and replaced it with a fresh glass. "Can I get you ladies anything else?"

"No, thank you," Beth said.

I only shook my head, as I had just stuffed my last two French fries into my mouth. The Tidewater's airy, nautical-themed dining room bustled with patrons. The summer tourists had arrived. In front of us, an enormous picture window overlooked Grand Traverse Bay, where the water glittered in the sunlight and waves crashed toward the sandy shoreline. I'd forgotten how the view of the bay could lift one's spirits. Still, I couldn't ignore the troubling thought poking into my mind.

I leaned closer to Beth. "It's hard to fathom how a young woman could have been murdered just down the road."

Beth pushed her napkin away. "Yeah. It's crazy they haven't identified her yet."

I clucked. "Maybe it was domestic abuse. Just horrible."

"Here's the check then. No rush." The waitress placed a narrow black folder on the table between us, cleared our plates, and hurried back toward the kitchen.

We both reached for it, but Beth beat me, snatching the bill toward her. "My treat, Gloria."

"Oh, no. At least let me split it." I didn't want Beth to think I was a cheapskate, although relief washed through me at having been a second too late. Despite her recent cash payment, my money didn't stretch as far as it used to.

Beth waved me off. "Don't worry. I can write it off as a business lunch. Plus, I wanted to thank you for giving me a shoulder to cry on yesterday. I'm not usually that emotional. I've had a lot on my mind lately."

"Well, we can blame the wine."

Beth smiled.

"Besides, I was happy to listen." I pointed to the check. "Thank you. My fish was delicious."

She nodded and signed. "I can see why your son likes this place."

Beth had barely touched her salmon-topped salad, so I wondered if she was only being polite. The mention of Ethan reminded me of the phone call I'd promised myself I'd make. I'd been too tired last night to follow through, but the call would happen tonight. Right now, the view demanded my full attention.

It had been such a lovely change of pace, sitting at the table facing the bay and chatting with Beth. She'd shared a little about her parents in Kalamazoo and mentioned a younger sister who'd spent several years battling drug addiction, but now worked as a hairstylist in Ohio. A glassy sheen covered her eyes when she told me they'd lost touch. I squeezed her hand and told her I was sorry; her insistence that I reconnect with Ethan suddenly made more sense. I changed the subject, describing the different varieties of vegetables I planned to plant in my garden this year. She told me more about her job as a travel writer and explained how a magazine called *American Traveler* had commissioned her to write an article on northern Michigan. Her task was to find unique angles on well-known tourist attractions and resorts, and to discover new destinations that people may not yet know about.

It sounded like a competitive business, but I wasn't surprised that Beth was successful. She was clever enough, that was for certain. Her article for *American Traveler* was the reason she was so eager to talk to Amanda. Beth usually interviewed the owners or managers of the resorts she visited and generally received the same canned information as everyone else. She wanted to pick Amanda's brain for another perspective on The Tidewater and ask her where the locals gathered. I'd rummaged through my own mind for any inside tips I could give her, but I hadn't ventured out much since Charlie had died.

The concierge desk had been empty when we arrived through the hotel entrance, and the man at the front desk told us Amanda's shift started at 1 p.m.

"Shall we go check for Amanda again?" I asked after the waitress had returned with the receipt from our meal.

Beth glanced at her watch. "Sure. I don't want to take up too much of her time, but an introduction would be great."

We stood up from the table and gathered our things.

"I have to make a quick trip to the ladies' room first," Beth said.

As she turned toward the hallway, a vibration from inside my purse startled me. Someone was calling. I fumbled through my purse. "My phone is ringing. I'll meet you in the lobby."

As Beth slipped away, I pulled out my cellphone; a number I didn't recognize appeared on the screen. I studied the glowing numbers, debating whether to answer. It was probably another one of those bothersome telemarketers. Still, the latest chapter I'd read in *The Thirty-Day Life Coach* encouraged me to take risks. I pushed the green button.

"Hello?"

"Hi, this is Joe Miles," a gravelly voice on the other end said. "I'm calling about the apartment for rent. Is it still available?"

I swallowed, excited at the prospect of another renter, but my skin turned cold at the same time. I'd only rented it to women in the past. Then again, maybe a man would be better equipped to repair the tricky lock or fend off mysterious intruders. Nonetheless, I hesitated, suddenly leery.

"Well, yes. I have someone else who is interested in it, but no lease signed." I exhaled. A little white lie never hurt anyone. Plus, it gave me a way out in case Joe Miles turned out to be someone less than desirable.

"Can I see it this afternoon?"

"Uh," I stumbled again, hoping I could schedule the showing during a time when Beth would be around.

"I'm an artist," the man said, probably sensing my unease. "I live in Detroit, but I'm doing all the art fairs in the area this summer and need a temporary place to live and store my paintings. I can pay upfront."

An artist. That sounded acceptable. The chill on my skin vanished, replaced by warm memories. Charlie and I used to love going to the art fair in Harbor Springs. We purchased a painting of a boat there one summer. It still hung in the upstairs hallway. "Well, yes. I guess you would need a place for your paintings, wouldn't you? I can meet you anytime after 2:30 p.m. today."

"How about 3 p.m.?" he asked.

"That sounds fine." I made a mental note: *Stand outside the garage at 3 p.m.* "My name is Gloria."

"Thanks. See you then."

I slid my phone back into my purse, overcome by the sudden urge to drive home and tidy up the apartment. It would be a relief to have the space occupied, especially after the unsettling door incident. How wonderful would it be to collect a full summer's rent for the apartment on top of the money Beth had already paid me? Maybe I could finally replace those drafty windows in my farmhouse. Charlie might not have approved of me renting out the apartment to a complete stranger, especially one who was a man, but he wouldn't have wanted me to be cold all winter either.

Dishes clanged behind me and a couple lingered nearby waiting to be seated. Remembering the plan to meet Beth in the lobby, I started down a hallway lined with framed photos of yachts and seagulls. Beth wavered in the distance, her hands shoved into her pockets, shifting her weight from foot to foot. Her eyes darted around the room the way they often did, as if she were searching for something. If I hadn't known any better, I would have guessed she was nervous.

I stepped next to her. "I'm back."

Her demeanor changed when she noticed me. She relaxed her arms and stopped fidgeting. Beth tipped her head toward the concierge desk. "I think that's her."

My eyes followed her gaze. Amanda stood behind the desk studying a computer screen. It had been quite a few months since she'd rented my garage apartment, and she looked different. Her hair was lighter than I recalled—almost white—and she'd cut it short, so it didn't quite reach her shoulders. She'd gained a few pounds, too. The weight gain suited her. I'd always thought she'd been too thin, not that I would have told her that. I hadn't been close with Amanda, not the way I'd already become friends with Beth. But Amanda had been nice enough. She'd kept to herself and paid the rent on time.

"Yes. There she is." I led Beth over to the desk to make the introduction. A cold sweat prickled my upper lip as we approached. I hadn't known Amanda well. Not at all, really. But it was too late to turn back.

Amanda's eyes met mine, their blueness reminding me of the sparkling bay outside. "Can I help you?" she asked.

"Yes, uh…" I said, freezing up. She didn't recognize me. "I'm Gloria. You used to rent an apartment from me."

"Oh." Amanda stepped back and put her hands to her face. She shook her head and sighed. "Hi, Gloria. I thought you looked familiar. Sometimes I don't know where my head is."

My heartbeat returned to a normal pace. "That's fine, dear. I know this is a surprise visit."

"Is this your daughter?"

"Oh, no." My cheeks blushed and I couldn't help but feel flattered someone would think Beth was my daughter. I turned toward Beth, remembering the reason for this whole encounter. "This is my friend, Beth. She's renting some land from me for the summer. She's writing a piece on The Tidewater for *American Traveler* magazine."

Beth stepped forward and held out her hand. "Hi, nice to meet you."

The two women joined hands in a brief handshake.

"I told Beth you worked here and might be willing to give her some information."

"I don't want to bother you while you're trying to work," Beth said. "But if you have time later, or another day, I'd really appreciate it."

"Yeah, sure. I can do that." Amanda puffed out her chest. "Or if you'd rather talk to the manager—"

Beth glanced toward the front desk. "Oh, thanks. I'll probably speak to the manager at some point, too, but I want a different perspective. Not just on this place, but on all the local hangouts."

"Okay. Yeah." Amanda nodded along. "I work until eight tonight. Or tomorrow I have the day off."

"Can I treat you to lunch tomorrow?" Beth asked. "It doesn't have to be here. Maybe another favorite spot?"

Amanda shrugged. "Sure. How about Barney's? It's a total dive, but they have great fish tacos."

"Perfect." Beth leaned toward Amanda and lowered her voice. "That's the kind of information I can't get from a boring manager."

Amanda and I chuckled.

"I'll meet you there at noon?" Beth asked.

"Yeah. Sounds good." Amanda pulled out her phone and typed the information into it. Then they exchanged numbers in case of any last-minute cancellations.

"Well, I'm glad I got to introduce you." I took a step forward and the two young women nodded in agreement. The introduction had gone wonderfully. They were about the same age. Maybe they'd even become friends. I'd done my good deed for the day. "I'm afraid I have to get going. There's a man interested in renting my apartment and I need to get it ready."

"It was a nice apartment. I'm sure it'll go fast." Amanda smiled. "Good to see you again, Gloria."

"You too." I turned and walked toward the front door of the lobby, Beth by my side. A man held open the door for us and we stepped into the sunlight, a brisk wind blowing off the bay.

"That went well," Beth said after we were out of Amanda's earshot.

"I'm delighted." The ache in my back began to ease. I'd been isolated for so long that I'd almost forgotten how rewarding it was to help people. It had been months since I'd last volunteered at the food bank in the basement of the church, or planted flowers as part of First Lutheran's beautification team. I'd just been getting acquainted with that nice couple, the Janssons, when Mary Ellen Calloway had left my name off the committee list. I'd hung onto Sunday services a couple of months longer, but stopped going to those, too, after I'd found myself sitting alone on Christmas Eve. As the choir sang carols of love and joy, my solitary status had been magnified by Mary Ellen Calloway's laughter two rows ahead. I'd tried not to stare in envy as four of her grandchildren piled on her lap, her husband squeezing her shoulder and chuckling along with her. In contrast, several inches of wooden pew stretched between my flabby thighs and the coats of the happy families on either side of me. I struggled to keep my eyes focused on the hymnal that weighed down my hands, but there'd been no mistaking I was all alone. I'd called Ethan the next day, desperate to reconnect. But when his voicemail beeped in my ear, my mouth had suddenly filled with cotton balls. I hung up, unable to think of the right words to say.

"I didn't realize you had an apartment showing today." Beth's voice pulled me from the distressing memory. She propped her sunglasses on top of her head, revealing her questioning eyes.

"Someone called when you were in the bathroom. His name is Joe Miles. He's coming by at 3 p.m." I smiled, not wanting to make it obvious I was concerned about meeting an unknown man at my property all alone.

Beth paused, eyeing me. "I'm going to wander around town for a while, but I'll come back to check on you. You can never be too careful, especially with what happened."

"He's an artist," I said, supplying her with more information in case of a future police investigation. "I'm sure it will be fine."

"Artist or not, I'll stop by later."

"Thank you. And for lunch, too."

Beth nodded and turned back toward The Tidewater. "See you later, Gloria."

My car was parked around the corner. I strolled through the sunshine, energized by the lunch. I hopped over the cracks in the sidewalk, thinking of my life since losing Charlie. I'd hidden away inside my farmhouse, inside myself. Sometimes I'd gone days without seeing or talking to another living soul. I thought of Ethan, my only child who I'd driven away. I'd been too prideful to pick up the phone and tell him I'd been wrong. Beth had only entered my life yesterday, but she had already changed me, given me a new way of looking at things. Her confidence was contagious, seeping into me in a way the self-help books never could.

The sun slipped behind a cloud, causing the temperature to drop and goosebumps to erupt across my arms. I hurried toward my car. A shortcut down the alley appeared on my right, but I continued straight, sticking to the sidewalk. There was a killer on the loose, after all. One could never be too careful.

CHAPTER EIGHT
Elizabeth (BEFORE)

A crib would fit perfectly against the far wall. With a hand on my hip, I stared in wonder at the beige guest room, seeing its potential for the first time. This room would soon be transformed into our baby's nursery. Natural light flowed through the windows opposite me. There'd be space for a changing table next to the closet door. I fanned out the dozens of color samples I'd collected from Lowe's and held them up to the wall. One by one, I tossed aside the shades of gray that appeared too yellow or too purplish in the glow of the overhead light. Five or six swatches of color remained, but I couldn't decide.

The back door slammed shut with a familiar clatter that shook our entire house. Jason was home. He was the only one who entered the house so forcefully, the floorboards booming with every step.

"Up here." I turned toward the hallway so he'd hear me. I'd called him earlier to see how his meeting had gone, but he hadn't picked up or called me back.

Footsteps bounded up the stairs. Jason appeared in the doorway, hands behind his back, panting. A smile crept onto the corners of his mouth. "Do you know anyone who picked up two investors today? A half-million dollars each!"

I tucked the paint samples into my pocket. "What? Did you…" I began to ask but was overcome with emotion, my throat constricting.

"Yes! I did it!" He lunged toward me and wrapped an arm around my waist, kissing me. "I've raised two million dollars. I'm going to make so much money for these people, they won't know what hit them. And guess who gets a percentage of it all?" His smile now spread wider.

"I'm so proud of you." His sweaty body pressed against me through his button-down shirt, the hard muscles in his arms twitching, and I wanted him to take me right there on the nursery floor. He stepped back from me.

"I got you something." He removed a Nordstrom shopping bag from behind his back.

I hesitated, and he shoved the bag toward me. "Go ahead."

My hand touched it before I saw it, something soft and luxurious. The scent of leather hit me next. I lifted out a purse. Even the color was decadent, a cross between gray and taupe with navy trim. It was more sophisticated than anything I owned. The kind of bag that no other writer for *The Observer* had ever carried. The tiny print on the attached tag read FENDI. Jason must have spent thousands of dollars to buy it.

"The mother of my child deserves the best." He jumped to my side, unable to contain his boyish excitement. "It can replace your old one."

My cheeks flushed with a mixture of gratitude and shame. The Banana Republic purse I normally carried sat on the kitchen counter downstairs, filled with credit cards, car keys, makeup, and other odds and ends. The interior pocket was frayed and the black fabric had lost its luster, but I'd never thought other people would notice. Especially Jason.

I was a failure at keeping up appearances, not understanding the way other women eased from trend to trend, and style to style. After we'd gotten engaged, Jason had mentioned how I might look better with lighter hair. I'd been humiliated at first; I'd worried he didn't find me attractive. But I'd gone to the salon the next day and had my dark tresses bleached. He'd been so excited by the change that I pretended to love it too… I just wished I'd thought of making the change on my own. Now I was angry at myself because I should have known I needed a new purse. *But a Fendi?*

"I love it, but…" My eyes took in the high-end bag as a pool of unease collected in my gut. Jason had been spending more and more money lately. Every time something good happened at work, he celebrated by making an elaborate purchase. A few weeks ago, it had been a silver necklace from a ritzy jewelry store. Today it was a luxurious purse. I would have preferred to save the money, especially now with all the home renovations we'd be doing to get ready for the baby.

"But what?" His shoulders slumped as he studied my face. "What's wrong?"

The positive energy deflated out of him, and I didn't want to take that away. I'd felt so little hope from him in the past months. I pushed away my lingering shame and anger, reminding myself he was only trying to do something nice for me. He'd bought me a gift most women would kill for and now I needed to be appreciative.

I clutched the bag and smiled, hugging him. "It's beautiful. I really love it." And I did love it. Maybe he was right. We both worked hard. I deserved to be spoiled a little after pinching pennies for so many years. My fingers traced over the smooth surface. "It's so nice. I hope I don't ruin it."

"You won't ruin anything, babe." He squeezed my hands in his. "We'll be millionaires soon. If you wreck that one, I'll buy you another one. No big deal." He kissed my neck and my skin bristled with excitement. He still had that effect on me. The paint samples brushed my hand and I began to pull them out of my pocket to get Jason's opinion on the color of the nursery, but he was already unbuttoning my shirt.

*

The fluffy pink teddy bear wore a T-shirt that read *Burlington, VT*. I squeezed it and set it back on the shelf. My flight had arrived into Burlington International right on time, and I'd managed to power through the morning sickness with soda water and crackers. I'd already dropped my bags at Smithson Manor Bed and Breakfast. Now, I had a few hours to explore the town before checking into my room.

I wandered down Church Street, the walkway bustling with a mixture of college students and empty nesters who were likely taking advantage of off-season rates. The eclectic mix of cafés, bistros, and clothing stores against the backdrop of the rolling countryside made for a picturesque setting. If only Jason had been there with me, it would have been a perfect afternoon. A hole-in-the-wall called the Whimsy Boutique lured me inside with its display of hand-sewn baby clothes in the window. My feet creaked across the wide plank floor, the flowery aroma of scented candles surrounding me.

"Can I help you find something?" A college-aged woman with curly black hair stopped folding scarves and smiled at me.

I noticed her eyes travel to my Fendi bag and I couldn't help but feel self-conscious. But also satisfied. No one ever stared at my old purse.

"Just looking," I said.

"Let me know if you need anything."

I nodded, sifting through a rack of calico dresses so small I couldn't imagine a human being fitting into them. I picked up a pair of baby booties from the shelf and inspected them.

"Those are knitted by a local woman," the saleswoman said. "She spins her own yarn from the wool she shears from her sheep."

The booties dangled in front of me. I couldn't believe how tiny they were. Even though I didn't knit, it was obvious the handiwork was exquisite. My finger brushed across the soft yarn. "They're adorable."

"They come in all different colors. Are they for a boy or a girl?"

"I don't know yet." My hand drifted to my stomach, a reflex. I hadn't been to see the doctor yet, but I knew from reading online that it would be at least a few more weeks before we would know.

The woman's eyes opened wider. "Oh. Congratulations!"

"Thanks." I could feel the color rushing to my face as I picked up a second pair of booties. "I just found out."

She waved her arm toward the back wall of the store. "Now you get to do the fun stuff. Shopping!"

"Yeah. It is fun." Biting back my grin, I browsed through additional shelves holding hand-carved wooden blocks and whimsical picture frames, but the booties called to me as if an outside force were pulling me back toward them. The $58 price tag seemed more and more reasonable, considering the woman spun her own yarn.

A pink pair weighed in one hand and a blue pair in the other. I debated. If Jason had been here, he would have bought both pairs, but that seemed silly. A white pair with pale yellow trim lay on top of the basket, solving my problem. They would work for a boy or a girl. I placed them on the counter and reached for my credit card. An unexpected hiccup caught in my throat and I swallowed back the surge of emotion. It was my first gift to our baby.

After I paid and thanked the sales lady, I clutched the delicate gift bag in my hand and meandered back outside, envisioning how cute our baby would look wearing the booties. I imagined people complimenting me on the baby's adorable footwear. I would tell them the story of the boutique in Vermont where I bought them, about how a local woman had stitched them together from yarn she had made from the wool of her sheep, and about how they were the first gift I ever bought for the baby before I even knew if it was a boy or a girl. I couldn't wait to get home and show the gift to Jason.

The walking directions on my GPS led me down a side street back toward the bed and breakfast. Despite being April, the weather was unseasonably warm, the searing sun feeling more like

August. My skin perspired beneath my misguided choice of heavy black pants, which I wore with the top button undone. I'd been reading about the changes happening to my body: my thickening midsection, enlarging breasts, and bulging veins. All of that on top of nausea and fatigue. The physical part of pregnancy was miserable, and the worst wouldn't hit until the third trimester. I might have to tell Gwen about the baby sooner than I thought.

Several minutes later, I let my weight sink into the quilted bedspread in my room at Smithson Manor Bed and Breakfast, where I'd already lined up an interview with the owner the following morning. I'd have the rest of the day for additional research into the history of the area and to locate other hidden gems of interest to tourists. I released the air I'd been holding in my lungs, kicking the shoes off my swollen feet. The room was stuffy, so I cracked the window open to let in a warm breeze. A jagged branch of an oak tree rustled in the wind and scraped at the window. I pulled back the quilt and lay down on the mattress. It was firmer than our bed at home and felt good on my back. It was just after 3 p.m. Plenty of time for a power nap before I chose a restaurant for dinner. First, I retrieved my phone, rested my head on the down pillow, and called Jason.

He answered on the third ring. "Hey, babe. Did you make it to Vermont okay?"

"Yeah. No problems." My eyelids closed as I breathed in the clove-scented smell of the room. "It's really nice here. I wish you were with me."

"I wish I was, too." Papers rustled in the background and Jason cleared his throat. "You get to the B&B yet?"

"Yeah. I'm here now. It's got a lot of character."

"Cool."

"I walked around Burlington earlier, and, guess what?" Every ounce of my body wanted to tell him about the booties, but I wouldn't let myself.

"What?"

"I found the cutest boutique and I bought our baby a little present." I smiled, relishing the secret.

"What is it?"

"I'm not telling."

"Come on."

"I'll show you when I get home. It's a surprise."

"Okay. I like surprises."

A woman's muffled laughter sounded in the background.

"Who was that?" I asked.

"A couple of the investors are waiting right outside. I'm getting ready to go over some numbers with them."

I squeezed my hands together, letting my head sink further into the pillow. Jason worked with both male and female investors, and he'd never given me reason to worry. "Oh. Okay."

"When are you coming back again?" Jason asked.

"Wednesday morning. I was hoping to come back tomorrow, but I don't think it's going to work out. I need to find some more 'diamonds in the rough' for Gwen."

"Ha. Right. I'll see you Wednesday night, then." More papers shuffling. "Hey. Sorry, but I've got to get ready for this meeting. Can we talk later?"

"Sure." I could tell he was distracted. "Good luck."

"Love you."

"Love you, too."

My phone dropped to the bed and I pulled the covers over me, exhausted. I flipped over on my side, unable to find a comfortable position. A nagging sensation tugged at my gut, but I couldn't pinpoint its source. Exhausted, I lay in bed with my muscles rigid and my eyes wide open. I didn't sleep at all.

CHAPTER NINE

Gloria (NOW)

A silver SUV with a crooked front bumper rumbled around the bend in my driveway. As the vehicle bounced closer, patches of rust around the wheel wells formed like black eyes. A cloud of dried dirt billowed out behind it. My heart thumped at the sight of the jalopy, which I could now see was a battered Ford Explorer. I cursed myself for being so naive. Why had I agreed to meet a strange man all alone? What if he wasn't really an artist? What if he was a murderer?

I glanced through the screen of trees toward the tiny house, but Beth's truck was gone. She hadn't returned from town yet. My fingers clenched, and I checked the time on my watch—3:05 p.m.

The Explorer lurched to a halt in front of me. I squinted my eyes, shielding them from the dust while trying to remember where I'd last seen my kitchen shears. Had it been in the dishwasher or the cutlery drawer? If necessary, I could make a beeline back into the kitchen and grab the weapon to defend myself.

The driver's door creaked open as an unshaven bear of a man emerged. His sandy-brown hair was flecked with gray and needed a good cut, not to mention a wash. The whole mop was pulled off his weathered face into a greasy ponytail. A shiny thread of a scar slashed through his left eyebrow. His age was a mystery. He could have been a thirty-year-old who'd had a hard life or a fifty-year-old who'd been blessed with a full head of hair. I was stumped.

"Hi. I'm Joe." He took two uneven steps toward me and held out his hand. I shook it.

"Gloria." I forced a smile, reminding myself to give him a chance. Recent events had made me paranoid.

"Beautiful land you have." He tipped his chin toward the pine trees in the distance. "I used to spend my summers up here, as a kid. Over on Walloon Lake. My aunt and uncle had a place."

"Oh, yes. Walloon."

The lake was situated a few miles from me. I nodded as if I'd been there, but my only knowledge of it came from the real estate fliers I sometimes picked up in town. I didn't recall ever seeing a house bordering the lake priced under $3 million, and I wondered how this man had gone from summering on Walloon to renting a garage apartment from a lonely widow.

"Can't afford to stay on Walloon now. Not with my artist's salary," he said, reading my mind.

"What kind of artwork do you do?" I asked.

"Oil paintings. Landscapes, mostly." He reached into his jeans pocket and pulled out a card. "This is my website."

I took the card and studied a thumbprint-sized image of a fiery sunset over a tree-lined lake. Although the painting was shrunken to the size of a quarter, the contrast of colors was breathtaking. Below the miniature painting was his name and an online address for an artist's studio. The card matched his story.

Rolling my shoulders back, I realized I'd gotten myself all worked up for nothing. I'd misjudged him. Yes, he was a little rough around the edges, but most starving artists were. The man had an easy way about him, and his half-moon shaped eyes were soft and kind.

"The apartment is this way, above the garage." I waved toward the exterior staircase that led to the second-story front door. Taking the steps slowly, I grasped the railing as I made my way to the open balcony. Joe followed a few paces behind.

"I bet you never get sick of this." Joe stood next to me, looking out at the rolling meadow bordered by trees. He turned to the north, facing Beth's trailer for the first time. "What's that?"

From up on the balcony, we had a clear look beyond the line of scattered trees; a bird's-eye view of the tiny house.

"That's a tiny house," I said, pushing my chest forward because I'd remembered not to call it a trailer. "I'm renting that field to a lovely young woman for the summer. She's a travel writer."

"Cool." Joe surveyed the landing. "This porch would be great for painting. Especially with that landscape." He pointed to the forest beyond my struggling vegetable garden and past the sprawling branches of the oak tree sheltering Charlie's ashes. The grassy color of the new leaves on the deciduous trees popped against the darker green needles of the pines. Songbirds chirped and flitted about. The dense vegetation was an endless yet comforting boundary, surrounding me like a hug. Tree branches swayed, their leaves rustling in the wind like hands waving at me.

I wondered if Joe was talented enough to capture the majesty of my land in a painting. Now, *that* would be something. I tried to imagine how the final image would appear, and where I would hang it. This unshaven artist was growing on me by the second. Hopefully, he'd approve of the apartment.

"Let me show you inside." Having left the front door unlocked on purpose this time, I opened it with an easy twist of the knob. I'd been there earlier to tidy up, turn on some lights, and spray air freshener. As we stepped inside, the aroma of vanilla and lavender wafted in the air. I swung my arm toward the couch, coffee table, and TV area. "Here's the living room. It comes furnished. I wrote that in the ad."

Despite finding the door wide open a couple of weeks ago, none of the contents had been taken or even moved, confirming my suspicion that a faulty lock was to blame, not a mysterious criminal. I'd examined every inch of the space, searching for clues like sticky fingerprints or missing furniture. Other than a loose window, I'd discovered nothing worth noting. I'd only come across some expired soup cans and stale boxes of cereal in the cabinet above the refrigerator and a few pieces of old mail Amanda had left behind in the drawer of the nightstand. The papers hadn't looked important, just a few ads and bank statements. I'd tossed the food away but set the mail aside so I could return it to her next time I ate at The Tidewater.

Joe wandered around the room, glancing out of windows. "Very nice."

"The kitchen is over here." I stepped into the galley kitchen. The white appliances and ceramic tile floor were dated compared to the sleek design of Beth's tiny house, but it was clean and fully equipped. "There's a big storage space here." I opened the door to a 10-foot by 12-foot walk-in closet.

Joe whistled. "Great storage. Perfect for my art supplies."

"The bathroom is there." I reached across the hall and opened the door so my prospective tenant could get a look. "And the bedroom is back here."

"That's a good-size room." Joe nodded his approval. He wandered around for another minute, inspecting closets and windows. "What about a washer and dryer?"

"I'm afraid you'll have to go to the Laundromat for that. There's one right in town, though."

Joe pressed his lips together. I hoped the laundry situation wasn't a deal-breaker and debated offering up the washer and dryer inside my farmhouse.

"Can I move in today?" Joe raised his scarred eyebrow. "It's June first. It'll make the math easy."

My body froze, delighted by his quick decision, but also taken off guard. He had a good point about the math.

"I promise I'll stay out of your hair and I'll be gone most weekends at art fairs." He grinned, waiting for my response.

Crossing my arms and shifting my feet, I wished more than ever that Charlie was here to handle this.

"I'll pay upfront like I said on the phone."

I wiped my palms on the front of my pants, glancing through the window at the nearby oak branches bobbing in the wind. Ideally, I would have liked to get a reference from a previous landlord and check out his website, but he seemed like a decent tenant, and I didn't have any other prospects. Besides, if he was paying upfront, there was little risk on my end. Still, I felt an obligation to warn him about the lock. "There's one thing you should know about."

Joe stared at me.

"The lock on the door may not be secure."

"Let me take a look." Joe paced past me and rattled the metal lock with his thick fingers. He closed the door, turned the deadbolt, and pulled the handle again. The fixture shifted a hair, but the door didn't budge. "Seems to get the job done. It's a little loose, but nothing to worry about."

My stomach reached into my throat. No faulty lock. *Did that mean someone had broken in? Or had I forgotten to lock the door altogether? Maybe the wind had blown it open.* My memory was jumbled.

"So, can I move in?" Joe asked, smiling.

"I guess that would be fine," I said, pushing away my tangled thoughts. At least I no longer had to worry about repairing the door.

Joe clapped his hands together.

"I'll need an extra month's rent as a security deposit."

"Thanks, Gloria," he said. "Do you take cash?"

"I do." I rocked back on my heels, my body stretching tall with the ease of someone ten years younger as all doubt about Joe's intentions vanished. The apartment was rented. Maybe I'd get those new windows, after all.

*

I slid my chair closer to the Formica counter of my breakfast nook and studied the pages of my *Thirty-Day Life Coach* workbook. I'd met Beth less than forty-eight hours ago, but she'd already helped me. In fact, I'd written her name in the *Number Two* spot as a "catalyst for change." Charlie's death filled the *Number One* spot, but the workbook suggested both positive and negative catalysts for change. Someday I'd have to tell her how she'd inspired me.

This workbook was making a believer out of me. It was pushing me to step outside of my comfort zone and create my best life. I'd taken some risks and now the rewards were paying off. For the first time since Charlie died, I'd have some extra money.

The stack of cash from Joe lay on the counter next to me, its inky aroma swirling with possibilities. I'd have to run to the bank tomorrow to make another deposit. Having all this money lying around made me nervous.

My fingers flipped to a dog-eared page of the workbook. It was my "Action Plan," which was really nothing more than a glorified to-do list. I checked the box next to "Rent garage apartment for the summer." The last item on the list stared back at me, the checkmark missing from the box: "Call Ethan."

A bubble formed in my throat and I hunched over the workbook trying to envision what I'd say to him and exactly which words I'd use. Our last phone conversation had been nearly a year and a half ago. It had been a disaster, even though I'd apologized to him straight away for keeping the pamphlet.

He'd let out a long sigh. "Are you still hanging out with the women who gave it to you?"

"Only once in a while. I see them at Bible study."

"You have to choose. It's them or me."

I hesitated, my fingers tightening around the phone. "Of course, I choose you. I'd still like to go to Bible study though."

Ethan coughed out a laugh. "That's what I thought. You can't have it both ways, Mom." He hung up the phone so abruptly it felt like I'd been punched in the stomach. I called him back in the days that followed, but he didn't pick up. My calls had been going to voicemail after that. Eventually, I stopped leaving messages. More recently, I'd stopped calling altogether.

I bought my first self-help book on a whim a few weeks after Mary Ellen Calloway had left me off the decorating committee and I'd abandoned Bible study for good. I'd skipped my regular trip to the IGA and, instead, traveled the four extra miles to Walmart for my groceries, eager for an excuse to stay out of the house a little longer. The shiny book with a sea-green cover and yellow lettering had been laying on top of the clearance bin: *Twelve Easy Steps to Positive Thinking*. The title had drawn me toward it, in the same way the Little Traverse lighthouse might have guided a sinking ship through a storm. For $1.99, the book was an affordable remedy for a desperate lady who'd lost grasp of every positive thought in her head. As shoppers shoved their carts past me toward the checkout lanes, my hand lifted the book from the bin and opened to a random page. The heading of the chapter jumped toward me and grabbed me by the shoulders: *When given the choice between love and hate, choose love.* I read it again. And again. The store dissolved around me, so only that sentence and I remained, a statement that so obviously referred to me and Ethan.

Was it really that simple? What were the odds I'd stumble across this book on top of the clearance bin? And to have opened it to that exact page? Surely, it had been some sort of divine intervention, a sign from God, as if the book had found me and not the other way around. But my wonder had quickly been squashed by the sinking feeling in my gut. I'd made the wrong choice with Ethan. It had been my duty as his mother to show him love. I'd failed. I'd saved the pamphlet instead of throwing it away. I'd sided with the unforgiving opinions of a few zealots over my own flesh and blood. No wonder Ethan had left. No wonder he hadn't answered my calls. I should have tried harder.

Now, I swallowed against the dryness in my throat, eyeing my phone and aware of my fingers squeezing the edge of the workbook. It was time to make amends with my son. I tried to think of the right words to say if he answered, words that wouldn't make him shut down or hang up. Drawing a blank, I calculated the time difference between Michigan and California.

A couple of solid knocks at the front of the house caused me to jump. I tossed the workbook aside and stepped toward the doorway, peeking through the peephole. Beth wavered on my front porch with her hands in her pockets. I opened the door.

"Hi." She shifted her weight. "I didn't recognize that car in the driveway and I wanted to make sure everything was okay."

"Oh, yes. I'm fine. Thank you." I ushered her inside.

"Sorry, it took me a little longer in town than I thought. There was so much to look at." She pointed toward the garage and cocked her head to the side, confused. "Is the guy who looked at the apartment still here?"

"Yes. He agreed to take the place for the summer." I smoothed down my khaki pedal pushers with my palms. "He's a painter. A little rough around the edges, but very nice."

Beth nodded but her eyes clouded over. I sensed her disappointment, which caused the temperature of my body to rise like the thermometers on the cartoons Ethan used to watch, heat collecting in a big red ball on my face. Had I made a mistake by renting the apartment so quickly and without getting Beth's approval first? Joe would be her next-door neighbor, after all. That thought hadn't occurred to me earlier. I hadn't even considered her feelings. It was no wonder I didn't have many friends.

I cleared my throat. "He said he won't be around much due to the weekend art fair schedule."

Beth scratched her elbow and nodded again. "Okay." She adjusted the shoulder strap of her multicolored fabric purse. The bag appeared to have been assembled by kindergartners but somehow looked stylish on her.

She shrugged. "My house is parked far enough away. It doesn't make a difference." Her voice was flat, though. Unconvincing. She picked at her fingernail. "What did you say his name was again?"

"Joe Miles. He does beautiful oil paintings. Landscapes, mostly."

"Okay." Beth motioned outside. "I need to unload a few groceries."

"Alright. Have a nice lunch with Amanda tomorrow if I don't see you before then."

She raised her hand in a wave. "I'll let you know how it goes." Beth opened the door and let herself out.

I hovered in the foyer, my previous elation at self-help progress deflated. Beth was miffed because I'd rented the apartment to a strange man. She was too nice to say it outright, but I could tell. Maybe she'd feel better after meeting Joe. Then, she could see for herself that he was nothing more than a giant, unkempt teddy bear. Or maybe I could do something to make it up to her.

My eyes traveled to the cluttered office nook that extended from the living room. I'd set up my home computer there years ago, although I couldn't remember the last time I'd used it. Perhaps I could pull up Joe's website and show Beth some of his paintings. I stepped toward my makeshift home office, noticing for the first time its utter disorder, my breath feeling thick as dishwater in my throat.

The area was a hodgepodge of rescued magazines, old tax returns, collected recipes, and scraps of paper containing grocery lists and phone numbers. Amanda's forgotten mail lay on top of the chaos. Piles of holiday cards sorted by year lay stacked on the limited desk space. They were from old friends back in Grand Rapids and some of Charlie's former co-workers. I hadn't had the heart to toss them out, the cards and pictures being my last glimpse into the friendships we'd once shared with their senders. I set the cards down, promising myself I'd find a better spot for them, and pushed a pile of papers off the keyboard. The computer made a humming sound as I turned it on, the screen flickering for a moment before the background appeared. Ethan had set it up for me when he'd been back for the funeral. It was a photo of me, Charlie, and Ethan on the beach in Florida from our trip at least fifteen years earlier. That had been a great day.

Remembering what I was doing, I sat down and clicked on the blue "e" to connect to the internet. I placed Joe's business card in front of me while I waited. Instead of the homepage I expected to see, an error message appeared: No internet connection found. Check your connection. Below that was a list of troubleshooting ideas, none of which was helpful or made any sense.

I blew out a puff of air and slunk back in my chair. *Honestly!* This outdated computer caused me nothing but headaches. It was worthless.

Raising myself up, I wandered back into the kitchen where the workbook on the counter caught my eye and reminded me what I'd been doing before Beth had knocked. *Ethan.* Beth was the one who suggested I call him and invite him for a visit. Her stinging words replayed in my mind, "*If I had a son, I wouldn't lose touch with him for any reason.*"

I'd been foolish to lose Ethan in the first place. Just because he hadn't turned out exactly according to my vision, I'd snubbed him, more worried about causing a fuss with the women at Bible study than protecting my only son. Heaven knew I wasn't perfect, either. I recalled the pain in Ethan's eyes when he'd discovered the pamphlet, the way the spoon had dropped from his hand. The horrible clatter of the metal utensil against the porcelain dish had never stopped ringing in my ears. In the weeks and months and years since that agonizing moment, I'd realized the obvious—the

Bible didn't approve of hurting others, especially my own kin. My actions toward my son hadn't been Christian at all. If I ever went back to Bible study, I'd be sure to point that out.

I stumbled toward my phone, shaking my head at my weak effort to reconnect with Ethan. Beth had lost her husband so young. Maybe she'd never get remarried or have children, and here I was wasting my good fortune. I scrolled through the address book, forgetting about the whispers of the ladies at church and the unknown time difference between Michigan and California, and I pressed Ethan's number.

CHAPTER TEN
Elizabeth (BEFORE)

Concealed inside of our double garage, I turned off the ignition and emerged from the car, catlike. Hopefully Jason hadn't heard the metal door clamoring open and closed. I wanted my early return home to be a complete surprise. My trip to Vermont had been cut short after I'd soon found plenty of little-known boutiques and restaurants to include in my Burlington article. This morning I'd completed in-depth interviews with the owners of two other destinations in the area, a kitschy 1950s-themed motel and a rustic cabin retreat five miles outside of town. Gwen had already reviewed my notes via email and praised me for hitting a home run in the "hidden gem" department. Around lunchtime, I realized there was no need for me to stay another night. I called the airline and switched my flight a day earlier. Visions of Jason's expression as I unexpectedly walked through the door played out in my mind. He loved surprises.

Now I lifted my suitcase from the trunk and closed it carefully. Jason was home. His SUV was parked in the garage, and warm lights shone from inside the kitchen and living room. It was 7 p.m. and I wondered if he'd eaten dinner yet.

My hand rummaged through the bag, searching for my house key and hitting the pair of wool baby booties instead. A tingle of anticipation prickled through me. The edge of the key poked my finger and I pulled it out, feeling my way through the darkness toward the lock on the back door. Our neighbor's golden retriever caught sight of me and barked from the other side of a slatted wooden fence.

"Shh!" I said to the dog in a loud whisper, which only caused him to bark again. I ignored the barking, finding the lock with my key and slipping inside. The kitchen was empty, except for a few beer bottles scattered across the counter. I rolled my eyes and hoped Jason hadn't been surviving on beer alone for the last forty-eight hours. A pleasant aroma emanated from the living room where my sandalwood candle flickered on the table.

"Hon?" He shouldn't have left a candle burning unattended. I'd need to talk to him about that. That was the kind of oversight we couldn't have once the baby arrived. Before I could blow it out, a white bag in the hallway caught my eye. I bypassed the candle and tiptoed toward the bag, a Nordstrom label appearing across the side. *Had he bought something for himself? Or was it another present for me?* I bent over and peeled back the tissue paper, unable to stop myself. My heartbeat quickened and I straightened up tall, confused. Another Fendi handbag, identical to the one he'd already given me, lay underneath the paper. Was it a joke? I'd told him I was worried about ruining my new purse. Maybe he'd already purchased a backup? It seemed wildly extravagant, and I forced myself to take a breath. I didn't want to ruin the night, the surprise. The conversation about his overspending could wait for another time.

The soft hum of music floated from upstairs and I realized Jason was probably taking a shower. He'd mentioned earlier that he was hoping to get a workout in tonight. I climbed the stairs, my hand clutching the booties inside my purse. I couldn't wait to show them to Jason.

I slunk down the hall and opened the bedroom door, the scene before me strangling my voice, my stomach convulsing. My hands automatically covered my abdomen, protecting my baby from the onslaught. Jason lay in our bed, naked, with a woman straddling him. Her ratty blonde hair bounced up and down. It seemed minutes or hours, or even my entire lifetime, passed before he saw me, his eyes growing so wide the whites showed all around. He shoved the woman off him and yanked up the sheet. The woman turned away, hiding her face and pulling on a T-shirt.

"What the…" was all I could say, my brain not able to catch up enough to form words, not able or willing to understand. My hands shook so violently that my bag dropped to the floor. He was in our bed with another woman. My eyes were fixed on her tangled blonde hair as I remembered Jason's insistence many months ago that I dye my hair lighter.

"Liz! What are you doing here?"

"What am I doing here? I LIVE here!" I screamed. My heart pounded in my chest, breaking me out of my frozen stance, allowing a tidal wave of emotions to crash over me. "How could you do this?" The tears flowed freely now. I saw my perfect life, my entire future, washed away. Our baby, our happy marriage, the dreams we shared, all destroyed. Something inside of me snapped, like a boat breaking from its mooring and smashing from wave to wave in the middle of a hurricane. "HOW COULD YOU?" I screamed again. A primal version of myself took over, someone I'd never known and didn't recognize. "IS THIS WHAT YOU DO WHEN I'M TRAVELING?"

Jason held up his hand. "Babe, this was the first time. I swear."

He was lying. I knew he was lying. I don't know which made me more furious, his lies or the fact that they flowed so easily from his lips. I lunged toward the pewter lamp on our dresser, the one we'd received as a wedding gift from my Aunt Bea, and yanked out the cord. I threw it directly at his face. He ducked just before it smacked against the wall, the light bulb fracturing into pieces.

"Holy shit." The other woman ducked and sprinted out of the room.

The confusing scene from a few minutes ago—the burning candle, the duplicate Fendi bag—rearranged itself in my mind, suddenly making horrifying sense.

"Was that purse for her?" I picked up a vase and chucked it at Jason. Again, it missed him by inches and split into pieces against the wall. "You bought us the SAME FUCKING PURSE?" I was screaming now, hysterical. I grabbed everything I could find, everything within my reach, and hurled the items at Jason—keys, jewelry, candles—hoping something would hit him and leave a permanent scar. If we'd owned a gun, I would have loaded it and shot him dead.

"Calm down," Jason said, his eyes pleading with me. "I can explain. This doesn't change anything."

"Get out. Get out. GET OUT!" He needed to leave or I would kill him. And that slut who was with him: I'd find her and kill her, too.

He didn't argue this time. He yanked on his pants as I chucked books at his back, the guttural noise emanating from my throat like nothing I'd ever heard. I was screaming for myself, for our unborn baby, for my shattered life.

Jason scurried out the door, careening through the hallway and leaping down the stairs two at a time. "We'll work it out, babe. I'll make it up to you." He yelled the words over his shoulder as he ran.

"GET OUT!" I screamed, chasing him.

He exited through the front door, slamming it behind him. A few seconds later, the garage door rumbled and his Mercedes zoomed out of the driveway. I didn't check to see whether she was with him, but the Nordstrom bag was gone, and I knew I'd been right. It had been a gift for her.

My legs gave out and I crumpled to the floor, sobbing. There was too much to process, so much lost in a matter of seconds. My mind shut down, my chest hollow. I hugged my belly, my baby, the one I could rely on. The only person in my life who I still felt connected with.

The number of minutes or hours I lay on the floor was a mystery. Missed clues and red flags surged through my mind. How many times had I traveled out of town for work? Dozens? No. It was more than that. Had he cheated on me every time I'd been away? I remembered the earring I'd found on the rug, the one I'd assumed belonged to his mother. It hadn't been Mary's. I knew that now. The muffled laughter I'd heard on the phone yesterday replayed in my mind. Had the other woman been at his office when I called? How stupid had I been? Did everyone know? The neighbors? His friends? Were they all laughing at me? My insides heaved again, and I felt exposed and raw as if someone had cut me open and turned me inside out. Why would he buy her the same purse? And insist on me dyeing my hair lighter? Maybe he wanted a crew of identical concubines to worship him. Cheating was some sort of sick game for him.

At some point in the middle of the night, I raised myself from the floor, shivering. I limped over to the candle in the living room. It barely flickered in a melted pool of wax and I blew it out. Then I dumped it in the kitchen trash. Just as I turned away from the garbage bin I doubled over, a new wave of despair crashing over me as I collapsed onto the couch. I hoped the baby couldn't feel my agony. I needed to go see my doctor, to make sure everything was still on track with the pregnancy. Maybe I could survive without my lying, piece-of-shit husband, but I couldn't cope with losing my baby, too.

Gathering my breath, I looked at the clock—2:30 a.m. Although every cell inside me screamed with exhaustion, sleep wasn't an option. I raised my shell of a body off the couch and dragged myself into the kitchen, sifting through the cleaning products under the sink until my hand landed on a box of oversized garbage bags. I stomped upstairs, ripped the soiled sheets from our bed and stuffed them in the bag. I caught a whiff of perfume, not mine. Grief filled my mouth. My muscles contracted, a frenzy taking over. Everything that was his was tainted by her. His stuff would vanish into the bags, removed from the house as if eliminating his belongings would somehow ease my pain. It was the only way I could think of to salvage what remained of my life. He'd hurt me, now I'd do something to hurt him. That's how karma worked. He loved his things—his toys, and clothes, and shoes, and watches—I knew that. He loved his stuff more than he loved me.

After the bed was stripped down to the mattress, I targeted his dresser, yanking open the drawers and scooping up his neatly folded designer clothes, the ones I'd told him he'd spent way too much money on, and dumped them into the trash bag. When the bag was stuffed, I filled another. And another. Within minutes, the dresser and closet were cleared of any memory of him. Thousands and thousands of dollars of his prized possessions, gone.

There were ten bags. I made five trips, dragging two behind me each time, down the stairs and out to the alley behind our garage where the dumpster sat. As I heaved the bags into the metal bin, I wondered how I'd ended up with a husband whose priorities were so out of whack. A man who valued brand names and arm candy over an honest relationship and a loving family.

The last bag balanced on the edge of the dumpster, teetering like it was scared to fall. With both hands, I shoved it over the edge, letting out a thick yelp at the same time. I stepped back, satisfied with my actions, a tiny bit of my dignity restored.

I stumbled back inside, my eyes hungry to locate more offensive items, but landing on the empty box of trash bags instead. The rest of my purging would have to wait. The contents of my purse lay strewn across the hardwood, the fuzzy edge of a miniature white sock visible beneath the mess. I crouched down and picked it up, the soft wool resting against my skin. An entire lifetime had passed since I'd made the purchase at the boutique in Vermont. The story of the woman who made the yarn from the wool of her own sheep seemed trivial now, a tale only a naive fool would tell herself to occupy her thoughts. Rocking forward on my knees, my forehead pressed against the cold floor, I clutched the knitted booties to my chest and sobbed.

CHAPTER ELEVEN

Gloria (NOW)

The hollow knocking of a woodpecker hunting for insects sounded from the forest. I boosted myself up from my hunched-over position in the garden, my eyes searching the distant trees for the noisy bird with the bright red head. I blinked, unable to locate it. Stretching out the kink in my back, I gave up my search and crouched back down. My gloved finger poked a hole in the soil, while my bare hand dropped in seeds.

Last summer, I hadn't had the energy to keep up with my vegetable garden, especially after the darn deer found a weak spot in my fence and destroyed my harvest. I'd arrived at my plot one July morning and discovered they'd devoured all my plants. The beans, peppers, cucumbers, and tomatoes were gone. They may as well have gnawed away what was left of my heart. I'd moped back to my living room and collapsed on the couch, defeated.

The wire mesh still dipped down where they'd trampled through it. My resolve had strengthened since then. I would figure out a way to secure the fence before the seeds began to sprout. The knocking sounded again from the woods, and I glanced toward the trees, my mouth dry. A sensation of watching eyes pressed on my back as if that bird was spying on me. Or maybe it was the deer.

By the way my stomach squeezed with hunger, I guessed it was close to lunchtime. I shrugged off my uneasy thoughts and spied through a gap in the birch trees beyond my dirt driveway.

Beth's truck was there, parked outside her tiny house. I'd secretly hoped she'd spot me working and come over to chat, but she was probably busy preparing for her important lunch with Amanda. I couldn't wait to tell her the news.

Ethan hadn't picked up my call last night; his recorded voice had asked me to leave a message, followed by a beep. I'd hesitated, a tangle of words caught in my throat, before leaving a long and rambling message. After talking in circles about topics like the weather and The Tidewater's fried perch, I'd finally gotten to the point and blurted out that I missed him and was sorry for not reaching out to him sooner. By the time I ended the call, my heart leaped around in my chest like a wild animal and my eyes stung with unexpected emotion. I'd hung up, pacing the room, wondering what in heaven's name I'd done, and how he'd react. Ten minutes hadn't passed before my phone rang. Ethan had called me back right away.

"It was good to hear from you, Mom," he said, a tinge of worry in his voice.

His statement hit me in an odd spot, like when I knocked my funny bone on the wooden arm of the dining room chair. "Yes. You, too," I said, but I dissolved into tears as soon as the words left my lips.

He'd been a patient listener, prodding me with questions and trying to understand. I explained how someone had left the pamphlet underneath my coat two years earlier, and how I realized I'd been wrong to keep it because he was perfect the way he was. I recounted how the self-help book from the clearance bin at Walmart had magically found its way into my hands and opened directly to the page about choosing love over hate. *Didn't he agree it was a sign?* He laughed and said he did. I steadied myself against the kitchen counter, apologizing for the unexpected tears. I explained how I'd been working on my life, healing from Dad's death, trying to become a better version of myself. But there was one thing, I told him, that I was missing more than anything—having him in my life. *Would he come home for a visit this summer? Just a week or two.*

He hadn't jumped at the invitation. He sighed and listed the obvious roadblocks: *Work, limited vacation time, tight finances.*

"I'll pay for your ticket," I said, interrupting. Other than replacing the drafty windows in my farmhouse, I couldn't think of a better use for the pile of cash stacked inside my pocketbook.

Silence hung on the line. Crickets chirped from the other side of the window screen.

"So, you're really okay with me being gay?" Ethan said at last.

"Yes, Ethan." I inhaled a deep breath and held it, working up my courage. "I was wrong to judge you. I hope we can talk more about it in person."

"Wow. Okay." He cleared his throat and breathed heavily from the other end. "Work has been kind of slow lately. I'll look into flights, but I'll pay for my ticket. I don't want you spending money on it."

My smile stretched wide. I bounced forward on the balls of my feet and patted my *Thirty-Day Life Coach* workbook. Ethan was coming home.

A motor grumbled and sputtered, bringing me back to the present. I raised my head, shielding my eyes from the billowing dust as Joe's vehicle clamored up the driveway. He'd already left and returned twice since I'd started working in the garden. Each time he passed, he waved to me and unloaded a new pile of boxes. The rusty Explorer lurched to halt in front of the garage and he emerged. From hundreds of yards away, he peered toward me and waved again.

I ignored the tremor in my gloved hand, lifting it in greeting. Then, I pretended to go back to planting. He swung open the back and removed an elongated duffel bag, its camouflage print ironically making it stand out more against the natural backdrop. My insides unraveled like a dropped spool of thread.

I'd seen a bag like that before, many years ago, when some acquaintances of Charlie had driven up one fall for a hunting trip. They'd convinced my husband to go with them as some sort of a male-bonding weekend. Charlie preferred books to guns and hadn't been thrilled about the idea, but he'd ultimately agreed. He'd felt obligated to accompany his friends who'd traveled hours in our direction to spend the weekend in the wilderness. I still remember the slackened expression of relief on Charlie's face when they'd returned on Sunday afternoon, empty-handed. He'd chuckled when he'd told me how they'd drank three cases of beer and played dozens of rounds of poker. They hadn't spotted a single deer the entire weekend.

I pictured the long, narrow bag they'd handed to Charlie when they'd arrived that weekend, the one containing the rifle. It was an exact match to the one Joe held now, camouflage print and all. The tremor in my hand now spread along my spine and into my core. It was true that plenty of people owned guns for lawful reasons—hunting and self-defense—but it was also true that just as many people didn't.

I swallowed against my parched throat and dug my toe into the dirt, cursing my malfunctioning computer. I hadn't even verified that Joe was an artist. What had I done? Oh, how I wished that Charlie had been here to handle this. I tried to think of anything in the lease that restricted guns, but I didn't recall seeing any such wording.

Joe climbed the stairs to his apartment, the rifle-shaped bag in one hand and a large black suitcase in the other. Where was he getting all this stuff? From a storage unit? An art studio? A Michigan Militia compound? I hadn't asked enough questions.

Yanking off my gardening gloves, I stuffed them into the pocket of my windbreaker and attempted to look casual. I wandered up the driveway toward Joe's SUV. As I got closer, I could see dozens of shoebox-sized boxes inside. The apartment door burst open and I jumped.

"Morning, Gloria." Joe's voice boomed against the calmness.

I stepped away from the vehicle. "Good morning. I see you're settling in." I wanted to ask him about the weapon, about why he had it, but I didn't want to make waves. People could be so sensitive about their guns, especially out here in the boonies.

"Yep. Yep. Lots of supplies, that's for sure." He motioned toward the SUV. "This is my last load."

"Oh, my. That's a lot of boxes." I shifted my weight to the other foot. "Where are you bringing them from?"

"Clearing out my storage unit in town. Brought all this stuff up from Detroit in a U-Haul a couple of weeks ago and needed somewhere to keep it until I found a place." He winked.

I smiled, the heat in my body cooling. Joe had a perfectly reasonable explanation. Art supplies. He wasn't a criminal or a terrorist. *Honestly!* I needed to stop expecting the worst from people, to stop jumping to conclusions. There was an exercise somewhere in my *Thirty-Day Life Coach* workbook on this very subject. I'd seen it and skipped over it, and now I was paying the consequences. His camouflage bag probably contained a roll of tracing paper or an oversized paintbrush, not a gun.

I shoved my hands in my pockets. "When is your first art fair?"

"Next weekend. Just a small one up in Cross Village." He folded his massive arms in front of his chest. His fingernails were grungy and black, and I wasn't sure if the color was from dirt or paint.

I pulled my gaze from his discolored nails. "That's wonderful. I'd love to see your paintings sometime."

"Doing two shows nearby in July. Harbor Springs and Petoskey. Or, if you want to see it sooner, most of my stuff is stacked in that huge closet inside." He pointed toward the apartment.

"Oh." A fist of anxiety tightened in my stomach at the thought of being alone inside the garage apartment with a giant man with a scar through his eyebrow who I barely knew and who may or may not have a gun. "I don't want to intrude. I'll come by one of the art shows. When you're all set up."

Joe stared at me, expressionless. I hoped I hadn't offended him.

"Sounds good." He returned to the stack of boxes.

A door clicked shut in the distance and I squinted, trying to make out activity behind the line of trees. It was Beth. A second later, the engine of her truck hummed and headed toward us. The truck followed the path of tire tracks through the gap in the trees and over the grass until intersecting with my dirt driveway.

"Have you met Beth yet?" I turned toward Joe, eager to change the subject.

"Nope."

The sun reflected off her windows, making it impossible to see inside. I waved anyway and the vehicle eased to a halt. The driver's window lowered. Beth's lipstick matched the hot-pink sundress she wore. A white knitted cardigan covered her shoulders, wooden beads looped around her neck, and metallic sunglasses shielded her eyes. If I hadn't known any better, I would have guessed she was a film star.

"Hi, Gloria."

"Don't you look nice!"

She grinned. "Thanks. I'm going to meet Amanda for lunch." She glanced at Joe, her smile fading.

"This is Joe," I said. "He's renting the garage apartment for the summer."

"Hi," Joe gave Beth a mock salute.

Beth stared, nodding slightly, but didn't speak. Her mouth pressed into a thin line. She must have been taken aback by his appearance. The shiny scar, dirty nails, soiled clothes, and greasy hair.

"He's an artist," I told her again, hoping to put her at ease. Guilt tugged at my insides for having done anything to make her uncomfortable.

"A starving artist," Joe said, laughing at his own joke.

"Nice to meet you." Beth didn't laugh. She looked at me. At least, I think she did. I couldn't see her eyes through those mirror-like glasses.

A motor rumbled, drawing our attention to the end of the driveway where a police cruiser crawled toward us.

"What's this?" I looked from Beth to Joe, but they looked equally confused. Beth cut her engine and stepped down from her truck.

The cruiser stopped a few feet in front of us, blocking the driveway. An officer with closely cropped black hair and a square jaw stepped from the car and held up his badge. "Hi folks, I'm Officer Bradley. How's everyone doing?"

"Just fine," I said, although my heart thumped inside my chest. "Is something wrong?"

"No, ma'am. There's no need for alarm. We're canvassing all the outlying areas today for leads relating to the death of the young woman found on the beach in Petoskey a few days ago."

Dread rippled over my skin. "Have they identified her yet?"

The officer dipped his chin. "Yes. The information was released this morning. Her name was Ella Burkholter. Only twenty-six years old. She was a hairdresser in town."

"Oh, my." My eyes traveled to Beth, who looked scared to death. Her mouth curved downward and her fingers clutched her keys so tightly her knuckles turned white. "What salon?" I asked, hoping it wasn't SpeedyCuts where I went for a trim every three months.

"It's called Fringe."

I nodded, releasing a breath. I'd never heard of Fringe.

The officer hooked his finger into his belt, surveying each of us in turn. "We're asking people if they've seen anything suspicious or noticed unfamiliar people passing through their properties."

I stepped closer to Beth. "Well, no. I don't think so. These are my tenants. Beth Ramsay. She's a travel writer." I motioned toward her and she forced a smile. "And Joe Miles. He's an artist."

Joe stepped forward and handed a business card to the officer. "I do oil paintings."

Officer Bradley inspected the card and nodded. "How long are you folks in town for?"

"They're staying for the summer," I said.

"Anyone notice any suspicious activity in the last few days?"

Beth shook her head. "No."

Joe shrugged. "I don't think so."

"Me neither," I said, deciding not to make an issue out of Joe's camouflage bag.

"Okay. Here's my card if you do notice anything." He fanned out three cards and we each took one. He tipped his head. "I appreciate your time."

"Thank you, sir," I said. "I hope you find whoever killed poor Ella."

"We're working on it." He slipped back into his car and pulled a U-turn, heading in the direction of my nearest next-door neighbor.

The three of us stood in silence.

"What a world we live in," I said.

Joe shook his head and kicked at the dirt.

Beth straightened her sunglasses and turned away from me. "I've really got to get going."

"Good luck with your lunch," I said as she climbed inside her vehicle.

She raised her window and shifted it into gear. Her truck sped away from us, a dust trail lingering in the air. Joe let out a raspy cough.

I tried not to take Beth's coolness personally. *Not everything is about me.* That's what *The Thirty-Day Life Coach* said, and I could see that it was true. Beth was probably worried about being late. Or nervous about becoming the next victim of a crazed killer who was still on the loose. No one could blame her.

Joe squared his shoulders toward me. "Don't worry, Gloria. I'll keep a lookout for you."

A breath of relief squeezed from my lungs. "Thank you."

"Well, time to finish unpacking." Joe stepped toward his SUV and opened the back door, pulling out a fresh stack of boxes.

I turned toward my farmhouse, steering my thoughts away from the unexpected police visit. Meandering toward my front door, I inspected the shoots of the irises and lilies pushing up from beneath the soil. It wouldn't be much longer before my front path would be lined with flowers. Maybe they'd even bloom while Ethan was here if the warm weather kept up. He'd emailed me his flight information this morning. A week and a half from now, a plane would land at Pelliston Airport and my son would be on it. He planned to stay for ten days. *Ten days!* That was more time with him than I'd dared to dream of. I wanted to share the news with Beth, but out in the driveway with Joe and the police officer hadn't been the right time.

CHAPTER TWELVE

Elizabeth (BEFORE)

It was Wednesday night. A full twenty-four hours since I'd stumbled across the land mine constructed by my cheating husband and his home-wrecking girlfriend. The parts of me that survived the explosion lay in a heap on the couch, my eyes puffy and painful from the tears that wouldn't stop. I'd called into work. No details for Gwen, only that I was "sick." My brain couldn't come up with anything more specific or convincing.

There were seventeen missed calls from Jason on my phone, nine messages. I'd only listened to the first few words before throwing my phone across the room so hard that it left a dent in the drywall. More recently, the texts had started flowing in, one after another. *I'm sorry, I love you, I don't want to lose you, Can I come over? Let's talk this out.* Lies. All lies. He disgusted me. My phone beeped again. I stared at another message from Jason. *I'm staying at Robert's house until we can work things out. Please call.*

I tried to think of what to do next, but my mind spun in a suffocating blur as if someone was holding my head beneath the water and demanding I make crucial life decisions. I wouldn't call Jason, but I did need to talk to somebody. This burden was too much to bear on my own. My closest friend, Lydia, was a willing shoulder to cry on, but I couldn't confide in her yet. Her life was just a little too perfect, every one of her dreams executed according to her master plan. She was happily married to her adoring husband with a one-year-old daughter who looked like the Gerber baby. Not the person whose shadow I wanted hovering over me at my most vulnerable moment. Besides, once I told her my situation, she wouldn't be able to keep it to herself.

My mom and I had never been especially close. We didn't spend time together or have much in common, really. Still, I knew she loved me, and I needed her more than ever before. I pressed her number on my phone and held my breath as it rang.

"Elizabeth?"

"Yeah." The emotion bubbled up in my throat, but I held it back.

"What's up?"

"It's just… um." The words refused to form. I hugged my knees to my chest and burst into tears.

"Elizabeth, what's wrong? Is it the baby?"

I panted, struggling to calm myself down. "No. No, it's not the baby. It's Jason."

"Is he alright?"

"He's been cheating on me." My voice cracked as I squeaked out the words. "I walked in on him and another woman last night."

"Oh my God," she breathed heavily.

I gasped for air, "I don't know what to do. My whole life is ruined."

"Ben. Ben!" My mom talked in a loud whisper, apparently trying to get my dad's attention. "Sorry. I'm here."

"I don't know what to do," I said again.

"Have you talked to him? How long has this been going on?"

"I don't know! I'm too pissed to talk to him." I gritted my teeth. "I chased him out of the house last night. He's staying at a friend's."

"What's going on?" I heard Dad say in the background.

"Jason's been cheating on her," Mom whispered, although I could clearly hear her. "Dad's here. I'm putting you on speaker."

"What? Wait, don't…" I was too late. The phone clicked and my dad spoke.

"I'm sorry, darlin'. I never trusted that guy. He was always a little too slick for my taste."

My tears began flowing again.

"You're too good for him, Lizzie," Dad added.

"You need to talk to him, Elizabeth," Mom said. "Find out why he did it. You have a baby on the way. You owe it to the baby to try to work things out."

"She doesn't need to work things out with that loser," Dad said.

"Ben, they're having a baby. The baby needs a father."

"Not a father like that."

My parents argued between themselves while I listened.

"I'm going to talk to him," I said, interrupting. "I just haven't been able to yet."

"Why don't you come home and stay with us for a while? Caroline would love to have you here. She's eighty-seven days sober and just completed her first session of cosmetology school."

"She's doing great," Dad said.

I cringed at the thought of heading back to my parents' cramped house in Kalamazoo where my twenty-five-year-old sister still lived in her childhood bedroom. I wondered why the conversation always had to circle back to Caroline, and why they talked about her like she was four years old.

"I need to stay here, in my house," I said. "I have a job."

My mom sighed. "Well. We can come to visit you, then. It sounds like you need some company."

Silence hovered between us. Dad cleared his throat. Maybe it would be good for me to have some other people around. People who had my back, even if they sometimes drove me crazy. Maybe my mom would make her homemade chicken soup like she used to when I had the flu.

"Fine. Okay," I said. "This weekend?"

"We'll drive over on Friday," Mom said. "Caroline will be so excited."

"Caroline's coming?" I asked, swallowing back my disappointment. I'd hoped it would just be my parents. Caroline could be so unpredictable, so high-maintenance.

"Yes. Of course. She's really excited about becoming an aunt." Mom lowered her voice to a whisper, "And we don't want to leave her on her own just yet."

"Okay." I slumped forward, too beaten down to argue about it.

We said our goodbyes and hung up. I tipped my head back into the cushion and closed my eyes. Nausea swirled in my stomach. I couldn't remember the last time I'd eaten. Had it been the Mediterranean wrap at the airport? That was over a day ago.

I inhaled, gathering my strength. My head was light and dizzy, but I needed to get this conversation over with. My arms trembled, my finger barely steady enough to press Jason's number. He picked up on the first ring.

"Liz. Babe. Please forgive me. I swear it will never happen ag—"

"Who is she?" I asked, interrupting. My voice was calm at first.

"It doesn't matter," Jason said. "I ended it with her. It's over."

"WHO IS SHE?" I screamed, unsatisfied with his answer. My voice projected a maniacal rage, "WHO IS SHE?"

"Her name is… Sarah. Calm down, Jesus Christ." His tone was exasperated, as if I was the one who'd destroyed our marriage.

"Sarah what? What's her last name?"

"That's all I'm telling you right now."

"How long?"

"What?"

"How long has this been going on?"

"It was just one time. I swear."

"You lying piece of shit. I don't believe you."

"Babe. I don't know what you want me to—"

"When did you meet her?" I was done with his fluffy bullshit answers. I wanted information. Just the facts. "*Where* did you meet her?"

He breathed through the phone, slow and steady.

"TELL ME!"

"Okay. Okay. I met her about three months ago at a restaurant."

Three months ago. I counted backward from April: March, February, January. Everything that had happened between us during the last three months had been a lie. Even the conception of our baby. My throat burned, dry and parched. I swallowed anyway. Some sadistic force inside me needed more information, more details. "Which restaurant?"

Jason sighed. "The Salted Olive. What does it matter?"

The Salted Olive. Each new revelation felt like another punch in the stomach. I'd been to that restaurant a year or so ago with Lydia.

"Who were you there with?"

"Some investors. Guys I barely know." Jason sighed. "Look, I made a mistake. It was the worst mistake of my life, but it's over. I'll do anything to make it up to you."

"You can't make it up to me. Don't you get it?" I paused, hugging myself with my free hand. "No amount of jewelry and cars and purses can fix this. You've destroyed me. You've destroyed our family."

"Liz, I'm sorry. I love you."

"I bet I'm the laughingstock of your friends. Right? Was this all a big joke to you? Buying us the same Fendi bag? Why would you do that? Is that why you wanted me to dye my hair blonde? Is that your *type*?" Hot tears streamed down my cheeks. I closed my eyes, but nothing could stop them.

"No. It wasn't like that. No one is laughing at you. I'm the idiot. Please let me come home."

"No."

"At least let me stop by and pick up some clothes."

"Ha," I chuckled an evil laugh, "you better come before trash pickup on Friday morning."

"Why?"

"Your clothes are out in the dumpster." I glanced out the window, proud that I'd gotten some sort of meaningful revenge.

"What? Are you serious?"

I smiled through my tears.

"Liz, what the fuck? Why would you do that?"

"You hurt me. I hurt you. That's karma."

"Oh, man." Jason sat silent on the other end. "Okay, I get it. Maybe I even deserve it. I can always buy new clothes. But you… You're the one thing I can't replace. And our baby. Please. Give me a chance." His voice sounded blurred and choppy, and I realized he was crying. I'd only seen him cry one other time: the day ten months ago when he found out his mom had died. This time, my heart didn't soften at his blubbering. The part of me that cared about his feelings, the piece that felt empathy, had been mangled beyond repair.

"Don't come near me."

*

The credits flashed on the screen as the episode of *Tiny House Nation* came to an end. I'd called in sick for the third day and I was on my fourth tiny house show. My chest swelled as each couple or family abandoned their belongings and motored away in their barren and economical mini home, smiling and open to life's possibilities. Unlike Jason, these people got it.

For a second, I wondered if I could become the people on TV. Maybe now was my chance, while my life was in complete chaos. No one could blame me for making a drastic change. A tiny house would never have worked with Jason and his aggravating attachment to stuff, his worship of physical possessions, and his need to impress every person he encountered. But with just the baby and me, it wasn't so crazy. We'd be free to roam and explore the country, never stressed by finances or weighed down with material burdens. My shoulders tightened as I remembered all the paraphernalia that comes along with having a baby. No way could I fit a crib, a changing table, a stroller, a highchair, and mountains of toys into a tiny house. Plus, once he or she started school we'd have to stay put. Homeschooling wasn't for me.

The front door creaked open. I bolted up from the couch. *Had I forgotten to lock it?*

"Elizabeth! We're here." Mom's voice bellowed through the house.

I stood and limped to the foyer where she rushed toward me and engulfed me in a bear hug. "Have you been eating? You look thin."

I took in her outfit, a deep-purple windbreaker with matching wind pants. She'd gained weight in her midsection and her hair was darker.

Before I could answer, Dad stepped through the door dragging two overstuffed suitcases behind him. He wore a similar windbreaker, but, thankfully, it was black, not purple, and his pants were regular jeans. In contrast to Mom, he'd gotten skinnier and the wrinkles around his eyes were more pronounced.

"There she is!" Dad kissed my head. "Things looking up yet, Lizzie?"

A half-hearted laugh slipped from my mouth. "Not really."

In truth, today had been slightly better than the previous two days. I'd forced myself to shower and eat small meals. In between fits of despair and rage, and episodes of *Tiny House Nation*, I'd managed to make up the bed in the guest room in preparation for their visit. I'd even written a first draft of the Burlington article and sent it off to Gwen. Not my best work, but hopefully enough to get me a pass until the next assignment.

"Where's Caroline?" I asked.

"She's getting her things from the car. She'll be here in a minute," Dad said.

My parents exchanged an awkward glance. Beyond the open front door, Caroline pulled two more overstuffed suitcases behind her.

"How long are you guys staying?" I asked, shaking my head.

"We just wanted to be prepared," Mom shrugged, "in case you need us to stay longer than you thought."

"Lizzie!" Caroline leaped through the entryway, leaving her luggage outside. She wrapped her bony arms around me and hugged tightly. She stepped back and we studied each other for a minute. I hadn't seen my younger sister since last Christmas when we'd gone to visit her at the rehab facility. Our relationship had grown more distant and strained with each one of her relapses. She'd lied to me countless times, stolen from me and my parents, and somehow still managed to charm everyone around her while acting like a child. She'd had her fourth relapse on Christmas Eve, putting Mom's preplanned holiday festivities into a tailspin. Addiction to heroin was fierce, not easily overcome. I'd spent plenty of time reading up on the science behind her addiction and had even attended a handful of family recovery meetings with Caroline. Still, I felt she hadn't learned from her mistakes, always choosing the short-term solution, the path of least resistance. At the end of the day, she was an adult, responsible for her choices. Caroline was ultimately to blame for the mess she'd made. And my parents, too, for enabling her. She was my sister, though, and I had to give her another chance. Nearly three months sober was nothing to scoff at. Maybe this time was different. Maybe she really had changed. She looked vibrant, her shoulder-length hair shiny, her eyes bright.

"I'm so sorry about Jason. What an asshole." Caroline rolled her eyes.

I forgot how much I missed her candor, and I gave her arm an extra squeeze. "Thanks. It's good to see you looking so healthy."

She shoved her hands in her pockets. "I wish I could say the same about you, but you're not looking so hot."

"You should have seen what I looked like yesterday," I said.

Caroline chuckled. I ushered them into the living room where they gawked at the surroundings.

"Nice house you've got here." Dad stuck out his chin. "Make sure that loser husband of yours doesn't take it from you."

Mom narrowed her eyes at him. "Ben!"

Apparently, they still didn't agree on the best course of action for me to take with Jason.

"Technically, we own it jointly." My face turned hot, as another wave of grief approached. I couldn't afford the mortgage on my journalist's salary. The thought of losing the house was too much to bear. I turned away from them and gathered myself. "We'll have to figure it out."

Mom stepped toward me and rubbed my shoulder. "You've got plenty of time for that. Let's work on getting your spirits up first. What do you say we go out for dinner?"

My insides recoiled at the thought of showing my face in public, of leaving the safe cover of my house. I wondered if exposure to sunlight would cause my body to shrivel up and blow away in the wind.

Dad nudged me with his elbow. "It'll be good for you to get out of the house."

All three of them stared at me, expectant. I'd have to leave at some point. Maybe it was better to venture out while surrounded by family.

"Okay. Sure." I shrugged, but my stomach turned over.

A smile crept across Mom's strained face.

"I can help you with your makeup," Caroline paused, picking at her nail, "I mean, not that you need it."

I pressed my lips into a smile and shook my head. We all laughed. It was a relief to find some humor in my situation. I'd caught a glimpse of myself in the mirror before they arrived and I knew she was right. I looked like a disaster. No amount of makeup could cover my swollen face and the redness in my eyes. But Caroline was welcome to try.

CHAPTER THIRTEEN

Gloria (NOW)

The steam from the muffins warmed my hands as I traipsed across the tire tracks to the tiny house. Hopefully Beth liked blueberries, because I'd added an extra cup of them to the recipe. The windows of her house were dark, but Beth's truck was parked in its usual spot. I didn't want to intrude on her, although I was bursting to share the good news about Ethan. A bag of flowers hung over my arm, and I ignored the way the handle dug into my wrist and pulled at my skin. After going to the IGA to stock up on groceries, I'd driven over to the nursery to pick up some snapdragons and impatiens for Beth to plant next to her house. Gardening would boost her spirits.

I set the flowers on the ground, then climbed the three steps to her front porch and pressed the doorbell. A tractor hummed in the distance. After waiting a few seconds, I couldn't make out any movement inside. Pushing the doorbell again, I paced toward the steps, wondering how her meeting with Amanda had gone. The faint melody of music seeped through the walls, rising and dipping in slow motion. My feet stuck in place and I cocked my head as a haunting female voice sang lyrics I couldn't understand followed by low chords on a synthesizer and the thumping of drums. The music must have drowned out the doorbell. I rapped my knuckles on the door, but Beth still didn't appear. Rocking my weight to my other foot I checked over my shoulder, deciding what to do. The muffins were getting cold.

Stepping around to the side of the house, I found a place to peek inside. Maybe I could catch her attention through the window. Balancing my hands against the wall, I pushed myself up onto my tiptoes and peered through a pane of glass. Beth's profile hovered below me, her features muted in shadows. She was turned to the side and holding something. An open shoebox was propped in her arms, but the contents were obscured by the darkness. She was spellbound by whatever the box held.

I'd caught her in a private moment and considered returning later. Before I could lower my face from the window, her eyes slid over to meet mine, her jaw dropping as she turned. She swung the box behind her back, grabbed the lid off the couch, and covered the opening. I averted my gaze and pressed my lips together.

She stared back at me and pointed toward the front door, so I backed away from the window and headed around to the porch, warding off the heat gathering in my face. A few seconds later, the lock clicked and the door opened. The music had been turned off. Beth's hair was disheveled and her eyes were red and swollen.

"I'm sorry to intrude." My cheeks burned. "I baked some muffins and I thought I'd bring them over before they got cold." I extended the foil-wrapped bundle toward her.

Beth stepped toward me, taking the package. "Thank you, Gloria. That's sweet."

"Is everything okay? I rang the doorbell and knocked, but I guess you didn't hear me."

Beth shook her head and sniffled. "Oh, yeah. The doorbell needs a new battery. I've been meaning to replace it."

An uncomfortable silence sat between us, and I suddenly wished she hadn't turned off that morbid music.

Beth must have sensed my unease. She waved me forward, "Sorry. Come on in."

I shuffled inside, admiring Beth's orderly house and surveying the room for the shoebox, but it had already been stored away in some nook or cranny.

Beth walked ahead of me, setting the muffins on her kitchen counter. She took two steps, which landed her back in the living room. "Do you want to sit down?"

"Yes. Maybe just for a minute." I was unsure if Beth really wanted me there, but she looked like she could use a friend. A framed photograph of a snow-topped mountain range was propped against the wall, so I carefully stepped around it. The picture with the metal frame had been hanging behind the couch the last time I'd been here.

She pointed to the picture. "Sorry about the mess. It keeps falling. I need a new wire for the back."

"That's no mess at all, trust me." As I went to sit on the sofa, the corner of something white poked out from beneath my foot. I stepped sideways and plucked an overturned photograph off the floor. Flipping it over, I found an image of Beth staring back at me, her arm looped around a taller and thinner version of herself.

"Oh! Is this your sister, Caroline?" I asked.

Beth's eyes widened. Her hand shot toward me and plucked the photo away before I barely had a chance to look at it. "Yeah. That's her." She slid open a drawer behind her and shoved the photo inside without looking at it. "It's an old picture."

"Do you get to see her much?"

"No. We lost touch, like I said. I haven't seen her in months." Beth's voice was sharp. I couldn't tell if she was angry at her sister for disappearing or at me for meddling. I lowered myself onto the denim sofa, finding the cushions firmer than expected. Beth pulled up a stool opposite me without making eye contact. She strummed her fingers against her thigh. Whatever had been inside that box still had a hold on her.

"Was your lunch with Amanda worthwhile?" I asked, deciding to change subjects.

Beth's eyes flickered in my direction. "Definitely." She straightened herself up in her chair and smiled, making an obvious effort to banish whatever worries had weighed her down. "Amanda was right about the fish tacos at Barney's. They were good. And she had some other insights into the town I never would have discovered on my own."

"I'm thrilled it went well."

"Thanks for introducing us. We had more in common than I thought." Beth played with the beaded bracelet wrapped around her wrist. "We're going to hang out again."

"It was my pleasure. I'm glad you found someone closer to your own age than me." I smiled, but the sudden weight of jealousy caused me to slouch. I worked the tightness out of my back and refocused. "Say, I've been meaning to share some good news."

Beth was still fidgeting with her bracelet, but she stopped. "What is it?"

"I called my son, Ethan, like you suggested. He's flying back from San Francisco in a few days."

She slapped her hands down. "What? Just like that? Is he staying with you?"

"Yes. For ten whole days!" I took a deep breath. "I apologized for hurting him. I think we're on the mend."

"That's great, Gloria. I'm so happy for you."

To my surprise, Beth popped up from her seat and hugged me. When she pulled away, tears had gathered in the corners of her red eyes.

"Maybe you can join us for dinner once he's here?" I said when she sat back down. "I know he'll adore you."

"Of course. I can't wait to meet him."

"It probably sounds silly, but I don't think I'd have had the courage to reach out to him if it hadn't been for our conversation the other day." I stared at my hands, inspecting the thin skin stretched over the tendons and veins, and wondering why I'd spent so many years trying to make Ethan fit into a box that didn't suit him, and why it had taken me another two years to tell him I'd been wrong. My eyes traveled back to Beth. "Thank you for giving me that extra push. He's my only child, after all."

"Sometimes you have to look at things from a new perspective. That can make all the difference."

I stared at Beth, gratitude filling my chest for her sudden appearance in my life. I wondered how she'd accumulated so much wisdom in so few years. My shoulders loosened as I stood up. "I'll leave you be. Enjoy your evening."

"You too, Gloria. Thanks again for the muffins."

As I opened the door to leave, the flowers I'd left at the base of the steps caught my eye. "I brought you some flowers, too." I pointed to the pink and purple impatiens and the yellow and blue snapdragons.

"Those are beautiful, Gloria. That was really nice of you."

"Plant them about four inches deep. Be sure to let me know if you need any help." I stepped off the porch as Joe's SUV lurched down the driveway in the distance. Beth stood next to me, and we watched the vehicle disappear around the curve.

I turned toward her bleary face. "I hope the visit from the police officer didn't unsettle you too much. I can assure you this isn't a high-crime area."

Beth shifted her weight. "He was only doing his job." The sound of Joe's motor faded. "How much do you know about your new tenant?" she asked.

"To be honest, not much. He seems harmless enough, though."

"Artists are usually a little weird." She raised an eyebrow and we both chuckled.

As I shuffled over the uneven ground toward my driveway, I registered the remoteness of our location and remembered the rifle-shaped duffel bag Joe had taken up to his apartment. It was better not to mention it to Beth. I didn't want to give her any reason to move away.

"You get that doorbell fixed so I don't barge in on you again," I said over my shoulder. My gaze traveled toward the garage apartment. "And lock your door."

A crease in my cotton sheets rubbed against my legs. I shifted my feet to try to work out the fold, but it only aggravated me more. The alarm clock on my nightstand glowed with giant green numbers—1:35 a.m. I'd bought the clock for Charlie several Christmases ago when his vision had begun to deteriorate. That was the same year he'd started reading large-print books. He'd never been one to complain, even when things started going downhill. One day, he'd simply replaced his latest Tom Clancy paperback with a hardcover version featuring larger letters and twice the number of pages.

"Got it from the library," he'd said when he saw me staring as I brushed my teeth in the doorway.

That was the thing about Charlie; he hadn't thought he was special or that he deserved to be immune to life's ups and downs. He adjusted and moved on. Even when Ethan had come out, Charlie had handled it better than me. He'd taken it in his stride.

Now, the clock's enormous digits covered the bedroom in an iridescent glow, as if a spaceship had landed next to my bed. I squeezed my eyes shut but couldn't blink away the neon imprint left by the numbers. I sat up, surrendering. Sleep wasn't happening for me tonight. At least, not anytime soon.

My insomnia wasn't uncommon. Sometimes, I could trace the problem back to a cup of afternoon tea, or a slice of chocolate cake after dinner, but at other times, like tonight, there was no obvious suspect. I'd never had sleep issues when Charlie was alive, so I guessed it had something to do with his absence, with not feeling secure, or having too many unspoken worries trapped inside my head.

My hands felt through the shadows to my closet, where I slipped my feet into my house shoes and wrapped myself in my terry-cloth robe, tying the belt snugly around my waist. Then I flipped on the hall light and made my way downstairs to the kitchen.

I removed a glass from the cupboard and filled it with ice and soda water. The bubbles tickled my throat as I swallowed. My hand raised the glass again, but then set it down. "What the heck," I said out loud, and added two fingers of scotch for good measure. The second sip was more satisfying.

The incessant chirping of cicadas and occasional screams of nocturnal animals sounded through my loose windows. Summer nights in northern Michigan were chilly, so I removed my coat from the hook in the kitchen and zipped it over my robe. My toes inched toward the front door as I carried my drink in one hand and a citronella candle in the other. Turning on the porch light would be a mistake; insects would swarm around the glow with me caught in the middle. The door creaked behind me, closing with a thump. I struck a match and lit the candle, its dancing flame mesmerizing me as I lowered my clunky body into the wicker rocking chair.

I'd relaxed on this porch hundreds of times in the daylight or at dusk, but the view in the dead of night was altered in the flickering glow of the candle. A three-quarter moon and a smattering of stars shone through the impenetrable blackness, but the air around me was thick and dark as if my chair had sunk to the bottom of the ocean. I pulled the candle closer and strained my eyes in the direction of the tiny house. Not a thing was visible beyond the railing of my own porch. Although Beth's lights were off, I knew she was out there, sleeping. I wasn't alone, and that gave me some comfort.

An owl hooted in the distance, triggering thoughts of Charlie and how much he used to love that sound. "Did you hear that, Charlie?" I said, speaking to a ghost who I wasn't sure was there.

I swallowed a mouthful of my drink and closed my eyes, embracing the familiar ache in my chest. I missed him. It had been two years, but the loss still shot through me as forcefully as it had the day he died. The closure mentioned in my self-help books had passed me over.

My hand squeezed the glass tighter, despair surrounding me. I'd been improving myself, making some progress by connecting with Ethan, talking to Beth, and using my workbook, but deep inside I understood that no amount of new friends and self-help books would take away the pain of losing my husband. Part of me relished the agony. The sorrow had become my most familiar and constant companion, a pit I'd willingly stumble into just to feel close to Charlie again. I took another swig. My throat burned first, then my eyes, as they filled with tears. I closed my eyes, letting the shadows from the candlelight dance across my eyelids.

A twig cracked from somewhere nearby. My eyes popped open and I stiffened in my seat. I set down my drink, wiping the moisture from my face. I leaned forward and listened. Another rustle of leaves from the direction of the woods, followed by more sticks snapping. My skin bristled.

A few weeks ago, I'd read about a mountain lion spotted in Charlevoix County. It was the first confirmed sighting in the lower peninsula in decades. Had the creature made its way to my property? I glanced over my shoulder toward the front door, planning my escape, as an equally terrifying thought edged its way into my mind. The police hadn't caught the murderer of that young woman in town. What if he was hiding out on my property? I froze, afraid to look toward the woods.

A deep, raspy cough echoed through the night and halted my imagination. It wasn't an animal. The cough was from someone familiar. It was Joe. The distant plodding of uneven footsteps confirmed my suspicion.

Slinking down in my chair, I peered above the railing and spotted a circle of light bobbing in the distance. Joe emerged from the edge of the woods, a flashlight aimed in front of him. I could only make out the shadowy outline of his body. A few steps later, at a point more than halfway up my dirt driveway, the light stopped bouncing and turned toward the ground. He lugged something heavy and bulky in one of his arms. I shielded the flame of my candle with my hand and then blew it out, wondering what he was doing and if I'd been spotted. Cold dread seeped through me as I waited, staying as still as I could manage. A mountain lion would have been more welcome.

Joe grunted, followed by the thud of something hitting the ground. *A bag?* The light swung wildly now as he picked up whatever he'd just dropped and continued trudging. I dug my nails into the base of the wicker chair, praying he wasn't headed toward the tiny house, toward Beth. My heart hammered so loudly I feared it might give me away.

He continued past my house, far enough down the driveway that I could no longer see the beam of light from my position on the porch. Still crouched down, I tiptoed down the front steps and felt my way through the blackness around the side of the house. I pressed myself against a forsythia bush, its angled branches scraping against my back like jagged fingernails.

The beam of light floated away from me up the driveway. He was now opposite the tiny house, only the thin line of birch trees and fifty yards separating them. My muscles twitched. I was prepared to tumble back inside and call 911 if he headed toward her.

His path continued straight, toward his apartment. I unclenched my teeth and exhaled as the light followed the slope of the stairs next to the garage, the circular glow rising higher with each step. Finally, the apartment door clicked open and a triangle of light from inside illuminated Joe. He lurched through the entryway and closed the door behind him, but not before I glimpsed a large duffel bag slung over his shoulder, along with a second bag, the camouflaged one I'd seen earlier—in the shape of a gun.

CHAPTER FOURTEEN

Elizabeth (BEFORE)

Dad slumped on the couch watching SportsCenter and playing games on his phone, while Mom stumbled around the kitchen searching for ingredients. She'd decided to make egg salad for lunch. I'd barely been able to choke down a quarter of my veggie quesadilla at the Mexican restaurant we'd visited last night and the thought of egg salad made me queasy, but I didn't have the energy to disagree.

"Do you have any green onions?" she asked, rummaging through the produce drawer of my refrigerator.

I sat on a kitchen bar stool, still wearing my pajamas. Caroline leaned next to me, checking emails on her phone.

"No." *Why would I have green onions?* I'd barely been able to brush my teeth for the past five days, much less go to the grocery store and stock up for recipes I didn't know I was going to make. "I don't think I have any eggs, either. Or celery."

"Might be hard to make egg salad," Caroline giggled, looking up from her phone. "Want me to run to the grocery store? I don't mind."

My sister's offer caught me off guard, and I was about to say, *sure*, but Mom spoke first.

"I'll go. I forgot my aspirin. And it looks like you need some fresh fruit." Mom shook her head and clucked, "I hope your kitchen isn't always this barren."

I inhaled and held the air in my lungs, ignoring her comment.

"I'll be back in a few minutes." She slung her purse over her shoulder and headed toward the front door. "Need anything, Ben?" she yelled to Dad on her way out.

"What?" Dad looked up from the TV. "Oh, no. I'm fine."

The door clicked shut behind Mom's purple windbreaker.

"There's no stopping your mom once she gets an idea in her head," Dad said, turning off the TV.

"Yeah," Caroline and I said at the same time.

"Can I help you do anything around the house?" Dad asked. "I saw you had a loose shingle out back." He slid toward the edge of the couch.

"No, but thanks for offering," I said. "There's a handyman who comes around a few times a year for stuff like that."

Dad's chin dipped. "Okay. How about your taxes? Should we take a look? It's never too soon to start preparing."

Dad was a semi-retired accountant who couldn't keep his hands off other people's tax returns. *The more complicated, the better*, I'd heard him say more than once. I knew he was only trying to help me in whatever way he could, but I couldn't handle going through my finances with him, especially after I'd already completed my filing for the year.

"I'm sorry, Dad, I can't deal with that right now." The smile on his face faded, and I felt like a horrible person. I remembered the furniture upstairs and backtracked, "I do have something else you can help me with, though."

He straightened his shoulders, the crinkles around his eyes returning. "Okay. Shoot."

"I need to rearrange the furniture in my bedroom. It's too heavy for me to move on my own."

He stood up and marched toward the stairs, a man grateful for a mission. "Let's take care of it."

I followed him, Caroline trailing a few steps behind me.

"Your bed was really comfortable," she said. "You should move back into it. I mean, you know, after we adjust the aura of the room." She waved her fingers through the air as if she were sprinkling glitter all over the stairs.

I hoped rearranging the furniture would be enough to do the trick. I hadn't been able to sleep in the bed since I'd found Jason and the other woman in it, but yesterday I'd dug out old sheets from the linen closet and made it up for Caroline.

We stepped into the bedroom where Jason's dresser sat picked over and abandoned. Only a few shards of glass from a shattered picture lay on top. The door to our walk-in closet was ajar, revealing a wall of hanging clothes and towers of shoes and sweaters on my side, but not a single item on Jason's half. I stared at the vacant shelves and exposed metal bar, an odd mixture of despair and satisfaction rising inside me. Not even a hanger had survived my wrath. The boxes of brand-named shoes, the rows of color-coordinated ties, the collection of button-down shirts and designer suits that he'd so neatly arranged, pressed together like the pages of a new book, now lay twisted and buried in a mangled heap somewhere in the back of a garbage truck, covered with soiled diapers, rotting food, and bags of dog shit.

Dad looked around, letting out a low whistle. "Holy moly. You really cleaned him out, didn't you?" He turned toward me, scratching his forehead and chuckling.

Caroline lifted a piece of glass from Jason's dresser and tossed it in the trash can. "Remind me to never get on Lizzie's bad side."

"Where do you want the bed?" Dad asked, still surveying the room.

I pointed to the skeletal dresser. "Let's move that piece to where the bed is and put the bed against this wall."

We tackled the dresser first, Dad at one end and Caroline at the other. Neither would let me pitch in due to the pregnancy. Adjusting their hands for a solid grip, they lifted it an inch or two off the ground and carried it out of the way. The bed sat on casters and was easier to move. They pushed it over to the open wall. A square of dust bunnies remained on the floor where the bed had been, so I retrieved the vacuum cleaner. By the time I returned, Dad and Caroline had already positioned the dresser nearby.

My hands guided the hose of the vacuum across the recently exposed floor. With every layer it sucked up, I reclaimed my room, cleansing it of each strand of hair, piece of lint, and speck of dust that may have originated from Jason or the other woman. When the area was spotless, I turned off the vacuum feeling as if I'd eliminated his filth.

"Okay," I said.

Dad and Caroline lifted the dresser and placed it against the wall. They stepped back, admiring our work. The room was a different shape now, encouraging a different flow.

"Looks good," Dad said. "What do you think, Lizzie?"

I nodded, my throat unable to produce words.

Caroline elbowed me, "We should buy some new sheets and a mattress pad. I'll help you pick them out. It'll be fun."

"Thank you." A hiccup formed in my throat, and—as had become a common occurrence—I began to cry. Only this time I wasn't crying because I was sad. The tears flowed because I was grateful for my family. For my dad and sister, who'd gone along with my silly furniture rearrangement without question, and for my mom who was out buying the ingredients for egg salad because she wanted to feed her family a nice lunch, and for all of them because they had my back, even after I'd only recently been conspiring to keep them at arm's length from my baby. They weren't perfect. No. None of us was, but they were mine. I stepped toward them and we hugged.

"I'm back," Mom yelled from downstairs. "What's everyone doing up there?"

Dad released his solid arms from around us and turned toward the doorway. "We'll be down in a second."

I wiped the tears from my face and Caroline rubbed my back.

"Let's go eat some egg salad," Dad said.

Caroline giggled.

"I'm going to put some clothes on," I said, glancing down at the rumpled flannel pajamas I'd been wearing all morning.

A couple of minutes later, dressed in jeans and a sweater, I joined them in the kitchen where Mom chopped green onions and already had a pot of water going on the stove.

"Thanks, Mom. That hit the spot." The plate in front of me was clean. I'd eaten every bite of my egg salad sandwich, along with the chips and apple slices Mom had served with it. It had taken a while, but my body had finally realized it was famished.

Dad scooted back his chair. "Delicious."

Caroline gave a thumbs up, her mouth full of food.

Mom leaned back and smiled. "I'm so glad you enjoyed it."

A knock sounded from the front door.

"I'll get it." Mom jumped from her seat and strode toward the door a little too eagerly.

Caroline's eyes found mine, and she shrugged.

Seconds later Mom stepped into the kitchen, her lips pressed together. "Elizabeth, you have a visitor," she said, without making eye contact.

"Who is it?" I asked.

Mom loaded dishes into the dishwasher, ignoring my question.

"Tell whoever it is to go away," I said, not caring if the person heard me.

"I'm not going to do that."

Something about the righteous tone of her voice caused my stomach to drop and my blood to reverse course. I slammed my hands on the table. "I don't want to see him. I don't want to talk to him."

"Is it that *loser*?" Dad asked, each word louder than the one before. He tossed his napkin on the table and stood up. "I'll talk to him."

Mom glared at him. "Sit down, Ben."

Dad froze for a minute, debating. In a burst of defiance, he pushed past her, a vein bulging in his forehead. "I'm not sitting down until I give this clown a piece of my mind."

My weight remained anchored in my chair, my head buried in my hands, my heart rate accelerating. The door yanked open with a forceful gust.

"What the hell is your problem? Is that how you treat my daughter?" Dad yelled.

Jason mumbled for a minute, his response not loud enough to hear.

"You know what I hope?" Dad yelled. "I hope she leaves your sorry ass, because you're never going to find anyone like her again. She's too good for you. I've always known it. She's one in a million and you're a sorry, insecure loser!"

My heart swelled with love for Dad, for the way he was fighting for me, protecting me. That was the way I already loved the baby inside me, fiercely and loyally. Jason said something back to him, but he wasn't yelling like Dad. I couldn't hear the words.

"Elizabeth, go talk to your husband," Mom said in a loud whisper. "Before Dad ruins it for you. You took a vow. For better or for worse. This is the 'worse.' You owe it to that baby to work this out."

"Why did you come here anyway? No one wants you here!" Dad screamed.

More talking from Jason.

"What? She did?" Footsteps descended the hall and into the kitchen. Dad stood with clenched fists, struggling to catch his breath. He narrowed his eyes at Mom. "You told him to come here?"

Mom locked eyes with him, her pallor growing. She bit her lower lip, not speaking.

"Dammit!" I'd never seen Dad so angry, not even when he'd discovered Caroline had stolen his class ring to buy drugs. Although he'd never been violent toward any of us, I feared he might hit Mom. Instead, he lunged forward and kicked the chair he'd been sitting in a few minutes earlier. Then he barreled through the back door, cursing under his breath.

I leaned into my chair, the wooden backing the only thing supporting me. My own mother had betrayed me.

"Whose side are you on?" I asked, dumbfounded. The nausea had returned, rising inside me.

"I'm on your side. I'm on my grandchild's side." Her voice sounded thin and weak. "He wants to work things out. Please go talk to him."

I shook my head in disgust and stomped toward the foyer. Jason wavered in the open doorway, his eyes hollow and arms crossed. He wore the black North Face jacket I'd given him for Christmas last year.

"Liz…" he began to say.

"I don't know what my mom told you," I said. "But I don't want to see you. You can't be here."

"Please talk to me." He inched toward me, his face gaunt, "I know I screwed up, but… this is my house, too."

"I guess we'll have to sell it then," I said, mostly to get a reaction out of him.

He took a step back. "What? No! I want to live here with you. And our baby. Please. I'll do anything to make it up to you."

My fingers fumbled with the hem of my sweater. "I don't know if I'll ever get over it."

"If you need more time, I'll give you more time." A sheen reflected in the corners of Jason's eyes. "We can go talk to someone. Like a marriage counselor."

"Ha." I turned away, a flood of despair rising in me. *How had we come to this?* "Do you love her?" I asked.

"Who?"

"Who do you think?" My voice carried a sharp edge now. "Sarah! Your home-wrecking girlfriend."

Jason raised his hands. "No. I don't love her, and she's not my girlfriend. I'm never going to talk to her or see her again."

I fluttered my eyelids, unwilling to believe anything he said.

"I know it's going to take time for you to trust me again, but I'll wait." His forehead filled with creases as he spoke. "I'll prove to you that I deserve you."

There were no words to respond. I hovered in the doorway, the world spinning around me.

He stepped toward me and reached for my hand. "Have you had a doctor's appointment yet? Is the baby okay?"

I twisted my hand from his grip. "For your sake, I hope the baby is fine. I'm sure the stress you've caused isn't helping. I'm going on Tuesday." I hated that he cared, that he was saying all the right things, that the stubble covering his strong jawline looked ruggedly handsome, and that the touch of his hand still sent a shock wave through me.

"Can I come with you?"

"No. My family will still be here. Caroline's going with me."

"Okay." He lowered his chin toward the ground before he looked up, desperation flickering across his face. "Can you call me afterward and tell me how it went?"

"Fine." I wanted him to suffer, but I wasn't a monster. It was his child, too. I turned to go back inside.

"Liz, wait…"

My legs froze. My husband appeared almost as broken as me.

"I love you," he said, his eyes glued to mine. "I'll never stop loving you."

I stared at him, stone-faced, knowing, on some level, I still loved him, too, but determined not to let it show. The metal handle rattled beneath my hand. I slipped inside the house and closed the door in his face.

CHAPTER FIFTEEN

Gloria (NOW)

"You'll never guess what I saw a couple of nights ago." I tipped my rocking chair toward Beth, clasping its wicker arms with my hands. She sat across from me on the front porch, a patchwork of late-afternoon sun filtering through the trees and across her body. The image of Joe slinking down my driveway in the dead of night caused my insides to flip-flop. For the past few days I'd been itching to tell Beth about what I'd seen, but she'd been busy researching her article. The third time I'd spotted her truck rumbling through the trees, I'd jogged out toward the driveway and waved until she stopped and lowered her window. She'd been off to meet Amanda at a new clothing store in Harbor Springs, but had accepted my invitation for tea this afternoon.

"What did you see?" She clutched a glass of iced tea in her hand. Her hair was pulled back in a ponytail and she wasn't wearing any makeup. She looked more like a teenager than a thirty-year-old woman.

"Well, I couldn't sleep the other night. Sometimes that happens." I glanced away from her and out toward the canopy of the oak tree. "So, I came out here to get some fresh air. It was past 1:30 a.m., mind you."

Beth nodded, encouraging me to continue.

"It was pitch-black, but I had a candle burning." I rocked back in the chair. Birds chirped in the distance. Beth sipped from her glass. I lowered my voice, "All of a sudden, I heard branches crackling in the woods. I couldn't see anything past the porch railing. The noise kept getting closer. It scared the living daylights out of me."

Beth set down her drink and leaned in.

"I worried it might be that mountain lion they spotted over in Charlevoix a couple of months ago."

Beth's mouth dropped open. "Really?"

"Yes. But it wasn't." I paused for dramatic effect.

"What was it?" Her eyes widened.

I leaned forward, turning the volume of my voice down to a whisper, "It was Joe. He came out of the woods carrying a flashlight and a couple of duffel bags."

Beth sucked in a breath. The color drained from her face. "Oh my God." She flattened her back against the chair and frowned. "What was he doing?"

"I don't know, and I don't mean to alarm you. It could have been nothing. I hid and watched him, like a spy."

"He didn't see you?"

"No, I'm fairly certain he didn't. He never even turned in my direction. Just marched straight back to his apartment."

Beth's hands fidgeted in her lap. "What was in the bags?"

"Well, I don't know. It was very dark like I said, and he never opened them."

"You should ask him." Beth's voice was tight.

"I'm not sure what good that would do." I'd made her nervous. That hadn't been my intent. I'd only wanted to make her aware, to remind her we couldn't be too careful.

Beth leaned forward. "Pretend you woke up in the middle of the night and happened to see his flashlight outside."

I glanced away, the thought of confronting Joe making my insides turn. "I don't want him to think I'm a busybody." I envisioned the rifle-shaped duffel bag he'd been carrying. "He could have been hunting, I suppose." I shuddered at the thought. Shooting defenseless animals wasn't much of a sport as far as I was concerned.

Beth frowned. "It's not hunting season. Just ask him what he was doing. It's no big deal."

My shoulders tightened as I pressed my lips together and stared at my tea. I didn't want to argue with Beth, but I wasn't comfortable questioning my new tenant when I was the one who'd been spying. I cleared my throat, realizing the most likely scenario. "He was probably working on some sort of art project."

Beth reached for her glass again, her fingernail tapping against it. "In the dark?"

"He had a flashlight."

We perched across from each other, my eyes not meeting Beth's gaze, and the creaking of my chair the only accompaniment to the awkward silence.

At last Beth sighed. "I guess artists do all sorts of crazy things to express themselves." She leaned forward. "But either way, there's something off with that guy. Make sure to lock your door at night."

"If I see him doing anything illegal, I promise I'll call Officer Bradley," I said.

"No," Beth's voice flung toward me like a slap. My hand jerked upward, splashing a stream of iced tea down my arm. Beth shrunk down in her chair and bit her lip. She handed me a napkin. "Sorry," she said, "what I meant was I don't think we need to freak out and call the police or anything. Joe might just be an oddball who enjoys nighttime walks. There are bad people everywhere. And they haven't caught the guy who murdered Ella Burkholter yet. Single women can never be too careful."

I exhaled, scolding myself for scaring so easily, yet happy that Beth had included me in the same category as her—*single women*. I gave her a half-smile. "I guess my imagination runs away with me sometimes."

"I'll keep an eye out." Beth raised her glass to me and took the last gulp of her iced tea.

The next time I saw Joe I'd consider asking him some casual questions about midnight walks and painting in the dark. I'd have to let him know I didn't approve of hunting on my land. Anything to confirm he hadn't been doing something illegal out in the middle of the woods.

"Ethan will be here soon. He'll help us keep tabs on Joe."

"When is he arriving, again?" Beth asked.

"On the ninth. Four days from now." I relaxed my shoulders, thankful for the change in topic.

"Any big plans while he's here?"

I shifted in my seat, the chair creaking beneath me. I'd been so busy cleaning the house and buying food that I hadn't thought to make big plans, or *any* plans for that matter. I'd pictured us relaxing on the front porch or exploring the waterfront. Maybe eating at some of Ethan's favorite spots, like The Tidewater.

"Not really," I said. "I guess we'll figure it out once he gets here."

Beth nodded. "Well, I'm looking forward to meeting him." She stood, lifting her empty glass. "Can I put this in the kitchen for you?"

I waved her off. "No. Leave it. Come back in a few hours and we can swap out the tea for some wine."

"Sorry. I can't tonight. I'm going out to dinner with Amanda. There's a new restaurant in town called The Castaways. I thought I'd check it out for my restaurant feature."

"That's exciting," I said, although disappointment at not having been invited rolled in my stomach. "You're welcome to stay a little longer now."

"I wish I could. I have to run."

"Busy day?" I asked.

"Yeah. I'm heading out to interview a local business owner."

I scooted forward. "Oh! Which business?"

Beth shrugged. "It's a bike rental place."

I pictured the only bike shop I knew of, over on Highway 31. I must have driven past the glass-and-concrete storefront with oversized red lettering hundreds of times on my way to the IGA. "Up North Bike Rentals?"

Beth nodded. "I think that's the one. I'm gathering information on summer sports activities to round out my article."

"That's a wonderful idea." I raised the pitcher. "Are you sure you don't have time for one more glass of tea?"

Beth flattened her lips. With her free hand, she held up her ponytail, then let it fall. "I also need to get my hair cut."

I took the glass from her hand. "You should go to Marcy over at SpeedyCuts. She's been doing my hair for ages."

Beth's eyes darted away from me but quickly found me again. "Oh. I'm already scheduled to see someone else. Amanda recommended her."

My back slumped under an invisible pressure, but I forced a smile. "I'm sure you'll look gorgeous no matter who you go to."

"Thanks, Gloria." Beth began to stand up, but then changed her mind and leaned toward me. She smoothed back a flyaway strand, tucking it into her ponytail. "What do you think of my color?"

Instinctively, I ran my fingers through my own gray, chin-length hair. "Ha. Well, I'm jealous of it, for one." I studied her shiny tresses, admiring the rich, chocolaty hue. "My hair used to be brown, believe it or not. But more of a mousy brown. Not as pretty as yours."

Beth laced her fingers together and stared at her feet. When she looked up, her eyes had turned on a different shade, their color shifting like the tide. "Jason always wanted me to have blonde hair. I used to bleach it every four weeks for him, whenever the roots started showing." She glanced at the woods in the distance. Something bubbled beneath her calm exterior. "I always liked my natural color better, though."

"I'm glad you went back to it." I squinted, trying to imagine Beth with blonde hair. Nothing about the scenario she just described sat well. *What kind of a man told his wife to change her hair color?* Charlie never would have dared.

Beth's lips parted slightly, but her eyes were glazed. It was as if she'd thought of another story to tell me but decided to keep it to herself. "I'll see you soon." She stood up and descended the steps, giving a wave over her shoulder as she wandered in the direction of her tiny house.

I exhaled. Beth's visit had caused a sourness to pool in my stomach. It was obvious she missed her husband, but he didn't sound like the greatest catch. She was a strong woman, though. She'd already done the right thing by reclaiming her natural hair color.

Carrying our dirty glasses in one hand, I nudged open the door with the other and set the dishes in the kitchen sink. *The Thirty-Day Life Coach* workbook sat on the counter. I picked it up and took it to the living room where I sank into the couch and flipped it open.

The book opened to the personality test identifying me as "Risk-averse" and "Conformist." I reread the line I'd highlighted: *Often, people who are "Risk-averse/Conformist" are insecure and afraid of disappointing people and/or not fitting in. As a result, they frequently end up disappointing themselves by living a life that is not truly authentic.*

Yes. That description fit me to a T. The author should have personalized the book: *To Gloria Flass, the most Risk-averse/Conformist person I know.* I wished I'd read it years ago. My eyes skimmed over the remaining exercises, encouraging me to *Do the opposite* or *Do something irresponsible.*

Outside, Beth's truck rumbled down the driveway. My head sank into the sofa pillow, feeling heavy as a pile of bricks. My sleepless night was catching up with me. I closed the book and rolled over on my side, my body begging for a nap. Just as my eyes closed, the old house creaked and groaned. Three sharp knocks landed on my front door. I slunk down and peered through the gap in the curtains, recognizing Joe's thick arm and part of his red T-shirt. I froze, slouching down further. An image of Joe emerging from the dark woods crept through my mind. The chill running over my skin warned me not to answer. Beth was gone, busy with her list of errands followed by dinner. She wouldn't be back for hours.

Three more knocks. The hair on my neck bristled as Joe's shadow passed in front of the living room window. A thousand pinpricks traveled across my skin.

I raised myself off the couch, pulse racing, and crept toward the window. My eyes edged around the curtains and I peered outside. No one was there. I exhaled, hoping he'd left. But just as my shoulders loosened, an alarming clatter sounded from the mudroom behind the kitchen.

Clink, clink, clink. Thud, thud.

Joe was hammering at the window. The loose frame shook and rattled, and I skittered forward to find Joe straining against it. *He was breaking in!* I gasped, my pulse racing. He looked up, his startled eyes connecting with mine, his mouth dropping open. I wanted to scream, but the sound was trapped in my throat.

Joe's eyes darted away as he lifted his free hand in a wave.

Out of instinct, I grabbed my phone and scooted out the front door and around the side of the house. "What on earth are you doing?" I asked, squaring my shoulders as I approached him.

Joe stepped back from the window, lowering a metal object in his hand. It was a box-cutter, the blade glinting in the sunlight. "Hi, Gloria. I knocked a few times. I didn't think you were home." He looked over his shoulder. "Your car wasn't here."

My lips stammered. "It's in the garage."

"Your window frame is in bad shape. I thought I'd fix it for you."

"Oh." A flood of relief washed through me as I tugged at my shirt. Maybe I'd misread the situation. My windows *were* in horrible shape. Maybe Joe hadn't been breaking in. Still, I couldn't help but notice the sheen of sweat on his upper lip and the jaggedness of his breath. I didn't know whether to believe Joe's story over the twisting in my gut. I jutted out my chin. "I'm going to hire someone to do that. I'd prefer you didn't touch the windows."

Joe's hands lowered to his side, his mouth curving down. He gave a salute. "Yes, ma'am. Enjoy your day." He brushed a few shards of paint from the windowsill, then turned and marched to the garage apartment, never looking back as he lumbered up the steps and through the door.

I exhaled, mild guilt eating away at my insides, but my heart thudding double-time. I feared I'd been rude to Joe. Still, what were the odds he'd work on my windows without getting permission first? Returning to the safety of my living room, I steadied myself against a chair and breathed in and out a few times. I pulled the curtains all the way closed and stepped toward the front door, locking the deadbolt with a satisfying click. Like Beth said, we single women could never be too careful.

CHAPTER SIXTEEN

Elizabeth (BEFORE)

The cold circle of the stethoscope pressed into my back.

"Take a deep breath in."

I inhaled, my socked feet hanging over the side of the examination table.

"And out." Dr. Hamouda stepped back. "Everything sounds fine." She flipped through my chart. She was up to date on my medical records, as well as my personal life. I'd spent the first half of the appointment giving blood, peeing in a cup, having my vitals taken, recounting the date of my last period, and explaining my marital situation—first to a nurse, and then, again, to the doctor—before she poked and prodded me.

She wheeled over her stool, holding a clipboard. Caroline crossed her arms and slouched in an extra chair near the wall. The chair that Jason should have been sitting in.

"Based on your results and our conversation I'm guessing you're about eleven or twelve weeks along."

I nodded, then looked at my hands, feeling like a failed mother already. "I probably should have come in sooner. I've just had so much going on."

"It's okay," the doctor said, rubbing liquid sanitizer on her hands. "You've been under tremendous stress. You're here now, and that's what counts." She patted my hand and rolled her chair back. "We'll do an ultrasound at eighteen weeks to confirm the due date and make sure the fetus is developing properly. You can also find out the sex of the baby at that time if you'd like."

I pressed my palm against my abdomen, still in disbelief that a tiny person existed inside me.

Caroline gasped, giving me a thumbs up, "You're going to find out, aren't you, Lizzie? I need to know if I'm having a niece or a nephew."

"Yes," I said. "Of course."

Caroline bounced in her seat.

The doctor turned to face me. "Your baby's about the size of a plum right now."

"A plum!" Caroline said, forming her fingers into a tiny circle.

I flashed her an annoyed look. "Caroline. Shh!" It was like she'd never been to a doctor's appointment before. In truth, though, I was touched by her enthusiasm. She was in love with the idea of becoming an aunt.

Dr. Hamouda grinned. "It's okay. This is an exciting time. Your baby's digestive system is developing, and little fingernails are forming. It's important that you eat a healthy diet, reduce stress as much as possible, and get plenty of sleep."

My own fingernails dug into the side of the table. I'd barely eaten anything the last few days, I hadn't slept much, and I'd endured the most stressful week of my life. I suspected, based on our earlier conversation, that Dr. Hamouda already knew all of this. I straightened up and nodded.

"I'll try to do a better job," I said. I couldn't let Jason's irresponsible actions affect our baby's health.

"Good. It looks like you have a nice support system with your sister, here." She tipped her head toward Caroline, who gave an exaggerated nod. Thankfully, her long sleeves covered the scars on her arms.

The doctor clasped her hands together and smiled, "Now, let's find your baby's heartbeat." She stood up and pulled out her stethoscope again. "Lean back and relax."

I rested my head on the exam table while she lifted my shirt, pressing the frigid circle in a variety of places. At last, she stopped.

"There it is." She stared at the wall. "Sounds very healthy."

Relief flooded through me as I released the breath I'd been holding.

"Take a listen." She removed the stethoscope and placed the earpieces in my ears. The sound was rapid and clear. *Baboom, baboom, baboom.*

I smiled. "It sounds like a train." I could have listened to that rhythmic beat all day. My baby was healthy and resilient. The heartbeat had embraced me, letting me know I hadn't messed up too badly. The little being inside me had forgiven me already.

"Can I?" Caroline had abandoned her chair and now hovered over me.

I nodded, handing her the stethoscope.

Her eyes stretched wide, her mouth hanging open. "Oh. I hear it. That's so cool." She tipped her head back and giggled.

I couldn't help but laugh at Caroline's excitement. But underneath the laughter, the competing image of what could have been seeped into my mind. As grateful as I was for Caroline's presence, it should have been Jason standing next to me. It should have been him laughing at the wonder of the heartbeat. It hadn't been my choice, though. He hadn't given me a choice.

Mom pushed a bowl of fruit salad toward me. "I'm thrilled the appointment went well. You've been under so much stress."

"It was so cool to hear the heartbeat." I scooped the sliced strawberries and melon onto my plate. Caroline had run out to the store to buy laundry detergent.

"Six months from now, I'll be a grandpa," Dad said, his eyes crinkling in the corners. "That's going to be one spoiled baby."

"No doubt," I said.

Mom cleared her throat. "Listen, Elizabeth. There's something Dad and I have been meaning to ask you."

I stopped chewing and studied their expressionless faces. "Okay."

"We've booked a two-and-a-half-week cruise to the Caribbean…"

My mouth opened. I couldn't remember the last time we'd vacationed as a family. That would be one way to relax and escape my reality.

"It leaves on Saturday," Dad said.

"In three days?" I slid to the edge of my chair.

"Yes," Mom answered.

I thought about the assignment I was working on for Gwen and hoped I could get away on such short notice.

"Anyway," Mom said, "we thought Caroline could stay here with you while Dad and I enjoyed some time away. It might be good for both of you to have each other to lean on."

My arms weighed heavily at my sides. I'd imagined myself diving into a deep ocean only to smash head first into the shallow rocks. I pulled in a breath, processing their message. The cruise was not for me.

I pressed my fingers against my temples to prevent my head from exploding. "So, let me get this straight. My marriage just fell apart at the same time I found out I was pregnant, and you want Caroline to stay here with me for three more weeks while you go on a cruise?"

Dad shifted in his chair. "Hon, you have to understand, we can't leave Caroline alone. Her risk of relapse is high, especially if she's not surrounded by good role models."

"She's twenty-five years old. She should be capable of living on her own."

"She's an addict, Lizzie." Dad fumbled with his shirt collar as if it was strangling him. "We need to keep an eye on her."

"Besides," Mom said, "you shouldn't be alone right now either. You girls can help each other."

I leaned back in my chair and crossed my arms, my face burning with betrayal. They'd known about the cruise. That explained why they'd brought those gigantic suitcases with them.

I swallowed, examining their faces, noticing for the first time the tired circles beneath their eyes, the empty stares behind their smiles. Maybe I was overreacting. Caroline had put my parents through hell over the past four years. She'd tested them over and over again, yet they'd refused to give up on her. Maybe they deserved a vacation, some time to themselves to not have to worry about anything. I remembered Mom's mission to make egg salad and the way Dad and Caroline had rearranged my furniture. I thought of Caroline's laughter at the sound of the baby's heartbeat. It wouldn't kill me to do this for them.

"Okay." My voice was barely audible. An odd mixture of emotion swirled inside me. "She can stay with me."

"Great!" Mom stepped toward me and kissed the top of my head.

"We appreciate it, Lizzie," Dad said.

"But just so we're clear, I have a job that requires travel." I folded my arms across my chest. "I may need to leave for a day or two at a time."

"You should take time off work. Really." Mom clucked and shook her head.

"I've already used four vacation days in the last week." The pitch of my voice became higher. "I can't use any more."

Dad held up his hand. "We understand. Caroline can manage on her own for a day or two."

"Does Caroline know about the cruise?"

Dad gave Mom a sheepish glance. "She knows. We asked her not to say anything."

Mom squeezed my shoulder. "She's excited to have some sister time."

My eyes dropped to the floor. Once again, I was the last person to arrive at the party.

My fingers traced the stitching of the new quilt in the master bedroom. *My bedroom.* I'd reclaimed the room as my own, the bed now facing the window overlooking the fenced-in backyard. Caroline had helped me choose the bedspread. The quilt soothed me, its alternating shades of blue reminding me of the playful waves of Lake Michigan in the summer.

I leaned back, two pillows propped behind me, my phone resting in my hand. Jason was probably on edge wondering about the results of the appointment. I could have called him hours ago, but I'd wanted to torture him. Gathering my strength, I pressed his number and he answered on the first ring.

"Hey," he said, "I've been waiting for your call. How'd it go?"

As much as I hated it, his words comforted me. His deep, smooth voice was like a drug. I caught a tiny glimpse into what Caroline must go through with her heroin addiction—knowing something is destroying you but needing it anyway.

"Good. Everything's good with the baby." My voice cracked. I swallowed, composing myself. "I'm about twelve weeks."

A gasp came from his end of the phone. "Wow. That's great."

"I heard the heartbeat." I sucked in some air, angry with myself. He didn't deserve the details.

"Really?" Jason's breath was heavy on the other end. "That must have been amazing."

I gripped my phone, my palm sweating. Part of me wanted to scream at him, but part of me missed him, needed him, loved him.

"I wish you'd let me be there with you," Jason said. "Can I come to the next appointment? Please?"

"I don't know."

"I know I screwed up, babe. And I promise you, it was the biggest mistake of my life. I'll never do anything like that again."

"That's what you keep saying."

"Because it's true."

"I don't believe you."

"Let me prove it to you," he said. "Let me move back into our house and be the husband you deserve and a loving father to our baby."

"I'm not ready."

Jason sighed again. "Okay."

"My sister is staying with me for the next three weeks while my parents go on a cruise."

"Caroline?"

"Yes. She's the only sister I have."

"Is that a good idea? I mean, given her… history?"

"She's been clean for a long time. Almost three months. Anyway, I don't think you get to judge."

"I'm not judging, I'm just…" His voice trailed off.

"Just what?"

"Glad to hear Caroline's doing better. I hope you two can reconnect."

Those weren't the words I expected to hear. Why was he making it so hard to stay mad at him? He'd always been understanding about Caroline's addiction, even when I'd lost all faith in her.

"We've been through a lot together, Liz." He paused, waiting for me to say something, but I could only dig my tooth into my lip. "No one else knows me like you do. I landed a big investor yesterday and the first thing I wanted to do was call you and tell you about it, but I couldn't. Without you, it's like it didn't even happen."

"Why didn't you call your girlfriend?"

Jason took a deep breath. "Because she's not my girlfriend. And because I don't care about her. I only want you."

My eyes burned, misting over. I squeezed them shut, understanding exactly how he felt because I'd felt the same way today at the doctor's office. If only I could have shared that moment when I'd heard the heartbeat with him or at least the version of him who hadn't cheated on me.

"Why did you have to destroy it?" I asked, my voice cracking. I pictured the woman named Sarah with the tangled mess of hair straddling him on our bed, the look of ecstasy on his face before he noticed me, frozen in the doorway. No matter what he did to make it up to me, I'd never be able to erase the scene from my mind.

"I don't know," he said. "I was stupid and selfish. I'll do whatever it takes to make things right. I'll wait as long as you need me to wait. All I know is that I'm not giving up on us."

"I have to go." I wanted to believe him, but the pain was too much to contain. I ended the call, tears streaming in rivers down my face.

CHAPTER SEVENTEEN

Gloria (NOW)

My weight pressed against the stone bench underneath the oak tree, the wind whipping my hair this way and that. It was one of those afternoons when the weather couldn't make up its mind. Clouds muted the sky one minute, only to have the sun's rays pop through a moment later. I flipped to one of Charlie's favorite verses—Isaiah 55:12—and pinned the page of my worn Bible down with my hand. I squinted my eyes and read out loud.

"For ye shall go out with joy, and be led forth with peace: the mountains and the hills shall break forth before you into singing, and all the trees of the field shall clap their hands." I gazed at the trunk of the tree, waiting for a response. The wind rustled through the branches and the sunlight dimmed again. "That verse always reminded you of our land, didn't it?" I tipped my head back.

Even in his current state underneath the oak tree, Charlie was much more agreeable than Mary Ellen Calloway and her crew of pious backstabbers.

Footsteps thudded behind me and I turned to find Joe carrying a large blank canvas down the steps. He loaded it into his SUV and offered a wave.

"Sorry about yesterday, Gloria. Sometimes I get ahead of myself."

"It's okay," I said, forcing a smile. Joe climbed into his vehicle, started his ignition, and drove past me. I'd convinced myself the window incident had been a misunderstanding, but I couldn't deny the way my body lightened as he drove away.

My muscles froze as a cough echoed from the direction of the tiny house. It was Beth. Leaning back, I spotted her moving behind the trees. I wondered how long she'd been there, and how I hadn't noticed her. She wore a gray shirt and crouched down near her front steps.

I didn't want to be a nuisance, but if Beth was planting the flowers I'd given her, she might want some help. My hand pressed into a sore spot on my lower back as I set the Bible down. My feet lumbered across the grass and through the line of trees.

Beth smiled in my direction as I passed through the gap, but she looked tired, purplish half-circles visible beneath her eyes. Her T-shirt skimmed her body, accentuating her slim figure and her hair was pulled back in a fabric headband. It was a richer shade of brown and the ends were neater.

"Hi, Gloria." Beth lifted the shovel, her hands hidden inside dirty rubber gloves.

"Good afternoon," I said. "Your hair looks beautiful."

"Oh, thanks."

"How was your dinner with Amanda?" I asked.

"Oh. She was…" Beth cleared her throat. "It was fine." She shook her hair back off her shoulders and looked toward the row of impatiens she'd planted near her front steps. "I thought I'd get the flowers going. Am I doing it right?"

"It looks perfect."

"You were right," Beth removed her gloves, "gardening is calming."

The sky darkened and a mist of rain began to sprinkle down. Beth and I craned our necks toward the menacing clouds gathering off to the west.

"Oh, dear. I was wondering how long the rain would hold off."

"Do you want to head into town with me?" Beth stared at me. "Amanda recommended a coffee shop in Petoskey. There's a bookstore next door, too."

I smoothed down my frizzed hair, flattered by the invitation. "That would be lovely," I said. "Let me get my purse."

Beth rested the shovel against the side of her house and started up her steps. "I'll pull my truck around in a few minutes."

I strode away, a smile creeping onto my face. I couldn't recall the last time I'd been out with a friend. That's what Beth was turning out to be—a true friend. And once I finished *The Thirty-Day Life Coach*, I'd need a new book to read. How refreshing to not have to browse the aisles of the bookstore alone. Maybe I could take a break from the self-help books and read a mystery instead. My step carried an extra bounce as I approached the oak tree, its sturdy branches blustering in the wind.

Thirty minutes later, I found myself perched on a rustic stool across from Beth inside a cozy coffee shop, yellow-and-white striped wallpaper surrounding us. I sipped my steaming drink and watched a trickle of tourists approach the counter as Beth revealed tidbits about her recent adventures around town. A notebook lay on the table in front of her. Every few minutes, she paused to jot down notes for her article.

"Mrs. Flass?" A gangly, dark-haired man in his thirties stood next to our table. He looked familiar, but I couldn't place him.

"It's me, Wes. Ethan's friend."

"Of course!" I could have kicked myself for not recognizing him. His hair was longer than the last time I'd seen him, but he was the same likeable young man whom Ethan had befriended when he'd moved back in with us after college. Wes had been a perfect combination of bookish, outdoorsy, and polite. "How are you, dear?"

"Great. And you?"

"Just fine."

Wes rested his hands on his hips. "Ethan texted me the other day. I heard he's heading back to town."

"Yes. He is."

"I'm hoping to get him out camping while he's here."

"I'm sure he'd like that. I didn't realize you still lived in the area."

"Yep. I got married a couple of years ago. My wife and I bought the bike shop on Highway 31. You've probably seen it. Up North Bike Rentals."

I straightened up in my seat, realizing the connection, and motioning toward Beth, "You must know my friend, Beth. She interviewed you yesterday."

Beth shifted in her seat and closed her notebook.

Wes stared at Beth, then narrowed his eyes and shook his head, "I don't think so."

I turned toward her, confused. "Didn't you interview the owners of Up North Bike Rentals yesterday?"

Beth's mouth pulled to the side, her fingers strumming the worn edge of her notebook. "I must have told you the wrong name. It was a different bike shop."

"Is there another bike shop on Highway 31?" I asked.

Wes crossed his arms. "There's Altitude Sports and Bikes over on Mason Road."

Beth nodded. "Yes. That's the one."

Wes raised his chin. "They're our biggest competitor."

My stomach turned. I hoped the mention of the interview hadn't made Wes feel bad. "Maybe Beth can include your shop in her article, too. She's a writer for *American Traveler Magazine*."

"Cool."

Beth lifted her cardboard cup, then set it down without drinking anything. "I can give you a call at the shop if you're interested in being featured. It's free advertising."

"Absolutely. That would be great." Wes nodded as he eyed the growing line at the counter and gave us a wave. "It was nice to see you again. Have Ethan text me when he gets here."

I raised my hand. "Will do."

"Nice to meet you, Beth."

"You, too," she said.

Wes wandered toward the counter, leaving Beth and I staring at each other.

Beth shook her head and looked down, embarrassed. "I've been doing so much research. It's hard to keep all the names of these places straight."

"Don't worry. I can't keep them straight either, and I'm not doing any research."

Beth smiled. I sipped from my cup, the hot liquid bitter against my tongue.

The next morning, I wandered through the aisles of the farmers' market drinking in the fresh air. I stepped quickly and lightly as if I was getting away with something. It always felt dangerous and exciting to walk down the middle of a street where traffic had been blocked. I'd invited Beth to join me, but she and Amanda had already made plans to try out an exercise class at a workout place in town. Even on my own, the energy of the outdoor market was contagious. The vibrant hues of the produce and the aroma of freshly cut flowers made my eyes pop. I hummed a hymn to myself, thankful for the warmth of summer. I'd finally escaped the grip of the previous winter when the endless shades of gray had chilled my bones and kept me pinned under my quilt alone with nothing but my circling thoughts.

I picked up a stalk of rhubarb, turning it over, and setting it back down. The six-dollar price tag was highway robbery. I was on the hunt for local ingredients to add to the new recipe I'd decided to make for Ethan, One-hour Paella. Paella was a Spanish rice and seafood dish I'd always wanted to cook, but had never had the patience to let it bake for an entire day. This "one-hour" recipe was the perfect solution. I'd hoped to locate some fresh fish or organic green onions at the market, or anything else I could add to the mix, but being early June in northern Michigan, the variety of produce was lacking.

I continued down the line of tents, strolling past a booth selling local honey and another featuring freshly baked bread, its yeasty aroma causing my mouth to salivate. A high-pitched squeal and giggle cut through the hum of the shoppers. A booth toward the end of the aisle drew a small crowd. A few people paused, gawking as they continued past, others were immediately pulled in. Curiosity lured me closer. I had to see.

"Mommy, can we get one? Please?" a little girl's voice said as I approached.

Beyond a makeshift wooden gate, five black-and-white puppies leaped and rolled, clamoring to climb on top of one another. The girl stuck her pudgy hand through the slat encouraging one of the puppies to lick and chew her fingers.

"Ha, ha, ha!" she squealed. "He likes me!"

A sign on the table above the puppies read: *Humane Society Adoption Mobile: Puppies looking for good homes.* In smaller print below, *$185 adoption fee, spay/neuter & vaccinations included.*

"Can we, Mom? Can we?" The girl turned her round eyes toward her mother, who crouched down beside her daughter.

"We already have two dogs, Lila," she said. "We'll let other people adopt these guys."

"Oh, but I love him. I love him." The girl's eyes filled with tears.

"Not today, honey."

Lila's hand gripped the wooden slat of the gate as her mom attempted to pull her away. "No. No!" she screamed.

My heart wrenched for Lila. I knew exactly how the little girl felt. These roly-poly puppies might have been the cutest things I'd ever seen. I stepped closer, amazed by their tiny noses and paws. One puppy tumbled off the top of the pile and sat down, revealing a white stripe down the center of its round belly. It stared directly at me, and—I'd swear on Charlie's grave—it winked.

"What breed are they?" I asked the woman who stood nearby wearing a purple Humane Society shirt.

"Our best guess is a Black Lab mix, but we don't know for sure. Someone dropped them at a farm out in Pleasantville. They were brought to us a few days ago."

My eyes traveled back to the winking puppy with the white belly. It now wavered on four stubby legs staring and me and wagging its tail.

"Look at the puppies!" A woman wearing a leather jacket and too much perfume shoved in next to me. Her eyelashes were thick and black like spiders. "Mike, we have to get one."

"Can we hold it?" asked the woman's husband or boyfriend. He leaned over the gate, chomping on a piece of gum and reeking of cigarettes.

The woman from the Humane Society entered the enclosure, bending over to collect a puppy. My muscles tensed, a terror ripping through me as she scooped up the dog with the white stripe on its tummy.

"I'd like to hold that one." The sound of my own voice astounded me. I lunged forward to fill the space between the couple and the woman from the Humane Society. I'd been there first. They couldn't just cut in front of me and steal my puppy.

The woman in the purple shirt nodded and handed me the furry bundle. "This one's a male," she said as she bent down to corral another puppy for the couple next to me.

"How old?" the perfumed woman asked.

"We think about nine or ten weeks."

The warm mound lay in my arms, tail flapping up and down. He rested his head back and gazed at me, docile and sweet. I noticed white markings on his two back paws as if he'd trudged through wet paint. With my free hand, I scratched behind his ears, my fingers sinking into the silky fur. I couldn't stop myself from leaning down and kissing him on his fluffy head. It had only taken a moment, but I'd fallen in love.

The Humane Society worker smiled at me. "Should we get the paperwork started?"

"Oh, I don't know about that." I glanced away, the rational area of my brain slamming on the brakes. I'd never owned a dog before, at least not since Barkley, the beagle we'd owned when I was in grade school. The puppy squirmed in my arms, his tongue stretching toward my face.

My empty farmhouse and the rolling acres of land would be a dog's paradise. Plenty of room to run. I thought of all the years Ethan had begged me for a pet, only to be denied because of Charlie's allergies. This puppy could be his dog, too. Ethan would be over the moon at the surprise. And at the end of the summer, after Ethan had returned to San Francisco, and my renters had moved south, I'd be all alone for the long winter. A dog might provide some security and deter trespassers. It would be comforting to have a constant companion.

The puppy wriggled in my arms and sneezed.

"Bless you," I said. He wagged his tail and blinked at me. I laughed.

My exercises from *The Thirty-Day Life Coach* workbook circled in my mind. *Do something irresponsible. Do the opposite.* Adopting a puppy wasn't the most responsible thing in the world. It would certainly be the opposite of what I'd normally do.

"I like the one she's holding." The heavily scented woman pointed to the puppy in my arms.

Her gum-chomping boyfriend shoved in next to me. "Yeah. He's cute."

My hackles went up. They were trying to steal my puppy! I stepped back and squeezed the dog tighter, my arms refusing to part with the warm bundle.

I turned toward the woman from the Humane Society. "Yes. Let's get the paperwork started."

My new puppy lay asleep in his crate, which I'd positioned next to the sofa. He had a knack for getting into trouble, so I'd named him Rascal. The woman from the Humane Society hadn't let me take my puppy home the morning of the farmers' market. She'd said I had to wait two days to allow time for them to neuter him and give him his shots. I'd been disappointed, worried I'd talk myself out of my decision, but I'd rushed straight home and told Beth the whole story. She'd been delighted by the news, reassuring me that adopting the puppy was the right thing to do. So, I'd stuck to my guns. That puppy had been intended for me, not for that awful couple. I couldn't wait to see the look on Ethan's face when he arrived tomorrow and saw the adorable creature.

The TV hummed in front of me with the voice of a local newscaster, a white-haired man in a charcoal suit: *A local woman has gone missing. Her family is asking anyone who's seen her to contact the police immediately.*

I straightened up, causing Rascal to roll over and groan. The picture on the screen sent a dread prickling through my bones. The photo had been taken a while ago, but I recognized the missing woman. She wore a black V-neck sweater and a silver necklace. It was my former tenant and Beth's new friend—Amanda.

"Oh, my Lord," I said under my breath. Beth had just been out for dinner with Amanda a few nights ago. They'd gone to an exercise class together the morning I'd found Rascal at the farmers' market.

Amanda Jenkins was last seen leaving The Castaways Bar and Grill in Petoskey late Friday night. The entire community, along with law enforcement, is hoping the young woman hasn't met the same fate as Ella Burkholter, the twenty-six-year-old woman who was discovered strangled to death last month on the public beach. No suspects have been named in that case.

I gasped for air, my throat constricting. *The Castaways*. That was where Beth and Amanda had gone for drinks. They'd met there on Friday.

The handle on my front door rattled and I knew without looking that Beth was on the other side. Rascal yipped. I ignored him, my shaking hand opening the door.

"Something horrible has happened." Beth's hands flew to her face.

"I know. I heard."

"I can't believe this."

"You saw Amanda the other day, didn't you? At the exercise class?"

"Yes. No." Beth closed her eyes and shook her head. "I was supposed to meet her there but she didn't show up."

"Did you call her?"

"I texted her. She never responded. I thought she was still mad at me."

"Mad at you?"

Beth grimaced. "When we went out for dinner on Friday I said something stupid. She ended up storming out."

"What did you say?"

"It was nothing." Beth bit her lip and stared past my shoulder.

"Well, it must have been something. Why did she storm off?"

Beth waved her hand in the air. "I said something negative about the town. She took it the wrong way."

"And you haven't seen her since then?"

"No." Beth's body quivered, tears streaming down her cheeks. Rascal yipped again and I lifted him from his crate and carried him out to the front porch. Beth followed me, placing her hand on the puppy's head for comfort.

I turned toward her. "You need to go to the police. Tell them everything you know."

Beth nodded through her sniffles, glancing at Rascal then out at the trees.

I suspected the unsolved murder in town was adding to her fears. "I can't imagine what's taking the police so long to catch the person who killed Ella Burkholter."

Beth's eyes were fixed on something in the distance. "They'll never catch the person who killed her."

My feet staggered backward at the certainty of Beth's words. "Why would you say that?"

Beth shook her head, her eyes snapping out of their trance. "I guess it's just a bad feeling. Small-town police aren't equipped to solve murders."

"Oh." I rubbed my palms on my pants, wondering how Beth knew anything about small-town police. "Maybe they'll surprise you."

"I won't hold my breath."

"But you'll go down to the station and talk to them about Amanda?"

Beth wiped her eyes. "Of course. I want to help," she said, her voice cracking.

I set down the puppy, who scrambled toward the grass, and patted Beth's shoulder. "I bet Amanda is fine. Maybe she wanted to get out of town for a few days." I motioned toward the tiny house. "She's probably jealous of how you can pick up and leave whenever you want."

Beth nodded.

"Let's hope she caught a last-minute flight to Maui. I bet we'll be laughing about this tomorrow."

Beth didn't respond. We stood shoulder to shoulder, observing Rascal who frolicked in the grass. Beth forced her hand into the pocket of her tight jeans. "I've been meaning to give you this." She held out a key attached to a plastic purple key ring and dropped it into my palm. "You should have a key to my tiny house. You know, just in case."

My fingers curled around the jagged metal object. "That's smart. You never know when you'll lock yourself out."

Beth stared at me, her face stained with tears. I shifted toward my front door. "Let me grab an extra key for you, too. Especially now that I might need help with Rascal."

As I stepped inside to retrieve a copy of my house key from the junk drawer, I envisioned the spare key pinned underneath my herb pot on the side of the house. My chest heaved, overcome by a wave of empathy for my former self. That was where lonely people kept spare keys, hidden in some secret spot in their yard. Peering through the window, I spotted Beth hunched over and stroking Rascal's head. Despite Amanda's mysterious disappearance, at least I wasn't on my own anymore.

I returned a minute later, handing Beth my house key. "Would you like me to go to the police station with you?"

"Thanks, but I can go on my own. I'm sure you're busy getting ready for Ethan."

I squeezed her arm, feeling the weight of her anguish. My fingers tightened around her key ring. Beth was a true friend, a next-door neighbor who'd come to my rescue if I was ever locked out. I hated seeing her so upset. I closed my eyes and said a silent prayer that Amanda would turn up soon.

CHAPTER EIGHTEEN

Elizabeth (BEFORE)

"This will be close to your natural color, but a little bit richer." Caroline sprayed warm water from the detachable faucet. "The dye is all-natural and non-toxic."

I balanced on a bar stool, head tipped back over the kitchen sink, as she massaged the water through my hair. When the last of the dye had been rinsed away, she wrapped my head in a towel and guided my head up with her hands.

"I feel like I'm in the salon," I said, admiring my sister's efficiency and the way she explained each step as she went along.

"I'm a quarter of the way through cosmetology school." Caroline used the towel to squeeze the excess water out of my hair.

"Should you be there right now?" I asked, suddenly feeling guilty. I'd been so trapped inside myself, so focused on making it through each breath, that I'd barely asked her about her life.

"No. We're on a break. I'll start up again next month."

"Do you like it?" I asked as she ran a wide-toothed comb through my tangles.

Our eyes met and she lowered the comb to her side. "Yeah. I really do. I want to open my own salon someday."

"I'll be your first customer," I said. "For real."

"Maybe wait to see what your hair looks like first." Caroline stretched her eyes into a shocked expression, followed by a giggle.

"Good point."

Mom and Dad had left four days ago to fly to Miami for their cruise. Eliminating my unnaturally blonde hair had been Caroline's idea. "Screw Jason," she'd said, "you looked better with dark hair."

Caroline held a hand mirror in front of my face. "What do you think?"

I studied my reflection; my wet locks were an intense hue of molasses. The new hair color had drastically altered my appearance. Although the darker shade was nearly identical to my natural color, I almost didn't recognize myself. That's what living a lie for so long did to a person. Jason had buried my authenticity. Now Caroline had excavated it. The woman staring back at me in the mirror was changed, hardened. She was someone who'd reclaimed a piece of herself.

"Wow." My fingers touched the strands near my face as if they might not be real. "Thank you."

"I'll go get the hairdryer. You'll look like a million bucks."

Darkness descended outside the living room windows as the local news droned on TV. The screechy voices of the two newscasters on Channel 7 annoyed me, but I couldn't be bothered to pick up the remote.

Caroline leaned forward from her seat in the armchair. "What are you doing?"

"I'm searching for evidence." My hands flew through the receipts that Jason and I had kept in our "paid bills" box. I couldn't stop thinking about my recent phone call with him, about how nonchalant he'd been about taking another woman into our bed. He was obviously a cheater, but I needed to know how big of a liar he really was. Had he only purchased two Fendi bags? What other presents had he bought for Sarah? If I could find a receipt for a piece of jewelry or a bottle of perfume—anything that hadn't been for me—then I could piece together the true timeline. I'd see if the proof matched the story he'd told me. He was holding things back. I was sure of it.

Something in my brain needed specific answers, not only the date he'd met Sarah but what had he been wearing? What had she been wearing? What had they talked about? Had he told her he was married? Who else knew about them? What was so great about her? I had to know everything about how my life with Jason had turned into a lie.

My eyes scanned each piece of paper, frantic. There had to be clues in this box. He must have gotten lazy somewhere along the line. But my zeal deflated with each itemized receipt that didn't back up my theory. Receipt after receipt showed purchases of groceries, gas, tennis shoes, smoothies from the café at the gym, and tools from Lowe's. Last February there'd been a purchase from Woodward Jewelers. I bit my cheek, inspecting the line item. I threw the slip back in the box, realizing the necklace had been a Valentine's Day gift for me, not her.

"Um." Caroline shifted in her seat. "Not that I'm an expert in relationships, but I don't think what you're doing is healthy."

"He's not telling me the whole story." The familiar sensation of heat rising through my body overtook me again. The tears waiting behind my eyes, ready to push through.

Caroline stood up and walked over to me, nodding toward the box. "I doubt you'll find what you're looking for in there. Jason wouldn't have been that careless. He probably has a separate credit card that you don't even know about." She paced toward the blackened window.

I peered up at her, a pulse of dread coursing through me, my muscles stiffening. Of course, she was right. She'd lived most of her adult life trying to hide her addiction from the ones she loved. I'd been so stupid to not have thought of a secret credit card before. So naive. I probably hadn't even scratched the surface of all the things Jason was hiding from me. I squeezed my hand into a fist, my fingers ice-cold.

Caroline turned toward me. "Where did you say he met her?"

"The Salted Olive. It's a restaurant on Main Street."

"And her name's Sarah?"

"Yeah." The mention of her name brought a new swell of emotion. I swallowed hard, forcing the tears to stay back.

"What do you say we go out to dinner at The Salted Olive tonight? Do a little detective work?" A sly grin crept onto Caroline's lips.

My back sank into the couch. "I doubt he'd be stupid enough to be there with her."

Caroline rolled her eyes. "I know that. But *she* might be there. It's Thursday night. Maybe that's where she picks up men. Or maybe she works there. You can confront her. Give her a piece of your mind."

I lifted my head and studied my sister's face. How had she become so savvy? Maybe she hadn't done well in school, but her street smarts were off the charts.

"I don't know if I'd be able to control myself if I saw her." I closed my eyes, wondering what I'd do if Sarah stood in front of me, smirking and feeling sorry for me. Would I dump my drink on her? Or stab her with my steak knife? No. Getting arrested or thrown in jail wasn't an option. I had the baby to think about now.

"How about this?" Caroline knelt in front of me and held my freezing hands. "If we find her, I'll do all the talking?"

I blinked and nodded, thankful for my kick-ass sister.

"Let's go." Caroline lifted the remote and turned off the TV. "By the way, your hair looks great."

An hour later, we stepped through the shadowy entrance of The Salted Olive. I'd eaten in this restaurant before, about a year ago with my friend Lydia, but the atmosphere seemed altered tonight. The lobby was dingier and more cramped than I remembered. Jazz music filtered through the speakers in the waiting area. The aroma of sautéed onions and garlic permeated the air. My heart pounded as I scanned the bar area beyond the hostess stand. An older couple sat at the midpoint of the counter sharing a plate of calamari and sipping wine. Two younger women occupied the far end of the bar. I couldn't see their faces, but wavy blonde hair hung to the middle of one of their backs. *Was it her?*

My parched throat refused to swallow. A neon sign above the bar seared into my eyes. Every clink of a dish sounded as if bombs were exploding. I grasped Caroline's arm to steady myself. This was where it had happened. It was one of the only solid pieces of information Jason had given me. This was where he'd met her.

"You okay?" Caroline turned toward me. A family stood with their backs to us, waiting for the hostess to lead them to their table.

"Yeah," I said.

My sister followed my line of vision toward the women at the bar just as an olive-skinned hostess in a short black skirt and high-heeled boots stepped toward us.

"How many tonight?"

"Two," Caroline said. "We'll sit at the bar, please."

"Of course." The hostess waved her arm toward the back. "Seat yourself."

I followed a half-step behind Caroline, bumping into her as she halted without warning. "Excuse me," Caroline turned back toward the hostess, "do you know if anyone named Sarah works here?"

My body froze, my breath trapped inside. My sister wasn't wasting any time.

"Sarah? Um, I don't think so." The hostess shook her head. "This is only my second week, though. I haven't met everyone yet."

Caroline nodded. "Okay. Thanks." She glanced back at me and moved toward the bar. I let the air escape from my lungs.

"It doesn't sound like she works here," Caroline said in a loud whisper once we'd reached the bar. She began to pull out a stool directly next to the woman who might have been the skank who slept with my husband.

I tugged Caroline's shirt and widened my eyes at her, mouthing the words, "Not so close."

We shifted down a couple of spaces and raised ourselves onto the tall stools. I leaned forward trying to get a glimpse of the woman's face, but she shifted toward her friend. They were laughing about something.

"Is it her?" Caroline asked.

"I don't know. I can't see her face." My breath clung to my throat, thick and stubborn.

A muscled bartender with a tattoo of a lizard on his neck placed two plastic-coated menus in front of us. "Can I get you ladies something to drink?"

"Soda with lime," Caroline said a little too quickly.

Bottles of liquor lined the mahogany wall behind the bar. I straightened up, feeling ashamed. My sister was a recovering addict. I shouldn't have put her in this situation. Mom and Dad had left a list of nearby Narcotics Anonymous meetings for her to attend. She should have been at one of those meetings right now, not sitting at a smoky bar with her pathetic sister. Still, we were already here, and it had been her idea.

"I'll have the same," I said.

"Two sodas with lime," the bartender said, his voice tinged with sarcasm. "Anything to eat?"

"We need a minute," Caroline said.

The bartender turned away.

"I just realized you shouldn't be hanging out a bar." I placed my hand on top of hers. "Is this hard for you? Do you want to leave? We can drive straight to one of your meetings if you want." My words tumbled out one on top of the other. I hoped she'd want to leave. Any excuse to get out of this room where the walls were closing in on me.

"No. It's fine. Relax." Her eyes darted to the rows of liquor and back to me. "Just between us, I don't find the meetings that helpful. And I don't crave alcohol, anyway. If this was a heroin bar, it might be another story." She picked up the menu and studied it. "Should we order something before the bartender has an aneurysm?"

I steadied myself against the counter. "Sure. Whatever you want."

The bartender returned, setting down two glasses of soda and wiping his hands on his jeans. "Ready to order?"

"We'll split the veggie nachos." Caroline handed the menus back to him.

"Anything else?"

"Nope."

He grabbed the menus and walked away.

"He hates us," Caroline said, smiling.

"We're the worst bar patrons ever—a recovering addict and a pregnant woman with no appetite."

Caroline giggled. The low din of conversation and clanking forks hummed around us. I swiveled in my seat, examining the spacious seating area in the dining room adjacent to the bar. A group of men dressed in suits huddled in a booth near the entryway. Cold sweat erupted across my skin as I wondered if that's where Jason had been sitting with his investors when he'd met her. Or had he been up here at the bar?

Laughter howled from the seats next to us. Caroline nudged me with her elbow. "I'm going to lean back. You look over and see if you recognize her."

My stomach lurched as Caroline angled her body backward, pretending to yawn. The woman with the blonde hair faced me, her smile fading as our eyes met. She looked away, but I couldn't shift my gaze. I'd wanted it to be her so badly, to prove to myself that she was back at the bar picking up men, that whatever she had with Jason didn't mean anything. I'd only glimpsed the woman in my bed for a second. She'd quickly hidden her face before running out and her features had blurred in my mind, but nothing about the person sitting a few seats down looked familiar. She had an angular nose, a blue streak in her hair, and her face was full and round. It wasn't her. I glanced away.

Caroline rested on her elbows, staring at me. "Well?"

I gulped the air as if I'd just surfaced from a deep dive. "It's not her."

Caroline's lips twisted into a frown. "Crap. I was all ready to tear into her."

I took a sip of my soda, simultaneously disappointed and relieved.

An oblong plate rattled down in front of us. "Here's your nachos, ladies." The bartender peered down. "Anything else you need?"

"No," I said.

"Yes," Caroline spoke over me. "Does anyone named Sarah work here?"

He angled his eyes at the ceiling for a second. "No." He picked up a dishrag and wiped off the counter next to me. "I don't think so."

"How about any regulars?" Caroline leaned toward the bartender. "We're looking for an old classmate. She has long blonde hair."

The bartender's lips twisted to the side before he shook his head. "Nope. Sorry."

Caroline nodded. "Okay. Thanks anyway." She turned toward me and shrugged.

I plucked a tortilla chip from the edge of the plate and nibbled the corner. It had been ridiculous to think we could randomly arrive at this restaurant and run into the woman who'd destroyed my life. I was no closer to finding answers than I'd been a week ago. Still, Caroline had gone all out for me and I didn't want her to sense my disappointment.

"The nachos are good." My teeth crunched into a loaded chip. I didn't think I'd be able to eat anything in this tainted place, but the smell of the cumin and roasted vegetables had revived my appetite. My baby needed food.

While we devoured our food, a busboy loaded dirty glasses into a cart at the end of the bar. A crash of shattering glass pierced through the air, causing me to straighten in my seat. Caroline swallowed the chip in her mouth and turned toward the commotion. The buzz of conversation ceased as nearby patrons gawked in the direction of the bar.

Just beyond our seats, a beer mug had smashed in pieces across the tile floor. With no change in his demeanor, the busboy removed the tray from the cart and placed it next to the mess, as if this happened to him every night. Using a dishrag, he scooped up the shards and emptied them into the bin. The conversation around us resumed as people forgot about the broken mug and remembered what they'd been talking about a minute before. Only Caroline and I stayed quiet, me biting into another nacho and Caroline fixated on the busboy.

"Sorry about that, ladies." The busboy looked up at us, but his eyes stuck on Caroline a moment too long.

Caroline glanced away, but then cleared her throat and leaned toward him, "Excuse me," she said.

"Caroline." I poked her arm. "She doesn't work here!"

My sister ignored me, repositioning herself toward the busboy. "This might sound weird, but were you at Hazelwood a couple of years ago?"

I stopped chewing, balancing my weight on the stool. Hazelwood was the rehab facility she'd been in and out of over the last four years. My eyes zeroed in on the busboy who now appeared paler and wirier than he had moments ago. His sinewy arm held the tray of broken dishes and his dark hair was shaved close to his head.

"Yeah," he said. "I thought you looked familiar. I'm Josh."

"I'm Caroline."

"Oh, yeah. I remember you now." He snapped his fingers and pointed at her, "Group therapy."

Caroline chuckled. "Right. You live in Royal Oak?"

"Yeah. Moved over to this side of the state last year. Share a house with some buddies." He adjusted the tray on his hip. "You?"

"I'm just here for a couple of weeks." Caroline waved toward me. "This is my sister, Liz. I'm staying with her."

"What's up?" he said, tilting his head at me, but his eyes remained on Caroline.

Caroline shifted in her seat. "Well. It's nice to see you again." She flipped back her hair and smiled.

"You, too. Hope to see you around." He grinned back at her, wiping his forehead with the back of his hand and exposing a jagged row of circular scars. They were the same scarred-over track marks that lined my sister's arms.

A prickling sweat covered me, my equilibrium thrown off as I almost toppled off the bar stool. I couldn't let this happen. My parents had entrusted me to protect Caroline while they enjoyed a long-overdue vacation. Instead, she was lounging at a bar flirting with a fellow addict under my watch. Maybe he was clean, but maybe he wasn't. Maybe, like Caroline, he was looking for any excuse to turn back to drugs.

"Bye." I pulled Caroline toward me as Josh sauntered away with his tray of broken dishes. "Let's go." My hand slapped a twenty-dollar bill on the counter. More than enough to cover the nachos. The bartender probably didn't deserve the extra tip, but all I cared about was leaving the restaurant.

"What's the rush?" Caroline tilted her head, her face flushed.

I slid from the stool, grasping her arm more tightly than I intended. A sense of foreboding flooded through me. The nachos had turned to acid and swirled higher in my stomach. My feet stumbled toward the door as my sister skittered after me. I leaned close, making sure she saw the warning in my eyes. "We shouldn't have come here. This was a mistake."

CHAPTER NINETEEN

Gloria (NOW)

The sun soothed the knots in my back as I plunged the shovel into the earth and scooped away as much dirt as I could manage. The hole was almost wide enough for the young tomato plant resting nearby. It was the warmest day of the year so far, and I hoped the nice weather would hold out for Ethan's arrival.

I hadn't seen Beth since she'd returned from the police station yesterday, but I'd heard a reassuring report on the news. According to the newscaster, the vast majority of adult missing person cases were false alarms. With the information Beth was providing, I was hopeful it was only a matter of time before Amanda resurfaced.

A scratching noise grabbed my attention. "Rascal! No!" I yelled.

His paws rifled through the pile of dirt, spraying debris into the air behind him. I laughed out loud, despite the mess. It was difficult to stay mad when he was having so much fun. I'd mistakenly imagined the fenced-in garden would be an ideal place to contain the wild puppy. The moment I planted a seedling, he immediately dug it up, tail wagging and with a proud look on his face.

"Morning, Gloria."

I jumped back, startled by the raspy sound of Joe's voice.

"Cute puppy." Joe wore a faded hooded sweatshirt, patchwork shorts, and flip-flops. His hair was pulled back into a ponytail and looked less greasy than normal. I suspected he'd taken a shower.

But when he turned to the side I gasped, my eyes snagging on the three red scratches marring his cheek.

I glanced down and pulled off my muddy gloves. "I brought him home yesterday. He's a handful."

Joe held out his hand. Rascal trotted over to him and sniffed. "What's his name?"

"Rascal," I said, my eyes darting back to the gruesome slashes on Joe's face.

"Hi, Rascal."

Rascal halted and crouched low. He growled, his ears pinned back, muzzle crinkled, and all his razor-sharp puppy teeth showing. I stood taller, never having seen such an unfriendly reaction from my little dog before.

"I'm your neighbor, buddy." Joe knelt down. Rascal backed off and sniffed the fence.

I rolled back my shoulders and cleared my throat, an image of Amanda's photo on the news popping into my head. "What happened to your face?"

Joe's hand raised to his cheek, "Oh, this? The brambles got me." He waved toward the woods. "I wandered down a bad path." He lowered his hand and squeezed three of his enormous fingers through the fence and attempted to rub Rascal's head. My puppy jumped backward and yipped, still leery of Joe's sudden movements.

I weighed the plausibility of Joe's explanation. The scratches could have come from thorns, but they could also have been caused by fingernails. With Amanda missing, everyone was a potential suspect. I wondered if the walk-in closet in the garage apartment was big enough to hold a woman captive and I shuddered at the thought.

"Puppies are a lot of work," Joe said.

"I'm starting to realize that," I said, blinking away my wild thoughts.

My first night with Rascal had been a challenge, to say the least. Between his howling and outdoor potty breaks, I'd barely slept three hours last night. Joe's SUV had arrived in the driveway sometime between Rascal's 1 a.m. outing and his 3:30 a.m. romp.

"How was your art fair?" I asked, digging for more information.

"Eh," he shrugged. "I didn't sell anything, but a few people took my card."

"That's something." I glanced away, wondering why he'd returned to his apartment in the middle of the night two days after the art fair ended.

Scratching an imaginary itch on my arm, I remembered my conversation with Beth. I was supposed to ask him about why he'd been in the woods the other night, but an overwhelming heaviness expanded in my gut, warning me not to intrude.

Joe lounged on the ground waving his hand until Rascal tried to pounce on it through the fence. "Oh. You got me!" he yelled, before starting the game over with the other hand.

"Looks like you made a new friend."

A crooked grin spread across Joe's face. "In Dog We Trust."

I pressed my lips together and stepped toward him. "My son, Ethan, is visiting from San Francisco. He's arriving later today, so you'll see him around."

"Cool. Thanks for the heads-up." Joe popped up and brushed the grass from his shorts. He raised his hand in the air, turned abruptly, and strode back toward his apartment.

Rascal yipped, trying his darnedest to dig a tunnel under the garden fence.

"Bye," I said, perplexed by the man's sudden departure. He was an unusual fellow. His behavior was suspicious, but I had no proof that his explanations weren't true. I'd read dogs were excellent judges of character. Rascal had growled at Joe but then accepted him. I wondered what that meant. I plunged my shovel into the dirt, determined to keep a closer eye on my tenant.

*

"Where do you want this, Mom?" Ethan held up a bowl filled with steaming rolls.

"Anywhere on the table, dear."

I stepped back from the counter, admiring my son. He'd grown since I'd seen him last. Not taller, but sturdier. He'd become more of a man. His movements, the tone of his voice, and the shape of his jaw all resembled Charlie. The sandy-brown hair that used to fall over his eyes was shorter and lighter. I wondered if he'd dyed it or if it was the result of the California sun. A few things were just as I remembered, though. His smell—a scent that reminded me of wood chips and cotton T-shirts. Then there were his lively blue eyes that sparkled like a swimming pool on the Fourth of July.

Before Ethan had arrived, I'd finished clearing my computer nook of all the clutter. Then I'd invited Beth over to eat paella with us. She'd declined at first, still shaken by Amanda's disappearance, but I'd been persistent. Ever the good sport, Beth eventually agreed to join us. So far, no one had noticed my orderly desktop.

"How was your flight?" Beth held a glass of Pinot Grigio in her hand.

"Great," Ethan said. "Right on time."

I lifted the good plates from the cabinet. "I wanted to pick him up from the airport, but he insisted on taking an Uber."

Beth nodded. "Uber is a lifesaver."

"I didn't know what Uber was," I said. "Ethan explained it was like a taxi he could call from his phone, so I let him do it."

Beth and Ethan glanced toward each other and chuckled. I stirred the paella, not realizing I'd told a joke. While I'd promised myself to accept Ethan "as is," a small part of me couldn't help thinking what a handsome couple he and Beth would make. My old way of thinking had a way of popping up, no matter how unwanted, like weeds in a garden.

"Can I set the table?" Beth asked, placing her wine glass on the counter.

"Sure. Thank you."

Rascal whined, followed by a yawn. He peered up at me from his crate in the corner of the kitchen.

Ethan bent down and scratched the dog's head, his face stretching wide with bewilderment. "I can't believe you adopted a puppy. What happened to you?"

"I've been reading a lot of books lately. Self-improvement-type books." I squeezed my hand into a fist, not making eye contact. "I've learned to take some risks. To do some things that I normally wouldn't have had the courage to do."

Ethan gawked at me as if I were wearing a clown costume. "Well, I like the new you."

Beth offered a kind smile. "I didn't know the old you, but I like the new you, too."

I carried the pot of paella over to the table. "Let's eat," I said as we sat down.

Beth fluttered her eyelashes. "I love paella. I went to Madrid for an assignment once. I ate as much paella as I could while I was there."

I leaned toward her, my lips parting in awe at her worldliness. "I've never been to Spain," I said, "but I've always wanted to make paella. It was a challenge from one of my books. Make a new recipe. So, that's what I did."

Beth's face beamed. "Awesome."

Ethan nodded vigorously. "I can't wait to try it."

One by one, we scooped the rice and seafood concoction onto our plates, along with some green salad and a roll. Ethan dug into his food as if he hadn't eaten in days.

"Wow. Really good, Mom," he said between mouthfuls.

"It's delicious, Gloria. Really." Beth methodically peeled the shell from a shrimp and popped it in her mouth. "Just as good as the paella I ate in Spain."

I puffed my chest out, pleased with the mixture of spices and textures in my mouth. "It's called One-hour Paella. The saffron is the key. It's hard to find and very expensive, but I'm happy to share the recipe."

"Did it really only take one hour?" Beth asked. "I can't believe it."

"More like three, but who's counting?" I replied, happy our dinner was distracting Beth from thoughts of her missing friend.

Beth smiled. "I'll take the recipe, anyway."

It might have taken three hours to create the meal, but it only took ten minutes for us to clean our plates. I leaned back and groaned, my stomach stretched to capacity.

Ethan scooped another helping onto his plate. "What's up with the weird guy in the apartment?"

"You met Joe?" I asked. My hands pressed into the seat of my chair. I'd hoped to introduce them properly.

"Yeah. When I took Rascal out earlier." Ethan shoveled a forkful of rice into his mouth. "He appeared out of nowhere. Scared the crap out of me. And Rascal, too."

"He's an artist," I said. "Oil paintings. He has a strange way about him."

Beth gulped the last sip of her wine. "The good news is he's not around very often. He spends the weekends at art fairs. The bad news is he creeps around in the woods at night."

Ethan stopped chewing and set down his fork. "Seriously?"

I nodded, dabbing my lips with my napkin and debating whether to mention the window incident and the scratches. I didn't want to send Beth into a panic.

"You did a background check on him, right?" Ethan said.

My arms dropped to my sides as I felt the blood draining from my face. *A background check?* It seemed an obvious precaution in retrospect, but I hadn't thought of it. Plus, I had no clue how to go about that type of investigation, especially without a connection to the internet. I lifted my eyes to meet Ethan's.

Ethan's eyes widened. "Mom. You didn't do a background check on a guy that lives less than a hundred yards from you out in the middle of nowhere?"

I swiveled toward Beth, whose face had lost its color. Now wasn't the time to reveal I hadn't done a background check on her, either.

"Oh, my stars." I suddenly felt sick. I'd put us all at risk. Maybe I really was useless without Charlie.

"It's okay, Gloria. Everyone makes mistakes." Beth's voice was as thin as a layer of ice about to crack.

Ethan shook his head. "I'll take care of it."

"I'm sorry," I said. "I wasn't thinking."

"Mom," Ethan held up his hand, signaling for us to stop talking about it, "it's fine. But from now on, you need to be more careful. They haven't found whoever murdered that woman in town yet. And now your former tenant is missing, too."

"I'll be more careful." I looked at Beth, noticing the way her lower lip quivered. "Amanda will turn up," I said. "I've been praying every day that her story has a happy ending."

"It doesn't." Beth spoke with no hesitation, her tone flat and certain.

Ethan threw a questioning glance at me. I pressed my spine against the back of my chair, my stomach turning at her pronouncement.

"Why would you say that?" I asked. "We have to think positive thoughts."

Beth looked down, fidgeting with her fork. "I'm sorry, Gloria. You're right. I don't know why I said that."

My eyes focused on the half-eaten pot of paella, an uncomfortable silence surrounding us. I stood to clear the empty plates. "Anyone care for another glass of wine?"

The rain blew sideways, invading the cover of my porch. I pulled the sash of my robe tighter against my waist to shield my skin. I'd left the front light off to escape the moths and gnats.

"Hurry up, Rascal," I whispered. "Do your business."

Through the downpour, an owl hooted from the direction of the woods. The night felt heavy and dark. Rascal foraged through my drenched flower bed a few feet away, the shadowy outline of his wagging tail barely visible. Ethan had offered to get up with the puppy, but I'd waved him off. The bags under his eyes betrayed his exhaustion after the long day of travel.

"Get out of there, Rascal," I said, imagining the mud dripping off his paws.

A car's ignition sputtered, then turned over. The taillights of Joe's Explorer lit up, casting an eerie glow in the distance. I sucked in my breath and crouched down. It was after 1:30 a.m. *Where was he going?* The SUV turned around and sped past me toward the main road. The curve in the driveway prevented me from seeing which way he turned. I struggled to swallow as I scolded myself again for skipping the background check. Rascal trotted across the muddy path, sniffing. At last, he crouched down to relieve himself.

"Good b—" I started to say when another engine rumbled to life. This time, the noise came from beyond the line of birch trees. I craned my neck and spotted more red taillights glowing through the curtain of rain, this time from Beth's truck. I ducked below the railing. Her truck cut across the grass to the driveway and headed toward the road. She was following Joe. Why else would she be going out on a miserable night like this?

This was all my fault. Maybe she'd been more spooked by the lack of background check than I'd realized. It would be just like Beth to take the initiative, to track Joe's movements and find answers on her own. I wished she would have left it to Ethan to perform the background check. There was no sense putting herself in harm's way.

The rain fell harder now and Rascal scampered up the steps to the porch, shaking the wetness from his coat. I scooped him up, ignoring his grimy paws. My eyes searched down the drive, but Beth's truck had disappeared into the blustery night. I squeezed Rascal tight, wondering if Beth had discovered something suspicious about Joe, something she hadn't wanted to tell me, perhaps something to do with Amanda's disappearance. It often seemed like an important secret balanced on the tip of her tongue but, instead of sharing it, she locked it away in some mysterious compartment. I thought about her husband's tragic death and her parents and estranged sister. Was it odd that she rarely spoke about them? That she hadn't wanted me to see her sister's photo? Did Ethan ever talk about me with his friends? I envisioned the box in Beth's hands when I'd snuck up on her the other day. What had been inside? I kept a special box on the top shelf of my closet. It was filled with mementos from Charlie—cherished cards, love letters, and photos. Beth's box probably contained memories from her husband, too. I bet that's why she'd been so distracted when I'd stopped over with the muffins. She must have been pining over his old cards and letters.

Gazing through the rain into the darkness, I promised myself to wake up early and check on Beth to make sure she'd returned home safely. Rascal squirmed in my arms. "Ha!" I said to myself. There was no chance he'd let me sleep past 6 a.m. "No one can accuse us of leading a boring life, now. Can they?"

My puppy's round eyes peered at me, his tail wagging. I rested my chin on his damp head and carried him inside, locking the door behind us.

CHAPTER TWENTY

Elizabeth (BEFORE)

I finished unloading the groceries while Caroline sat in front of the TV messing with her phone.

"I'm heading into the office." I closed the pantry door and peered toward her.

She nodded without looking up.

"Remember, I have to fly to Charlotte tonight. I'm going straight from work."

Caroline didn't speak, just gave me a thumbs up.

"There's pizza in the fridge," I said.

She didn't respond. She was giving me the silent treatment. Last night, I'd asked her to stay away from the busboy at The Salted Olive, and my concern had offended her. Unease prickled through me. We had to resolve this before I left.

"Caroline, can you put your phone down for a second?"

She lowered the phone and glowered at me.

"I'm sorry for what I said about the guy from rehab."

"His name's Josh."

"Right. Josh." I shifted my weight. "I just don't think it's good for you to hang out with him, especially when I'm not around. And when Mom and Dad aren't around."

"I'm twenty-five, not twelve." Her lips turned down in disgust. "I can decide who I hang out with."

"Okay. I agree." I touched my abdomen, calming myself. "This is my house, though. And I don't know this guy. Can you please not have him over while I'm gone?"

She crossed her arms and sighed. "Fine."

"Can you go to one of your NA meetings today? I know you think they're not helpful, but I promised Mom and Dad you'd keep it up."

Caroline stared at me. "I'll try."

I took a deep breath, willing to take what I could get. "And if Jason stops by for any reason, don't let him in."

"Don't worry."

"Great." I slung the new purse I'd picked up at the bohemian store on Main Street over my shoulder. It fit my personality so much better than that pretentious Fendi bag. "I'll only be away two nights. I'll call you when I get to North Carolina."

Caroline picked up her phone again. "Safe travels."

"Love you," I yelled over my shoulder as I exited through the back door.

Loading my suitcase into the trunk, I tried not to think about the last trip I'd taken, and the shock that had awaited me when I'd returned. I pulled out of the driveway, but instead of heading toward the office, I turned in the opposite direction, toward Jason's friend Robert's house. The story I'd told Caroline about going into the office had been a fib. I'd lied to Gwen, too. She thought I was working from home today, at least until my flight at 3 p.m.

Gwen didn't need to know there was no chance I'd be able to focus on my assignment. I couldn't get anything accomplished until I knew what Jason was doing, where he was, and who was with him. It was as if he'd locked me inside a horrific room of mirrors, leaving me unable to decipher the difference between reality and illusion, truth and lies. If there was a part of my life with him that had been real, I didn't know what it was. I needed to sort out the facts for myself.

I lowered my sunglasses over my eyes and navigated through traffic, at last reaching the other side of town. My car crept along White Oak Drive. I eased to a stop before reaching a compact Tudor house with overgrown shrubs: Robert's house. This was where Jason claimed he'd been staying, but he could have been lying about that, too. I lay in wait, my hands clenching the steering wheel. A car parked in front of me blocked my view of the driveway, so I reversed into a better spot.

I let out a breath, noticing Jason's SUV parked near the garage, the morning sun reflecting off its polished windows. He was telling the truth about staying with Robert. I checked the clock – 8:22 a.m. He'd be leaving for work soon. A sickening sensation settled in my stomach. *Would he be alone?* I slunk down in my seat, feeling exposed. Idling in front of the house was too risky, so I circled around the block.

The next time I passed Robert's house, the front door was open. Jason emerged carrying his briefcase. I slowed the car as he turned to lock the door and then strode toward his car checking his watch. My hands relaxed on the wheel. He was alone. I sped past him, ducking down and circling the block again.

The third time I turned the corner, Jason's car was gone. My breath lodged in my windpipe as I scanned the street in both directions. Brake lights flashed in the distance. His Mercedes pulled to a stop at the corner. I accelerated after him, my car following a few car lengths behind down Woodward Avenue until he pulled into the parking lot of the red-brick building where he leased an office for his one-man company. I drove past his lot and into the raised parking area of the building next door, hoping he hadn't noticed me.

Through the slats of a metal railing, I had a clear view of the main entrance to the building, as well as the office windows. The building's windows were tinted, obscuring everything inside from my view. I waited, slouching down in my seat while Jason disappeared through the front door. I straightened up and breathed, my heart still pounding from my covert operation. I'd wait here and I'd watch. I'd see for myself if he was still lying to me.

All morning, cars pulled into the parking lot below me. My pulse quickened each time the drivers revealed themselves—a middle-aged man, a curly-haired woman, a mother with a toddler, a bald guy. None of them came close to the memory of the woman in my bed.

I opened a bag of pretzels, crunching on them as two men in charcoal suits entered the building. A few minutes later, an elderly woman hobbled out through the front door, balancing on her walker with each labored step. By the time she reached her car, my pretzels were gone, and I'd swallowed the last gulp of my caffeine-free green tea. I huffed, annoyed with myself for wasting an entire morning on a fool's errand. As I ripped open a granola bar, Jason barged through the front door of the building, his head turning in my direction. My eyes stretched wide as I dove down, hiding behind the steering wheel.

Shit! Shit! Had he spotted me? I tilted my phone toward my face, the clock reading 11:50 a.m. My eyes blinked, double-checking the numbers. It was lunchtime already. He was leaving to meet someone. I'd been spying for over three hours.

Through the windshield, I watched Jason back out of his parking space. With one hand I fumbled for my seat belt, while I started the car with my other hand. He turned right onto the side road leading to Woodward Avenue. I waited, letting a car pull between us, then I exited the neighboring lot, following.

Was he going to meet Sarah? Was this their routine? Meeting for a midday tryst? I gulped air as I drove, struggling to keep my car from swerving over the centerline.

Two miles later, his right blinker flashed and he turned into the parking lot of a restaurant called Coney Island. The place was a dive, its neon sign burned out on one side. I pressed my back into the seat and turned into the hardware store next door. Pulling into a spot facing the restaurant, I spied on Jason as he entered the diner. A Prius parked in the spot next to his SUV and I braced myself, but relaxed when a squat woman with salt-and-pepper hair emerged.

There were no windows in the cinderblock wall of the restaurant opposite me. Wondering if Sarah was already inside, I squeezed my eyes closed, feeling as if I was losing my mind. This must be what it felt like to go insane, everyone a suspect, the world spinning around me as I struggled to maintain my balance.

When I opened my eyes, Jason was passing through the front door carrying a white, grease-soaked bag in one hand, and a soda in the other. He ducked inside his car, reversed out of his space, and zoomed back into the traffic.

I tipped my head back, angry with myself for letting my imagination run wild. He hadn't been meeting anyone at all, only picking up some unhealthy carry-out.

After relieving myself in the restaurant's dingy bathroom and confirming the absence of the other woman, I drove back to my position in the camouflaged parking space overlooking Jason's office, his Mercedes now parked in the same spot it had been this morning. Two more hours passed with no action. I made another pit stop to a nearby McDonald's to use the bathroom again and buy some lemonade. Now, parked in my "secret" lookout spot for the third time in one day, I nibbled on the salty fries I'd also purchased.

A text beeped on my phone. It was from Gwen: *Don't forget to visit the new lounge in the Elderberry Hotel.*

Will do. I sent back.

I massaged a tight spot in my shoulder, realizing I needed to leave for the airport. As far as I could tell from my one day of surveillance, Jason had been telling me the truth.

*

The monotone hum of the hotel's air ventilation system filled the room. I sat in bed, two pillows propped behind me and my laptop resting on my legs. I clicked to the next image, browsing through profiles of men within five years of my age on Match. com. A sickening taste filled my mouth like I'd swallowed a mouthful of vinegar. *Were these the only men left to choose from?* It was shallow of me to judge them by their looks alone, but I didn't have much more to go on. Appearance-wise, Jason blew them out of the water.

I clicked on a guy who seemed okay. He had kind eyes and straight white teeth. He was thirty-five, an attorney, divorced with two kids. Additional photos showed him playing baseball and sitting on a giant rock with his kids and an attractive woman. Was it his ex-wife? I rolled my eyes. He couldn't have found another photo? I stared at the family portrait. They looked so cute, his pretty wife holding his hand, the children's eyes beaming. Had he cheated on her, too? I wondered if this was the fate awaiting every married woman. Maybe it didn't get any better no matter who I was with. At least Jason wanted to work things out. And who was I to be so picky? I was twenty-nine, pregnant, and working as an underpaid writer. Not exactly a hot catch.

Almost on cue, my phone buzzed, Jason's name flashing across it. I slammed my computer shut.

"Hey," I said, feeling slightly guilty for tracking his every move earlier in the day.

"Hey. I just wanted to hear your voice. Are you feeling okay?" he asked.

"Yeah." My voice cracked, and I sat up straighter, "I'm in Charlotte right now. Checking out a new hotel."

"Oh. That sounds nice."

"It's not."

Jason laughed, and I couldn't help but smile.

A strange sensation rippled through my abdomen. "I think the baby just moved." I needed to share the moment with him, even if he didn't deserve it.

"Really?" He breathed heavily. "Man. I wish I could feel it."

Hot tears formed behind my eyes and I struggled to blink them back. Why had he put us in this situation?

"Can I move back home, babe? Let's work things out."

I pressed my fingers on my eyelids, not sure what to do.

"If you can't do it for me, then do it for our baby," he said. "He or she deserves to have both of us."

His words were so unfair, as if I was the one who'd been in the wrong.

"Yes. Our baby does deserve to have us both." My voice clawed through my throat, vicious and raw. "Too bad our baby's dad is a self-centered dick." I shielded my abdomen with my hands, my breath jagged.

Jason sighed. "I was. You're right." He paused, leaving a thick silence hanging between us. "When my mom died, it really messed with my head. I didn't deal with my feelings the right way. I know I messed up, but I've learned from my mistake. I wish I could go back in time and do things differently, but I can't. All I can do is be the man you deserve going forward. I'll treat you better this time. Please. Give me one more chance."

My emotions shifted at the sincerity of his voice. The tears leaked out now. I sniffled, nodding my head. "Will you go to counseling?"

"Yes. Anything."

"I'm so mad at you," I said, as the tears continued to flow.

"I know. I'm mad at me, too."

"I just… I just need to have a little more time away from you." Each word felt like a boulder on my tongue. "But maybe when Caroline leaves, we can talk about you moving back in."

"Okay." He paused. "That sounds fair."

"I'll let you know when I'm ready to have that discussion," I said, trying to maintain some control.

"Okay. I'll be waiting."

"Bye." I lowered the phone.

"Love you."

With my hand stretched down, his muted voice barely reached my ears. *Did he really love me?* I wanted to believe him, but his actions would have to prove it. I stared at the phone debating whether to say it back, but something slithered inside me, wrapping itself around my throat and squeezing, refusing to let my mouth produce the words.

The back door rattled shut behind me. "I'm home!" I called. "Caroline?"

As I stepped into the kitchen, a chill of déjà vu prickled my skin and left my tongue dry. My flight home from Charlotte had landed thirty minutes ahead of schedule, and I suddenly feared my early arrival would lead to another shocking surprise. It couldn't be as devastating as the last time I'd arrived home unannounced. I rolled back my shoulders, bracing myself against the painful memory.

Caroline didn't answer. I hoped she hadn't eaten yet, so we could go out for dinner or even catch a movie. For the first time in weeks, a spark of hope flickered within me. The phone call with Jason, along with my investigative work, led me to believe he was no longer seeing Sarah, that she hadn't meant anything to him. Maybe there was a real chance we could save our marriage.

I wandered through the kitchen where a few dirty dishes lay in the sink. A white box sat on the counter with a red card on top, my name written across the front in Jason's handwriting. I opened the card. *Liz, I miss you. Remember the first time we ate these? That was one of the best days of my life. Love always, Jason.*

I recognized the box from the Uptown Cookie Factory. We'd gone there on our first date after a two-hour dinner at a tapas restaurant. The chocolate-chunk cookies had melted in our mouths as we strolled down Main Street nibbling them and wandering into a city park. Jason had sent me home with an entire box of them, along with a long kiss. We'd been inseparable ever since—until I walked in on him and Sarah.

I opened the box finding a dozen chocolate-chunk cookies stacked inside. The aroma hit me, emotion swelling in my mouth. I blinked away tears and closed the lid, wondering if Caroline had let Jason inside.

The clock ticked from the mantel in the living room. I dragged my suitcase upstairs, poking my head in the guest room. The sheets lay in a tangled pile on the bed, the shades drawn. Caroline wasn't here.

I continued to my bedroom and deposited my suitcase on the floor. Outside the window, a squirrel hung from a tree branch flicking its tail. I crossed my arms, an unconscious effort to contain my growing panic. I'd spoken to her last night when I'd interrupted her binge-watching a new series she'd found on Netflix. We'd talked again this morning. She'd seemed fine. Happy, even. She didn't have a car, so she couldn't be far away. Maybe she'd walked up to the Walgreens on the corner. That's what I hoped, at least.

The image of the busboy's eyes burning into Caroline flashed in my mind. Had they found each other? Had he picked her up and taken her somewhere to get drugs? I shivered, a surge of dread weighing down my limbs. I stumbled back downstairs, finding my way into the kitchen where I leaned on the counter.

I'm at home. Where are you? I sent the text to Caroline. My fingers strummed the counter as I waited for her response. None came. I paced back and forth across the room, my jaw muscles locking into place.

Unable to focus, I got myself a glass of water and broke off a piece of one of the cookies, too distracted to notice how it melted in my mouth. I wandered into the living room, balancing on the edge of the couch as I flipped on the TV. The annoying woman from the local news screeched about the weather. I switched the channel to HGTV, relieved to find an episode of *Tiny House Nation*. A guy who looked as if he'd barely graduated from high school pressed his palms to his forehead as he stepped into his tiny living room for the first time.

"I can't even speak," he said, looking around.

I wondered where he'd parked his tiny house. On a farm? Out in the woods? On the edge of a lake? The sudden urge to run away and escape civilization overtook me.

The lock turned in the front door and I jumped from the couch into the foyer. Caroline poked her head through the opening and then stepped forward. A windblown strand of hair dangled in front of her eye.

"Hi. Sorry. I thought you'd be back a little later." She motioned toward the counter. "Jason left that box for you on the porch. I brought it inside." She pulled the door closed behind her, but not before I glimpsed a beat-up sedan squealing away.

"Who was that?"

Caroline averted her eyes and strolled past me into the living room, ignoring my question. "How was your trip?" she asked.

"Caroline." I bolted after her. "Don't even tell me that was the guy from the restaurant."

"So, what if it was?" She turned toward me, her voice sharpening. "And his name's Josh."

I dropped my head. I shouldn't have gone to Charlotte. She was making bad decisions, heading down the wrong path. Mom and Dad would be so disappointed. Again. I locked eyes with her and held my breath. Was it my imagination or were her pupils as tiny as pinpricks?

"What are you doing?" I said.

"Hanging out with a friend. Someone who understands me." She squared her shoulders. "We're not corrupting each other, if that's what you think."

"Did you go to the NA meeting?"

"I was going to, but it didn't work out." Caroline turned her head toward the stairs.

My body seethed. My heels dug into the floor. I couldn't speak.

"Anyway, Josh said the meetings here aren't that great."

I closed my eyes, replaying Caroline's chance encounter with Josh at The Salted Olive, the way they smiled and stared at each other too long, the chemistry between them tangible. No one could stop them from having sex or doing drugs if they both wanted it.

"At least tell me where you were."

"Ha! That's funny." Caroline rolled her eyes. "How about you tell me where *you* were before you left for Charlotte. You weren't at your office. I called."

I stepped back, heat rising in my face. I glanced toward my feet. "I was spying on Jason."

Caroline nodded. "Okay. I believe you. Now I'll tell you where I was. Josh and I went out for coffee. Drip Café on Main Street."

I pressed my lips together, weighing the competing thoughts in my head. I didn't want to accuse her of doing something she hadn't done, but Josh was bad news. I could feel it in my bones.

"I'm sorry," I said, deciding to avoid confrontation. We only needed to make it through a few more days before Mom and Dad returned from their cruise. Then she'd head back to cosmetology school in Kalamazoo, far away from Josh. And I'd make a fresh start with Jason.

Caroline flashed me a sheepish grin, her olive branch. "I forgive you."

"Do you want to go out for a bite to eat? There's a new Italian restaurant down the street."

"Oh, I'm not really hungry. Sorry." She placed her hand on her stomach. "I ate a pastry and drank too much coffee."

The hair on my neck stood on end. *Not hungry?* That sounded like something a heroin addict would say after hitting up. I'd witnessed Caroline's behavior enough times over the years to recognize the warning signs—lying, stealing, wearing long sleeves, shrunken pupils, loss of appetite, sleeping excessively. I turned away from her to hide the worry that surely crept onto my face.

"Okay," I said, reminding myself to rein in my imagination. Her story was perfectly plausible. I needed to give her the benefit of the doubt. "I'll just heat something up then."

"I'm wiped. I'm gonna go lie down." Caroline scurried up the stairs.

I walked toward the refrigerator, pulling open the door but closing it a second later. My appetite had disappeared.

CHAPTER TWENTY-ONE

Gloria (NOW)

"No!" Ethan raced across the living room and scooped up Rascal. By the way his shoulders deflated when he reached the puppy, I could tell he was too late. "He peed again."

I shook my head and tore some paper towels off the roll. Just when I thought the little guy was getting the hang of it. After mopping up the puddle, I followed Ethan out to the porch where we watched Rascal sniff and then chew the flowers. This dog was giving me a run for my money.

Ethan tossed a tennis ball nearby, luring Rascal out of the greenery. "You need to get him in a puppy training class. He's gonna walk all over you when he gets bigger."

"I suppose you're right." I adjusted the elastic waistband on my sweatpants, wondering where on earth I'd find a puppy training class.

"I'll look into it for you," Ethan said. "There's gotta be a high school or a YMCA that has one."

I smoothed down a rumple in my shirt, thankful for my son's presence. He was a problem-solver, just like Charlie.

"I talked to my buddy, Wes, yesterday. He said he ran into you and Beth at a coffee shop."

"Yes. It was nice to see him."

"Beth never called him back about that interview."

"She probably forgot. She's been so busy." My eyes automatically traveled to Beth's tiny house and the red truck sitting next to it. It wasn't like her to not keep her word, but she'd been distracted. I'd been extra-worried about her ever since her midnight adventure following Joe the other night. Although, by the time I'd gotten up with Rascal at 5:30 a.m., her truck had been back in its usual spot. I'd been meaning to ask her about her late-night outing and warn her against taking unnecessary risks, but we'd been missing each other.

"Anyway, Wes and his wife, Vicki, invited me to go camping over at the state park for a couple of nights next weekend." Ethan swatted at a fly buzzing near his elbow, before adding, "If you don't mind."

"Yes. You should go," I said.

My last three days with Ethan had been wonderful. We'd puttered around the land admiring the trees and wildflowers. We'd strolled through downtown Harbor Springs, wandering out to the farthest spot on the pier and sneaking glimpses inside the fancy yachts. We'd even revisited the exact spot on the side of the street where I'd adopted Rascal. Then Ethan had treated me to ice cream at Kilwin's where I ordered my favorite flavor, Mackinac Island Fudge. Yesterday, after repairing my internet connection, he'd helped me tackle the mess in the guest room closet. That closet had always overwhelmed me, but somehow Ethan had sorted through the clutter with detached and efficient precision. He'd made all the difficult decisions for me, leaving no room for haggling. He'd even driven a carload of donations over to the Salvation Army. As if that wasn't enough, this morning he'd spent three hours rebuilding the mangled fence around my vegetable garden. He'd made more than one trip to the hardware store to purchase new fencing and sturdier posts. The result was a magnificent, rodent-proof fortress, complete with a hinged gate that opened and closed.

"Let's see those darn deer try to get through that," I'd said, my hands on my hips, challenging the deer in the woods in case they could hear me.

Ethan had put in his dues with me. He was getting restless. In truth, I'd been craving an hour or two alone to work on my *Thirty-Day Life Coach* exercises. I missed Beth, too. I'd been so busy with Ethan, I'd barely seen her, not even in passing.

"Check the weather report first, though," I said, my thoughts returning to Ethan's camping trip. "You don't want to be stuck outside all weekend in the rain."

"Yeah, yeah." He leaned on the porch railing, keeping his eyes on Rascal. "And Beth asked if I'd grab a drink with her tomorrow night."

"Really?" I stepped back, a ripple of excitement traveling through me.

Ethan picked at his nail. "She wants to go back to The Castaways. Something about needing more research for an article she's writing. I wouldn't mind checking it out, too."

"That's wonderful." I clasped my hands together, surprised Beth would return to the place where she'd last seen Amanda. But she was committed to her work. Or maybe she was hoping to find a clue. Regardless, I stifled my grin at the thought of their date. Beth was so much more worldly and sophisticated than anyone Ethan had ever dated in high school. I held my breath, heeding the warning in my gut that told me not to push him, not question him.

Ethan must have noticed my silly smile and the misguided look in my eyes. He dropped his chin and shoved his hands into his pockets. The air left my body, and I felt like I'd been found out, like I'd forced him to read that pamphlet all over again.

"Mom, there's nothing romantic between me and Beth."

My mouth fell open.

His lips pulled back in disgust. "I thought you changed, but you haven't."

I stepped toward him. "That's not true. I have changed. I love you just the way you are."

Ethan rubbed his temples, pain pulsing through his face. "What about your friends at church?"

"I told you. They're not true friends."

"Do you still have that pamphlet?"

"What? No. Of course not. I burned it, if you want to know the truth."

Ethan looked away, considering my response. "Okay. Wow. Well, in that case, I've been wanting to tell you something." His voice was low and calm. "I have a boyfriend in San Francisco. His name's Sean." Ethan pulled his phone from his pocket. He scrolled through some photos and held the screen in front of me. "I was going to tell you about him yesterday, but I wasn't sure how you'd react."

The image was of a handsome young man with shiny black hair and olive skin. He stood on a rocky beach wearing a blue-and-white striped bathing suit. His body was fit and muscular, his smile charming. This was someone else's son, a man whose parents had also found out that their son was gay. I wondered if they'd handled it better than me.

I swallowed and forced myself to smile. "Sean?"

Ethan nodded. "He's a financial analyst. And an amazing piano player. He's smart and funny."

I rocked back on my heels. There was so much I didn't know about Ethan's life. "Does he treat you well?"

"Yeah. He does." Ethan put his phone away. "I want you to meet him sometime."

"I'd like that."

I studied Ethan, the flecks in his aqua eyes, the dark shadow of stubble around his mouth, his confident posture. In so many ways, he'd turned out to be the perfect son.

I grasped Ethan's hands in mine. "Thank you for telling me. I'm happy for you." Hot shame rose into my face, as I realized how courageous my son was. How brave he was to stay true to himself in the face of people who tried to make him be a certain way. People like Mary Ellen Calloway. People like me.

By the time I released Ethan from my embrace, Rascal had disappeared. "Rascal," I yelled, stepping toward the yard. I peered over the railing and found him staring up at me. He'd eaten the tops off my lilies.

Ethan laughed. "Oh, man."

"That little devil," I said, giving up on the dog and facing Ethan. I squeezed his arm. "I'm so glad you're home."

"Thanks." His eyes hung onto mine and I knew we'd made progress.

"You know, it's the strangest thing," I clasped my hands together, then glanced in the direction of the tiny house, "remember how I told you I saw Beth leave in the middle of the night? Right after Joe pulled out of his driveway?"

"Yeah."

"I just can't stop thinking about it. I can't shake the feeling she was following him."

Ethan stared off into the distance. "I'll ask her about it."

A knot tightened in my gut. "No. Don't. I don't want her to think I'm spying on her."

Ethan rolled his eyes. "Fine. Then I'll do that background check on Joe. Maybe that's what she was worried about."

I nodded. "That would certainly put my mind at ease, too."

Ethan stepped toward the door. "Hungry?"

"I suppose so."

"I'll make some sandwiches for us before I leave."

The last of the morning dew clung to my sneakers as I wandered over to Beth's tiny house. It was 9 a.m. and I hoped it wasn't too early for a visit. Although I hadn't talked to Ethan, I heard him return from The Castaways before ten o'clock last night, earlier than I'd expected.

I raised my hand to knock on her front door, but it swung open before my knuckles hit. I blinked at Beth's rumpled appearance. She was fully dressed but looked as if she'd slept in her clothes. Her face held hints of last night's makeup.

"Would you like to join me for coffee?" I asked, eager to make our coffee outings into a regular routine.

She closed her eyes and pulled her hair back into a ponytail. "Sure, Gloria."

"Ethan took my car to buy camping equipment. Can I trouble you to drive?"

"Yeah." She leaned against the wall and inhaled a deep breath. "Give me fifteen minutes and I'll pull my truck around."

Her voice lacked the enthusiasm I'd been hoping for, but at least it was a date.

Fifteen minutes later I locked Rascal in his crate and opened the passenger door to Beth's truck.

"Sorry about the dirt." Beth pointed to a layer of mud on the side of her normally shiny truck. "These country roads are killing me."

"No problem, dear." The roads leading to my house were all paved, and I suspected my dusty driveway was the real culprit. I heaved myself up beside her, noticing a streak of dried mud where my pant leg had skimmed against the step below the door. The truck rumbled past rolling fields dotted with makeshift wooden signs advertising fresh eggs and bundles of lavender while I chatted about the weather report and my garden. My midsection strained against the seat belt as I bent to brush the smudge of dirt off my clothes. The twenty-five-minute drive had passed so quickly that I hardly noticed when Beth pulled into a street-side parking spot downtown.

I'd hoped to return to the same café we'd gone to the other day—the cozy one with the striped wallpaper next door to the bookstore—but Beth had parked in front of a different coffee shop a few blocks away. She must have seen the disappointment on my face.

"I'm comparing all of the coffee shops in Petoskey for an article. I haven't tried this one yet." Her voice was scratchy and I realized I'd been doing all the talking during the drive.

Nodding, I followed her inside. She raised her eyebrows at the metal cut-out sign and wide-plank wood floors. We ordered our drinks and waited at the end of the counter. I preferred the cottage-like atmosphere of the other café over this one's modern feel, but I kept my grumblings to myself.

The hiss of the espresso machine churning steamed milk into my vanilla latte made my spine straighten. If the caffeine didn't wake up Beth, then that noise certainly would. I leaned against the exposed brick wall, Beth flipping through texts on her phone and fidgeting beside me as we waited for the barista to produce our drinks. Then we found a small table by the front window.

"It sounds like you've been keeping Ethan busy." Beth lowered her eyes and took a long sip of her chai.

"He's been a big help," I said. "I'm glad he got to do something fun with you last night. Did you have a nice time at The Castaways?"

Beth squeezed her cup and stared past my shoulder. "Yeah. A part of me was hoping I'd see Amanda there again. I know that's crazy." Her face was pale and her voice was soft as if she barely had the energy to speak.

"That's only natural. It was the last place you saw her. I admire your commitment to your career. I wonder what on earth is taking so long for her to turn up." I sipped my drink and uncrossed my ankles. Beth remained silent. "I'm thinking about going back to my church. Just on Sundays. Not the Bible study, of course. I used to love going to the Sunday service, but I stopped going months ago because I was afraid of running into those terrible women. Then I was thinking, why should I let Mary Ellen Calloway ruin my faith?"

Beth's eyes flickered toward me. "You shouldn't. You need to take back your power."

"I think I might finally dare to do it."

Beth cradled her cup between her hands. "Isn't it crazy how one person can ruin your whole life if you let them?" She leaned back and looked past me again. I got the odd sensation she wasn't talking about Mary Ellen Calloway.

"Well, I don't know if she ruined my *whole* life."

Beth stared at her hands. She closed her eyes and I noticed again how tired she looked. Her normally radiant skin carried a grayish hue and the hollows of her eyes were carved into her head. She must have had one too many beers at The Castaways last night.

"Are you feeling okay?"

Beth's eyes popped open. "Yeah. Sorry." She tapped her finger against her cup for a second and then took another sip. "I haven't been sleeping well lately."

I remembered Beth's truck creeping down the driveway the other night and wondered if she made a habit of going for a drive whenever she couldn't sleep. I had a friend who used to do that.

"I can relate to sleepless nights," I said. "I've had trouble sleeping ever since Charlie died. And now with Rascal needing to go out…"

Beth's mouth tugged down at one corner and I thought she might cry. She seemed especially fragile. I wondered if today was the anniversary of an important date, like her wedding day or her husband's birthday. I decided to stop talking about unpleasant things, to not ask her any more favors or questions that might upset her. Tipping my cardboard cup toward my lips, I sucked in a gulp of hot liquid. Beth rested her elbows on the tiny bistro table, studying the people who strolled past on the sidewalk outside.

Silence hung between us, the lull in our conversation magnified by the clamor of the bustling coffee shop. To fill the uncomfortable hole, I continued talking: "I've been reading a book called *The Thirty-Day Life Coach*. It's been very helpful. I know it sounds crazy, but it's like the author wrote it just for me." I leaned into the back of the metal chair marveling at the book's classification of me as a "Risk-averse/Conformist."

More patrons streamed into the shop. The line of people waiting for drinks had grown to at least half a dozen. Beth focused her eyes everywhere except on me, as if I'd grown a massive wart on my forehead and she couldn't bear to view it.

I continued telling my story. "Whenever I can remember, I write a list of five things I'm grateful for before I go to bed. That idea came from the workbook. Sometimes it helps me fall asleep. For example, last night I wrote—"

Beth's chair scraped across the floor, the blood-curdling screech causing my head to jerk back. "Let's go to the bookstore now," she said, slinging her fabric purse over her shoulder. "I'm feeling claustrophobic." She stood up, clutching her cardboard cup and angling herself toward the door.

"Okay." I fumbled for my purse, searching the café for the source of Beth's strange behavior. Sleep deprivation could cause people to have a short fuse. I'd experienced that myself. But something else had spooked her. At the end of the coffee line, an overweight man leafed through a free stack of real estate fliers. In front of him, two women about my age laughed loudly about something. A couple in their twenties stood at the front of the counter placing their orders. Nothing looked out of the ordinary. Outside the window, a young mother pushed a baby stroller past the entrance. Beth almost collided with her as she shoved her way out of the shop. I lagged a few steps behind, trying not to spill my four-dollar cup of coffee, and wondering why on earth Beth was in such a tizzy to leave.

CHAPTER TWENTY-TWO
Elizabeth (BEFORE)

Hunched over the living room table, I shoveled leftover salad into my mouth as a house-flipping show played on TV. I'd planned to make spaghetti tonight, but Caroline had disappeared into her room as soon as I got home, saying she wasn't feeling great and needed a nap.

Steady rain battered the windows. In between bites of salad, my eyes traveled to the open window in the kitchen. Water pooled on the sill in front of it. Our neighbor's golden retriever barked. Setting down my fork, I raised myself off the couch and moped into the kitchen to crank the window shut, the simple task draining the last of my energy.

Thirty minutes passed while I lay motionless staring at the people on TV and their brilliant real estate investment, a dilapidated ranch in an upscale California neighborhood they'd effortlessly transformed into a high-end model home that would sell for top dollar.

Ding-dong.

The ring of the doorbell pulled me back into the present, the neighbor's dog resuming his barking. I clicked off the TV and looked around at my messy living room, wondering who would be at my door at 8:15 p.m. on a Tuesday. Hopefully not someone trying to sell me something or asking for a political donation.

I ambled toward the foyer, ready to send away whoever stood there. When I cracked open the door, my stomach lurched. Jason balanced on the edge of the bottom step, ignoring the rain that pelted his face. He clutched a dozen red roses in his right hand.

"Hey." He blinked at me through the curtain of water. "Sorry to show up without any notice. I just had to see you."

A thousand competing emotions swirled through me, my mouth unable to form any words. His drooping eyes clung to me, the rain falling harder now and plastering his hair to his forehead. He looked defeated, making no effort to shield himself from the downpour.

Climbing one step closer, he held the flowers out to me. "These are for you."

My teeth gouged into my lower lip, my hand clutching the edge of the door. I nodded, taking the flowers from him.

"Can I come in? Just for a minute, so we can talk?" His eyes flickered with something close to desperation, and his shoulders hunched forward like an old man.

My muscles tensed, but I nodded again. I'd never seen Jason like this before, so vulnerable and unsure of himself. I waved him inside where he removed his soaked jacket.

"Should I take off my shoes?" he asked.

"Yeah. Please," I said, wondering what it must feel like to be a stranger in your own house.

He slid off his waterlogged loafers and followed me into the living room where Caroline's clothes, shopping bags, phone chargers, and bottles of lotion were strewn across the floor and furniture. I grabbed a dish towel from the kitchen and handed it to him.

Jason's eyes traveled around the room as he dried his face. "I see Caroline is still staying with you."

"How did you know?"

Jason chuckled, his thick fingers smoothing back his hair. "Did you get the cookies?"

"Yeah. Thank you." I set the flowers on the counter, not bothering to put them into a vase just yet. Jason surely knew he couldn't win me back so easily. He hovered in the opening between the kitchen and the living room, his hands fidgeting.

"You look good," he said.

Holding my body still, I inhaled, making a conscious effort to not return the compliment.

"How are you feeling?"

"Okay. Considering."

Jason waved toward the couch, "Can we sit down?"

I nodded, striding past him and removing the leftover box of salad from the table. He lowered himself onto the couch. I positioned myself a cushion away, being careful not to touch him. His eyes locked onto my abdomen and he scooted a couple of inches closer.

"How's the baby?"

"Fine, I think. I haven't had any more appointments since the last time we talked."

Jason gave an almost imperceptible nod. "How's Caroline doing?"

"She's good," I said, ignoring the mess she'd created around us. "Are you still staying at Robert's?"

"Yeah."

"Oh. I wasn't sure if you'd moved in with your girlfriend yet."

Jason sighed and tipped his head back, his eyelids closing. "I screwed up, babe. I know I did, and I hate myself for it." He opened his eyes and peered directly into mine, a droplet of water sliding down his forehead. "I miss you so much. I don't want to lose you, or our baby, or any of this." He waved his hands at the living room.

I raised my chin, my voice hardening. "I didn't want to lose any of it, either."

"What do I have to do to make it better? Please don't throw away our future because I'm an idiot. Tell me. I'll do anything."

"I don't know if it's possible."

Jason pressed his palms into his forehead, his face scrunching up as if he was struggling not to cry. My stomach dropped. I hated myself for feeling bad for him, for still loving him, but I did.

"Can we start over?" He lowered his palms and grasped my shaky hands in his steady ones. "Can I take you out for dinner? It will be like our first date all over again."

Heat built up behind my eyes as I blinked back the tears. Nothing would be better than starting over, yet I wasn't sure he deserved the chance.

"I'm not sure," I said.

"Please let me take you out for dinner, just for starters. We can talk about everything else. I'll do whatever it takes."

I squared my jaw at him. He couldn't earn my trust with a dozen roses and a fancy dinner. "We'd need to go to marriage counseling."

"Okay. Yeah." Jason squeezed my hand and shifted his position on the couch. "I totally agree. That's a good idea."

I focused my eyes on the blank TV, a sick feeling tunneling through me. Would I let him get away with it? Was it worth sacrificing my principles to save our marriage? To keep this house? To ensure an intact home for our future child? The answer wasn't clear. I'd lose so much either way.

Jason leaned toward me. "So, what about dinner?"

My gaze darted away from his. "I said I don't know yet."

"Will you think about it?"

"Yeah. I'll think about it." I pulled my hands from his and stood up, ushering Jason to the front door.

He followed silently, sliding on his soaked shoes and draping his dripping jacket over his arm. My hand grasped the metal handle and pulled the door open, a thunderous wall of rain pouring on the other side. Jason hesitated for a moment as if waiting for me to ask him to stay, but I pressed my lips together and stared at the floor.

"I'll be in touch," he said as he stumbled out into the rain and then jogged toward his car.

I watched from the shelter of the doorway, a pang of guilt shooting through my chest because I hadn't offered him an umbrella.

*

A week after Jason's surprise visit, Caroline had officially overstayed her welcome. The stench of stale garbage surrounded me as I entered the kitchen. I gagged, my hand covering my mouth. My pregnant body had lost all tolerance for foul odors. The lid on the garbage can tilted upward, unable to close against the mass of trash underneath. Caroline hadn't bothered to take it outside. Her dirty dishes lay stacked in the sink. It looked as if she'd crumbled an entire loaf of bread across the counter.

I marched into the living room searching for my ungrateful house guest.

"Caroline!" I yelled up the stairs.

The door to the guest room creaked open and Caroline peeked through, rubbing sleep from her eyes.

"Seriously?" I said, wondering if she'd been asleep all day. "It's after 5 p.m."

I'd been working since the crack of dawn, revising articles, conducting a phone interview with a casino owner in Windsor, and attending lengthy meetings with Gwen to discuss an upcoming article on the vegan restaurant scene in Detroit. Meanwhile, my sister had been trashing my house and napping. Our parents would be returning in five days to retrieve her, but I wasn't sure I could make it.

Caroline blinked. "Sorry. I must have dozed off."

"Can you clean up the dishes and take the garbage out?"

"Relax. I'll take care of it." She rolled her eyes as I turned away.

Closing myself into my bedroom, I kicked off my sandals and collapsed on the bed. At least Jason had cleaned up after himself. I'd need to get the house back to myself if I wanted a shot at repairing our marriage. I pulled a card from my pocket and turned it over—*Isabelle Brennan, Licensed Psychologist.* She'd come highly recommended from Lydia, who I'd finally called a few days ago. I'd underestimated my friend, who had not only talked me through my pain but had gone out of her way to get a babysitter for her daughter so she could meet me for lunch. I was still reeling from her revelation.

We'd sat across the booth from each other at Panera eating our grilled paninis while she'd listened to my story. I recounted all the important points, how I'd discovered the pregnancy, found the stray earring, bought the booties at the boutique in Vermont, and arrived home a day early to the horrible surprise.

She'd nodded along, asking all the right questions, a pained expression on her face. Her black hair hung past her shoulders, straight and shiny, and I wondered how she always stayed so put-together.

"Jason keeps saying it was a mistake," I said to her about halfway through our meal. "That it was just one time and she meant nothing to him. He showed up at my doorstep in the rain a couple of nights ago pleading for us to start over and saying that he'll be a changed man. I want to believe him, but I just don't know if he's telling the truth."

Lydia shifted uncomfortably in her chair and set down the chip she'd been about to eat. "Everyone makes mistakes," she said, nervously touching her unused silverware with her manicured fingers. "This was obviously a really big one, but I think it might be worth it to give him another chance."

I raised my eyebrow at her. It wasn't the response I'd been expecting.

"You know," Lydia said, leaning toward me, "I cheated on Mike once."

Her words punched me in the stomach. The noise of the restaurant muted around me. "What? When?"

"Just after we got married." She shook her head, her mouth stuck in a grimace. "It's not public knowledge, so…" She pressed her lips into a thin line and pretended to turn a key next to them.

I nodded, but once again, the world I thought I'd lived in had been knocked off-kilter. *My perfect friend had cheated on her perfect husband.*

"I didn't mean for it to happen," Lydia continued, "but there was this guy at the gym who was always flirting with me. He wasn't even that good-looking, but I liked the attention. I started working out at times when I knew he'd be there." She paused and glanced out the window. "One night, he asked me out for drinks afterward. I knew it was wrong, but I said yes. I guess you could say one thing led to another."

"But why? You and Mike always seemed so happy."

"There is no answer, except that I screwed up. I definitely didn't love the guy. I never stopped loving Mike."

"Does Mike know?"

"Yeah." Lydia stared at her hands for a minute before looking up. "I felt so guilty that I ended up telling him everything a couple of weeks later. He was so pissed. He didn't talk to me for three days. I thought he was going to leave me." A deep crease formed in the center of Lydia's forehead. "That's when we started seeing a marriage counselor."

"And that helped?"

"Yes." She played with the ends of her hair and smiled. "I'm so grateful Mike gave me another chance. We wouldn't have McKenzie now if he hadn't."

McKenzie was their ridiculously cute one-year-old daughter. Tears gathered in the corners of Lydia's eyes. "Our sessions with Dr. Brennan made our relationship so much stronger in the end." Lydia dug a card out of her purse and slid it across the table to me. "This is the person who helped us. I think you and Jason should meet with her."

By the end of the meal, I felt guilty for not confiding in Lydia sooner. Her married life hadn't been as ideal as I'd believed. Lydia had made a mistake, but she was a good person. Hearing her story reassured me that I might be doing the right thing by giving Jason another chance. Maybe we could work through our issues just like Lydia and Mike had. Maybe Jason could finally deal with his mom's death, too.

Now, a week later, I stared at my closet, wondering what to wear for dinner. At Lydia's urging, Jason and I had already attended a session with Dr. Brennan, who had allowed us to open up to each other in ways we never had before. Jason had sat next to me, holding my hand and listening to me describe the pain he'd caused as my tears hardened into anger and back into tears again. He apologized, again and again, his watery eyes showing remorse for his actions. He'd admitted he'd been selfish. He was insecure, he said, afraid I'd leave him, just like his mother had disappeared from his life without warning. It had taken a horrible mistake to make him see how lucky he already was.

After we'd bared our souls to each other inside the safety of the psychologist's office, I'd finally accepted Jason's dinner invitation. He'd planned a date at our favorite French bistro. It was meant to be our first attempt at reconciliation, a time to reconnect on neutral ground before I considered whether he could move back into our house. I rifled through the hanging clothes and selected a low-cut black dress with white trim. He loved this one. It would show off my enhanced cleavage and it was made of stretchy material to accommodate my thickening midsection.

After freshening up, I slipped on the dress, smoothed back my hair into a low ponytail and reapplied my eyeshadow, liner, and lipstick. I tried to remember the last time I'd attempted to make myself look sexy but couldn't recall. Maybe I needed to put in more effort, too.

Wearing my three-inch heels, I stepped down the stairs to check out the progress in the kitchen.

Caroline was pulling the overflowing garbage bag out of the bin but stopped when she saw me. "Ooh la la!" Caroline whistled. "Hot mama. Who's your date with?"

"Jason." I glanced away, feeling guilty I hadn't shared more of the events of the past week with her.

"Are you serious?" Caroline loosened her grip on the bag, her mouth turning down. "That asshole doesn't deserve you."

"Maybe not," I said. "But we've been talking. We had a session with a marriage counselor. I think he's truly sorry. I have to try and move past it." I patted my stomach. "For the baby."

Caroline bit her lip, studying me. At last she nodded, her face softening. "I hope you guys can figure it out."

She dragged the garbage bag out the door. I watched in awe, my feet cemented to the ground. *How was Caroline so accepting of me?* Suddenly, I felt like the bad sister, the ungrateful one. She reappeared a moment later and washed her hands.

Two short beeps jolted me from my thoughts.

Caroline grabbed her purse from the counter. "See ya!" she said. "I'm gonna go hang out with Josh. Be back later."

My muscles constricted, but I held back my impulse to object. She wasn't giving me a hard time about Jason. I could let her get away with this. Plus, maybe it was healthy for her to hang out with someone who'd gone through the same experiences.

The sink still teemed with dirty dishes, but at least she'd taken out the garbage. I held my tongue. "Bye. Don't stay out too late."

She looked back at me and raised an eyebrow. "Right back at ya. Make him earn your trust."

I gave her a slight nod and locked the door behind her, noticing my bare fingers. I'd pulled off my wedding band and engagement ring after discovering Jason's lies. Maybe it was time to start wearing them again. It would show him I hadn't given up.

Back in my bedroom, I opened the jewelry box where I'd stashed the rings. I'd been so desperate to get them out of my sight that

I'd shoved them into one compartment or another. I dug through the piles of bracelets and earrings, searching. They weren't there.

My breath quickened as I recalled my frenzied trips to the garbage dumpster on the horrible night I'd returned from Vermont. Was it possible I'd thrown them out? Closing my eyes, I struggled to think back to that night. The rage and despair that had driven me to clear out the bedroom had also dulled my memory. While my body retrieved the agonizing emotions I'd experienced a little too easily, my mind had responded to the trauma in the opposite way, by blacking out my words and actions. I'd lost entire minutes and hours from that night.

I stepped back and glanced around the room, choosing to believe I hadn't thrown away the rings. That would have been too extreme, too final, even for me in my damaged state. If for nothing else, I would have held onto them for the resale value. My eyes landed on the clock. It was 6:30 p.m. There were still thirty minutes until my date with Jason. *Where were they?*

Maybe, in my haste, I'd tossed the rings into the top drawer of my dresser instead of into the jewelry box. My fingers sifted through my underwear and bras, reaching back into the far corners of the shallow drawer, but came up empty.

My jaw stiffened as an indescribable coldness leeched into my body, the sickening realization setting in. My rings weren't here. What if Caroline had taken them? I hated myself for having the thought, but her past behavior had trained me to think this way. What if she'd swiped them to buy heroin for herself and her new friend? She'd done the same with Dad's treasured class ring a couple of years earlier. I steadied myself against the dresser and breathed deliberately in and out, in and out. No. Caroline wouldn't have done that. I couldn't believe it. Not after all we'd been through in the last couple of weeks.

Despite her less-than-desirable new friend and her laziness, she hadn't shown most of the common indicators of drug use. At least, not that I could tell. I straightened my shoulders and shook my head. The rings would turn up. My imagination had been spiraling out of control lately. I smoothed down my dress and went downstairs.

As I reached into the cupboard for a glass, something moved in my peripheral vision, a dark shape passing outside the window. The neighbors' dog barked. Electricity bristled through me as I replaced the glass and slunk toward the window, pressing myself against the wall. It wasn't Jason. We'd agreed to meet at the restaurant. I peeked outside but didn't see any movement.

Ducking down, I tiptoed to the front of the house and peered through a tiny gap in the curtain. A black Escalade idled next to the curb. A stream of exhaust floated from its tailpipe and vanished into the air. I held my breath as a broad-shouldered man paced across our yard directly in front of me. His thinning hair was slicked back and a gold chain hung around his neck. The leather coat he wore couldn't conceal the gut that hung over his belt. Despite the evening hour, tinted sunglasses covered his eyes. Everything about the man was greasy. Three loud knocks pounded on the door. My heart pounded just as violently.

"I know you're in there!"

I crouched down lower, my hands shaking.

"Yo! Give me my money!" More pounding.

I waited, staring at the wall and trying not to breathe. My eyes darted around, searching for my phone. I'd left it in the kitchen. I could make a run for it if it came to that. At last, a car door slammed and an engine revved. I released a breath as I straightened up. My heart raced. I peeked through the curtain. He was gone.

I'd never seen the guy before, but he wasn't someone to mess with. He looked like he could have been connected to the mafia. I thought of Caroline and her new friend. Her unusual sleep patterns and irregular pupils. My missing rings. *Not again.* I pressed my hands to my forehead as I imagined the call I'd have to make to my parents. *What had she done?*

CHAPTER TWENTY-THREE

Gloria (NOW)

It was a lazy summer morning, the kind that normally encouraged lounging on the couch and basking in the melody of birds chirping through an open window. But I was finding it more difficult to relax the longer Amanda remained missing. Ethan was sleeping upstairs. I closed the *Thirty-Day Life Coach* workbook, proud of myself for how much I'd accomplished.

I'd hoped to find another book by the same author at the bookstore yesterday, but it had been difficult to browse while holding a full cup of coffee. Beth's odd behavior had left me flustered, even after she apologized for leaving the café in such a hurry. The crowd in the enclosed space had made her feel claustrophobic and had caused her to panic. I'd patted her shoulder and told her it was fine, but I worried about what kind of review she must be planning for the little shop.

My head sank into the cushion behind me, the morning sun casting a gentle light across the living room floor. Weeding the garden had been on my agenda, but Rascal had me trapped on the couch. He groaned and shifted position in his sleep, his warm head resting on my thigh.

Lifting the remote, I clicked on the TV. The familiar white-haired newscaster spoke in his usual dire tone: *Breaking news. Another murdered woman has been found in Petoskey. The victim has been identified as Amanda Jenkins, a local woman who has been missing since last week.*

I leaned forward, my stomach lurching. I couldn't breathe.

A farmer discovered the body early this morning in an irrigation ditch outside of town. The cause of death is cited as a single gunshot to the head. Police haven't commented on whether the murder might be related to the recent death of local hairdresser, Ella Burkholter, the twenty-six-year-old woman who was discovered strangled to death last month on the public beach. No suspects have been named in either case.

I gasped for air, my throat constricting.

"Ethan," I said. He was upstairs in his room. "Ethan!" Rascal sprang from the couch and ran to the window.

My son's figure appeared in the stairway. "What's wrong?"

I pointed to the TV where Amanda's photo hung on the screen with the words *Body of Missing Woman Found.* It was the same photo they'd displayed when she'd first gone missing. She wore a black V-neck sweater, and a delicate silver necklace hung from her neck. Her lips held a mischievous smile.

"Oh, my God." Ethan stepped toward the TV. His eyes bulged as he ran his fingers through his hair. "Is that her?"

"I'm afraid so."

Ethan pulled on his shoes and craned his neck toward the window again. "We should go over and see if Beth is okay."

I followed him, stumbling toward the tiny house with Rascal trailing behind. Beth would be devastated when we told her, but it was better if she heard it from us. We ducked through the trees, discovering her truck was gone.

"She's not home," I said.

Ethan ignored me and pounded on the door. "Beth!"

"Her truck's gone." My voice was calm, even though my chest heaved. I'd gone out for coffee with Beth yesterday, so I knew she hadn't disappeared. Still, I hoped she was somewhere safe. "Maybe she's gone back to the police station."

Ethan stepped away from the door, placing his hands on his hips and breathing heavily. We trudged back through the trees, the garage apartment rising before us. Joe's truck was missing, too.

Ethan motioned toward the apartment. "Where's this guy running off to all the time?"

"Art fairs, he says." My stomach flipped as I remembered his peculiar emergence from the woods and his sudden departure, both in the middle of the night, plus the mysterious scratches on his face. Was it possible he was hiding something in the middle of the forest?

Ethan shook his head, disgusted. "This is all my fault."

"What do you mean?"

"I should have done the background check on Joe, but I put it off. I forgot." He marched toward the farmhouse. "I'm doing it right now."

He barged through the front door and took the steps two at a time up to his room. As he left, I pulled out my phone and wrote a text to Beth. *Are you okay?* I hit send and waited, but there was no response. A moment later, Ethan clomped down the stairs, set up his laptop on the kitchen counter and began typing.

"Joe Miles, right?" he asked.

"That's the name he gave me."

Ethan pulled out a credit card and entered the numbers. He leaned back.

Squeezing my eyes closed, a vision of Joe forcing my window open flashed in my mind. I tried not to let my imagination wander down a dark path. "Did you find anything?" I asked.

"It's searching." He crouched in front of the screen, tapping a key. "Nothing on Joseph Miles. He lives in Detroit. No aliases.

Forty-three years old. Got a speeding ticket four years ago. That's it." Ethan started typing again. "Is Beth's real name Elizabeth?"

"Yes. Elizabeth Ramsay. But I really don't think…"

Ethan held up his hand and continued typing. He leaned back and waited. He studied the screen. "She lived in Royal Oak."

I nodded. "I know that."

"She used to go by a different name—Liz McCormack."

"Yes. That was probably her married name. Her husband died in an accident. She told me all about it."

Ethan ignored me. "No criminal record for her either."

"Well, of course there's not." I shook my head at the thought. The keys continued clicking.

"She has a younger sister, Caroline Ramsay." His eyes widened. "Holy crap! Look at her rap sheet."

I edged closer, but Ethan's shoulder blocked the screen.

"Assault, Reckless Endangerment, Public Indecency." He said each word under his breath.

I grit my teeth but shook my head. "Beth mentioned her sister struggled with drugs. She's changed her life around, though. She graduated from cosmetology school and lives in Ohio."

"Yeah. That could be true. Her last arrest was almost two years ago." Ethan straightened his shoulders. "Let's do a simple Google search on Joe." His fingers clicked across the keys. "Wow."

"What?"

He turned the screen toward me, and I lost my breath. Dozens of images of oil paintings formed a mosaic across the screen. The brightly colored natural landscapes popped as if painted in 3D.

"Beautiful," I said. I'd never seen any of Joe's artwork other than the thumbprint image on his business card.

"This is Joe's website." Ethan reclaimed the screen. "I guess he has some talent."

I exhaled, relieved my reckless decision to rent the apartment to Joe hadn't put anyone in danger. He was a real artist with no criminal record. The storage closet was probably filled with his art supplies just as he'd told me, not kidnapped women who he planned to murder. Still, it didn't explain his unusual midnight excursions.

"Holy shit."

"Ethan!"

"Sorry." Ethan's eyes darted back and forth, reading frantically. "Look at this article."

I stepped behind him and took in the words. *Royal Oak Woman Named Person-of-Interest in Death of Husband.* My arms dropped to my sides as if my hands were attached to anchors. An image of Beth and her late husband appeared just below the headline, but the person in the photo barely resembled the Beth I knew. It was a wedding photo. Her hair was blonde and flowing, she wore heavy makeup around her eyes and an elegant white dress. A tall, handsome man in a tuxedo stood next to her, his arm draped over her shoulder. I shuddered, although I didn't have the faintest idea why. Beth had told me about this already. Nevertheless, I couldn't stop my eyes from swallowing the words.

Jason McCormack (33), a rising star in the financial invest-ment industry, died Saturday afternoon after falling from a privately owned 130-ft yacht into the frigid waters of Lake Huron. While the official cause of death has been identified as drowning, police are investigating whether McCormack fell overboard accidentally, or whether he may have been pushed. The coroner reported a blood-alcohol level of .18, indicating that McCormack had been drinking heavily prior to his fall. A small amount of blood discovered on the back of the boat suggests McCormack may have hit his head on his way into the water.

The exact time of McCormack's death is unknown. Passengers stated they'd gathered for lunch inside the upper cabin where loud music was playing, preventing them from hearing anything unusual. McCormack wasn't discovered missing until after the boat had docked at Lakewood Marina in Port Huron. A search and rescue team was immediately dispatched and his body was discovered six hours later.

McCormack's wife, Elizabeth, was on board and was questioned as a person of interest before being released. She stated that she was in the upper cabin when her husband fell. Other passengers have accounted for her whereabouts. The couple had recently reunited after a brief separation. According to a family friend, Robert Langdon, they were "loving and happy toward each other." Police will further question Elizabeth, which is the normal course of action in cases where one spouse has died under suspicious circumstances. Additionally, Elizabeth had been named as the sole beneficiary on a $2 million life insurance policy recently purchased by her late husband.

The owner of the yacht, Conway Stratton, was an investor in McCormack's financial fund and is also being questioned.

I stepped back: *$2 million?* Beth hadn't mentioned anything about an insurance payout. She'd paid me in cash, but she certainly lived frugally. Maybe she'd stashed the money away for a rainy day or donated it to the less fortunate.

Leaning forward, I squeezed Ethan's shoulder. "This isn't a surprise. Beth was very open with me about her husband's death. On the very first day we met she told me her husband drowned in a boating accident."

Ethan narrowed his eyes at the screen. "Look at these comments."

I squinted at the words, acid rising in my throat as I read the horrible words underneath the article.

He fell off a boat? Yeah right. The wife is SO guilty!
I guess someone wanted to cash in on life insurance.
It's ALWAYS the spouse. Police, do your job!

I turned toward Ethan. "Who are these people?"

Ethan shrugged. "Anyone can leave comments on these online articles."

"Well, I don't think these people know what they're talking about. Beth said everyone, even her friends, suspected her. She was cleared, though. That's why she decided to buy a tiny house and move to a new town."

"Why did she change her appearance?"

"To get a fresh start, I suppose. Also, her husband was the one who told her to dye her hair blonde." I examined Jason McCormack's photo on the web page again. "Just between you and me, he didn't sound like the nicest man. I'm glad she's back to her natural color."

Ethan ignored me and typed something on the keyboard, his head hovering inches above the screen. "You're right." He wiped the perspiration from his forehead. "She was cleared."

I peered over Ethan's shoulder. A different article spread across the screen. *Death of Successful Financier Ruled an Accident.*

The article described how Beth's whereabouts had been accounted for during the cruise, and how Jason had wandered toward the back of the boat where the railing ended to smoke a cigarette over the water. The police concluded that his actions, paired with his excessive drinking and the violent waves on the lake that day, had resulted in his tragic death. No foul play involved.

I nodded my approval at the article. "Maybe we need to stop worrying about Beth and start worrying about catching Amanda's killer."

Ethan closed his laptop.

"Let's get down to the police station. I bet Beth is there. I'll tell the detective Amanda used to rent my apartment. They might want to search it for clues."

Ethan stood. "Okay. Yeah. This is crazy."

We looked at each other, and his eyes wavered with the same watery depth as when I'd dropped him off for his first day of kindergarten. I was more thankful than ever that he was back home.

He strode toward the door. "Let's go."

I scooped up Rascal and put him inside his crate, turning a deaf ear to my puppy's high-pitched cries. It was harder to ignore the shaking of my fingers as I secured the metal latch.

CHAPTER TWENTY-FOUR

Elizabeth (BEFORE)

"You're wrong about me, you know?" Caroline dragged her suitcase toward the front door. "I haven't been doing drugs. I don't need to go back to rehab." Tears streamed down her cheeks. My heart wrenched for my sister. I wanted to believe her.

"I'm sorry, Caroline. I just want what's best for you." I stepped forward to hug her, but she pulled away, leaving me teetering over an empty space.

It had been two days since the mobster had been lurking around the house. That same night, Caroline hadn't returned home. I'd paced the hallways, checking the multiple texts I'd sent to her. She hadn't responded. I'd been terrified by the possible horrors that could have befallen her. By yesterday morning I'd been ready to call the police. She'd stumbled through the door, her normally shiny hair sticking out in all directions, and long sleeves covering her arms despite temperatures in the eighties.

"Let me see your arms," I'd said.

"Screw you." Caroline stomped past me toward the guest room.

"Where are my rings?" I screamed at her through my sleepless haze.

"Hell if I know." Caroline slammed the door.

I'd had enough. Jason had been there for me, talking through everything on the phone, listening. He agreed that I had too much on my plate. I could no longer balance salvaging our marriage, nurturing my unborn baby, maintaining my career, and babysitting my irresponsible twenty-five-year-old sister. He was worried about my safety, but we decided it was best not to call the police. Jason insisted on moving back home so he could protect me and the baby from the mobster, should he return. We didn't want to implicate my sister in whatever shady scheme she and her new lowlife friends had gotten themselves involved in. Besides, Caroline didn't need jail time. She'd been down that road before and it had only made things worse. It was best to get her out of town and into a treatment center. Last night, I'd pressed Mom's cell number on my phone and asked her to come and pick up Caroline.

Now, Dad stood next to me in the foyer, rocking his weight from foot to foot. Mom exited the bathroom, a frown pulling down her tanned face. Their cruise ship had already docked the day before but they still had to cut their trip a day short.

"You did the right thing, Lizzie," Dad said after Caroline had reached the car. "We need to get her away from this Josh fellow."

Mom tipped her head back and sighed. "We'll take care of Caroline. Her doctor will be able to sort this out. I'm just glad you and Jason are getting back together."

Dad kicked the ground and grunted. I wondered if he'd ever sit in the same room as Jason again.

"We're taking things slowly. It's a trial period." I glanced at Dad. "I'll keep you updated on the baby," I added, attempting to turn the conversation to a happy subject.

"Please do," Mom said.

We hugged and made our way outside. They climbed into their minivan. I waved as they drove away. Caroline only stared out the window at me, her eyes swimming with anger.

Later that afternoon, I motioned toward the beige walls of the nursery. "Looks like we better start painting."

"We'll hire someone." Jason massaged my shoulders. "You shouldn't breathe those fumes. We need to pick out a color."

He held my hand as we strolled into the master bedroom, his touch sending an intoxicating jolt through me.

"Wow. This looks different." Jason surveyed our altered room.

"I rearranged it. You know… for obvious reasons." Despite my agreement to let Jason move back in, my anger surfaced at unexpected moments. He would have to earn my trust over months and years, not days, and I wouldn't hesitate to remind him of the pain he'd caused. The day after our date night at the French bistro, we'd completed another session with Dr. Brennan where we'd told her about the missing rings and expressed concern about Caroline living with me. Dr. Brennan agreed it was a good time for Jason to move back in, at least on a trial basis. The sessions with the psychologist had helped, but only time would tell if he'd really changed.

"Sorry, babe." He wrapped his arms around me and squeezed. "I'm sorry I put you through all of this."

"I know. And I'm sorry I threw away all your clothes."

"And my watch." Jason's mouth formed into a lopsided smile.

"Yeah. That, too."

"I'm going to run down and bring up a load of clothes from the car," Jason said.

"Do you want me to help?" I asked.

"What? No. You shouldn't be lifting anything."

We'd spent the previous hour back at Dr. Brennan's office, opening up and sharing our feelings. She suggested that we plan regular dates together, maybe even a vacation. She promised these shared experiences would strengthen the foundation of our marriage. Even a weekend getaway would give us the time to focus on our relationship away from our everyday stresses.

"Relationships are often tested once a baby arrives," she'd said, a dire look in her eyes.

We'd agreed to plan a fun outing, something we wouldn't normally do. We'd only begun talking about our hopes for the future when the hour was up. Lydia had been right; Dr. Brennan was a lifesaver. In the span of only a few weeks I'd gone from losing everything, spinning in a freefall off a cliff, to landing unexpectedly back onto the secure foothold of my family and my dreams of the future. Imperfect as our marriage was, at least it was truthful.

I waited on the bed as Jason returned with an armful of suits, shirts, and pants. He hung them on the empty side of the closet.

"I ordered some new shoes and belts online. They should be arriving in the next few days."

"Okay." I wondered how mad he really was about me trashing his belongings. I got up and looped my arm through his. "I was thinking about what Dr. Brennan said. It would be fun to plan a vacation. Maybe we could fly somewhere for a weekend?"

"Yeah." He wrapped his solid arms around me again. "We should definitely do that."

"Any ideas?"

"Maybe California? Or up north?" A smile stretched across his face. "I know. One of my investors has a yacht. It's sick. Like, 130 feet or something. Maybe he'll take us out for a cruise."

"Where?" I asked.

"He docks it on Lake Huron. We could make a weekend trip out of it. Let me talk to him."

"Okay." My palm rested on my belly. A cruise sounded fun, although I wondered how my nausea would hold up on a boat.

"By the way, I bought something else." He led me over to the bed where we sat down. "For you." Jason reached in his pocket and pulled out a tiny square box. He opened the lid, revealing a massive diamond set on a silver band. Next to it sat another ring encrusted in tiny diamonds. "Since we don't know what happened to your other rings, at least not for sure, maybe it's better to start fresh."

"Oh my God." My hand shielded my gaping mouth. I'd never seen a diamond so enormous, so beautiful. I ignored the familiar tightening of the knot in my stomach, the one that worried about how much it had cost, and whether we could afford it. A smart remark about whether he'd bought the same rings for his girlfriend balanced on my tongue, but I swallowed the words, not wanting to ruin the moment.

Jason nudged me. "Put them on."

My hands quivered as I removed the rings from the box and forced them over my knuckle onto my ring finger. They were tight, probably because of the pregnancy weight. I held up my hand, admiring the way the light reflected off the precision cuts in the gems. "They're gorgeous," I said.

Jason leaned in and we kissed. He pulled me closer. "I love you," he whispered into my ear.

"I love you, too." My hand caressed his back as I tried to ignore the way the silver bands cut into my finger.

CHAPTER TWENTY-FIVE

Gloria (NOW)

I followed Ethan across the steaming asphalt toward the police station. Beth's red pickup truck was already parked in the far corner of the lot. My shoulders loosened and I looked at Ethan.

"That's what I thought. She's already here."

Ethan stared at the truck and nodded. He opened the glass door to the nondescript beige building and ushered me into the lobby. The smell of burned coffee and stale cigarettes filled my throat. We approached the front desk, my stomach bubbling with nerves.

"Can I help you?" asked a woman with a gap in her front teeth and severely cut bangs.

Ethan stepped in front of me, his fingers tapping on the counter. "Yes. My name is Ethan Flass. We're looking for our friend, Beth Ramsay."

"Oh." The woman puckered her lips. "She's speaking to the detective. You'll have to wait."

I stepped forward. "I also have some information I'd like to give to the detective. It's related to Amanda Jenkins, the woman who was just found. She used to rent my garage apartment. That was over six months ago, but you never know what clue might help solve a case."

The receptionist twisted her mouth to the side. "I'll let the detective know. Would you two like some coffee?"

"No, thank you." I made a face at Ethan. I couldn't imagine anything less helpful than filling up on caffeine just as I struggled to get my heart rate under control.

We sat in seats against the wall. I clutched my purse in my lap as the receptionist ogled us from behind her desk. She only averted her eyes when I stared right back at her.

A moment later, a portly man with a balding head opened the door of a side room. He wore a white button-down shirt and a tie the color of untilled soil. The receptionist whispered something to him, and I presumed he was the detective in charge. He glanced toward me and nodded. Then he ducked back into the room.

Beth's eyes were rimmed with red, her face puffy. She stared at the ground as she stumbled back toward the lobby. It took a second for her to notice us standing there.

"Ethan? Gloria?" She rushed toward us and embraced me. "This is horrible."

"We were looking for you this morning."

"I just saw your text," Beth said.

Ethan leaned in close to her. "I'm sorry about your friend."

Beth bit her lower lip and nodded. She tugged on her sleeves and looked as if she might burst into tears again. "I drove straight here when I saw the news. I'm sorry. I should have stopped by your house first. I was in a panic."

"It's okay." I patted her shoulder, remembering how she hadn't been sleeping well.

"Gloria Flass?"

We turned our heads toward the deep voice that boomed through the room. The detective stood in the doorway, his thumb hooked over his belt.

I stood and approached the man, eager to assist with the investigation.

Beth stepped in front of me. "Gloria. What are you doing?"

"I have some helpful information for the detective. I'll be back in a minute."

"She wants to tell him Amanda used to rent her garage apartment," Ethan whispered as I maneuvered past them.

It only took a minute to pass on my clue to the detective. I made sure to include the part about the apartment door swinging open just before Joe moved in, although I admitted I may have been the one who'd left the door unlocked. When I told the detective Amanda had moved out of the apartment months earlier, he sighed. It was clear he didn't give much weight to the information. Still, he smiled and thanked me before sending me on my way.

Now Ethan, Beth, and I walked toward the door, away from the prying eyes of the receptionist.

"What did you tell them?" I asked Beth once we were outside.

"The same thing I told them last time." She crossed her arms and shook her head. "I mean, we were just hanging out, having a couple of drinks the night she disappeared. Amanda was in a really bad mood. It was uncomfortable. I made a stupid comment about the backward people in this town. She took it personally and stormed out. That was the last time I saw her."

I patted Beth's hand and felt it quivering underneath mine as we walked through the parking lot. She was shaken. I remembered feeling the same way after Charlie died.

"I'm parked over there." Beth tilted her head toward her truck.

I crouched toward Ethan and lowered my voice. "Do you mind driving my car? I thought I'd ride with Beth. She seems traumatized."

"Sure." He took the keys from me. "I'll see you back at the house."

"I'll ride with you," I said, stepping toward Beth. "You look like you could use the company."

Beth nodded, her eyes focused on the ground as she neared her truck. It sat like a sparkling ruby in the morning sun.

"I see you got a car wash." I nodded my approval as I hoisted myself into the passenger seat.

"It needed it." She pulled onto the street and accelerated in the direction of the highway.

I glanced at Beth. "I'll try to think of more information to pass on to the detective."

"Please don't." Beth's voice was blunt, her eyes trained on the road. Her words sent a prickle of dread through me, like spiders skittering down my spine. Her truck continued to pick up speed.

"I guess you're right. We'll let the police do their job."

Beth stared ahead without looking at me. Her face was gaunt and her complexion had taken on the shade of milkweed. "The police are useless."

"Are you okay?" I asked, leaning toward her.

"Yes, Gloria. I'm great. My life is fucking wonderful." She turned and glared at me, her eyes as dark and empty as two holes dug in the dirt. "I know you think you're helping, but you're not. You need to stop talking."

I shrank down, shocked by Beth's sudden change in demeanor. She'd turned on a dime yesterday in the coffee shop, but I'd never seen this ugly side of her before. Since the day she'd arrived on my land, I'd built her up to be a sophisticated and independent woman, someone who knew the world and how to deal with people, someone who had no use for silly self-help books, the kind of woman I'd never had the chance to become. Now I realized I may have ignored some red flags. I may have glossed over the parts of her that hadn't fit my idealized images, like her late husband's suspicious death, her desire to live off the grid, and her peculiar behavior. Once again, she wasn't telling me her whole story. I pressed my shoulder blades against the seat as the truck squealed through a sharp turn. My purse tipped, spilling some of its contents at my feet.

"Darn…" I started to say, but let my voice trail off. I bent over, straining against the seat belt to collect the pens and keys and compact that had toppled from my bag. Beth ignored me, accelerating onto the two-lane highway, and passing cars in the lane next to us as if they were standing still. My left hand clutched the center console, as my right hand reached down again to make sure I'd retrieved everything.

Stretching my arm beneath the seat, my finger caught on something stringy and metal. I bent over to see what I'd discovered. A necklace hung in loops from my fingers. It was silver with a pendant shaped like a butterfly. Each wing had been crafted from two shiny jewels. Topaz, if I had to guess.

The necklace wasn't mine. It hadn't come from my purse, but it looked familiar. I wondered if I'd seen it on Beth, but the dainty silver butterfly didn't match Beth's bohemian style. It didn't fit with the wooden beads and messy tangle of black cords that normally encircled her neck and wrists. I was certain she wasn't the one I'd seen wearing it.

The silver strand balanced in my palm as the truck screeched around a turn into the entrance of my driveway, pinning my body back against my seat. My hand clenched the necklace as my brain caught up, an image of Amanda on the local news flashing in my mind. My stomach lifted and crashed as the memory formed. The picture flickered before my eyes, as clear as if I'd recorded it and was now watching it back on the television screen. In the photo, Amanda had been wearing a black V-neck sweater. I squeezed my eyelids shut, conjuring up another detail… one I didn't want to see. She'd also been wearing a necklace. A silver necklace with a turquoise butterfly, identical to the one in my hand.

I hoped Beth wouldn't notice the perspiration covering my brow. With the smallest movement I could manage, I slipped the necklace into my purse and zipped it closed. By the time the truck skidded to a halt in front of my house, it felt as if all the blood had leaked from my body. The pieces of Beth's past fluttered through my head and settled on a disturbing picture: Beth's dead husband, her off-the-grid tiny house that held no photos or clues to her past, her dyed hair, her changed name, her mysterious nightly excursions, her erratic behavior the last few days. And now, her new friend—who I'd introduced her to and who'd been angry with her—was dead, and the missing woman's necklace was under the seat of Beth's truck.

"I didn't mean to yell at you, Gloria." Tears welled in Beth's eyes, but she stared straight ahead clutching the steering wheel. "I'm not a bad person. It's just that my life didn't turn out the way I thought it would."

"Oh, that's not—" I started to say.

Beth held her palm up to my face. "You don't need to pretend to be my friend, Gloria. I don't deserve it."

I had a thousand questions for Beth, but I was too terrified to learn the answers. My parched throat constricted and my heart thudded so loudly in my chest I could barely hear my own thoughts. Instead of speaking to her, my fingers fumbled for the door handle, opening an exit route. Without looking back, I jumped from the truck, hoping Ethan was right behind us.

"Maybe you should take it to the police, Mom." We huddled in the living room, the curtains drawn, the doors and windows locked. We'd placed the necklace in a zip-lock bag to preserve any evidence. Ethan pinched the corner of the bag and held it next to the police photo of Amanda he'd pulled up on his laptop. The resemblance between the two pieces of jewelry was heart-stopping. Just as I'd suspected, they were identical.

"I don't want to jump to conclusions." I massaged my forehead as I paced behind Ethan, Rascal biting at my heels. Although Beth had been rather rude on the drive home, I had no real reason to betray her trust. My imagination had been on overdrive. It was only a day or two ago that I'd been ready to accuse Joe of kidnapping and hiding bodies in his closet. I paused in front of the window and peeked through the curtain. The back of Beth's truck was visible beyond the tree line. Hopefully she was inside her tiny house drinking some tea and calming down. "Did you see Beth arrive back here the other night after you two left The Castaways?"

Ethan tipped his head back and sighed. "No. She drove separately. Said she had to stop for gas on the way home. I wish I'd been paying attention. I have no idea when she got back."

"When I knocked on her door the next morning, she looked like she'd slept in her clothes. Why didn't you drive together?"

"We were going to, but Beth texted me and said she needed to run a couple of errands first. I told her I'd meet her at The Castaways at eight. She was already there when I got there."

"Was she acting like her usual self?"

"I don't know. I've only known her for a few days."

"Think, Ethan. Did you notice anything unusual?"

Ethan stared toward the window. "Yeah. I guess she seemed distracted. She kept looking around the restaurant, almost like she was waiting for somebody else."

"But no one else approached her?"

"No."

I clasped my hands together, remembering Beth's misguided hope that she'd run into Amanda at the restaurant again. "She mentioned Amanda was mad at her the night she disappeared. I don't know what their tiff was about, but they were spending a lot of time together. Amanda's necklace must have fallen off at some point when Beth gave her a lift. Or maybe Amanda lent it to her. Besides, what possible motive could Beth have?"

"I have no idea." He closed out the screen and turned toward me. "Still weird, though. The fact is, Amanda is the second woman in this small town to be murdered in less than a month. There were no murders before Beth arrived."

We sat in silence for a moment before Ethan began typing on his laptop. "What magazine did you say Beth is working for?"

"*American Traveler.* They commissioned her to write an article about northern Michigan resort towns."

"I'm going to call them."

"What? You can't just call them."

Ethan raised his eyebrows at me, pressed some numbers on his phone, and then switched it to the speaker so I could hear the ringing.

"*American Traveler*, can I help you?" a woman asked.

"Yes," Ethan cleared his throat and lowered his voice, "my name is Tom Weller. I own a hotel in Petoskey, Michigan, and I was approached by a journalist named Beth Ramsay who says she's writing an article for your magazine. I just wanted to verify that she's been commissioned by you before I agree to an interview."

"Of course, sir. You said Beth Ramsay?"

"Yes. Or it might be under Elizabeth Ramsay. Or Elizabeth McCormack."

"Just a minute, please."

Music played over the speaker and Ethan smirked at me.

"Do you really think this is necessary?" I asked him.

He shrugged. "We'll see."

A minute later, the music cut out and the woman returned. "Sir?"

"Yes."

"No one by Elizabeth Ramsay or McCormack has a contract with us."

My heart sank as a chill traveled over my skin. *No contract?* Beth had been lying to me this whole time. I remembered the awkward encounter with Wes at the coffee shop. She hadn't gotten the name of his bike shop wrong at all. She'd lied about the whole thing. That was why she never followed up with him for an interview.

"Okay. Thank you." Ethan hung up, his mouth gaping open. He flopped back against the couch and I lowered myself down next to him.

"Holy shit."

"Ethan!"

"Sorry, Mom, but this is messed up. Beth is a liar."

I closed my eyes, feeling as if I'd been duped. If Beth hadn't been researching local attractions for her article, what was she doing here? Where did she go every day? Why was she really parked in my field? I straightened my shoulders, remembering the Beth I knew, the good friend she had become.

"This doesn't prove she had anything to do with Amanda's disappearance. Maybe she writes under a pseudonym." I squeezed my hands together, a stubborn knot of loyalty within me refusing to believe my new friend had transformed into a lying murderer. There was probably a logical explanation.

Ethan raised his voice. "You need to keep your distance from her. We both do. At least until they arrest someone else. Beth is nice on the surface, but we really don't know her at all."

I rested my head on the cushion behind me, wondering how I'd keep my distance from someone who lived just a few hundred yards away.

Ethan leaned forward, a concerned look in his eyes. "Listen, I'm supposed to go camping with Wes and Vicki tomorrow. I'm going to cancel the trip."

"No. Don't do that." I shook my head and patted Ethan's knee. "You're worrying too much. I'm perfectly capable of taking care of myself. Besides, you deserve to have a little fun while you're here. You should go and get your mind off all this."

Ethan stood up and paced across the room. He peeked out the window and then let the curtain drop. "Do you promise to keep away from Beth while I'm gone? Stay inside, keep the door locked?"

"Oh, honestly." I shook my head. Ethan was acting ridiculously. "Yes. I'll keep to myself as much as I can. Rascal will have to go in and out, of course." I thought of the house key I'd given to Beth and my insides quaked. Locking my door wouldn't do any good, but I wouldn't mention that to Ethan. I shoved my hands into my pockets and tightened my jaw. Beth may have lied about writing an article for the magazine, but it was absurd to think she planned to harm me. I didn't want Ethan to miss out on his camping trip.

A throbbing pain squeezed through my head, coupled with an unrelenting ache in my back. My suspicions and unanswered questions were taking a toll on my body. "I've got a headache. I'm going to go lie down."

I scooped Rascal up in my arms and carried him upstairs. He might not have learned any of his manners yet, but he was the closest thing I had to a guard dog.

Morning sunlight speared through a gap in the curtains and across the kitchen floor. Brakes screeched from the driveway. Rascal perked his ears toward the door and barked. I set down my second cup of coffee on the counter, my heart racing. I wasn't sure if the deafening noise had come from Beth's truck, Joe's SUV, or a police car. My uncomfortable encounter with Beth the day before replayed in my mind. I sidled up next to the window, glancing back toward the empty staircase. Ethan had left an hour earlier with his friends to go camping, but only after I'd promised him, again, to keep my distance from Beth.

A car door slammed. It wasn't the police. It was Joe, a trail of dust floating behind his SUV. Rascal barked and raced in circles around me. Beth's truck was gone.

"Let's get you outside, boy." I shooed Rascal in front of me as I made my way through the door. I envisioned Joe's paintings. He was a talented artist, that was certain, but some of his actions puzzled me—the gun-shaped bag, the midnight hikes into the woods, his urge to fix my windows, the scratches on his face, and the field trips to who-knew-where in the middle of the night. Now, in light of Amanda's death, I had to be bold. I had to find answers; answers I hoped wouldn't lead back to Beth.

Rascal wove through the bushes next to the house while I waited near the garage. The apartment door swung open and I crossed my arms in front of me, my muscles strung as tight as shoelaces.

"Hey, Gloria." Joe bounded down the steps two at a time. "Beautiful day, huh?" He seemed blissfully unaware that the woman who used to live in his apartment had been murdered.

"Yes." I swallowed and buried my hands in my pockets, unsure how to begin.

"I'm unloading a few supplies. Then I'll get out of your hair."

"Joe," I said, my voice hoarse. I cleared my throat and started again. "I was out here with Rascal the other night. It was late. More like early morning, really."

Joe stared at me, deadpan, and I shifted my weight.

"Anyway, I couldn't help but notice you coming out of the woods. It's not hunting season yet, is it?"

"What?" Joe set down the box he was lifting from his trunk. "No. You thought I was hunting?" He squeezed his eyes shut and bellowed out a laugh from his gut. "That's funny," he said, catching his breath. "I'm a vegetarian. Have been for years. I wouldn't kill a bear if it was attacking me."

I exhaled, relieved and embarrassed that I'd misread him so badly. "Oh, that's a relief. Your bag was shaped like a rifle, so I thought—"

Laughter erupted from Joe again. "You mean my easel? I guess I could use it to whack someone on the head if I was desperate."

Giggling along with him, I glanced toward the trees feeling like a dimwit. *Of course it was an easel.* It was no wonder I'd spent my life as a housewife and not a detective.

Joe lifted a box from his vehicle and placed it on the ground. "I've been working on a new technique: night painting. These woods are the perfect setting. It took me a few hours of wandering around in the dark to find the best spot, then I realized I needed a headlamp, not a flashlight. Duh!" He bonked his forehead with his palm. "I can't hold a paintbrush and a flashlight at the same time. So I've made more than a couple of treks out there. At least now I know where to avoid the brambles." His thick fingertips touched the scratches on his face.

I nodded and raised my chin, trying to preserve my dignity. "That does sound like a lot of work. I'd love to see the finished product."

Joe motioned toward the apartment. "I've got a rough start upstairs if you want to take a look."

"Oh," I said, caught off guard by the invitation. "Sure."

I followed him up the wooden steps and into the living room. Canvases were stacked against the far wall, a T-shirt and socks were strewn across the floor, and an open pizza box lay on the counter. The scene was a startling contrast to Beth's pristine tiny house. The door to the walk-in closet was closed, but I was relieved to hear no frantic banging or cries for help coming from within.

"Sorry about the mess." Joe picked the clothes off the floor and tossed them into the bedroom.

"Is the apartment working out for you?"

"It's great. Except for the whole Laundromat thing. But beggars can't be choosers." He smiled and turned toward the stack of artwork. "Let's see." He thumbed through some half-painted canvases and shook his head. "I must have put it in the closet."

As he wandered around searching for the night painting, I took in the cluttered apartment. It had been barren when Amanda had lived here several months earlier. I tried my darnedest to remember why she'd moved in but couldn't. Or maybe she hadn't told me. I regretted never having sat down for wine or coffee with her as I'd been doing with Beth. Amanda had been polite the day I'd shown her the apartment but hadn't offered any more information than necessary. The four months she lived here had gone by fast. She'd kept to herself, barely offering a wave when we'd passed.

One day I'd run into her on the driveway, her eyes had been puffy as if she'd been crying and she'd obviously tried to disguise it with makeup. I'd hemmed and hawed about knocking on her door and having her over for dinner but hadn't followed through with it. The drama with Mary Ellen Calloway and my Bible study group had distracted me that day. That was before I'd started reading *The Thirty-Day Life Coach*. I would have handled the situation differently now.

"Here it is," Joe's voice echoed from within the closet.

He stepped into the living room holding a large canvas. Thick black smudges crisscrossed the white background. A yellow circle hovered in the left corner.

"Oh, my," I said, not sure how else to respond.

"It's a work-in-progress. I started it when the moon was full." He pointed to the yellow circle. "The moon was only three-quarters full when I was out there Thursday night. That's where memory comes in. These lines will be trees, and I'll fill in the night sky in the back."

"Did you say Thursday night?" I leaned forward.

"Yup."

"What time did you return from the woods?"

Joe stared at the ceiling. "Hmm, probably around midnight. Maybe later. You can ask Beth. She almost ran me over in the driveway. Didn't even have her headlights on." Joe laughed and shook his head.

My muscles tightened, my blood curdling like forgotten milk. Beth had returned home at midnight? Ethan said they'd left The Castaways around 10 p.m. What had she been doing for two hours? She'd looked like a mess when I'd asked her to go out for coffee the next morning, still wearing her clothes from the night before. Amanda's lifeless body was discovered soon afterward. "Are you sure, Joe?"

"Yes, ma'am. I know it was pretty late on Thursday because Friday morning I had to help a friend set up his display at the art center and I remember wishing I'd gone to bed earlier." Joe rested the canvas against the wall. "Why?"

"Oh, nothing." I wavered on unsteady feet, hoping my face didn't betray my horror. I swallowed and steadied myself.

The doorway beyond Joe's shoulder caught my eye. It led to the bedroom. Joe slept there now, but it had been Amanda's bedroom before him. The pile of forgotten mail she'd left behind in the nightstand surfaced in my mind. I'd collected it and set it aside, never having gotten around to returning the papers to her.

"Thank you, Joe." I scurried through the apartment door, picturing the bundle of mail, and taking the steps as fast as I could without slipping or jarring my knees. I was anxious to close myself inside the privacy of my house and examine the papers before Beth returned. It was a long shot, but maybe, somehow, they held a clue to who killed Amanda.

CHAPTER TWENTY-SIX

Elizabeth (BEFORE)

I ended the call with the doctor's office, my hands cradling my abdomen. The baby inside me was almost the size of a cantaloupe melon and my twenty-week checkup was scheduled for next Thursday at 10 a.m. Jason promised he'd clear his schedule that morning so we could experience the moment together. A week from tomorrow, I'd get the ultrasound and we'd find out if we were having a boy or a girl.

A petal dropped from one of the yellow lilies resting in a crystal vase on the counter. I reached for it. Jason had surprised me with the bouquet of colorful flowers the other night. It had been over a month since he moved back home and our relationship was healing. Turning the delicate petal over in my hand, I smiled at the irony of his affair somehow having brought us closer together. Lydia had been right. Our visits with Dr. Brennan had opened our lines of communication. Jason listened to me now. He'd even been willing to talk about all the pain he'd suppressed surrounding his mom's death.

Jason still worked longer hours than I preferred, but because of our conversations with the therapist, I now understood he was only trying to secure our future before the baby arrived. Because of his schedule, we hadn't been able to plan a getaway to the Caribbean or Mexico, but we did have a daylong cruise on a yacht scheduled for three weeks from Saturday. It wouldn't be just the two of us, as I'd originally hoped, but it would still be fun. The owner of the yacht was one of Jason's investors. He'd invited us on a private party cruise with about thirty other guests. I didn't love boats, especially at nearly five months pregnant, but Jason was excited about it.

My stomach twisted with hunger, even though it was barely 11 a.m. The Detroit article I'd been writing for Gwen had been put on hold pending some fact-checking, so I had some free time. Jason had done so many thoughtful things for me lately—buying jewelry and flowers, arranging dinner dates, and having long talks into the early hours of the morning—I decided to do something nice for him, too.

I flipped through the carry-out menu from his favorite sandwich place, Lou's Deli, and called the number. I'd surprise him with lunch at the office and tell him about next week's doctor's appointment when we'd learn a little bit more about the future member of our family. If I left now, I could catch him before he ran out to get his own food.

Twenty minutes later, I pulled into an empty space near the far corner of his office parking lot. I'd ordered his usual, corned beef and Swiss cheese with coleslaw. The savory aroma permeated the car. My stomach couldn't hold out much longer. Clutching the handle of the brown bag in one hand, I opened my door with the other.

As I stood, Jason emerged from the front door of the building. I grinned, relieved I'd caught him in time. My arm began to rise in a wave but stopped mid-air as a woman sidled up next to him, her head tipping back in laughter.

A sickening sensation traveled through my bones, pinning my arm down to my side. I recognized her face and the shape of her body and her blonde hair, even though it was pulled back into a ponytail. She wore a short blue skirt and heels. It was the other woman—Sarah. My body was frozen, my mouth dropping open but no sound escaping. He'd lied to me. Nausea flooded my stomach, squelching my hunger.

Jason draped his arm around her shoulders the same way he'd done to me so many times. He turned toward her with his charming, boyish grin. They walked away from me toward his Mercedes, where he opened the passenger side door for her before climbing into the driver's side. The brake lights lit up and he began to pull away.

I steadied myself against the car door, my body shaking. I thought I might throw up. How could he? Had it all been a lie? Again? I ducked into my seat and slammed my foot on the pedal, my rage accelerating along with my car. His SUV turned right. I'd catch him in the act. Then what would he say? What excuse would he have? He wanted to keep his wife and baby at home while he screwed his girlfriend, too. No! I was done playing the fool. I was smarter than him, and I wouldn't let him get away with it.

His SUV traveled down the street where he paused at a red light before turning onto Woodward Avenue. I followed, my heart thumping out of control, my body cold and heavy, plunging to unknown depths. Three lanes of traffic sped around me as I took the turn without stopping. A car honked and swerved out of my blind spot and away from me. Jason drove fast. He switched to the left lane, the space between us lengthening. I tried to move over, but a moving truck blocked the lane and my view.

A frenzy of thoughts swarmed in my head. *Where were they going? Lunch? A hotel? Back to her place?* I was desperate for proof. My foot pressed on the pedal, my car shooting ahead. As I passed the truck, Jason's Mercedes was no longer in view. In the rearview mirror, I spotted him heading in the opposite direction on the other side of the median. He'd pulled into the turn-around lane to take a Michigan left.

"Shit!" I screamed. My foot plunged down, rocketing my car ahead as I dodged traffic. The next turn-around was up ahead.

My car veered through the U-turn, only pausing slightly for the stop sign. I couldn't waste any time if I wanted to catch up with them. A car in the oncoming lane headed toward me, but it was slow. I could beat it.

I accelerated into the turn, realizing immediately that my timing was off. The other car was on top of me, brakes screeching and metal twisting. A punch in my gut, and then in my head. Everything went black.

"I'm here, babe."

My eyes struggled to open against the fluorescent lights above. Jason peered down at me, his face hazy. His hand was squeezing mine.

"You've been in an accident. You're in the hospital."

I lifted my head and gazed around at the sterile room. A blur of white walls surrounded me. A puke-colored curtain had been pushed back to reveal a window with a view of a half-empty parking lot, but the images overlapped each other. There was two of everything, the second square of the window drifting over itself and back again. A dull ache spread through my abdomen and my head seared with pain. An IV bag hovered near me, the tubes pumping fluid into the veins in my arm. I wondered what kind of drugs they'd given me.

I focused on Jason's face but seemed to be peering at him through layers of spiderwebs, the edges of his features muted, his voice still ringing in my ears. He was a stranger to me, the room wobbling around him. *What happened?* I tried to ask, but only an inaudible grunt escaped my mouth.

"Your car got broadsided on Woodward yesterday. Your head hit the windshield." Jason swiped the back of his hand across his eyes. "They said you weren't wearing your seat belt."

My muscles tensed as a bleary recollection from the shocking scene flashed through my mind. I'd been following Jason and Sarah.

My gut heaved at the memory, not letting me forget the extent of the betrayal. I pressed my back against the soft mattress and averted my eyes. I wanted to yell at him, call him a liar and berate him, but my mouth filled with wet cement. The words refused to form, replaced by a series of grunts and drooling.

A nurse entered the room. Even through my cloudiness, I caught the worried expression flashing across her face. "I'll get the doctor," she said, looking only at Jason.

A heavy sort of panic rippled through me as I noticed for the first time the hollowness inside. There was a twisting of cramps where there'd previously been a warm fullness. Pain burned through my abdomen.

I clutched Jason's arm, my eyes stretched wide and a scream struggling to escape my mouth. *Is the baby okay?* I tried to ask, but my tongue and throat weren't cooperating.

He shook his head as if he understood what I'd been trying to ask, his fingers pressing around my wrist. "Your body hit the steering wheel. The trauma was too much for the baby." He bit his lip and pressed his eyes closed. "They couldn't find a heartbeat."

My hand brushed against my abdomen and I flinched. Through the hospital gown, I felt the bandage. They'd cut me open. I swallowed repeatedly, gasping for air.

Jason squeezed my hand. "They said you'd die unless they did an emergency C-section."

"*No. No!*" I tried to scream, but only a tangle of muted grunts came out. I clutched my stomach, praying it wasn't true.

My body felt like it was floating above itself. I became a spectator watching my own disaster. My baby hadn't survived. The one person who I'd never met but had already loved more than anything in the world was dead. I couldn't look at Jason. More memories of the moments before the car crash came flooding back—my surprise visit to his office to deliver sandwiches, the short blue skirt, and the blonde ponytail. He was a liar and a cheat. I'd lost my husband

and my baby in one day. My chest heaved and a sob bellowed from within me. My lungs needed air, but I couldn't breathe.

"Why weren't you wearing a seat belt, Liz?" Jason's voice cracked. "Where were you going?"

He hadn't seen me. Even if I was capable of speaking, I wouldn't tell him. He didn't deserve the truth.

My eyes bore into his. My body was weak and quivering. Although the weight of the drugs held me in place and kept me quiet, I understood what had happened and swallowed back my disgust at the realization. Jason was blaming the baby's death on me. This devastation was *his* fault. He hadn't even realized I hadn't had time to buckle up because I'd been chasing him. I pushed away his hand and closed my eyes, pretending to sleep. Even through my spinning and blurred vision, I couldn't bear to look at him.

A few hours later, I woke up in the same hospital bed, thankful that Jason was no longer sitting beside me. A white-coated woman entered the room and introduced herself as Dr. Langonson. She balanced on a stool next to me and placed her warm hand on top of my cold one.

"Can you talk?" she asked.

"Yes," I said, surprised by the word that now slipped easily from my mouth.

"Sometimes the drugs can have unexpected side effects, but they should be wearing off now. There are other things we can give you for the pain."

"Okay." My hand traveled to my abdomen, my mind still refusing to accept the absence.

The doctor explained how severe trauma can terminate a pregnancy, and described how normally when a fetus dies they prefer the mother to deliver vaginally. Because I'd been knocked unconscious by the crash and my life had been at risk, they'd been forced to perform an emergency C-section.

I listened but felt as if I wasn't really there, as if I was witnessing a scene from someone else's tragic life.

"We're going to keep you here for a couple of nights," she said. "Your vitals are strong, but we need to run some additional tests in case of concussion." She pointed to my head. "That laceration on your scalp required two stitches."

My fingers raised to a tight area beyond my hairline, the prickly thread poking my skin.

"Many women find support groups helpful after suffering this kind of loss. The nurse will bring you some pamphlets. You need to take care of your mental health."

I nodded again, although I wouldn't bother with the pamphlets. No support group could help me. I was too far gone.

"Where is the baby?" I asked. "Can I see my baby?"

"Would you like to wait for your husband to return?"

"No."

The doctor's eyes softened, the corners of her mouth turned downward. "We can bring him out to you if you'd like. Then you and your husband can decide what to do next. The hospital can send the fetus to a funeral home or some people choose to donate for medical research."

"Him?" I asked. "You said 'we can bring him out to you'."

Her lips curved into a sad smile. "Yes. Your baby was male."

My heart plummeted to the floor as I sucked for air. I felt as if I was drowning, as if Jason's hands were holding my shoulders down beneath the murky water. Images from that bright place above the surface hovered just out of reach—the booties my son would never wear, the teddy bears he'd never hug, the baseball games he'd never play in. *My baby. My little boy. Gone.* And it was all Jason's fault. I swallowed against my parched throat, my fingers curling into fists. I wouldn't let Jason emerge from this disaster unscathed. Once again, he'd left a trail of destruction in his wake while he sailed on, untouched and blameless. He was nothing more than a cockroach that skittered into a hole in the wall whenever anyone came close to finding him out. This time he wouldn't get away with what he'd done to me: to my baby. I didn't know how yet, but I was going to blindside him just like he'd done to me. I was going to make sure he paid.

I uncurled my fingers, my eyes finding the doctor. "I'd like to hold my son now."

*

Mom had arranged a small memorial service at the Methodist church where Jason and I had attended only once before on Christmas Eve. The service had ended a couple of hours earlier. I lay in bed, nothing more than a warm corpse, staring at a speck on the ceiling while Mom, Dad, and Caroline milled around downstairs. Jason was down there, too, but I imagined he and Dad were sitting in separate rooms.

Despite the fog of grief, anger, and painkillers that enveloped me, I was aware it had been a nice ceremony, simple and loving. Jason had sat next to me, his leg pushing into mine. As the pastor spoke about God working in mysterious ways, Jason held my hand and squeezed his eyes closed every few seconds. I wondered if his grief was real or merely a performance of what he thought a grieving father-to-be should look like. I wasn't sure if he was even capable of feeling the depth of love a father should feel for a child or a husband for a wife. His whole emotional life had been a performance, one act after another concocted from all of the TV shows and movies he'd watched over the years. Jason was whatever the people around him wanted him to be. A chameleon. He was a fake yet still so believable. So charming. He'd even fooled Dr. Brennan. A more astute psychologist might have diagnosed my husband as a sociopath.

In contrast, there was no doubt about Caroline's pain. She'd been a wreck of raw emotion, hunched over and sobbing throughout the service, devastated by the loss of the nephew she'd never meet.

At the end of the service, I'd left Jason's side and said my final goodbye to my baby, but I wasn't ready to lay him to rest yet. For the last five days, laying in the bed in the hospital, and then in my bed at home, I'd existed in a haze, only conscious enough to not reveal the cause of the crash, to not tell Jason that I'd witnessed him cheating on me again with Sarah.

The secret crouched within me like a tiger waiting to pounce. He had destroyed my life. I hadn't figured out how yet, but it was only a matter of time before I'd destroy his life, too.

Two soft knocks at the door caused my neck to strain upward. A pain ripped through my abdomen where the bandage from my C-section remained. The door creaked open and Caroline poked her head through.

"Hey. Do you want some company?"

I released my head back into my pillow, the burn in my midsection subsiding. "Sure."

My sister eased the door closed behind her and slunk over to the bed where she climbed in next to me, the way we sometimes used to sleep when we were kids. Her eyes were raw and puffy from the crying, and her body excruciatingly thin.

It turned out I'd been wrong about her and the drugs. She'd voluntarily gone in for a drug test as soon as she and my parents had returned to Kalamazoo, and the test had come back clean. She and Josh broke up shortly afterward. The guilt over my wrongful accusation was crushing, especially seeing her now, so frail and breakable. Yet, somehow, Caroline was still strong enough to be here for me. Loyal to a fault.

"You okay?" I asked as Caroline lay motionless next to me.

She snorted, a half-laugh, half-cry, "No. You?"

"Not even close." I reached for her hand and held it in mine.

Caroline turned her face toward mine. "You'll get through this," she said. "We both will."

I lowered my voice to a whisper, focusing on the solid black pupils of Caroline's eyes. "I need to tell you something about the car accident. You have to promise you won't say anything to anyone. Not even Mom and Dad."

She stared at me, expressionless. "Yeah. Okay, I promise."

I told her the whole story, from picking up the sandwiches at the deli to my ill-timed turn onto southbound Woodward Avenue and the moment of impact. Her eyes widened and her mouth opened in horror.

"He's the reason my baby is dead." Tears leaked from my eyes. "I didn't have time to put on my seat belt because I was chasing him."

"Oh my God. That bastard!" Caroline propped herself up. "How can you be around him? Why is he still living here?"

I held my finger to my lips, "Shhh! He doesn't know that I know. No one does."

She cocked her head at me. "You haven't said anything to him?"

"No. We need to keep it that way."

Caroline huffed.

I rolled toward her. "Don't you get it? I'm going to surprise him, to make sure he ends up as devastated as I am. I need time to get my strength back and make a plan."

Caroline tucked a piece of hair behind her ear, then fixed her gaze on me and nodded. "You better come up with a good one."

"I will."

"If you don't take down the bastard, I'll do it."

We stayed in bed for another hour, brainstorming Jason's downfall.

*

It had been almost two weeks since the memorial service. I'd taken extended time off work to let my wounds heal. I lay on the couch, my feet propped up on two pillows as *Tiny House Nation* played on the TV. This episode featured a single woman who'd rejected her career as an attorney and decided to go back to nature.

"Do you want some tea?" Jason appeared in the doorway dressed in a black suit. "I'd stay with you, but I've really got to get into the office."

"No. I'm fine," I said without looking at him. It had only been in the last few days, and only because of my secret plan for revenge, that I'd been able to poke my head above the surface and gulp some air. Jason had worked from home the two days following the memorial service but had quickly gotten back into his old routine, saying he preferred to keep himself busy, that people grieved in different ways. I didn't understand how he could go on as if nothing had happened. Then again, maybe losing the baby had been a relief to him. Now he'd have more time to cheat on me.

He stepped toward me. "Listen. You don't have to go out on the yacht this weekend. Connor would understand if you didn't feel up to it."

"I want to go," I said, my voice flat. My body had recovered relatively quickly from the C-section. I could walk normally and drive again. The insurance company had replaced my car. It was my mind and my heart that were irreversibly mangled. My hatred for Jason consumed me from the moment I'd awoken in the hospital. Each time he fluffed my pillows, brought me toast in bed, accepted condolences from neighbors on my behalf, or told me he loved me, the beast inside me growled and gnashed its teeth, waiting to become strong enough to free itself from the cage. On the surface, I forced sad smiles, peeped out thank yous, and pretended that I believed him. When the time came to expose his lies, he'd be completely blindsided.

"I need to get out of the house," I said in the airiest voice possible. "The cruise will be a nice change of pace."

Besides, Caroline and I had drawn up a plan for revenge, and it was going to happen this weekend on the cruise in front of all of Jason's colleagues. I bit back my smirk.

"Okay. Be sure to rest up today. There's soup in the fridge." He bent down and kissed my head. "Love you."

"Love you, too," I said, but I didn't mean it. I hated him.

He hustled out the back door. A minute later his SUV backed out of the driveway. An insurance commercial came on TV so I raised myself off the couch and made my way into the bathroom.

Jason's iPhone lay on the bathroom counter next to the sink. He must have forgotten it. That phone was his lifeline, never out of his reach. He'd freak out and return as soon as he realized, but I'd seen him drive away, so I knew I had at least a few minutes to search. This was my opportunity to discover more dirt on his girlfriend, Sarah.

My fingers shook, pressing in the security code—his birthday—but it didn't work. He'd changed it. I tried the four digits of our street address, but that didn't work either. My heart raced. He'd be back soon. I remembered him using the last four digits of his social security number for another pin several months earlier. I pressed in the numbers and the screen glowed, unlocked.

My breath escaped, heavy and labored. I tapped on the text message icon and scrolled through. Messages to Robert and other work colleagues appeared. Disregarding the male names, I focused only on the texts he'd sent to females. Steadying myself against the counter, I realized no one named Sarah existed on his phone. There was an Ellen and a Margaret, but their messages related to investment questions.

There was another name that stood out, though. It was one I'd never heard him mention, about seven deep in the messages. Amanda Jenkins. I clicked on her name.

The words from a recent exchange ripped through me, tearing open wounds that hadn't yet healed. *I still love you,* Jason wrote. *I miss you already.*

Then Amanda wrote, *Then choose me.*

My stomach curled in on itself. Of course he wouldn't have told me her real name. How stupid had I been? I should have known that Sarah was a lie, too. My fingers scrolled their messages back further. They went on for weeks, even months.

When are you leaving her? Amanda wrote. *I want to live with you.*

Soon. Need to wait until the baby arrives. Then I'm gone.

He told her he was leaving me? Why had he gone to all the trouble of working on our relationship? Was it just to save face? To protect his perfect image among his conservative investors? Or, was he lying to her, too?

I scrolled back further and found partially nude photos they'd sent to each other. Bile rose in my throat as I wondered where I'd been when they were sexting each other. Off on assignment? Or had I been in the same room as they secretly joked about how dense I was? Another photo showed them lying on the beach together. She was wearing a black string bikini and holding up a margarita. My stomach flipped. They'd gone on vacation together. The date on the photos was over six months ago. I recognized her as the woman in my bed the night I'd arrived home early. The same woman who'd been in the car with Jason when my car crashed, killing my baby.

My eyes swam forward through the messages as fast as they could, finally reaching the ones from the past few days.

I'm leaving town. I can't stand to be around this place anymore, Amanda wrote. *Come and find me when you finally have the balls to leave.*

I'm sorry babe. I love you, Jason had replied. *I know I disappointed you. I'll send money… diamonds to follow. We'll be together soon.*

A few days later, another message from Amanda: *I was a jerk about your baby. I really am sorry for your loss. I found a new job in*

Petoskey. Moved into an apartment above an old lady's garage. My new address is 4027 Waters Rd. Bed's big enough for two:) Miss you.

The handle of the back door rattled. Jason was back. There were more messages following that one, but I didn't have time to read them. I held my shaking fingers still long enough to click off the phone, setting it back on the counter exactly where it had been. My hand shielded my healing abdomen as I leaped across the living room. I laid back on the couch, my breath trapped in my lungs. Jason barged into the kitchen.

"Hey, what are you doing back already?" I asked in my most casual tone. A cold sweat covered my skin.

His eyes scanned the kitchen. "Forgot my phone."

"Haven't seen it."

Jason bounded upstairs and stomped around, cursing. Then he headed into the first-floor bathroom. "Got it. Bye again." He jogged out the back door.

"Bye." My heart pounded as I grabbed my phone to record the information. *Amanda Jenkins, 4027 Waters Rd., Petoskey.*

CHAPTER TWENTY-SEVEN

Gloria (NOW)

Rascal darted in front of me, my feet tripping over him as I entered the living room and locked the door behind me. I pulled the curtains closed and hurried through the kitchen to my office nook. Thanks to my recent decluttering, the area lay before me, clean and organized. I opened the cabinet below the computer and retrieved the manila envelope containing Amanda's forgotten mail. My hands pinched the edge of the envelope, my jittery body rushing toward the sofa. A prickling dread traveled through my limbs as I sat down and emptied the papers onto my lap.

I pushed my reading glasses onto the bridge of my nose and held up the pieces of mail one by one. The first two items were credit card statements from clothing stores—Athleta and Loft. The statements were dated eleven months ago. That was last July. That was the month Amanda had moved into the apartment. Beneath the bills was a bank statement from Chase. The balance in Amanda's checking account had been $485. No savings account was listed. Behind the bank statement lay a couple of receipts from the post office.

My fingers leafed through the papers, landing on an envelope with my address handwritten across the front, but addressed to Amanda Jenkins in Apt 1. I did a double take, the wind leaving my body. It wasn't Amanda's name on the envelope that caused my blood to reverse course, but the name stamped on the return address label—*Jason McCormack, McCormack Investments, 29488 Woodward Ave., Royal Oak, MI 48073*. The envelope shook in my hand. Jason McCormack was the name of Beth's dead husband. How had Beth's husband known Amanda? What in heaven's name was going on?

My trembling fingers fished into the envelope but found nothing inside. Amanda must have taken the letter with her when she moved. I inspected the front of the envelope again. Amanda's address was handwritten in chicken scratch, the way a teenage boy would write.

My back pressed into the cushion as I absorbed the shocking connection. Had Jason overseen Amanda's finances? That hardly made sense, seeing as Amanda hadn't had any extra money to invest. She wouldn't have been living in my garage apartment and working as a concierge if she had. My stomach plummeted with my next guess. Had the envelope contained a love letter? What if Amanda and Jason McCormack had been lovers? The realization pinned me down and squeezed my throat.

I closed my eyes, the muscles in my face twitching. As much as I didn't want to believe it, that scenario made the most sense. It explained Beth's sudden arrival on my land with her altered name and appearance, her eagerness to meet Amanda. I gulped, steadying myself against the cushions. It could even explain Amanda's death. *Hell hath no fury like a woman scorned…*

The version of Beth I thought I knew was transforming, slipping through my fingers like sand. What if her husband's death hadn't been an accident at all? If my suspicion was correct, Beth had a motive for killing both her husband *and* Amanda. A strong motive. Honestly, I couldn't say I blamed her. On the other hand, I couldn't believe it was true. Plenty of wives caught their husbands cheating, but very few chose murder as the solution. Divorce, maybe. Or marriage counseling, but not murder.

Up until my ride in her truck yesterday, Beth had been so insightful and compassionate. A true friend. She'd been so upset at the police station. Her distress hadn't seemed like an act. Then there'd been her odd statements in the car: *You need to stop talking, Gloria... I'm not a bad person. It's just that my life didn't turn out the way I thought it would.* What had she meant? And what about her earlier insistence that Amanda's story didn't have a happy ending? How had she known the outcome before Amanda's body had been found?

I felt raw and exposed as if someone had peeled off my skin. I wrapped my arms around myself thinking back to Beth's strange behavior in the coffee shop. I hadn't realized it at the time but Amanda was already dead when Beth had darted out of the café like she'd seen a ghost. And she'd all but told me she hadn't slept the night before. Why hadn't she slept? And why hadn't she arrived home until two hours after she and Ethan had left The Castaways? Was it possible she was disposing of a body she'd hidden somewhere before returning here and almost running over Joe in the driveway?

Without thinking, I stood up and migrated toward the window, remembering the way Beth's truck sparkled in the parking lot. She'd gotten it washed just before Amanda's body had been discovered. Was she hiding something? Destroying evidence?

And there was another question. What did Ella Burkholter have to do with any of this?

I paced into the kitchen, no longer able to ignore the dryness in my throat. Retrieving a glass from the cupboard, I tried to think of what to do next. Recent events had proven that my imagination could get the best of me, and I didn't want to overreact. After all, the police had already cleared Beth of her husband's death. I could call Ethan. He'd know what to do. I set the glass on the counter and squeezed my hands together, debating. It wouldn't be fair of me to ruin his camping trip, though, especially over a hunch. He'd only be gone for two days. My discovery could wait.

The Thirty-Day Life Coach workbook lay in front of me. I flipped through it searching for the section entitled, *What to do when you suspect your new friend is a murderer*, but came up empty.

Be Bold, Take Calculated Risks, Do the Opposite. I rested my elbows on the counter as the highlighted words in the workbook sprang out at me. The old Gloria would have ignored the incriminating clues, not wanting to get involved. Or perhaps I would have taken my information directly to the police, even though Beth could be innocent.

But I wasn't the same person anymore, and I couldn't deny much of my transformation was thanks to Beth. I valued her friendship. She'd helped me rediscover joy, to live again, and reconnect with Ethan. I cared about doing right by her. I needed to dig a little deeper on my own.

Rascal lapped water from his bowl, splattering drops across the floor. He'd have to go outside soon. And, again, tonight. That's when I'd hide on the porch under the cover of the darkness and watch Beth's movements. Despite what I'd promised Ethan, I'd have to follow her if she left. I couldn't go to the police until I knew for sure. She was my only friend and, if I was wrong, she'd never forgive me.

The porch light was off. I crouched down in the wicker rocking chair using the black night as my cover. Rascal lay curled in a ball, asleep at my feet. I slid my phone from my pocket to check the time: 10:47 p.m. It was much earlier than when she'd left the other night, but I didn't want to risk missing anything. A light inside an upstairs room of the tiny house glowed through the gnarled branches of the trees. Beth was awake.

I tipped back in the chair and stared at the nearly full moon. A clicking noise sounded in the distance. I craned my neck to try to make out movement from the tiny house, but I couldn't see anything. Moments later, Beth's truck rumbled alive, followed by the crimson glow of her taillights. I crouched down, heart pounding, before scooping up Rascal and depositing him in his cage inside the front door. He whined.

"I'll be back soon, boy," I whispered as I whisked my purse off the counter. Ducking out of the house and through the shadows, I slipped into my car, only turning on the ignition once the red truck had zoomed past me. I followed with my headlights off, going by memory of the dirt drive I'd traveled down so many times.

Around the second curve, Beth's truck turned right toward town. I paused at the end of the driveway, waiting until she was a good distance away before turning on my headlights and driving in the same direction. She was far ahead now, but on the barren country road, the lights of her truck were the only ones shining in the distance. She turned left on Mason Road, passing the nature preserve toward downtown Petoskey.

Each mile seemed to drag on for ten as I grew more paranoid she'd spotted me. I breathed in measured breaths, reassuring myself that I could be any car pulling out of any farm or vacation house. She wouldn't have been able to identify my Buick in the dark.

As we approached town, a few more vehicles joined us on the road and I found my breath again. I thought she might be going back to The Castaways, but my hunch was wrong. She continued past it, stopping at a red light, then turned left onto Highway 31. I made it through the light a couple of cars behind her. A mile or so later she merged onto another highway, heading north. We were leaving downtown. I didn't have a clue where she was going.

The brake lights flashed and she turned left into a private condo development. A rustic wooden sign read, *Waterside Condos. No trespassers*. Keeping my distance, I turned in a few seconds after her, barely catching her taillights as she angled left down a dirt road.

Heavily wooded land surrounded the condos. A ways ahead, Beth parked her truck in the driveway of an end unit. At the top of a hill, I eased my car behind a clump of trees near the side of the road and turned off the headlights.

From my hideout up the hill and halfway around the bend, I could glimpse Beth's truck through the shadowy trees. A row of solar lights lit the pathway to the front door, which was painted forest green. She emerged from her vehicle, approached the door, and knocked. I crouched low and clutched the steering wheel so hard my knuckles turned white. Beth reached up and knocked again.

The door cracked open and a man's head peeked out. He towered over her with broad shoulders. With his slicked-back hair and gold chain, he appeared to be a rough fellow, like a gangster from one of the mafia movies Charlie used to watch. He glanced from side to side as if making sure Beth was alone. They exchanged a few words, and then he waved her inside.

I swallowed and realized I hadn't been breathing. Who was this man? I had no clue, but the tightness in my gut told me he was bad news, that he might have had something to do with Amanda's murder. "*Just give me some time to figure out what to do*," Beth had said after she yelled at me yesterday. What was she figuring out?

After several minutes of waiting in my hidden spot, my heart rate returned to a normal pace. I stared at the closed door of the condo praying for Beth to re-emerge. Fifteen minutes passed. Then thirty. What was she doing? Was this seedy character her lover? I couldn't imagine it.

My fingers fumbled through my purse, looking for my phone, something to occupy my time. Instead, my hand hit the spare key Beth had given me a couple of weeks earlier. A shiver formed deep inside me and bristled across my skin as I thought of Beth holding the key to my house. If Beth had seen me tailing her, she could let herself into my house at any time. She could silence me if she needed to. I pressed my head against the cool glass of the car window. Ethan had been right. My plan to follow her had been reckless. I wasn't safe.

Beth's spare key rested in my palm, its silver finish glinting in the moonlight. I pictured the tiny house in the darkened field, sitting vacant. All at once, a new plan formed in my head.

There were probably more clues lying within her house than I'd discover by waiting here. Beth wasn't home, that was certain. She could be inside that room all night, and even if I saw her leave, I'd have no way of knowing what she and this man had been discussing. If I left right now, I'd have time to drive back and search through her drawers and secret compartments, time to read her mail. Maybe I'd discover a missing piece of evidence or something that would explain away her odd behavior and clear her name. At the very least, I could take back my house key. I'd be out of there before she returned.

The hairs on my arms and neck prickled, adrenaline surging through me. I was about to cross a line and break the law, but I wasn't harming anyone. My foot rattled against the pedal as I backed out of my hiding spot and sped away.

Minutes later, the faint beam from my flashlight guided the way as I tiptoed across my grass. The line of trees loomed in front of me like soldiers standing guard over the tiny house. Crouching down, I glanced over my shoulder toward the garage apartment. Joe's SUV was gone and the lights in the apartment were off. The ache in my back distracted me and I stumbled over a protruding rock. A humbling reminder that I was no svelte cat burglar. Thankfully, there was no one around. After regaining my balance, I kept the light angled down and felt my way over the rugged ground toward Beth's front steps. The key was ready in my hand, and I poked it around the handle until it slipped into place. The door opened without any fuss.

Instinctively, my hand reached for a light switch, but I stopped myself, remembering I was breaking the law. I wondered what they'd charge me with if I was caught—*Breaking and Entering*? Perhaps I could lie and say I heard a strange noise and needed to check it out. The tiny house was parked on my land, after all.

Besides, I had the key. Or maybe Beth wouldn't press charges, but she'd spend the rest of her life remembering me as a false friend, the woman who had betrayed her. That would be worse. Then again, maybe I'd discover she was a murderer, and that would be the worst of all. My body quaked but I pushed through the fear.

The circular ring of light from my shaking flashlight scanned across Beth's living room and into the kitchen. As usual, everything was in its place. It was hard to believe a human lived in this immaculate and compact space, especially compared to the books, clothes, dust, and dog fur strewn about my farmhouse.

The carved handles of the storage drawers beneath the stairs caught my eye, and I stepped toward them, pulling out the lowest one. It contained cleaning supplies, the all-natural, plant-based kind, and a few rolls of paper towels. The drawer above it revealed a collection of matching towels. My hands dug through, searching for evidence of either innocence or guilt, but coming up empty. The third and fourth drawers held clothes for the winter—sweaters and heavy pants and coats. The fifth drawer held nothing but shoes.

I sighed, scolding myself for believing I could solve the mystery so easily. I'd sent myself on a wild goose chase. I didn't even know what I was looking for. My eyes scanned the kitchen where cabinets and storage cubbies lined the walls. Rifling through them, one by one, I found only dishes and cans of organic food. My heart thumped faster as I wondered how long I'd been inside already. Beth could be returning at any minute. I glanced out the window for any sign of headlights, but only darkness loomed beyond the panes of glass.

Carefully, I made my way up the railing-less staircase, clutching the edges of the steps as I ascended. My feet wobbled at the top and I leaned forward, falling into Beth's loft bedroom. The bed was tightly made, and only a book and an empty glass lay on the built-in nightstand. I picked up the paperback, noting the title, *Mindful Living*. Out of reflex, I flipped through the pages, finding a receipt doubling as a bookmark. My eyes caught on the name of the store printed at the top of the narrow strip of white paper. *Fringe Salon.* I lost my breath as I reread it, making sure my mind hadn't gone to the birds. Fringe Salon was where the murdered woman, Ella Burkholter, had worked. Officer Bradley had told us as much, and I'd seen it on the news. I held the paper closer, dread dripping through my veins. The thirty-two-dollar charge was for a pedicure. The next line made me gasp: *Technician: Ella B.*

My knees collapsed, my legs supported only by the firm mattress behind me. Did Beth know Ella? She'd never once mentioned it. The date printed on the receipt was faint, but I could make it out. *May 24.* That was the Friday of Memorial Day weekend. But Beth hadn't pulled her tiny house onto my field until May 29. She said she'd driven up from downstate, but she'd lied. She'd already been in town. The receipt in my hand was proof. She'd gotten a pedicure from Ella a day before the young woman was found strangled on the beach.

I breathed in and out, squeezing the piece of paper in my hand. What did this mean? Had Beth been involved in Ella's death? But, why? I didn't know what to make of the information. I shoved the piece of paper into my pant pocket, hoping Beth would think the bookmark fell out on its own.

My knees creaked as I got down on all fours, peering underneath the bed. To my surprise, the bed's base was constructed from more storage compartments. I pressed on a small cutout rectangle near the front and it popped out as if connected to springs.

I gulped in a mouthful of air, registering the contents of the hidden compartment. The beam from my flashlight illuminated dozens of bullets. It was as if someone had tipped my rocking chair all the way forward and left me dangling. *Beth had a gun.* The bullets rolled in circles around the drawer, at last coming to a standstill. A smaller wooden compartment rose from the center of the drawer, the perfect size for a handgun. I thought of Amanda, killed by a single bullet to the head. Despair shot through me.

With shaking hands, I lifted the lid, expecting to find a revolver lying before me. The box was empty. I bit my lip, both relieved and frantic. A squeaky laugh escaped my mouth. *How had I gotten it so wrong?* All this time I'd been worried about Joe hiding a gun inside his camouflage tote. It hadn't even crossed my mind that Beth was the one who was armed and dangerous.

I shoved the compartment closed and shone the light around the loft. There was nothing left to search up here.

The spark of a memory boosted me from my position on the bedroom floor. When I'd delivered muffins to Beth a couple of weeks ago, I'd witnessed a private moment through the window. She'd been startled, quickly concealing a cardboard box and hiding it away. I'd convinced myself the box held nothing more than love letters from her late husband, but that was before she'd lied to me about her job with *American Traveler*, her husband's connection to Amanda, and who knew what else. I cursed myself for not thinking of it sooner. The picture had been removed from the wall that day. Maybe it covered a secret compartment.

I inched my way down the open stairway, shielding the ray of light from my flashlight with my hand. Slinking across the kitchen and into the living room, I approached the framed photograph of the mountains. I set the flashlight on the couch and hoisted the picture off its hook, laying it on the floor. It only took a moment to spy the abnormality in the siding. One wooden panel protruded a few millimeters further than the others. Using both hands, I pushed it. Sure enough, a hidden compartment popped out from the wall, just like a Chinese puzzle box. Inside the alcove lay the worn Nike shoebox Beth had been holding the day I'd interrupted her. With trembling hands, I lifted the box and set it on the couch. I raised the lid with one hand and shone my flashlight on it with the other.

A variety of items reflected under the beam of light—an important-looking document, a church program, a pair of white baby booties, and the photo of Beth and her sister I'd found on the floor the day I'd brought over the muffins. My hands clutched the booties first, my fingers inspecting the soft yarn and the quality stitching. I'd done some needlework over the years. Someone had taken great care to craft them. I wondered who the tiny socks had belonged to but was stumped.

I set them down and lifted the church program. It was from a memorial service at the First Methodist Church of Royal Oak. *In loving memory of our unborn son. He brought us infinite love, although he never had the chance to live.* There was no birthday, only a memorial date.

I dropped my head and closed my eyes, a surge of sorrow flooding my chest. Beth had been pregnant, but she'd suffered a miscarriage. The booties must have been meant for her baby. She'd endured even more heartache than I'd imagined. I couldn't believe she'd never mentioned it to me. She'd been so insistent about me reconnecting with Ethan. "*If I had a son, I'd do everything possible not to lose touch with him.*" It made perfect sense now. If only I'd understood the loaded meaning behind the words when she'd said them.

My quivering fingers raised the document lying beneath the program. A life insurance form outlined the payout of $2 million to Elizabeth McCormack as a result of the death of her husband, Jason. I reread the form. The information in the newspaper article had been true: *$2 million!* What in the world had Beth done with the money? This tiny house couldn't have cost more than thirty or forty thousand. She lived frugally on her writer's salary, although maybe she'd never been a writer at all. Next, I lifted the photo, studying the image. Beth's arm was draped around her taller sister, who had long sandy hair and hollowed-out features.

Hardware clicked, my head swiveling toward the noise. The door pushed open and bright lights stung my eyes. My heart reached into my throat. I stumbled backward, still pinching the photo between my fingers. The lanky woman I'd been studying in the photo a moment earlier now hovered in the doorway, her eyes boring through me, distant and cold. It was Caroline.

"What are you doing in my sister's house?" Her voice was sharp, her body blocking the door.

How had I not heard her? Or seen the headlights outside? I stammered backward, the walls of the tiny house closing in on me. There was nowhere to run. "I was just…" I couldn't think of what to say. This wasn't supposed to have happened. I was supposed to have been locked inside my farmhouse by now. "I was only trying to figure out…"

Caroline's arm swung forward from behind her back. I swallowed my words as a glint of shiny metal reflected beneath her palm. The handle of a revolver was gripped within her fingers, its barrel pointed at my head.

CHAPTER TWENTY-EIGHT

Elizabeth (BEFORE)

It wasn't the bright summer day I'd envisioned when Jason had first mentioned the cruise on Lake Huron, but nothing about my life had turned out the way I'd pictured it. Still, the weather was appropriate for what I had planned. The clouds hung low in the sky, a thick and ominous weight that churned with the wind. I steadied myself against the railing on the deck outside the main cabin as the yacht cut through a series of choppy waves, a sliver of land disappearing behind me. The storm was blowing in, but we'd beat it. The forecast said no threat of lightning until after 6 p.m., and we were due back to the marina two hours before that.

"Care for another drink?" The same doe-eyed waitress who'd brought me an earlier glass of wine stood before me holding two empty beer bottles.

"Yes, please. Another Pinot Grigio," I said, although my stomach felt sore and queasy from the undulating motion of the boat.

The waitress nodded and skittered between some of the forty-plus passengers on board. Under different circumstances, the yacht would have been impressive. It reminded me of the mid-size cruise ship we'd sailed on during a weekend visit to Navy Pier in Chicago a few years earlier, except the multi-level decks on Connor's yacht were open to the outside, rather than encased in tinted glass, and the interior of the sprawling main cabin on the upper deck resembled the lobby of a five-star hotel, complete with crystal chandeliers, museum-quality artwork, and a full bar. Appetizers were arranged across an oblong table in the middle of the room—shrimp cocktail, crab dip, an assortment of cheeses, and caviar. This was how the other half lived. I twisted the massive diamond ring on my finger, leaned against the railing, and stared out toward the endless view of the lake.

Jason's laugh echoed from across the deck, and I turned toward him. He held a plate full of appetizers and chatted with two other couples, stopping talking only long enough to shove a meatball in his mouth and take a swig of beer. I caught his eye.

"Liz, come over here." He waved me over. I approached him, my feet wobbly. He looped his arm around my shoulders and rubbed my back. "This is my lovely wife. She's a journalist with *The Observer*."

I forced a smile and made small talk about the weather and the food, going along with his act. I wondered if the others knew about his girlfriend, about our sham of a marriage. Before the cruise was over, I'd expose him for what he was, a liar and a cheat, the man who caused the death of his own baby. He'd be humiliated, his business connections destroyed. Our marriage would be officially over. We'd have to sell the house. I'd stay at a hotel tonight, take an Uber home, recounting over the phone to Caroline how everything had gone down. The plan was in motion.

"Anyone want a smoke?" asked Alan, a man with tanned skin who was sporting an expensive-looking haircut. He towered over the group, a good six inches taller than the next person. His tailored pants, collared golf shirt, and boat shoes matched the uniform of the other men on board.

"Sure." Jason's eyes crinkled with his smile, a trait I'd once found attractive, but now found phony.

I gave him a sideways glance. Jason wasn't a smoker, but I knew his game. He wanted to fit in with this man. Anything, no matter how false, to make a new business connection.

Alan flicked open his lighter and lit his cigarette.

"I'm sorry, sir." The waitress had appeared with my glass of wine. "The captain requests no smoking on the upper deck. Feel free to light up on the lower deck. Right down the stairs." She motioned toward a stairway at the back of the boat.

"Sure thing." Jason turned toward us. "I guess we'll see you back here in a few minutes."

As they stepped away, the boat lurched. I wobbled, thrown off balance and spilling some of my wine. A splitting pain shot through my abdomen, which was still tender whenever I moved too quickly or in the wrong direction. I clutched the arm of the woman next to me and gasped. A tray of dishes crashed from the direction of the back deck.

"Must have hit a rogue wave, there," Alan said, widening his eyes.

"A storm's moving in," the woman next to me said.

I looked up at the darkening sky and nodded, straightening myself. *It sure is.*

Jason and Alan disappeared down the stairway. Needing to take the edge off, I gulped down the remaining half of my drink. The skirt of my sundress billowed in the wind. I went to find a seat, realizing how tipsy I'd become. Slowing down on the alcohol would be necessary if I wanted to make a coherent toast to my wonderful husband. I didn't want anyone questioning the veracity of my claims.

Setting down my glass, I entered the cabin. I filled an appetizer plate with just enough food to settle my stomach, then located an empty sofa along the far wall. All alone, I sat and chewed and swallowed, silently rehearsing the speech in my head—*Attention, everyone! I'd like to make a toast to my husband, Jason McCormack of McCormack Investments. He wants you to think he's a great guy, but it's all a lie. He's an actor. He lies to me, his wife, and he lies to his clients. He has no moral compass. He never worked at Goldman*

Sachs like he's told all of you. No. Not even close. Look into it if you don't believe me. He didn't go to the Ross School of Business or any business school, for that matter. He lied to you about that, too. Your money is not safe with him.

I'm leaving him today, and you all should leave him, too. He thinks I don't know that he's still cheating on me, but I do. I found out a few weeks ago, the day I almost died in a car accident. He's the reason our baby is dead. He's a liar and a cheat and a murderer!

I wasn't worried about embarrassing myself, or people thinking I'd gone off the deep end. I'd already lost everything. The point of the speech was to humiliate Jason in front of his peers, to make people question his character and withdraw their money from his fund. If he could treat his wife and unborn child with so much disregard, how would he handle their money? Jason had ruined my life; now I would destroy the only thing that mattered to him—his reputation.

The group of people I'd been standing with a moment earlier migrated to more important conversation partners. Minutes later, Alan strode over to the railing and draped his arm over the shoulders of his petite wife. Jason wasn't with him.

Although I was committed to my plan, my nerves were catching up with me, my heart thudding louder with each passing second. Shifting in my seat, I felt the time nearing. Via email, we'd received a detailed schedule of the cruise, including a map of the exact route we'd take, the timing of the food and drink service, and a complete menu. I'd make the toast right before the crew opened the buffet lunch. That's when there'd be the most people gathered in the main cabin. Hopefully, I'd cause such an uncomfortable scene that the captain would cut the cruise short and return to port. But first, I needed to run to the restroom. The alcohol had gone straight through me.

Standing, I teetered along the side of the cabin, using the wall to balance against the rocking motion of the boat. I made my way down the stairs and turned the corner into the bathroom. A minute later, relieved, I emerged on the lower deck, finding my bearings. The floor was even shiftier down here, the boat tilting and straightening with each wave.

I rounded the bend. Jason lounged in the distance all alone. He could have been mistaken for a model from a J.Crew catalog, the way he rested his elbow on top of the railing, gazing out at the expanse with his chiseled features and windblown hair, the turquoise waves tossing beyond him. He flicked ash from his cigarette into the water as if he didn't have a care in the world. I tried to remember any reason to still love him but couldn't come up with a single one. If only he knew his charmed life was about to come to an end.

A few feet from where he stood, the railing ended, leaving only a low ledge at the back of the boat. Beyond the ledge lay a drop of at least fifteen feet to where the water displaced by the yacht's propellers churned and splashed creating a frothy white current behind us.

How easy would it be, I thought, *just to push him off the back of the boat, to never have to look at his lying face again?* He deserved it. I'd be rid of him forever. Everyone would assume it was an accident.

Planting my feet, I squared my shoulders and took a deep breath, remembering the plan. The speech Caroline and I had written. Despite everything Jason had done, I didn't have it in me to kill him. Maybe I'd just give him a hint about the downfall awaiting him. That would be fun. An ominous statement to foreshadow his doom. Then I'd walk away without explanation.

Slinking up behind him, I folded my arms in front of my chest. He still hadn't noticed me when I was about a foot away. I stepped toward him, my heartbeat throbbing in my ears. "I know what you did." My voice cut through the gusty sea air.

His head swung toward me, eyes and mouth stretched wide. "Liz. You scared the crap out of me."

"I'm going to destroy you."

He shook his head and narrowed his eyes. "What are you talking about?"

"You and Sarah." I leaned close to him, speaking in barely a whisper, "Or is it Amanda?"

His smile disappeared and he dropped his head. His knuckles turned white as his hand clutched the railing.

"I was following you that day. That's why I didn't have time for the seat belt." I ignored the spit that flew from my mouth with each painful syllable. My voice shook with anger, the words stinging me.

His shifting eyes latched onto mine, solidifying in a moment of realization. "Liz…" A wave crashed against the boat, causing his beer to slip out of his hand. He fumbled, reaching to catch it, but wasn't fast enough. The bottle spiraled downward and splashed into the water. He turned back toward me, his mouth pulled low at the corners, a sheen of sweat covering his forehead. He looked like he was going to throw up. I'd said enough. I needed to get away from him before he tried to justify his behavior. I'd save the rest of my surprises for the speech.

I turned to leave but paused as Jason's eyes popped open, his stunned expression transforming into panic. I wondered if he'd somehow figured out the speech I had planned, but he was no longer focused on me. Something beyond my shoulder had drawn his attention.

A hand shoved me to the side, my stomach splitting with pain as a heavy-set man with gelled-back hair barged past me. A gold chain peeked from beneath his button-down shirt, his shadow darkening Jason's face. "Let me save both of you a lot of trouble." He lunged toward Jason, grabbing him by the shirt collar and forcing him several steps backward, toward the opening at the back of the boat. The yacht lurched against a wave and slammed down. A glass shattered in the distance, followed by laughter from the upper deck.

"Shit!" Jason's face stretched with terror. The man picked him up like a bag of garbage and heaved him head first over the ledge, slamming Jason's skull against the side of the boat before he released him. Everything happened in an instant, yet also in slow motion. Jason's limp body splashed into the water below, the choppy waves gobbling him up in a frenzy.

My body froze. *What the hell just happened?* My feet remained cemented in place, shocked by the scene playing out in front of me. Before I could cry out, the man's fingers clenched my arm. I struggled to pull away, searching for an escape route, for other witnesses, but his grip only tightened. Music, conversation, and laughter buzzed from the upper deck, but the lower deck was empty, except for us.

Something about him was familiar. He forced me toward the ledge where we peered beyond the commotion of the propellers into the water behind us. Jason's body floated motionless in the white froth of the boat's wake and then began to sink. I gasped, still not believing what had happened. Jason was drowning. I'd lain awake at night wishing for karma to catch up with him. A part of me had wanted him to go overboard, but now that it was actually happening a sickening sensation rose in my stomach.

"Don't say nothin'." The man leaned close to me, heat radiating from his face. My stomach dropped, my body visibly shaking.

My brain told me to ignore the man's warning and yell for help, but my gut twisted with fear. *What if I was next?* I couldn't find my voice. I didn't want to help Jason. Someone else would have to do it. Backpedaling, my breath clogged my throat. I waited for someone to scream out in panic, or yell *man overboard!* but no one had noticed. Reggae music vibrated through the speakers, the bass thumping. Laughter echoed from the party upstairs.

Searching over my shoulder, I checked again to see if there'd been any new witnesses descending the stairway, someone to come to my aid. We were still alone. I yanked my arm, attempting to free it from his hand, eager to get away from the scene as quickly as possible, but he'd now grasped both of my arms, his thick body blocking my path. I swallowed, trying not to think of the last glimpse I'd caught of Jason's face as he disappeared beneath the wake.

The man grunted, and a jolt of recognition tore through me. He'd been the person creeping outside my house when Caroline was staying with me. His hair was shorter and he wore a collared shirt today, instead of the leather jacket he'd had on back then, but his voice, his gut, his gold chain, were all the same. He'd pounded on my front door demanding money. My jaw clenched, my stomach tightening itself into a knot. A vision of Caroline wailing at the memorial service, crumpled and broken, flashed through my head. She'd yearned so intensely for a niece or nephew. She was the only person who hated Jason just as much as I did. Had she moved off script from our plan? Had Josh introduced her to this thug? Had she gone behind my back and hired her seedy contact to take care of business in some sort of misguided attempt at sisterly love? Or maybe she owed this guy drug money.

I shook my head and squeezed my eyelids closed, only sure of one thing. I was afraid for my life.

CHAPTER TWENTY-NINE

Gloria (NOW)

Beth's sister blocked my path to the front door of the tiny house. She raised the revolver in line with my forehead, a crazed sheen in her eyes. "Who are you?" The calmness in her voice was unsettling, like the lull of the sea before a storm.

"I'm Beth's friend, Gloria. I live next door." My eyes wouldn't budge from the gun in her hand, the dark hole of the barrel staring back at me. A sinking feeling in my gut wondered if it was the same gun used to kill Amanda.

"Why are you sneaking around her house in the dark?"

My jaw locked, my eyes glued on the dime-store version of Beth. I unwittingly took a step closer. "Beth told me about you, Caroline. Are you visiting from Ohio?"

"Stay back!" She lifted the gun higher, aiming at my face.

I whimpered, the photo of the two sisters slipping from my hand and spiraling to the floor.

Headlights flashed through the window, traveling over the young woman's tormented face.

"Get down!" she said in a loud whisper as she waved the gun at me. She pressed her back against the wall, her nostrils flaring with each breath she inhaled.

I slid to the floor and pulled my shaking knees toward me, reciting a silent prayer that I wouldn't become her next victim.

The doorknob rattled and the door opened beside her. Beth tumbled inside with her mouth stretched open.

"Caroline. I told you to stay away." Her eyes bounced from Caroline to me.

Caroline tipped her head toward me. "I caught her snooping around in here."

Beth frowned, her features hardening. "You shouldn't be here, Gloria."

I swallowed and lowered my chin. "I'm sorry. You're right. I should have just asked you about Amanda."

"Did you think that I kidnapped her? Or murdered her?" Beth stepped next to her sister, towering above me as I cowered against the wall. "I thought we were friends," she said. A stream of tears glistened on Beth's cheek.

"I found her necklace under the seat of your car," I said. "The one she was wearing in the photo on the news."

Beth's eyes bulged before she covered them with her hands. "That wasn't Amanda's necklace." She lowered her hands. "It was mine. Jason bought us the same one." Beth shook her head, her lips quivering. "He bought us the same purse, too."

"Oh." My chest deflated.

"He was having an affair with her."

"I suspected as much," I said. "At least, about the affair."

Beth cocked her head at me, swiping her free hand across her cheek.

I laced my knotty fingers in front of me to stop the trembling. "I found an envelope Amanda left behind in the apartment. There was nothing inside, but it was from your husband."

Caroline grunted and kicked the floor. "That piece of shit."

I sucked in a breath, worried I might have angered the unstable young woman again.

Beth hovered in front of me, wavering back and forth like a tree that might topple. "Yeah. He was cheating on me. I was stupid enough to take him back, and then he did it again. Fool me once, shame on you. Fool me twice…" The whites around Beth's eyes showed.

"I found a receipt from Fringe Salon," my voice squeaked out like a mouse. "It had Ella's name on it. It was from the day before she was killed. You never mentioned you knew her."

Beth shook her head and let out a hollow laugh. "So, you think I killed all of them? My husband and his lover and some random woman who worked at a salon? Got my revenge. Is that it? Did you already call the police?"

"No, dear. Of course not," I said. But my eyes flicked toward Beth's sister, and I couldn't help wondering if she was the one responsible for their doomed fates. Beth had mentioned her sister was a hairstylist and that she battled a drug problem. Caroline was unhinged. "I'm only trying to understand what's going on. You've been acting so oddly. You lied to me. That's not what friends do."

Beth watched me. Her gaze followed mine toward the gun in Caroline's hand. She turned toward her sister. "Lower the gun, Caroline."

Caroline stepped back and lowered the revolver, her shoulders relaxing. "I saw the flashlight from outside and I didn't know who was in here."

Beth nodded.

I exhaled, slumping forward into a heap. "Please tell me what's going on. Tell me you didn't kill those women."

Beth's face tightened into a grimace. "It's a long story."

I tried to ignore the way my stomach turned. "I only want to know the truth."

Beth pinched her lips together, her nervous eyes darting toward her sister.

"Can we trust her?" Caroline asked.

Beth eyes locked onto mine, tears pooling in their corners. "Yeah. We can trust her."

CHAPTER THIRTY

Elizabeth (BEFORE)

The boat lurched beneath my sandaled feet. I blinked toward the churning water, Jason sinking somewhere beneath. My fingers gripped the railing as I slumped in front of the large man who'd just thrown my husband overboard. "Listen. Whatever my sister did, I can make it right. Does she owe you money? I can pay you back. Please don't hurt her."

The man lowered his chin and laughed. "I don't care about your addict sister. Your husband's the one who scammed me." The man's breath smelled of cigarettes and alcohol, his words nowhere close to the explanation I'd been expecting. "He was running a Ponzi scheme. I don't like being scammed."

Ponzi scheme? So, this had nothing to do with Caroline. My knees buckled. Jason's deception extended further than I'd imagined. I thought back to the increasing deposits to our bank account, the sums growing astronomically by the month. All at once everything made sense: the luxury cars, the expensive jewelry, the endless dinners out, the designer clothes. Jason had lied to me about his business, too. His outrageous spending had been with other people's money. He probably hadn't invested their money at all.

I remembered calling Jason after I'd hidden from the man lurking outside our house. At the time I'd assumed the thug was looking for Caroline, but I'd been wrong. It was Jason he'd been after. Jason had let me think the man had been there for my sister.

"Who are you?"

The man tightened his grasp on my arm, still blocking the stairwell. A wry smile formed on his face. "You mean your husband never mentioned me?"

My entire body quivered.

"Listen closely." He tipped his head toward the stairs. "We gotta get outta here before anyone sees us. We're gonna head up and finish our little chat while we enjoy lunch. Then you're gonna talk and laugh with your country club friends. It'll be a while before anyone notices he's missing. When they do figure it out and try to account for our whereabouts, we'll say we ran into each other coming out of the bathrooms on the lower deck. We never saw him. Understand?"

My jaw clenched, my eyelids lowering.

The man pushed his face next to mine, tipping his head toward the railing. "You've seen my work. I got no problem doin' the same to you, unless you do exactly what I say."

I nodded, my throat too dry to speak. He stepped away, lowering his hands to his sides, but never releasing the grip of his stare. Smoothing down my dress and tucking my hair behind my ear, I climbed the stairs to the upper deck, envisioning Jason's lifeless body sinking beneath the waves and feeling as if I might throw up.

The man's breath heaved behind me as I shuffled toward the lunch buffet.

"Get some food." He shoved a small plate toward me and took one for himself.

Hands shaking, I lifted a pair of metal tongs and dropped a few crackers and a piece of cheese onto my plate. My eyes darted around the deck, wondering if there'd been any witnesses. The other passengers were standing in small groups, eating and laughing. No one gave us a second glance. The man guided me over to a tiny space beyond the appetizer table, within eyesight but out of earshot, of the closest group of people. He leaned into me. "Smile," he said.

I forced my mouth into a smile, struggling to mirror his false show of happiness.

He moved even closer. "I been doing some diggin', okay? I know you're involved in Jason's company. I know your pretty-boy husband has a two-million-dollar life insurance policy. You're going to collect the money and pay me—Vic Callis—back first. Understand?"

"No." I shook my head, my free hand clutching the railing behind me, the metal bar the only thing keeping me upright. My legs felt as liquid as the lake surrounding us. "There must be some mistake. I don't know what my husband did. I wasn't involved. I've never heard your name before."

"You're a member of his LLC. It's in the records. You don't pay me, and you'll be the one who'll end up in the joint. Or worse." He chuckled and thumbed toward the hungry waves.

I doubled over as a vague memory from almost three years earlier surfaced—Jason asking me to sign his business papers the day he'd formed his LLC. I'd never had an active role in the company, but I'd agreed to be listed as a member just in case anything ever happened to him. I cursed my naivety. Now he'd left me holding the smoking gun.

"How much?" I asked, my voice shaky.

Vic's eyes narrowed into sharp slits. "$1.2 million. ASAP."

A yelp escaped my mouth at the staggering amount. Jason probably owed other investors money, too. I feared $2 million wouldn't be enough to reimburse everyone.

Vic glared at me as he jabbed a thumb into my arm. "Act naturally." He grinned and laughed loudly for the sake of the people around us. Then he slung his arm around my shoulders and whispered in my ear, "Your life depends on it."

I followed Vic's instructions exactly. We separated after our conversation near the appetizer table and mingled with as many people as possible, making sure to call the waitress over for frequent drink refills for our lunch companions. With no assigned seats for the meal, the guests had gathered in shifting clusters of four or five throughout the main cabin and the upper deck. Having never met most of the people on board, almost no one picked up on the fact that Jason wasn't with me. I made a point of asking questions of my new acquaintances and smiling frequently, commenting on the ominous weather and the delicious seasoning in the seafood salad. My facial muscles twitched in defiance, struggling to mask the terror that surely crept into my eyes whenever Vic caught my gaze from the other side of the room.

When Alan sidled up to me and asked after Jason, I shrugged and told him I hadn't seen him in a while. "Maybe he went to the bathroom?" I added for effect. A moment later, Alan was swept into a nearby conversation and I released my breath.

Just as Vic had predicted, no one noticed Jason was missing from the yacht until we returned to the dock. Then it was me, in the performance of a lifetime, who was unable to locate my loving husband. "*Where is he? Has anyone seen him?*" My questions quickly turned to panic and grief.

After the yacht was searched and the police called, I was escorted to the Port Huron police station and led to a room where the dropped ceiling, beige-tiled walls, and concrete floors pressed in on me, making each breath I took a conscious and drawn-out effort. Other passengers on the cruise were at the station, too, although they were ushered into separate rooms. A pale man with a bulging stomach and gray hair entered the interview room soon after me, introduced himself as Detective Schmidt, and offered his condolences.

Through fits of shaking and occasional uncontrolled sobs, I answered his questions, sticking to Vic's story when necessary. I explained how I'd been drinking and caught up in conversation with new friends, and that's why I hadn't noticed Jason's absence. I was upfront about Jason's recent affair but explained how he'd ended it weeks earlier. We'd reconnected and were making progress with the help of our marriage counselor. I even told him how I'd only just suffered a miscarriage, leaving out the reason for the car accident and adding that Jason and I had already started talking about trying for another baby. Detective Schmidt tipped his head and offered more condolences, but his face gave nothing away.

An hour or so into my interview, Detective Schmidt left the room for twenty or thirty minutes while I hugged my arms around myself and cried. I told myself I was having a nightmare, that I'd wake up soon and tell Caroline about my long and horrible dream. But I didn't wake up, of course. The detective returned and resumed his post across from me. He cleared his throat and stated they believed Alan was the last person to have seen Jason when he'd left my husband leaning on the railing near the opening at the back of the boat, smoking a cigarette. The detective said several other passengers had corroborated my story. Almost everyone remembered the rogue waves that had hit the boat throughout the afternoon, coupled with Jason's heavy drinking. Alan recalled how Jason had wandered toward the back of the boat more than once when they'd been smoking together, and how Jason was mesmerized by the churning water. A few women who had used the restroom on the lower deck around the time Jason was thought to have gone overboard confirmed no one was down there. Several other people remembered talking and eating lunch with me on the upper deck, positive I'd never left.

The facts led investigators to reach a preliminary conclusion: Jason must have wandered too close to the rear ledge, lost his balance, and fallen into the water on his own. They'd already called the Coast Guard to work on the recovery effort and hoped to find the body soon. I was released just after 9 p.m.

A uniformed officer insisted on driving me home, and I accepted, too weak and drained to argue. I slumped in the passenger seat of Jason's Mercedes, staring blankly through the window at the passing lights as the officer's partner followed behind us in a squad car.

At last, when the Mercedes was parked in the garage and the police car had backed down the driveway, I staggered through the front door of our house, a shaking, hollow shell. I dug out my phone and called Caroline, holding in my tears and explaining how our plan had gone terribly wrong, how Jason had lost his balance and gone overboard before I could give the speech. It was better to stick to Vic's version of events than to put my family in harm's way. The less they knew about Vic Callis, the better.

Caroline laughed at first, thinking I was joking but fell silent when I began to cry. "Oh my God!" she said. "Is he really dead?"

"Yes."

"Do you think someone pushed him?"

I bit my lip, wondering if she meant me. "No. It looks like it was an accident." My voice was tight, my throat fighting against the lie. "He was drunk. A rogue wave hit the boat."

"Wow." Caroline gasped. "Maybe karma *is* real."

I swallowed, thankful to my sister for not questioning my story.

Hours later, the morning light reflected off my phone, highlighting the accumulated messages from family and friends. I listened only to the one from Detective Schmidt, informing me the Coast Guard had recovered Jason's body late last night; the wallet and driver's license in his pocket confirmed his identity. Yet they still needed me to return for formal identification. His recorded voice explained how, after the identification was complete, they could send the body for an autopsy and would inform me of the results as soon as possible.

A cry escaped my mouth and I doubled over. The nightmare was real. I couldn't erase the memories—Jason's face sinking below the bubbling water, Vic's scowl, or the pressure of his hand around my arm.

Hungry and shaky, I stumbled into my car and drove to the office of McCormack Investments. I felt like a burglar, spying over my shoulder and my heart pounding as I let myself inside Jason's office with the spare key, preparing myself to discover whatever secrets he had taken to his watery grave.

The room was laid out like a time capsule of Jason's last day. Papers were stacked in neat piles on his oversized desk, a sticky note with a phone number hung from the screen of his computer, and an extra pair of dress shoes were positioned near the far closet. The modern office I'd helped him decorate two years earlier with potted plants and framed black-and-white pictures now looked staged, nothing more than a back-alley racket dressed up in disguise, a calculated attempt to camouflage Jason's money-making scam. The lack of any photos of me, his wife, struck me as another missed sign of his infidelity, so obvious in hindsight.

I drew in a breath, my hands sifting through every folder and piece of paper I could find, my eyes scanning back and forth through correspondence and rows of numbers in search of some sort of proof that either Vic or my husband had been lying. At last, I came across a list of computer passwords tucked inside an unused day planner. The third password I typed gave me access to Jason's computer, where I began opening folders and examining the contents. Finding nothing worthwhile in the first few folders, I clicked on one labeled *Family Photos* expecting to see pictures of either me, Jason's mom, or the other woman. Instead, a list of spreadsheets outlining recent transactions appeared. My breath blocked my windpipe. It was a hidden file.

My mouth fell open as I absorbed the numbers. At first, the data was difficult to decipher, but after taking a closer look it was clear Jason had not invested anyone's money in stocks or real estate. Vic's tale of Jason's Ponzi scheme had been true. The spreadsheets told the real story. Money from investors had flowed in. Millions of dollars. That same money had flowed out, but none of it had been invested according to Jason's "proprietary formula." A small portion of the money had been paid back to the investors from his first fund, tricking them into thinking they'd made a twenty percent return. The rest of it had been deposited into our personal accounts, where we'd quickly spent it on cars, home renovations, vacations, clothes, and jewelry. I bit down hard on my lower lip, wondering how I could have been so stupid. The depth of Jason's deception knocked the breath from my lungs as if I was the one being thrown overboard and sucked into the current, too weak and battered to swim to shore.

Jason's funeral was held five days after his body was recovered. My mom had stepped in once again and planned the ceremony at the same church where Jason and I had memorialized our unborn child. The service had been well attended, as I'd never had a chance to expose Jason's lies. They were buried along with him. Only Caroline and I knew what kind of man he really was.

The police were still questioning me then, but with less fervor. It hadn't been difficult to play the role of a grieving widow. My shock at Jason's unexpected death and the extent of his betrayal had been real. I'd worn my black sheath dress with a matching brimmed hat pulled down low to hide my puffy eyes. The police had been at the funeral, watching. And I'd been watching for someone, too. The other woman, Amanda Jenkins. I'd wanted to confront her, to tell her how she'd ruined my life, to question her involvement in Jason's fraudulent scheme. Only she hadn't shown.

I spent the days after the funeral praying for the police investigation to be completed, desperate to receive the insurance money so

I could pay off Vic but dreading the possibility that an overzealous detective would uncover Jason's scam, or even try to pin his death on me because of his recent affair.

Time passed slowly, the rumor mill running at full capacity. Somehow, I'd become the criminal while Jason rested in peace without a blemish to his name. My neighbors ducked away when they saw me, rather than offering condolences. People I didn't even know wrote horrible comments on my Facebook, Twitter, and Instagram posts. I deleted my social media accounts, but the whispers continued. One afternoon, Lydia had arrived at my door holding a Tupperware container filled with chicken soup. She'd balanced next to me on the couch as I recounted the details of the cruise, or at least Vic's version of the details. She was supportive and empathetic, but, maybe sensing my lies, she left in a hurry and without our usual hug. When I called her a week later to see if she wanted to retrieve her Tupperware and stay for a glass of wine, she never responded.

Finally, I received the long-awaited phone call from Detective Schmidt. The autopsy results were back. The report determined the injury to Jason's head was consistent with him hitting his skull on the side of the boat during his descent into the water. A few droplets of blood had been located on the backside of the boat, confirming the theory. The impact had left him unconscious and unable to swim. The official cause of death was listed as accidental drowning. I was cleared. I filed the life insurance claim the same day.

Three weeks later, the payout had arrived, $2 million payable to me. With that kind of money, I should have been able to pay off the house and secure my future. Instead, I struggled to come up with enough money to reimburse the innocent people Jason had swindled, along with the not-so-innocent, like Vic Callis.

The day following Jason's death, I'd researched Vic online. A cursory search located nothing more than a few online business profiles listing Vic as the CEO of a regional property management company. There was a photo of him at a charity dinner in Detroit, where he stood shoulder to shoulder with some other investors who'd been on the yacht. But digging deeper into the search results revealed more than one social media post questioning the legitimacy of Vic's property management company. Alarmingly, there was no online trace of the man older than three years, the same year his company had been formed. I questioned whether Vic Callis was his real name. Regardless, my life was at stake. I had to comply with his demands.

The business insurance Jason purchased for McCormack Investments had lapsed over a year earlier, so using the life insurance money was my only option. I funneled the payout through McCormack Investments and paid the investors back as soon as possible. No. They wouldn't make any money as Jason had promised, but they wouldn't lose any money either. They could go on believing they'd made a smart investment, that they would have made their twenty percent return if only Jason had lived.

The life insurance wasn't enough to cover the reimbursements, though. I sold my second set of wedding rings and listed the house with a neighborhood realtor. It sold in only ten days and I netted just over $100,000 in proceeds.

I paid off Vic first, as his threats toward me continued to escalate, but it was only a matter of time before other investors demanded their money, too. The guilt of being oblivious to Jason's scam ate away at my insides. I needed to pay everyone back, to make things right, and to put the whole thing behind me. I used the remaining $800,000 of the insurance money, plus the proceeds from the house, my rings, and Jason's Mercedes, to reimburse the remaining investors. Luckily, Jason's first fund—the one worth $4 million—had been another one of his lies. It had only been worth $100,000, and he'd paid those people back already with the money from the new investors.

Each check I signed and letter I completed on the official letterhead from McCormack Investments describing Jason's untimely death and the dissolution of the fund brought me one step closer to freedom. There'd been just enough money to satisfy everyone. On a Wednesday afternoon in late August, I filed the final paperwork dissolving the LLC. Then I called the owner of the building and requested paperwork to cancel the office lease. I deleted Jason's secret folder, drafted new versions of the spreadsheets showing everyone's investments repaid, and emailed them to my dad, who had offered several times to take care of the LLC's final accounting. I smashed Jason's computer with a sledgehammer and tied it in a garbage bag, waiting until nightfall to drop it in a dumpster behind a McDonald's a few miles away.

I'd been through hell—the cheating, the miscarriage, the accident on the boat and the whispers about my guilt, the Ponzi scheme and the efforts I'd made to cover it up—but it wasn't too late for me to reclaim my life. It was time to leave Jason in the past, time to forgive him and start healing from my baby's death.

I thought about the pang of jealousy that shot through my gut every time someone on an episode of *Tiny House Nation* drove off in their tiny house, free from the chains of consumerism and open to new experiences. Now I could actually do it. I could escape and create a new version of my future. I had $50,000 reserved for myself, enough to buy a used tiny house and get out of town with $15,000 left for spending money.

A few hours of online searching led me to a nearby builder with a perfect tiny house. The house resembled a quaint log cabin reminiscent of my childhood, the kind my parents used to rent during our summer trips up north. It was in my price range and move-in ready. Two days later, I traded my car for a red pickup truck, paid in cash for my new home, and drove west, hopeful my nightmare was finally ending.

Little did I know, it was only the beginning.

CHAPTER THIRTY-ONE

Elizabeth (BEFORE)

Six months later

My tiny house looked awkward crammed into the backyard of my parents' suburban quarter-acre lot. Caroline was graduating from cosmetology school tomorrow. I wouldn't have missed it no matter how many inches of snow fell across the Midwest during February's deep freeze. I'd returned two days ago from a six-month tour of Utah and Colorado, my neck still stiff from the tedious, icy drive. Traveling far away from the memory of Vic Callis, where no one knew me, and where no one whispered about whether I'd pushed my husband overboard, had been a relief. I'd changed my name to Beth, surrounded myself with mindful and interesting people, and threw myself into my new freelance career.

My heart still ached for the son I'd lost, the despair rising within me at unexpected moments, like when I'd seen a display of board books at a local bookstore and raced out of the store in a panic, or when I'd started sobbing uncontrollably at the sight of two young mothers pushing side-by-side jogging strollers down a park pathway. I never mentioned my baby to anyone, though. It was more bearable to keep his memory private, stored safely inside.

I thought of Jason, too, but more fleetingly and with less emotion. Sometimes it was better to leave the pain behind.

Now I sat inside my tiny house replaying last week's conversation, the one that lured me back to my childhood home.

"They'll be a whole twelve people at the party," Caroline had said, trying to downplay her accomplishment.

"Well, now you'll have thirteen." I'd already begun mapping out the fastest route back to Kalamazoo. I hadn't forgotten how she'd been there for me. More importantly, she was almost nine months clean and had just put a security deposit down on an apartment in town. My sister had overcome the odds and had proved everybody wrong. She deserved to celebrate.

It was after 11 p.m. Mom, Dad, and Caroline were getting ready for bed fifty feet away in their normal-sized house. As I reached to turn off my bedside light, a fist pounded on my door. I sighed, thinking Mom or Dad had traipsed across the frigid backyard when they could have just as easily sent me a text. I raised myself out of bed and clomped down the steps.

A rush of cold air whipped inside as I opened the door, my throat seizing up. The shadow hovering in the opening belonged to someone I hoped to never see again, the ghost of someone I thought was dead to me.

"I finally tracked you down." Vic Callis sniffed in air through his nose, his gloved hands stuffed into his jean pockets, and his gut hanging over his belt.

At first, I couldn't speak. I didn't want to let him inside, but I couldn't risk having my family see him, either.

"Why are you here?" I asked, my fingers gripping the doorknob.

"I want the rest of my money."

My feet inched backward as my heartbeat accelerated. There must have been some misunderstanding. A light went on from within my parents' house. I opened the door wider and waved Vic inside, out of sight.

"How did you know I was here?"

Vic snorted. "I got people working for me, like I said. Plus, it's amazing what you can find out about a person on Google." He shook his head and chuckled. "Nice blog, by the way."

My insides went cold. I could have kicked myself for my recent post about traveling back to my hometown. I should have been more careful. "I paid you back already, $1.2 million."

Vic shook his greasy head. "No. Your smooth-talking husband promised me a twenty percent return on my money. You were short. By $240,000."

I stepped back, wrapping my arms around myself. I would have laughed, except I felt as if I were plummeting through the floor of my tiny house. Vic had never mentioned the twenty percent return.

"My husband's company doesn't exist anymore. I don't have that kind of money," I said. "I'm a writer."

"Then get it from someone else." He waved in the direction of my parents' house. "Maybe Mommy and Daddy can help you out."

"No." My bones chilled at the thought of Vic involving my parents in this, especially after their years-long ordeal with Caroline, their tight finances, and everything else they'd been through. "They don't have that kind of money, either."

Vic shoved me up against the wall, his forearm squeezing my windpipe. "Look, sweetheart. I don't fucking care where you get the money, but you better figure it out. I'll go to the police about your crooked business and your husband's little fall if you don't. I got connections like you wouldn't believe." He tilted his head in the direction of my parents' house and smiled. "And now I know where your family lives."

He stepped back, releasing the pressure on my throat. I doubled over, gasping for air, my hands covering my neck. Through the tiny window behind Vic, a light glowed from within my parents' bedroom.

My stomach wrenched. "Okay." I held up my hand, signaling for him to stop talking. "Please. I'll think of something. Give me some time to figure it out."

"You've got six months to pay me two hundred and forty grand. Then all bets are off. You miss my deadline and people will die."

I slumped against the wall, already defeated, but not wanting him to see it. "How can I reach you?"

"Don't you worry about that. I'll find you." He turned and walked outside.

My fingers pinched the deadbolt, locking it. I covered my mouth with my hand and fell to my knees, having no idea how I'd ever be able to get that kind of money.

CHAPTER THIRTY-TWO

Gloria (NOW)

I gasped, Beth's story turning my skin so cold I wished I'd worn my wool cardigan. "A Ponzi scheme," I said, shaking my head. My eyes traveled to the insurance document I'd found in the secret compartment. I wondered if the man who opened the door at the Waterside Condos was Vic. A sickening feeling spread through my body. "Did you pay him the interest?"

Beth stared at her hands. "No. I tried to hold Vic off for as long as possible. I told him I was securing a loan. It worked for a few months. I took an equity line out on my tiny house and paid him $30,000, but it wasn't enough. I was desperate."

"Oh, no." My eyes dropped to my shoes.

Beth nodded toward her sister. "I ended up telling Caroline everything about Jason's scam and about how Vic threw Jason off the boat and how I didn't have the interest money. I knew she was loyal, but I had no idea how far she'd go to protect me, or how far Vic would go to send a message."

Caroline squirmed. "I'm sorry, Lizzie. This is all my fault. Following Amanda up here was a big mistake."

I teetered backward, my head spinning. "You followed Amanda up here?"

Caroline's eyes stretched as wide as dinner plates. She nodded. "Lizzie didn't know what I was doing until it was too late. We'd missed Vic's first deadline. He wanted the first $100,000 by May twenty-fifth. We didn't have it. I wanted to confront Amanda here." She nodded toward the garage apartment. "Only she didn't live here anymore."

My head swung between Beth and Caroline. "But why?"

Caroline crossed her bony arms in front of her, the gun, blessedly, pointed at the floor. "Jason sent money and jewelry to Amanda while he was cheating on my sister. I started thinking, what if that asshole sent her *a lot* of money? What if Amanda had a bunch of diamond necklaces and earrings laying around? It was only fair that she should have to pay her share to Vic, especially if she knew about Jason's scheme."

Beth shifted her weight and stepped closer to me, resting her hand on one of the storage bins that doubled as a step. "I didn't know Caroline was poking into Amanda's whereabouts. The last thing I wanted was to get her involved, to have my dead husband's girlfriend back in my life. I'd already come to terms with everything. I'd bought my tiny house and moved on. But my sister was right about one thing. When it came to finding more money, I was out of options. We'd already missed Vic's first deadline and we only had three weeks left to get the rest. I drove up here as soon as Caroline told me where she was. She hadn't thought things through. I told her to wait for me before contacting Amanda. We needed a better plan." Beth sputtered out a labored breath. "Caroline told me about your field and the ad in the paper. It was a good spot to hide my tiny house, far away from town." She glanced out the window toward the garage apartment again.

Caroline followed her gaze. "I'm sorry about the break-in. I thought I'd find Amanda there, but she was already gone."

"Oh my Lord." Just as I'd suspected, Beth's arrival on my land hadn't been a lucky coincidence at all. I remembered the haunting way the apartment door had swung in the wind. Beth's sister was the one who'd forced open the door. "So, when I introduced you to Amanda at The Tidewater—"

Beth swallowed. "I already knew who she was. But she didn't know me. I wanted to get close to her to figure out if she had the money to pay Vic, or if she'd been involved in Jason's scheme. I had to keep my true identity hidden or she wouldn't have talked to me." Beth paused, studying her feet. "I used to go by Liz McCormack, not Beth Ramsay. Amanda only saw me once for a few seconds and I looked totally different then. My hair was longer and blonde. My social media accounts had my old photo, before I deleted them altogether. And if Jason told her anything about me at all, he would have told her I was a journalist with *The Observer*, not a travel writer."

"And Ella," my voice cracked as I forced out the next question, "the young woman they found on the beach?"

Caroline sniffled. Her slender fingers covered her face. "It's all my fault."

Beth pressed her lips together, her head drooping. "No. It's not."

Caroline's face scrunched up like a prune. "Ella was the assistant manager at Fringe Salon. My second day in town, I saw a *Help Wanted* sign in the salon's window and went inside to apply. When I couldn't find Amanda at first, I thought I might need to stay up here for a while. It seemed like a good place to hide from Vic. Ella told me how much she loved my hair and asked me to dye hers the same color. She liked my work and hired me on the spot."

Beth squeezed her eyelids shut. "Vic, or someone who works for him, must have followed me into town, I parked my tiny house at the state park. Then I took an Uber to the salon to visit Caroline. Ella insisted on giving me a pedicure." A sad smile pulled Beth's lips. "Caroline and Ella looked a lot alike. They were the same age with identical hair color." Beth's voice trailed off, her eyes glazing over. "We'd missed Vic's first deadline. He was sending me a message by killing my sister. Only he got the wrong person."

"Oh my stars." I breathed in and held my breath. It was a case of mistaken identity.

Beth wrapped her arm around her sister's fragile body. "Caroline's been in hiding ever since. She doesn't live in Ohio. I only told you that in case Vic or one of his thugs figured out I was here and started asking questions. I snuck out to meet Caroline a week or so ago when I told you I was getting my hair cut. She took my gun for protection. She wasn't supposed to come back here."

Caroline tossed her head back. "I was worried about you after they found Amanda's body."

I balled my fingers together, my head aching with a flood of realizations. "Are you a travel writer? Ethan called the magazine and..." I let my voice trail off. I needed to know which parts of Beth were real.

Beth's eyes stuck on something behind me. "I'm a writer. Only I haven't been commissioned by *American Traveler*. I'm writing freelance pieces and trying to sell them as I go." She glanced at the ceiling, then looked at me. "I'm sorry I lied. I didn't want you to think I didn't have a real job, or wondering where I was going every day." Beth sniffed and pointed in the direction of the garage apartment. "When Joe moved into the apartment, I was really worried. I thought he might be connected to Vic. You know, helping him out. So, I followed him when he'd leave in the middle of the night."

"Where did he go?" I asked.

"The Laundromat. Every time. It's open twenty-four hours."

My breath rushed from my lungs. "Did Vic kill Amanda too?"

Beth wiped the wetness from her eyes. "Yeah. He did. The night I met Amanda at The Castaways, I knew right away that something was wrong. She looked horrible, like she hadn't slept. She told me she was worried her former boyfriend had been involved in some kind of illegal business. I was so stunned by her words, I couldn't speak." Beth blinked several times, composing herself. "Amanda said a sleazy guy had shown up at her apartment the day before demanding money and threatening her family. She'd withdrawn money from her bank account and sold a few pieces of jewelry, but it wasn't enough. I knew it was Vic. My plan had gone totally sideways. He'd found Amanda because of me." Beth squeezed her eyelids closed and shook her head. "I was worried for Amanda's safety, so I came clean with her right then. I told her who I really was and what I was doing—that I thought she might have the money I needed to pay Vic, but obviously I'd been wrong. I begged her not to mess around with Vic and to leave town, but she said she wouldn't. She threatened to go to the police. I told her not to do that. I warned her it would be a death sentence. That's why she was angry and stormed off. She thought I was tricking her or was out for revenge, but it wasn't true. I was only trying to warn her. I realized she was another one of Jason's victims. He used her and threw her away just like he did everyone else in his life." Beth shook her head. "But my warning came too late."

I hugged my fragile arms around myself. "Oh dear."

Beth blinked away tears. "I know it sounds terrible, but when I first met Amanda, I wasn't sure I wanted to help her, especially after Ella was murdered. A part of me thought the woman who ruined my life deserved to have karma catch up with her." Beth grimaced and pointed to the booties that lay on the floor between us. "Those were for my baby. I lost him when he was only nineteen weeks along. A car accident."

"Oh, Beth. I'm so sorry." My eyes flicked toward the church program on the floor. I wanted to stand up and hug her, but an invisible wall separated us.

"I'd been following them—Jason and Amanda—when it happened. I didn't have time to put on my seat belt. It's their fault my baby's dead."

"Ah."

"So, maybe you can understand why I hid my identity, why I didn't rush to warn her. Meeting her in person tore open so many old wounds." Beth stared beyond me in a daze, then shifted her eyes to her fidgeting hands before speaking again. "Once I got to know Amanda, I actually kind of liked her. Isn't that funny?" Beth pressed her lips together.

I swallowed against my scratchy throat, once again not sure of an appropriate response.

Beth pressed her palms to her eyelids, then lowered her hands. "When Amanda disappeared after our dinner at The Castaways, I assumed the worst. Still, I hoped she'd outsmarted Vic and skipped town or gone into hiding like Caroline. I hoped Vic realized he'd killed the wrong person with Ella and got spooked by the police presence. I hoped he'd finally moved on." The watery sheen of Beth's eyes reflected in the light. "But, of course, I was wrong."

"This is all so unbelievable." I rubbed my eyes, more questions flooding my mind. "Why did you go back to The Castaways with Ethan the other night?"

"Because I was desperate to find Amanda. I knew it was a long shot, but I texted her and begged her to meet me back at the restaurant if she was okay and still in the area. I told her to wear a disguise. Texting her was risky. I was scared Vic might have her phone, that he would come for me instead. I thought I'd be safe as long as I was in a public place with Ethan."

"I see."

"I'm sorry I put Ethan at risk. I wasn't thinking straight. Anyway, Vic never showed. He must have ditched Amanda's phone along with her body."

I swallowed.

"After Ethan and I left the restaurant, I made a quick stop at the gas station, then headed over to Amanda's new apartment to look for any sign of her or talk to her neighbors. Of course, she wasn't there. No one had seen her." Beth stared at the floor and shook her head. "I spent hours driving around town looking for her."

I exhaled. Beth hadn't returned home until after midnight on Thursday because she'd been searching for Amanda, not disposing of her body.

Beth continued, "I finally went home, hoping Amanda was hiding several cities away. I didn't even know for sure if Vic was still in the area." Tears streamed down Beth's cheeks and her lower lip quivered. "But then I saw him the next day when I was with you at the coffee shop."

My mouth gaped open as I remembered Beth's strange behavior, her urgent need to leave after we'd just barely gotten our drinks.

"I should have confronted him then, but you were with me and I didn't have his money. I panicked. By the next day, Amanda still hadn't answered any of my texts. Then I read online that she'd been murdered." Beth's voice was shaky. "I knew Vic was responsible."

"Have you talked to him?" I asked, thinking of the man she'd visited earlier.

Beth nodded. "I've spent days calling every hotel, motel, and vacation rental service in the area. I've even driven to their offices and described him to the people at the front desks. I finally traced him to a rental at the Waterside Condos. That's where I went tonight."

Caroline jutted out her chin. "You shouldn't have gone. You're lucky he didn't kill you."

My eyes darted away from Beth, trying to hide my guilt from having followed her.

Beth narrowed her eyes toward her sister. "I didn't have a choice, Caroline." She massaged her forehead and released a breath. "Vic repeated what Amanda had told me, that she emptied her bank account and sold her jewelry. She paid him $10,000, but it wasn't enough. He killed her after she threatened to go to the police. I have three more days to pay $200,000." Beth swallowed, letting out a high-pitched squeak. "He said he made an example out of Amanda."

My gut twisted like a wet dishrag: *$200,000?* How could Beth possibly find that kind of money in three days? A jolt of adrenaline raised me from my seated position on the floor. "Let's turn him in. We need to call the police."

"No, Gloria!" The color disappeared from Beth's face as she squared her shoulders at me. "Vic knows too much. He's involved in bad stuff. Illegal gambling. Money laundering. I think he's even connected to the mafia. He'll do anything to stop the police from investigating. He threatened to pin Jason's death on me if I even thought about contacting anyone. And he'll tell them I was involved in the Ponzi scheme."

"But you didn't know about his scheme. And Jason died in an accident." I dug my heels into the floor, trying to make sense of dire information.

"The thing is…" The words were lodged in Beth's throat. She took a moment and massaged her temples with her fingers. "I was there when Vic threw Jason over the back of the yacht." The look in Beth's eyes shifted to sheer panic. "I was so scared and shocked, I didn't yell out for help. It was just after I'd discovered Jason's affair and lost my baby."

"Oh, my." I couldn't stop my mouth from hanging open.

"And most of the money Jason stole from his investors was deposited into our personal account. I didn't know where it came from, but maybe I should have. I was a member of his company, on paper at least." Beth's features appeared sunken. "After he died, I created fraudulent accounting statements to cover up Jason's crime. What I did was illegal. I don't want to go to prison, Gloria."

Beth was in a horrible predicament. My insides wrestled with competing emotions: shame, for suspecting Beth of being a murderer; sadness, for the loss of her baby; anger, at her selfish husband; grief, for the families of Ella and Amanda. Most of all though, my insides trembled with fear, the fear of Vic Callis and the depths he would plunge to collect his money. It was only logical that Beth would be his next victim.

CHAPTER THIRTY-THREE

Gloria (NOW)

The light from my nightstand cast a curved shadow across the bed, and my shoulders pressed into the pillow propped behind me. It was 2 a.m., but sleep wasn't a possibility. Every chirp of a cricket and groan of the decrepit house caused me to tilt forward, my senses hyper-alert, my blood pumping faster. Rascal was curled at my feet, and *The Thirty-Day Life Coach* workbook lay open in my lap. I sighed and pushed the book away, giving up on completing any exercises. I imagined my current situation was way beyond anything anticipated by the author of the self-help tutorial.

An hour earlier, after double-locking all the doors and windows, I'd made up beds for Beth and her sister on the couches downstairs. We'd agreed it was safer for them to stay inside with me and Rascal. Plus, Beth had hidden her gun under the cushion where she slept in case of any uninvited visitors.

I thought of Ethan on his camping trip and hoped he was sleeping soundly. It was a small relief to have him out of harm's way and oblivious to the horrible man named Vic Callis. At the same time, I couldn't wait for him to return, to confide in him about Beth's experiences, and to feel less alone.

My instincts told me to march down to the police station and report Vic as a possible suspect in the murders of Ella and Amanda, but Beth had made me promise not to contact anyone. She was convinced the police couldn't touch him, especially small-town police who'd probably never investigated a real crime before. She said Vic was a professional criminal who didn't leave behind evidence. He didn't make mistakes. There wouldn't be enough to hold him. She doubted Vic Callis was even his real name. Alerting the police would only guarantee prison—or a death sentence—for Beth.

I reached for the glass of water next to me and the gleam of a jewel caught my eye. Beth's necklace, the one I'd discovered in her car and had assumed was Amanda's, lay in a shimmering coil inside the zip-lock bag on the corner of my nightstand. Amanda had sold her jewelry to pay Vic the $10,000. I picked up the bag and examined the silver chain through the plastic; the turquoise wings of the butterfly reflected like sparkling water under the light. *What if?* I thought. *What if?*

Under normal circumstances, a "Risk-averse/Conformist" like me never would have considered the illegal act. But facts had changed. Piece by piece, I concocted a plan.

The next morning, my eyelids struggled to stay open as I poured water into the coffee maker. I hadn't slept a wink. Opening the refrigerator, I rummaged for something to offer Beth and Caroline for breakfast. Half of a loaf of bread and some eggs lay on the shelf. French toast would be the easiest.

A torturous sob drew me into the living room. I found Beth on the couch next to Caroline. I looped my arm around her shoulders and squeezed. Her body radiated heat beneath my embrace, and my heart wrenched. I knew from experience that grief surged in waves, crashing over a person at unexpected moments.

"It's my fault. I caused those women to die." Beth lowered her hands, revealing her watery, red-rimmed eyes.

"No. It's my fault," Caroline said, burying her head in a pillow.

"That's not true," I said to both of them. "It's Vic's fault. It's Jason's fault. But it's not your fault." My hand shook as I rubbed Beth's back.

"Why didn't I warn her sooner?" Beth asked, her voice frail and cracked.

"You didn't know it would come to this. You didn't even know Vic was in town. You told me that yourself. Besides, it doesn't sound like it would have made a difference."

Tears flowed down Beth's cheeks as she heaved and sniffled. I didn't know what to say to comfort her as thoughts and emotions tumbled through my mind.

At last, Beth squeezed my hand. "You guys," she said, alternating her stare between me and Caroline. We looked at each other. Beth's eyes were stretched round and wide like a doe. Her lower lip trembled. "He's going to kill me next."

"We're not going to let that happen." I stood up, pulling Beth's arm. "You both need to leave. Right now. Hook your truck up to your tiny house and drive somewhere far away."

Beth raised herself off the couch but shook her head. "It won't matter. He'll figure out where I've gone."

I squared my shoulders. "You need to trust me on this. I have a plan."

"What plan? You can't call the police. He'll know it was me. They won't be able to pin Amanda's death on him."

I grabbed her hand and squeezed. "Please, Beth. You can't stay here. It isn't safe."

"She's right, Lizzie. We're putting Gloria in danger by being here."

Beth's mouth dropped open, her complexion fading. "I don't want to put you in danger. Or Ethan."

I envisioned my meager bank account and the depleted stack of cash I'd spent on dog supplies, gardening equipment, and groceries. "What could Vic want with me?" I cleared my throat and spoke with authority. "I need you to trust me. Get into your tiny house and drive far away. I'll call you when it's safe."

"What if I don't hear from you?"

"You will."

Beth stared at the wall, finally nodding. I peered through the windows to make sure no one was lurking outside, then ushered Beth and Caroline through the front door and hustled behind them toward the tiny house.

It didn't take Beth long to pack, as she only had to disconnect a hose and remove a folding chair and a flowerpot from the front porch. She reversed her truck, and I signaled for her to stop when the hitch was within an inch of the house. I'd been directing her into the same spot only a few weeks earlier. If only I'd understood how she would change me—the depth of friendship, confidence, and excitement she'd breathe into my life—then maybe I wouldn't have charged her for the land. Now I had to protect her. That's what friends did.

Rascal ran circles around Beth as she exited her truck.

"I'll miss you, Rascal." She leaned down and kissed his head. "Don't give your mom too much trouble." Tears leaked down her pale cheeks.

I stepped toward her with a hug. "Keep yourself safe."

"I'm sorry I got you involved in this."

We pulled apart. "I know, but I am involved now and I'm going to fix this mess."

"What's your plan, Gloria?" She spoke in a strained whisper, her lip twitching.

"I'm going to make sure Vic gets caught. That's all I can tell you."

I expected Beth to argue or to dig for more information, but she only pinched her lips together and stared at me. She closed herself inside her truck and pulled it forward with her sister following a car-length away in a dented silver hatchback. A rectangle of yellowed grass and a strip of flowers were the only clues Beth and her tiny house had been here. She stared straight ahead as she drove down the dusty driveway, the miniature log cabin rattling behind her.

Several hours later, my car eased to a halt on the side of the dirt road. I parked in the same spot as the night before, partially hidden behind a dense cluster of trees. Through the branches, the Waterside Condos stretched out beyond the bend. A few windows glowed from within the row of vacation homes, but the darkened condo on the end loomed like a monstrous shadow. There was no car in the driveway. Presumably Vic had either gone out for the night or had left town.

I crouched down, reciting a prayer in my head, asking God to grant me the courage to exit my sedan, as well as for forgiveness for the law I was about to break. Breathing ever so slowly, I inched open my car door and ducked out into the night, my hand clutching the zip-lock bag that contained the secret weapon. Despite the vacant-looking condo, I couldn't calm my nerves or shake the sensation that someone was watching me. Aside from sneaking into Beth's tiny house the night before, I'd never disregarded the authority of the law. At least, not on purpose. Being out of options didn't prevent my thoughts from circling downward.

A man's voice bellowed from somewhere outside, followed by a woman's laughter. I froze, pressing my back against the rough bark of a nearby tree and scanning for movement. Glasses clinked. The noise was coming from a patio or balcony on the opposite side of the condos. They wouldn't be able to see me from there.

My gut urged me to dart up to the front door and get out of there as quickly as possible, but I didn't want to appear suspicious should anyone catch sight of me. I forced myself to inhale and stretch my shoulders back, pacing calmly toward the end condo as if out for an evening stroll. As casually as possible, I walked toward the condo where I'd seen Beth talking to Vic. My heart beat so wildly I thought it might burst out of my chest. My fingers turned over the bag holding the necklace I'd found in Beth's truck. It hadn't belonged to Amanda. Amanda would have sold her necklace to try to pay back Vic, but the police wouldn't know that. They'd believe this belonged to her. She'd been wearing an identical necklace in the police photo. The next time I talked to Beth, I'd ask her to tell a white lie and confirm Amanda had been wearing the same necklace at The Castaways the night she disappeared.

I hunched over, clearing away a handful of wood chips next to the bushes by the painted green door. The necklace dangled from my hand. I'd already pulled it apart, breaking the clasp to make it appear like it had been ripped from Amanda's neck. Now, I removed a cloth from my pocket, pulled the necklace from the bag, and wiped any stray prints off it. Using the cloth, I draped the silver chain across the ground in a spot underneath the shrubbery. Lightly covering the necklace with a sprinkling of wood chips, I surveyed my work. The jewelry wouldn't be noticeable at first glance, but even a mediocre small-town detective doing a cursory search wouldn't be able to miss it.

Stepping back from the planted evidence, I glanced from side to side, scanning for any witnesses. Aside from the conversation echoing from the cocktail party, the night was quiet and still. I crossed my arms in front of me and strode back to my car, only allowing myself to breathe once I was safely inside.

My hands shook as I shoved the cloth and empty plastic bag into my purse, grasped the steering wheel, and accelerated past the row of condos. The faster I drove, the faster my mind raced. I thought of Amanda's family and Ella's family, and how they must be aching with grief and searching for answers. I wondered how far Caroline and Beth and her tiny house had traveled since this morning, and whether Vic knew they'd left town. I envisioned Ethan sleeping in a tent, oblivious to everything that had transpired in the last twenty-four hours. I wondered what Charlie would think if he could see me now. Would he have recognized me? I swallowed, believing he would have accepted my need to make things right, no matter how illegal my actions.

A memory from years earlier popped into my head. Our local banker had been held up at gunpoint. I'd been so livid with Charlie when he'd defended the robber.

"You don't know what his situation was," Charlie had said. "Maybe the guy's kids were starving."

I'd been stunned at the time. My own husband defending an armed criminal! But now I could see he'd been correct. Charlie hadn't believed in good or bad, black or white. He'd realized how complex people could be, how events outside of their control could influence their behavior. Surely he would have understood my actions. Maybe he would have even been proud. I blinked back tears.

A car honked and I swerved wildly. I'd traveled across the centerline and hadn't even noticed. Now, back on my own side of the road, I breathed in jagged breaths, taking stock of my surroundings and where I needed to go.

"Pull it together, Gloria," I said to myself.

I followed the signs to downtown Petoskey and pulled into an empty parking space a block away from The Tidewater. Slinging my purse over my shoulder, I exited my car and ambled toward the restaurant. I didn't stop until my sedan was out of sight. A well-dressed couple strode through the front door, chatting about their plans for the following day. From a half-block away, I could see they were city folks.

"Excuse me," I stepped in front of them, "do either of you have a cell phone I can use to call my husband? I have a flat tire and I left my phone at home." I'd watched enough *Dateline* episodes to know it was foolish to make the next call from my own phone.

The woman studied me for a second before her face relaxed, probably realizing that I resembled her mom or, possibly, her grandma. "Oh, sure." She reached into her purse and slid out a phone, a half-dozen silver bracelets clanking on her arm.

"Can I help you with your car?" the man next to her asked. His hair was gelled to his head, and he wore plaid shorts, a braided leather belt, and boat shoes.

The woman rolled her eyes at him. "Yeah, right. Like you know how to change a tire."

"I could do it." The man shrugged. "I mean, probably. Or I can call Triple A."

I smiled. "No. Thank you." I motioned to a bench about twenty-five feet away. "I'm just going to step over here. I've got a bad back. Don't worry. I'm not stealing your phone."

The woman chuckled. "You're fine."

The couple went back to their conversation as I plodded toward the bench and sat down. My heart clamored inside my chest. I pressed the 1-800 number I'd committed to memory. It was the tip hotline the police had set up to gather information relating to the recent Petoskey murders. I waited as the phone rang three times.

"Petoskey Murder Investigation Hotline, how can I assist you?" asked a man with a gruff voice.

"Hello. I'm calling about the woman who was found in the ditch, Amanda Jenkins."

"Okay. Your name, please."

"I have some information that may be helpful to the police."

"What's your name, ma'am?"

"I prefer not to give my name." My muscles tensed. I hadn't realized they'd be so intent on learning my identity. "I know who murdered Amanda and my life is in danger."

"Do you need police assistance?"

"No! I need you to listen to me." The volume of my voice had increased enough that the couple glanced my direction. I gave them a wave and a smile and took a deep breath.

"Okay," the man said. "Please continue."

"I heard a woman screaming last Friday night. It was a week ago. The night Amanda went missing. I was walking my dog past the Waterside Condos in Petoskey. The screaming was coming from the end unit. The one with the green door. There was a large man with black hair in the doorway, and he slammed the door shut when he saw me."

"What time on Friday?"

"It was very late. I don't know when exactly, but probably around midnight. I was going to call earlier, but I thought it was a domestic dispute. Then they found that woman, Amanda Jenkins, in the ditch. I realized I may have witnessed something important." I let my voice trail off for dramatic effect.

"You said the Waterside Condos in Petoskey?"

"Yes."

"Do you know the unit number?"

"No, but it was the end unit, as I said. Green door."

"Anything else?"

"Promise me someone will go over and investigate?"

"I assure you this information will be checked out by the police as soon as possible."

"Thank you."

I ended the call before he could ask me any more questions. My legs wobbled as I stood up, but I steadied myself and forced a smile as I walked back to the helpful couple.

"Mission accomplished." I handed back her phone.

CHAPTER THIRTY-FOUR

Gloria (NOW)

"One pound of shrimp, please," I said to the man behind the seafood counter at the IGA. Ethan stepped next to me, plopping a bag of rice into the cart. We were collecting the ingredients for my famous One-hour Paella recipe, as well as some fresh vegetables to put in the gazpacho so Joe would have something to eat. It was Ethan's last night in Michigan before heading back to San Francisco.

It had been three days since I planted the evidence outside the Waterside Condos and called the police hotline, and two days since I cheered in front of my television as Vic Callis was led away in handcuffs on the local news. It happened the same day Ethan returned from his camping trip. I'd spent at least an hour filling him in on the truth about Ella and Amanda, my late-night encounter with Caroline and Beth, and all the dreadful events that Beth endured during the past year.

Once they had Vic in custody, I'd urged Beth to call the police to fill in the blanks. By then, they'd discovered Vic's true identity: Leonard Brunkso. He was connected to an illegal gambling ring in Detroit and had been using Jason's fund to launder large sums of money. Jason had promised Vic huge returns for investing in the fledgling fund.

Beth had gone along with my plan, falsely confirming with police that the necklace recovered in front of Vic's condo was the same one Amanda had been wearing at The Castaways the night she disappeared. Amanda's parents, unaware Jason had given both women the identical necklace, further confirmed the necklace was the same one frequently worn by their daughter. A local police officer had found Amanda's car in an abandoned parking lot bordering Pelliston Airport, the keys still inside and the vehicle wiped clean of prints. Together, it had been enough to charge Vic with Amanda's murder, in addition to multiple counts of fraud. Using DNA evidence that had been collected from Ella's body, they connected Vic to Ella's murder several hours later.

With her safety secured, Beth and her tiny house arrived back at the empty field earlier this morning, without her sister. Ethan and I greeted Beth with hugs and a few tears.

"I'm heading into the station," she'd said. "Amanda's family deserves to know what happened to her. So does Ella's. She clenched my arm and lowered her voice, "I'm not going to tell them about the necklace. That stays between us."

I nodded and exhaled. Some things remained sacred between friends. We understood the importance of protecting each other.

While Ethan and I roamed the aisles of the IGA for ingredients, I envisioned Beth sitting under fluorescent lights in a tiny interrogation room answering an endless stream of questions. I imagined her voice cracking and her forehead glistening as she recounted the unbelievable turmoil she'd been through over the past year. And finally, I imagined the detective being satisfied that she'd connected all the dots, cementing Vic's arrest. Beth would stand and shake the hand of the detective and walk back to her truck, her shoulders five tons lighter than when she'd arrived.

"Well, if it isn't Gloria Flass. I haven't seen you in ages!"

My head jerked up, my body startled by the familiar, screechy voice. Even before I saw her sculpted hair and bejeweled sandals, I knew Mary Ellen Calloway had encroached upon my space. She flashed her mechanical grin and gave me a hollow hug, the kind reserved for people you don't really know or like. My fingers squeezed the handle of my shopping cart as my mouth forced a smile.

Mary Ellen leaned back, gawking at Ethan. "And is this... No, it can't be! Ethan?"

Ethan nodded his head and smiled. "Hi."

I noticed the boyish way he shoved his hands in his pockets and looked at the floor. The fake tone of Mary Ellen's voice made him uncomfortable, too.

"I can't wait to tell Lacey I ran into you." Mary Ellen's fingers fidgeted with the giant beads on her necklace. "We have a mother-daughter brunch together every Sunday after church. She's pregnant again, you know. It will be grandbaby number eight."

"Wow." Ethan raised his eyebrows. "Congratulations."

"And where are you living again? Was it San Francisco?" Mary Ellen asked.

I sucked in my breath, gritting my teeth at the smug tone of her voice, and the way she was digging for dirt she could later use against us.

"Yeah," Ethan said.

"How is that?"

"It's great," Ethan said. "I love it."

While Mary Ellen tolerated a don't ask, don't tell policy, I no longer did. That archaic way of thinking was hurtful to Ethan. *When given the choice between love and hate, choose love.* I'd chosen love for my son. While I'd never accused her, I suspected Mary Ellen was the one who'd left the pamphlet under my coat. She was nothing more than a schoolyard bully. Someone who took verses from the Bible and twisted them to fit her personal agenda. Someone who left a lonely widow's name off the decorating committee list just because she could. Someone who enjoyed excluding anyone different from herself. Bullies never stopped tormenting others until they were confronted. I'd read that in *The Thirty-Day*

Life Coach, but I'd known it all along. I stepped closer to Ethan, my instinct to protect taking over.

"He's very happy in California. He has a terrific job and a wonderful boyfriend named Sean. I've heard so much about him. I'm hoping to meet him in person soon."

Mary Ellen's complexion lost its rosy glow. "Oh, well…"

She was at a loss for words for what I guessed was the first time in her life.

Ethan glanced at me with his mouth ajar, as if I'd just performed a double backflip off the side of the grocery cart. He placed his hand on top of mine and squeezed, acknowledging my feat. My chest swelled with pride for my son. He had more character, compassion, and grace in his little finger than possessed by Mary Ellen Calloway's entire extended family.

I saw so much of Charlie in him. And me. I was in him, too. I couldn't fathom what had taken me so long to come around to Ethan's side. So slow to admit I'd been wrong? I'd been so insecure that I'd lived my life trying to please other people, people who I didn't even care about. I was a different person now. A strong woman who did right by the ones she loved. A mother whose son could be proud of her.

"See you at church." I collected the bag of shrimp and pushed my cart past Mary Ellen's gaping mouth. I planned to sit in the front pew next Sunday, *"taking back my power"* as Beth had put it. Ethan strode next to me, pinching his lips together, trying not to smile.

"You should have seen the look on her face." Ethan heaped another spoonful of paella onto his plate.

Our two dinner guests, Joe and Beth, sat across the table. Ethan's eyes crinkled in the corners as they met mine and I thought again of how handsome he was.

I couldn't mask my grin. "I finally figured out how to get Mary Ellen Calloway to shut up: talk to her about my gay son." The others chuckled and nodded.

Beth recounted the details of her police interview, which had gone even better than I'd imagined. They'd decided not to charge her for any crimes related to Jason's Ponzi scheme, convinced by her successful efforts to repay all those who'd been swindled. Her actions matched her story of trying to stay one step ahead of Vic's threats. After describing the end of the meeting with the detective, Beth's demeanor suddenly changed.

"I kept a few things to myself."

"Not every detail needs to be revealed," Joe said, winking at Beth. "That's a little something I learned in art school."

I leaned back in my chair.

Beth gave us a sad smile. "Caroline reached out to Ella's parents yesterday. She said it was something she had to do."

I nodded, unable to imagine the guilt Beth and her sister must be feeling. "You and Caroline are lucky to have each other."

"She's a good person. The best sister. After hearing what she did, I drove to Amanda's parents' house to talk to them," Beth said.

Everyone ceased chewing and peered at her. I shouldn't have been surprised by Beth's gesture, yet her unannounced visit so soon after Amanda's death seemed ill-advised.

"They live about forty minutes from here," Beth said. "I felt like I owed it to them to stop by in person and offer my condolences."

I swallowed, nervous to hear how she'd been received.

"I expected them to yell at me, but they didn't." Beth's eyes became glassy. "They hugged me and cried. Said it wasn't my fault, and that Jason and Vic were responsible for Amanda's death, not me. Amanda had told them we were becoming good friends." Beth's voice cracked.

"It wasn't your fault," I said.

The memory of the two murdered women weighed so heavily in the room I almost pulled two extra chairs up to the table, one for each of their ghosts. Their faces would be etched in my mind until my final breath.

Beth dabbed her mouth with her napkin and looked away. "I'm going to help Amanda's parents with the memorial service." She looked at me. "That is, if you don't mind me parking my house here for a while longer?"

Pinching my lips together and tipping my chair back slightly, I tried to conceal my delight amid the heavy atmosphere. With Ethan leaving in the morning, it would be especially nice to have Beth around. Judging by her puffy eyes and her fragile emotional state, she could also use a friend. "Of course not, dear. You can stay as long as you like."

A smile flickered across Beth's face and she slouched down in her chair. "Thank you, Gloria."

"What about me, Gloria?" Joe asked in a teasing voice. "Can I stay as long as I like?"

The glint in his eyes and the crazy trajectory of his hair made me chuckle. "You can stay, Joe, but you'll need to pay upfront."

"In cash," Ethan added.

"I decided I'll let you fix those windows for me, too." I winked at Joe.

Everyone laughed, finally breaking the morbid spell cast around us. It was nice to see Beth smiling, despite what she'd been through. She was even tougher than I'd realized.

At last, Joe cleared his throat. "Seriously, Gloria, I guess I missed a lot of what's been going on around here lately, but it seems like this has been a rough week for everyone. I wanted to thank you for sharing your beautiful land with me this summer. I have something for you." Joe held up his finger. "Just one minute while I go get it." He backed up his chair and scooted out the door, leaving Rascal whining in his crate and the rest of us making confused faces at each other.

As promised, Joe returned a minute later carrying a large canvas, which he'd flipped backward. "I've been working on this during my off-hours. I hope you like it."

Joe turned the canvas around and handed it to me. I gasped, my hand flying to my mouth. It was the most breathtaking painting I'd ever laid eyes on. Bright hues of red, orange, green, blue, and brown combined to form a sunset over the trees. I recognized the landscape as my own backyard, and the large tree in the foreground could not be mistaken. It was the oak tree that guarded over Charlie's ashes, the tree whose shade provided a refuge for me to sit and spend time with Charlie's memory. Charlie's spirit still lived in that tree, just as much as it lived in me and in Ethan. Joe had even included the stone bench.

I stared at Joe. How could he have known about the tree? I'd never mentioned it to him. A swell of emotion rose in my throat.

"Thank you," I said at last, as Beth and Ethan oohed and ahhed in the background. "I truly love it."

"You're welcome." Joe winked at me. "And if you don't like it, you can give it away as soon as I leave. I won't know the difference."

"I'll never get rid of it." I pointed to a bare wall above the fireplace. "I'm going to hang it right here in the living room."

"I used the oak tree as my focal point," Joe said. "I saw you sitting under it a number of times. Figured it meant something to you."

Tears stung the corners of my eyes, but I blinked them away. "Yes. You're right about that. It does."

I wondered if Charlie was watching us right now. Was he floating above us, peering over my shoulder? Or maybe he was waving from the branches of the oak tree outside. I wondered what he'd think about this haphazard crew assembled inside our old farmhouse: a quirky, starving artist who wandered through the woods at night; a drifting writer recently suspected of murder; our kind and strong-willed son who'd taught me the true meaning of love; an adorable, but untrained mutt who dug up my lilies; and me, his wife, who had finally discovered how to stand confidently on her own two feet.

I didn't have to ponder too long because I already knew the answer. It pulsed through my bones and embraced me with the warmth of the room. It played in my ears with the ease of Ethan's laughter. It appeared in the brushstrokes of the painting propped in front of me, and in the bright futures rolled out like place mats before every person sitting at my table. Charlie was here, and he was smiling. And perhaps more importantly, I was smiling, too.

A LETTER FROM LAURA

Dear reader,

I want to say a huge thank you for choosing to read *Two Widows*. If you'd like to keep up to date with all my latest releases, just sign up at the following link. Your email address will never be shared, and you can unsubscribe at any time.

www.bookouture.com/laura-wolfe

I wrote *Two Widows* with the intent of keeping the reader guessing until the final pages. I wanted to see what would happen if two women of different ages and from divergent backgrounds and life experiences were thrown together in a remote location with plenty of secrets. Ultimately, *Two Widows* became a story about standing in one's truth. It was important to me that each character's truth prevailed in the end.

Over the last few years, I've become slightly obsessed with tiny houses and the idea of minimalist living. Beth's character provided a perfect opportunity to incorporate a tiny house into the setting. While tiny houses aren't inherently creepy, they have a claustrophobic quality, are transient by nature, and contain nooks and crannies that make great hiding places. The tiny house contributed to Beth's mysterious past and allowed for a quick getaway when her secrets caught up with her.

In Gloria, I hoped to portray a woman transforming into the best version of herself. She was meant to be someone readers could easily relate to and root for, despite her faults. Gloria's changing relationships and circumstances unleashed the powerful inner strength that had been waiting inside her all along. (Credit to Dorothy from the *Wizard of Oz*!)

I hope you loved *Two Widows*, and if you did, I would be very grateful if you could write a review. I'd love to hear what you think, and it makes such a difference in helping new readers to discover one of my books for the first time.

I love hearing from my readers – you can get in touch on my *Facebook page*, through *Goodreads*, *Instagram*, or *my website*.

Thanks,
Laura Wolfe

LauraWolfeBooks

lwolfe.writes

www.laurawolfebooks.com

1908042.Laura_Wolfe

ACKNOWLEDGMENTS

So many people supported and assisted me in various ways along the journey of writing and publishing this book. First, I'd like to thank the entire Bookouture team, especially my editor, Hannah Bond, for taking a chance on me. Her insights into my story's structure, pacing, and characters made the final version so much better. Thank you to those who read the early versions, or portions thereof, and provided valuable feedback and/or other inspiration and encouragement: Karina Board, Stephanie Bucklin, Torrey Lewis, Alexia Andoni, David Peterson, Lisa Richey, Nancy Richey, and Helen Zimmermann. Thank you to my "writing partner," Milo, for forcing me to take at least one frisbee break per day. Thank you to my parents for instilling a love of books in me from a young age. I'd like to thank my kids, Brian and Kate, for always cheering for me. Most of all, I am grateful for my husband, JP, for supporting my writing. He read every version of this novel over the years, and I wouldn't have made it to the end without his encouragement.